CARLISLE: JOURNEY TO THE WHITE CLOUDS

WALLACE J. SWENSON

THORNDIKE PRESS

A part of Gale, Cengage Learning

GALE
CENGAGE Learning·

Farmington Hills, Mich • San Francisco • New York • Waterville, Maine
Meriden, Conn • Mason, Ohio • Chicago

GALE
CENGAGE Learning

LIBRARY OF CONGRESS CATALOGING-IN-PUBLICATION DATA

Names: Swenson, Wallace J., author.
Title: Carlisle : journey to the white clouds / by Wallace J. Swenson.
Description: Waterville, Maine : Thorndike Press, 2016. | Series: Thorndike Press large print western
Identifiers: LCCN 2016039998| ISBN 9781410495440 (hardcover) | ISBN 1410495442 (hardcover)
Subjects: LCSH: Frontier and pioneer life—Nebraska—Fiction. | Families—Nebraska—Fiction. | Large type books. | Domestic fiction. | GSAFD: Western stories.
Classification: LCC PS3619.W4557 C37 2016b | DDC 813/.6—dc23
LC record available at https://lccn.loc.gov/2016039998

Published in 2016 by arrangement with Wallace J. Swenson

Printed in Mexico
1 2 3 4 5 6 7 20 19 18 17 16

To the mothers and fathers who
devoted themselves
to their children.

ACKNOWLEDGMENTS

In the real world, I bow in gratitude to my wonderful wife who now recognizes me best in the glow of a computer screen, who kept the love, and the support, and the coffee coming, and who always knew which I needed most at any given time. In the literary world, I am repaying those who have gone before, took me places I'd never dreamed of, and showed me things I never thought possible. Ruark and Hemingway, Dixon et al and Tarkington; London, Cooper, and Defoe; Twain and Dickens, all whisper to me as I create. For those of the more modern era, I thank Cormac McCarthy, Larry McMurtry and Craig Johnson for their robust voices. At the practical level, I will forever be in author Patti Sherlock's debt. I also owe a lot to a special group of people, strangers at first and now friends, the Five Star Publishing folks, most especially Tiffany Schofield, who took a chance on me. Thanks.

CHAPTER 1

Carlisle, Nebraska Territory, early winter,
1858.

The incessant moan of the storm tore at
Paul Steele's nerves as an icy wind searched
for a way into the sod house. He scowled at
the latch keeping the door firmly closed;
doing more for his family than he was, the
simple device mocked him.

The snow had caught him by surprise. It
started at noon, thick and steady, bearing
down out of the northwest. Something in
the air had compelled him to go home, and
he'd no sooner set foot in the house than
Ana sent him back to town to find Simon,
their oldest at seven, and over an hour late
from school. And he'd found him curled up
in the road and nearly unconscious — they
barely made it home. For two full turns of
the clock it'd snowed, until, in the depths of
the night, the storm had moved on to torment those east. A suffocating blanket of

white lay three feet deep on the level, blurring the landscape. Then the wind had picked up, piling the treacherous powder high, and packing it in everywhere. And last, the temperature plummeted to twenty-one degrees below zero the first night, thirty-one below the next, and there it stayed, so frigid a layer of thin ice formed in the bottom of the forty-foot well.

"Ma, could you rustle up some rags?" Paul asked. "We've got snow sifting in through a dozen places."

His wife, Ana, rose from her chair by the table and handed her baby to Simon who sat by the stove with two of his two younger brothers, Axel and Abel, and a toddler sister. "Hold Eric for a minute," she said, and stepped through a curtain in the rear of the house. She soon returned with several pieces of cloth and handed them to him. "Not much difference between what's a rag and what's not," she said with a wan smile, retrieved the baby, and sat back down at the table.

Paul mentally winced, but recognized the truth of her comment — it still stung. The space he provided for his family of seven measured twenty feet square, a sod house with the rear quarter screened off by makeshift curtains. In there stood the wardrobe and dresser, a bed with a night table along-side, and a four-legged stool; their bedroom.

He started in the northwest corner, stuffing bits of cloth into the seams of the earthen blocks wherever he saw a telltale streak of white. In the north wall was the door, flanked by two small windows. To the right of the door and under the window, benches sat on either side of a sturdy table. The only two chairs in the place stood at either end. He worked his way across, and then down the east wall, past the cupboard to the black iron stove. Beyond it stood a washstand and some rough shelves for storage. Firewood, stacked knee-high, occupied the space below some more shelves on the back wall.

The forty-inch-wide cookstove served as the focal point in the tiny home, and as he worked his way around the room, the eyes of his skinny children followed him from their positions in front of it. He finished the west wall where a two-tiered bed stood, and turned back to his wife. She puffed a lock of soft-brown hair out of her eyes, fallen from the scarf she wore around her head, the bright blue and white checkered cloth an incongruous splash of color in the drab interior. It struck Paul that it was the only bright spot in the whole place, and he suddenly felt tired and useless.

Ana came to his side and put her hand on his arm. "This will ease pretty soon."

"Well, if it doesn't, we're going to have a problem. I'm worried about the chickens." He had decided to raise poultry the year before because his experience raising pigs the year before that had been a disaster. Those that hadn't been sun-scalded were lost to the flu, along with all the invested time and money. "I'm going to move some more wood in. We're burning it at an awful rate." He shrugged into his coat, wrapped a long wool muffler around his face, and jammed his hat on. "Listen for the door." He pulled it open and went out. For the next hour, he carried load after load of wood in, stacking it nearly chest-high on the back wall. When he was finished, he stuffed more rags over the ill-fitting threshold, and then sat down at the table. He'd done what he could.

Even kept fully stoked day and night, the iron stove barely kept up with the invasion of frigid air. By the end of the third day, the two windows were completely covered, blocking the meager winter light. The shriek of the wind taunted them, and the uncertain light of the coal-oil lamp offered scant comfort. Closed in, they were safe from freezing, but when Paul looked at the meager stores on the shelves, a chill rippled through his body — it wasn't from the cold.

On the fourth day, he pulled the front door open to reveal a solid wall of snow. Packed, it had a beautiful light-blue hue that did little to temper its dangerous appearance. His groin tensed. Ana handed him her biggest frying pan, and he started to dig near the top of the door frame, letting the snow pile up at his feet. He dug as far as he could, and then stood on a chair to continue. He was soon digging outside the house; up and out, he struggled as he neared the limit of his reach. Finally, a rush of cold air blasted in. He climbed off the chair and turned to face his family. He'd thought he'd never see his wife scared, but fear now contorted her face.

Together, they scooped the snow away from the door to make room for the next assault on the cold, white wall. He started to dig again, lying on the shelf he created as he dug. He threw the snow up and out, the shrieking wind grabbing it and sweeping it away. Scoop after scoop he dug, until a way was cleared, and he slid back into the house, wet, frozen, and exhausted. They closed the door against the wind and the terrible sound it made.

Paul sat by the stove in his long under-wear, and his shivering muscles fought against the cold. Ana held a wool blanket up to the heat for several minutes, and then wrapped the trapped warmth around him. He tried to drink the cup of coffee she of-fered, but his trembling arm spilled most of it on the dirt floor. He knew his smile of apology turned into a grimace; his face tight with worry and fatigue. Ana knelt to rub his feet and calves, and gradually, aided by the hot coffee, the blanket and the stove nearby, the trembling subsided, and he felt some of the relief he'd prayed for.

He sat for nearly an hour before he got out of the chair and put on dry clothes. When he pulled on his still-wet shoes, he glanced at Simon, the boy's face screwed tight with anxiety. Paul wondered what the boy might be thinking. He'd watched his father dig them out and now he expects us to just wait until it stops blowing. "Gotta get to the stock, especially the chickens," Paul said to him, knowing the boy would not understand. "You help Ma get that snow into the washtub and the water bucket. Melt it down so we can use it." His wife had the same mosaic of worry etched on her face as she nodded assurance. He realized the body language was for the children, because her face acknowledged the danger he faced. She wound the long scarf around his neck and over his wool hat.

They had two ropes in the house, and Paul tied them together, fixing one end to a nail in the door frame and securing the other to his belt. He had length enough to reach the cowshed. He coiled the slack, and with a reassuring wink at his huddled fold, opened the door and hiked himself up on the snow ledge. Ana closed the door over the rope, and Paul was alone in the storm.

He punched and kicked through the fresh snow the storm had blown back into his hard-won trench. When he broke through, the depth of the cold and the ferocity of the wind stripped the breath from his throat, and icy grit stung the skin around his squinted eyes. He turned his head away from the onslaught and gathered his courage. The cold drove straight to his core, and the tears that streamed from his eyes froze on the scarf. Head down, he leaned as far forward as he could, then, planting one foot in front of the other, moved down the slope of the roof-high drift. The incline dropped him onto the ground between the cowshed and the coop, the area scoured bare by the wind that whipped between the two buildings. He heard the cow bawling.

Paul pulled at the door to the shed and forced it open against the gale. In the surprisingly warm gloom, the cow stood on the south side breathing heavily. She looked at him and bawled again. He let the door close, plunging him into near darkness. "How ya doin', Meg?" He spoke quietly as he moved toward her. "Blowed up quite a storm didn't it? Took us completely by surprise." He heard the cow shift slightly as he felt for the pitchfork that stood just inside the fodder box. He used it to turn a forkful of hay into the manger and then, catching the cow's halter, he moved her to the food. After locking her head in the stanchion, he located the one-legged stool and the milk bucket, and then settled down beside her. Running his hands over the velvet of her udder, he winced at the hardness of the bag; her blood veins stood out like small ropes. "Poor girl," he murmured, "I couldn't help it. Here, we'll get that out for you."

He warmed his hands by rubbing them vigorously on the coarse wool of his trousers before starting to rhythmically stroke the cow's front teats. The milk, willing to flow, sang into the bottom of the tin bucket, and the cow visibly started to relax. He worked methodically, and soon the twin streams made a swooshing sound as they cut through the generated froth. The tension in Paul's shoulders slowly dissipated. He wouldn't try to get the milk back to the house; this bucketful would go to the chickens.

When he'd finished, Paul put the stool back, unlocked the cow's head, and pitched another batch of hay into the manger. Mentally preparing himself to face the blizzard again, he wrapped the scarf around his neck. Ready, he grabbed the rope lifeline, and pushed open the door.

Though he expected it, the wind still took him by surprise. He had no sooner shoved past the door than it slammed shut, leaving him with nothing to hold onto and standing sideways to the screaming storm. The wind caught the bucket and twisted it out of his grip. Paul made a frantic grab at the handle, only to be swept off his feet. The loose bucket bounced once to send the milk flying, and then disappeared from sight. He attempted to break his fall, lost his grip on the rope, and watched in dismay as his lifeline disappeared as well. On his knees, he looked across at the barely visible coop, just fifteen feet away. Offering the back of his head to the icy blast, he crawled to the door and stood. The fierce wind fought his entrance and slammed the door as he stepped inside. Paul's fists clenched and he clamped his teeth: "Oh, Lord, no."

He saw no movement in what looked like all sixty-six chickens jammed into the far corner of the coop, and his shoulders slumped. The drafty coop had better light than the cowshed, but the same cracks that allowed air to move in the July heat, also let the snow go everywhere. The lethal blanket of white had sifted onto the pile of chickens. Paul went to them and found those on top frozen solid. After moving some of the dead, he took off his gloves to feel further down into the pile. Something moved to his touch, and Paul quickly put the frozen hens back. The clammy hand of desperation gripped him as he stepped away and stared at the pitiful pile. He found six more live hens in the laying boxes, their heads buried under their wings.

His chest constricted with dread as he tightened the scarf up and put his gloves on. Taking a deep breath, he punched back the door and charged into the storm. He could see nothing but a confusing swirl of flying snow, and half a dozen steps later, he tripped on the milk bucket and sprawled facedown. The blizzard howled in triumph as the assault of blinding white robbed him of all sense of direction. Panic stricken for a moment, he struggled to his hands and knees, his breath a ragged pant. Then, he swallowed hard, and anger drove out the debilitating fear. He snatched hold of the bucket handle and stood.

The relentless wind at his back pushed him, and he staggered forward, blind. The damp shoes had frozen solid around his numb feet, and his face felt strangely tight. Furious at his sense of helplessness, he forced one foot before the other. "Dammit to hell," he screamed, the oath instantly swallowed by the wind. Suddenly, he lost his footing and pitched forward into the loose snow of the trench. Floundering, arms flailing, Paul slid headfirst down the short incline and banged into the door. Vaguely, he heard the latch lift, and he tumbled inside covered in snow and heaving for air.

"Thank the Lord," Ana said.

Her strong hands under his arm, she helped him farther into the room. Someone pushed the door shut. "Cow's all right," he croaked. "Think we lost most of the chickens." He tried to hide his dismay as Ana helped him up, and he started to pull off the frozen clothes. The children sat clustered around the stove, eyes wide and staring. Abbey, the toddler, clutched Simon's leg, and started to whimper.

Late in the morning of the fifth day, the wind dropped to leave an unsettling silence. Paul shoveled his way out to the front yard, and then he, Simon and the next oldest boy, Axel, went to work. They uncovered the woodpile, cleared the haystack, and moved the chickens into the cowshed; the cow didn't appreciate the company. By late afternoon they had exposed the two windows, and light streamed again into the interior of the sod house.

An uneasy calm prevailed over the usual cheerful banter around the supper table, and Ana put the children to bed early. With them tucked away and sleeping, Paul and Ana sat sharing the last of the day's coffee.

"That was good supper, Ma." His wife looked tired and haggard.

"And the last of the squash." Ana smiled at him, but it looked forced. "Simon sure likes that. Abe too."

"Soon as some of this snow melts off and settles, I'll get back to cutting wood, and we'll be okay." He said it, but didn't believe it for a minute. The storm had buried everything deeper than he'd seen in his lifetime, and he could see it lasting through the rest of the winter.

Ana stood and came to his side. "It could be worse. We still have the cow and a few chickens. And, thank God, the little ones aren't sick. We'll be all right." She wrapped her arms around his head and pressed his face to her bosom.

The familiar feeling of deep respect overwhelmed him, and his eyes stung. *No matter the trial, she's with me.* He gave himself up to her tenderness for a few moments, and listened to the steady beat of her heart. *How much more can we take and still manage to survive?* His father had taught him that hard work and honesty would always see a man through. Taken to heart, he'd always done his best, but he harbored a secret fear. Buried deep and long suppressed, it now filled his mind; failure's cruel fist hung over his head, poised to crush him.

CHAPTER 2

Simon was glad to see things get back to something like normal. He didn't understand why his mother had been so upset. He had gotten confused and lost, and Pa had come to find him, simple as that. They'd been snowed in, and that was scary, but Pa had dug them out. He was ready to get back to school, but the frigid air and drifts piled as high as twenty feet made wanting and doing two different things. Simon read, practiced his letters, and ciphered with chalk on a slate board at the kitchen table. It was what he was doing now, his fingers dry and scaly from rubbing the board clean between problems. He missed school, at least, most of it. He lowered his chin into his cupped hands, and the slate board drifted out of focus.

A young single woman named Margaret Fritz taught at and maintained the Carlisle

School. In dark clothes, hair tied back in a bun so tight it made her squint, she always had a scowl on her face, and Simon thought she looked like a witch. His mother said that Miss Fritz was a good teacher and a good person too. *Miss Fritz just missed a few good chances early on, and life had kind of left her behind,* was the way his ma put it. When she'd said that, Simon had nodded like it made sense, but in fact he wondered, if Miss Fritz had been left behind somewhere, how come she was here? And so, every day, with every intention to please and learn, Simon applied himself.

At first, the older kids in the school caused enough trouble for Miss Fritz that she more or less ignored Simon. But, eventually, she either whacked the bigger kids into submission with her ever-present hickory ruler, or they got tired of standing in the stuffy cloakroom and settled down. Unfortunately for Simon, the result of their improved deportment was that she then had time to direct her full attention toward him, and apparently, for no reason that he could see, she particularly disliked Simon.

This interest caused him no end of confusion and hurt feelings; he'd carefully write the alphabet, the letters perfectly formed, all even on top and spaced just so, only to have the inevitable backward "d" or "b" send her into a fit. He knew he wasn't stupid because Pa said he wasn't, and that was good enough, but after six weeks of constant criticism, Simon started to doubt his worth.

Simon got along quite well with most of his classmates, especially Buell Mace, a skinny kid with coal-black hair and eyes that were just as dark. His pa ran the blacksmith and livery in town. Buell didn't have a ma, the why of that something Simon hadn't pursued. Buell didn't say much to anyone, not even Miss Fritz. When recess came, he'd usually go to the sunny side of the school-house to just sit, and watch.

Simon kind of liked the boy who sat next to him. Named Gus, after his pa, Werner Gustav Swartz, who ran the trading store, he was nine years old, fat, unkempt, and rowdy. If you heard a girl squeal, you could be sure Gus was either there, or in the act of leaving quickly. Simon couldn't under-stand how, but Gus seemed completely unaffected by Miss Fritz's temper. Every fifteen or twenty minutes, she would whack, pinch, or ear-pull him, and every fifteen or twenty minutes, Gus, big grin on his face, would flick another spitball, or slam another hand in a book, or belch. He seemed to enjoy school immensely, and he thought flicking spitballs was a cracker. Therefore, Simon reasoned, if Gus could do it, so could he, and so came the day he learned that life does not treat everyone equally.

His very first spitball went astray, and the cold, spit-soaked wad of paper caught Miss Fritz square in the ear hole. His face in his hands, Simon barely glimpsed Miss Fritz's head snap around, but to his horror, he saw quite clearly out the corner of his eye, Gus, grinning so widely it must have hurt, point his pudgy finger, and direct Miss Fritz to an object for her wrath. Simon squeezed his eyes closed, but could not shut out the sound of the four giant strides that brought her to his desk.

She grasped his ear firmly in her bony fingers and brought him out of his seat. Straight up he rose, as if levitated, his head tilted awkwardly, and then skipped directly toward the cloakroom, his feet barely touching the wood floor. His panic rose with each long step as his fellow students tracked his course, mouths agape. He had attacked Miss Fritz! What had he been thinking? Had he been thinking? Even hulking Armand Swaggart, fourteen years old and almost a man, had always stopped short of physical contact.

Through the curtain and into the cloakroom she marched him, until he stood alone and out of sight with the witch; alone and at her mercy, a sentiment, Simon was sure, she knew nothing about. Along the outside wall, coat hooks, four and a half feet off the floor, and eighteen inches apart, stuck out like so many skinny fingers, tips turned up. Miss Fritz grabbed Simon by the pants waist and lifted him off the floor like he weighed nothing. She hooked the back of his trousers on one of the skinny fingers and dropped him. He stopped with a jerk. Her eyes sparked, and she didn't utter a sound as she turned and marched out of the cloakroom, digging at the gloop in her ear.

Simon counted the clack-clack of Miss Fritz's sturdy brogans as she crossed to the front of the room. He hung there dumbstruck for several seconds, the classroom as silent as a rock. And then she went at them, railing for what seemed like forever, the whack of her ruler on desktops splitting the air to emphasize her points. Her voice got higher and screechier as she chastised the class, her steam really up. Simon actually felt he had the better of the deal, just hanging there, looking around at lunch buckets, various hats, coats, and girls' vests.

It was after Miss Fritz had blown off sufficient steam, and settled back into her sing-songy, put-a-polecat-to-sleep voice, that Simon started to feel the intended effects of being strung up by his waistband. The pants-seam that runs from front to back had found its way into the valley that separates one butt cheek from the other. As Simon squirmed to relieve the binding, the rough wool cloth of his trousers chafed the tender skin of his crotch. And when he tried to support himself with his hands on the hooks either side, the points dug into his palms and he quickly gave up on the idea. He leaned forward and tried to get some purchase with his heels, but that didn't work either; it just chafed more. It soon occurred to him that the coat hooks were not that at all, they were torture tools, installed by the evil witch in the next room to punish spitball-throwing boys.

After half an hour, Simon started to regret his mischief. "Dern Gus," he muttered to a coat, three hooks down. "He didn't tell me the wad might stick to my finger." He squirmed. "That wadder was meant for Sarah." Once more, he tried to relieve the crotch pressure by using the hooks beside him. No use; his hands were too tender from previous efforts, and besides that, when he straightened up, the hook he hung on dug into his spine. As he sagged back down, his full weight continued the process of cutting him in two.

"This isn't fair," Simon complained out loud to the floor, and conveniently forgot whose fault it was. *I'm going to be damaged forever if I don't get down. I'm a good kid. Ma says so all the time, and so does Aunt Ruth. This isn't right, and besides, I can't take much more.* His throat tightened.

The first tear welled up, squirted out of his eye, and cut through the recess-dirt like a swipe of a mother's spit bath. He could imagine the clean pink line all the way to his chin. One tear begat another, and soon Simon, in full flood, was sobbing silently. Suddenly, Miss Fritz threw back the curtain and reentered the cloakroom to unhook Simon — recess. Snatched from the hook like a fetched ham, she set him down, and then stomped out. Both Simon's legs and spirit failed at the same time and he slumped to the floor, his dignity gone. The tears of self-pity became tears of frustration and embarrassment, the pain in his crotch enhanced by her having seen him cry.

Of course, every kid in the class, eager to see what had happened, crowded around to get a closer look. Their attention to his tearful plight made it all the worse. He was about to explode with humiliation when Jacob Luger appeared. Jake, as he was called, sat in the back, on the boys' side of the room and rarely said a word. Gus said Jake was a dummy because, at eight, he hadn't even finished the second McGuffey's reader. His sudden appearance didn't make Simon happy.

"What're all you ninnies lookin' at?" Jake bawled. "Get on outta here, before I thump a couple of ya."

The smaller children scattered like chickens in a hawk's shadow, out the door in seconds. The outburst shocked and frightened Simon some, but he felt grateful and mortified at the same time. Jake had never said a word, or even looked at him, in the two months since school started, so Simon thought the rescue a bit strange.

Jake clumped up to Simon, grabbed him by the arm and stood him on his feet. "Guess you showed the ol' witch a thing or two didn't ya? She kept looking at the curtain, expecting you to start hollerin', and by gum, ya never did."

"Yeah, I'm not afeared of her." He couldn't completely keep the quaver out of his voice. "Shucks, I was just getting comfortable before she came in and dropped me on the floor." His voice felt stronger.

"That's what hurt . . . that dropping." He liked his story more and more. "Thought my leg got busted there for a minute. And her finger in my eye didn't help . . . made it water something awful."

Jake grinned his approval, and punched him in the shoulder, which hurt — Jake was a big boy. "Let's go out and throw rocks at the outhouse," he invited and headed for the door.

Simon could hardly believe his good luck. Jake had bought the finger-in-the-eye story, hook, line and sinker. He did his best to stride as he followed Jake out into the dusty yard. Buell gave him a shy smile from his place by the wall. Simon smiled back at him, and nearly ran over the girl standing in his path.

"I'm sorry, Simon," she said in her melodious voice. "She was mean to do that." It was Sarah, the prettiest girl in town, and Judge Kingsley's only child. Simon was afraid of the judge.

"She didn't hurt me none," he said. "I could've stayed there all day."

"Well, I think it was mean. Do you want to walk me home after school?"

He couldn't speak until Jake punched him again, on the same spot, and headed for a cluster of kids on the other side of the playground. "Su-su-sure," he said, rubbing his arm. "I know where you live. It's right on my way."

"I know. I'll see you after." She ran off to the girls' cluster, leaving him to stand, stunned.

Remembering that day caused a flutter in his chest that made it hard to breathe. His gaze picked up the slate again, and then he looked around the sod house, and his family. It was so crowded.

As the days passed, small things started to niggle. To stay cooped up in a twenty-by-twenty-foot-square house with six other people is hard enough if they are all able to somehow keep themselves busy. But with three babies, two youngsters and two adults, the harmony was soon lost in the cacophony of squabbles and tearful complaints. His pa had made one trip into town already to tell his customers that he had lost his chicken flock, and that he could no longer deliver the eggs they counted on. He'd also gone to see Mr. Swartz at the trading store about getting credit until some work came available. The customers understood and were very appreciative of his father coming by to let them know, but the same could not be said for Mr. Swartz.

More often than not, Simon lay awake after bedtime with thoughts about something he had learned in school, or heard his folks say. And because of this, if his folks had a discussion around the kitchen table at night, the chances were good he heard it. And so it was that the dire straits they found themselves in were shared with Simon.

The beans and rice might hold out until spring, and they had a couple hundred pounds of spuds and some parsnips and rutabagas in the root cellar. But they needed flour, salt, soda, coffee, and sugar, in that order. Normally, his pa would have had another month to cut and deliver wood to his regular customers for winter. The storm had fixed that. And normally they could count on selling ten or twelve dozen eggs a week, and that, too, was gone as they ate the few eggs that the dozen underfed hens laid. And they certainly couldn't eat the chickens. He'd heard them say the cow and chickens plus a few staples would see them through, but an odd, unsteady tone in his mother's voice told Simon they were in trouble.

CHAPTER 3

Paul watched helplessly as his family submitted to their fate and struggled on, through the end of November and into December. He sent Simon to school when it was not deadly cold, and he went to town nearly every day to look for work, but he didn't find any.

Ana cooked her vegetables, rice, beans and potatoes in every conceivable fashion: rice pudding, rice with milk gravy, creamed rice, refried rice, creamed potatoes, fried potatoes, baked potatoes, scalloped potatoes, boiled potatoes and baked beans. And so it went into January, Christmas more or less ignored except for a red candle that Ana had been saving. She lit it on Christmas Eve and allowed it to burn all the way down as Paul read the Christmas story from the Bible. And then came February and the night they faced the inevitable.

That evening Ana had refried some baked

spuds. Normally, when they were nice and brown, she'd pour half a dozen whipped eggs over the top to cook for a few minutes. It made a thick potato pancake that everyone really liked. Except tonight there had been no salt on the spuds, and there had only been three eggs to pour on, a skimpy meal that tasted flat. However, the hungry kids didn't seem to mind, but Paul noticed that Ana hadn't eaten anything; instead, she'd stood by the stove with Eric nestled against her breast. And after the meal, she'd pushed the children off to bed instead of letting them listen to one of his stories or hear him play some old songs on his zither.

After the usual jostling and fussing, the children grew quiet and Paul leaned his elbows on the kitchen table. Ana absently turned her wedding band round and round on her finger. "I see you didn't eat again tonight, Ma," he said quietly. He tried to keep the concern out of his voice.

"Can't seem to get up much of an appetite. I've been feeling kinda strange the last couple of days. Can't quite figger it out."

"Have you felt the baby moving around?"

"That's the problem, I haven't. I sat real still for almost an hour today and waited. Nothing." Ana's voice sounded unsteady.

"Do we know for sure how far along you are?"

"About four months." She paused. "Why are we being punished, Paul?" She pinched her brows together. "I'm feeling a bit lost tonight. Usually we can count on things working out, but I'm having some doubt." Tears welled up in her eyes.

"I think the problem's our eating. You need something that meat gives us, and we haven't been eating meat." He felt his anger rising, and he didn't know where to direct it. "I think we're paying for my foolishment with Grandpa."

"Your choice was the only one that could be made then, and you were forced to make it. Please don't blame yourself."

"It still rips my guts to watch you and the little ones go without. It's my job to provide, and I ain't getting it done." He lowered his head into his hands.

"You're a good man, and I wouldn't have another. You're good to the kids, and nobody is more willing to bend his back than you. We'll be okay."

"I don't think so." He sighed. "I really don't think so." He paused for a long time. "I'm going to go see Matt tomorrow," he said finally. "He'll help if I put it to him right."

Ana didn't look convinced. "I hate to see you go through that."

Simon could hear she meant it. *What in tarnation is going on here? Uncle Matt can be kind of mean once in a while, but he is Pa's brother. I'd help Axel, no matter what.*

His uncle Matt lived way on the other side of town. Pa and him were brothers and Aunt Ruth and Ma were sisters. They said that made Cousin David as close to being his brother as you can get without being brothers. Simon didn't care much for David, who was two years older. He liked to boss Simon around. Simon thought his pa and Uncle Matt were as different as pudding and pickles. His pa said Uncle Matt's farm covered eighty acres and Grandpa Steele had settled it in 1835. He said it was fine land, right along the river with plenty of well water, and flat as the bottom of a skillet. Why Uncle Matt had the whole eighty acres instead of sharing it with his pa was a vague question that floated around Simon's head, but it had never concerned him enough to ask. He accepted the fact his cousin David had it a lot easier than he did, and that was that. And when they came to visit, the differences were apparent, and Uncle Matt pointed out often who was the rich side of the family.

Simon loved his Aunt Ruth almost as much as his own mother. During the infrequent visits, the three of them would work in the kitchen while the men sat outside on the bench under the window. The women folk would laugh and talk for hours about recipes, babies, faraway relatives, and stuff Simon couldn't hear that caused them to just hoot, and cover their mouths to muffle it. Once in a while they would stop and listen when the giggles got real loud. Simon thought they were checking to see if Uncle Matt had heard. Sometimes they'd get their heads back together again and continue to laugh, but sometimes they'd sit quietly for a while. Simon was sure it depended on whether they heard a grumble or not. Uncle Matt, a real religious man, always prayed long and loud before they ate, and he didn't think it was right to laugh or have fun. That made him altogether different from his brother — in that way and many others.

In the end, the women would prepare food and wait on the family. They'd serve coffee, cup after cup of the stuff, which Simon couldn't understand because it tasted awful, and then they'd eat. A feast of fresh-baked bread rings stuffed with cinnamon, sugar, raisins and butter; molasses cookies, egg custard, and gooseberry pie. Just the thought raised a torrent of saliva in Simon's mouth that nearly choked him. And potatoes, roast chicken, parsnips, rye bread, and gravy that made his pa groan. He could almost taste it.

But Uncle Matt always had to say something bad: about how ragged Paul's family looked, how small the house was, how come they could put that much food on the table, yet not manage to save enough to buy a horse and wagon. And he'd always add that it was probably God's punishment for something, but he'd never say what, except to remind them they were all sinners. Ma would wind up looking at her plate, while Pa sat silently, and the little ones wondered where all the laughter had gone. Soon after, Uncle Matt would say they were leaving, and his aunt Ruth would look real sad, and then later he'd hear soft gasps coming from behind the curtain; his mother crying, while his father worked at the woodpile, smashing the sawn lengths to splinters. And Simon would go to sleep confused, like he was right now. He knew he shouldn't listen to grown-up talk but he couldn't help it.

"Let me talk to Ruth first," Ana said. "Maybe she can calm the waters a little."

"I don't want you gettin' into it," Paul replied. "Besides, how would you get over there, nearly two miles?"

"You could ask them over for coffee." She was silent for a moment. "But we don't have any coffee." Her voice cracked and she started to sob quietly.

Paul watched his wife cry, his fists bunched tight. Then his hands sought hers. "Don't cry, Ma. Please, don't cry," he whispered. For several minutes he let her weep until, with a long shuddering breath, she seemed to get her tears under control. "Matt hates the sight of me, Ma, and I'm at fault for it. I never should have bucked Pa when we had to figger some way to help Matt out."

"For a father to ask that, and a brother to go along, was more than a real man can take," Ana said, her voice raised slightly. "Your father was a hard man, and Matt was like a harlot, doing whatever, without a thought for his soul. Your father knew Matt was weak, and saw this way as Matt's only chance." She slapped her hand on the table. "The fact that Matt turned out to be a lot weaker than Grandpa had bargained is Grandpa's fault, not yours!"

Paul felt helpless in the face of her anger. "I should've agreed to work for Matt, and taken what Matt was willing to give us, just like it said in the will. Instead, I go off in a huff, and now we got nothin'. I just wish I could have had one last talk with Pa before he died. Ruth's sitting all fat and sleek over there, and you're here with nothing but dirt around you. And me with no work." He tried but couldn't keep the sound of defeat out of his voice.

Ana grasped his hand. "Please don't do this. I went where my heart led me, and I'm happy with my choice. We have five wonderful children, and come spring everything will look better."

"No, I gotta go see Matt. We're gonna starve if I can't get a pig or a beef to help us through. I'm going to ask for a loan too. No salt or sugar or coffee. Good Lord, woman, we gotta eat!"

CHAPTER 4

The next morning Paul opened the door and stepped into the house, bringing with him a blast of cold air. Simon pulled the quilt over the tops of his ears. Ana stood at the stove with her back to him and she turned as the air hit her. He'd watched Ana scoop rice out of the sack last night, put it in the kettle, and then pour several ladles of water over the top. The rice would now be soft and swollen, and it wouldn't be long before she'd pour in milk and add sugar and lots of eggs and raisins. It would be delicious. He sighed. *Except there isn't any sugar or raisins, and few of these.* He glanced at the basket he held and then handed it to Ana. She took out the four eggs and put them in a rack he'd carved. The six empty spots made the four brown orbs look small and lonely.

Half an hour later, the family sat around the table, each engrossed in their bowl of creamed rice. "I'm going to take Simon with me today," he announced. Simon almost choked on his rice. "If I can arrange for a steer, I'll need some help herding it home. If I get a pig, I'll see if I can use Mace's wagons, and maybe Simon can help me drive the horses. What do ya think, Simon?" His son just stared. Not so Axel. "I'll help, Pa. I'll help ya drive," he offered, his excitement making his voice squeak.

"Only got enough eyes to watch one of you, Ax, maybe next time."

Axel deflated instantly, his disappointment showing like rain clouds.

"You can help me churn that sweet cream, Ax, I'd appreciate that," Ana said.

The boy looked dubious. "Can I shake it all the way? Till it's just a lump in the jar?"

"Yes, all the way."

Axel squinted at his mother, thought for a second, and then treated them with his smile. His cheeks rose to a crinkle, his eyes sparkled, and the grin he displayed was so big you'd have thought his ears moved back to make room. "Deal," he said. "All the way to the lump." Axel looked pleased.

Paul and Simon set out at noon after the wan sun had done what it could to warm the air. Though Paul could cover the two miles in about forty minutes, Simon's

42

shorter legs slowed things down considerably. As they passed Judge Kingsley's house, the upstairs curtains moved aside, and the judge's daughter, Sarah, peeked out. Simon saw it too, and with his neck craned up and to the side, tripped on a pile of frozen horse manure and went down in a heap, right in front of the house. Paul almost burst out laughing as Simon scrambled to his feet and hurried ahead. He knew Simon walked Sarah to school.

At the livery in town, Paul pushed open a narrow side door to let them into the ironworking part. Paisley Mace, the blacksmith who owned it, stood facing them, his anvil clanging as he worked. The smithy wasn't as tall as Paul, but looked just as powerful, his impressive arms and wide shoulders the result of countless hours lifting and dropping the heavy hammer. He greeted them with a wide smile. Paul loved the smell of the livery: grain, hay, horse manure mixed with sweat, dust, and Mace's tobacco. And it was Mace, never Paisley — he hated being called Paisley.

"Hello, Paul. Hello, Simon," Mace greeted them and stuck out his hand.

Obviously pleased to be called by name, Simon took the work-hardened hand and his expression said he was wondering if he'd get it back. Mace pumped it a couple of times and let go.

"Phew, Paul, that little guy has got a grip," Mace said.

Simon looked at the ground, tapped his foot and the scuff of dust he'd formed exploded into the air. He started to make another pile with his toe.

"Yes'ir, gonna be like your pa, lucks to ya." Mace was Paul's best friend and vice versa.

"Don't hurt none to ask, Mace, any work about?" Paul shook the smithy's hand.

"Afraid not." Mace looked uncomfortable. "This blasted cold weather is keeping everyone's head down. The stage and freight has even slowed to four or five trips a month. I'm having a hard time myself. Be glad when this breaks."

"That's for sure. I'm goin' to see Matt about some meat. If I get a pig I'd appreciate the use of one of your rigs."

"You know I'd do'er in a minute, but the wagon's out at the McQueens' and won't be back for another four days, and both small rigs went first thing this morning. Sorry."

"That's okay, I appreciate it."

"Can't you use Matt's?"

"Hate to ask."

"I understand. Wish I could help."

The side door opened and Buell came in.

"Hey, son." Mace's pride showed in his face, "Say hello to Mr. Steele."

Buell walked up to Paul. "Hi," he said, his voice barely a whisper. He didn't offer his hand.

"Fine-looking boy, Mace. Gonna make a blacksmith outta him?"

"Not if I can help it. This one's going to school, maybe even back to Ohio to one of them colleges."

From the look on his face, Buell didn't think much of the schooling idea. The boy turned to watching what Simon was doing. Tap, poof.

"Well, best be getting to it." Paul hoped the reluctance he felt wasn't apparent in his voice.

"Luck," Mace said. He stuck out his hand again. "Don't be a stranger."

Paul shook the hand, nodded and then he and Simon stepped out of the warm barn and into the crisp air.

A few minutes later they arrived at Matt Steele's farm, a place as fancy as Paul's was plain. Set away from the river and situated on the south side of the road that divided the farm east to west, eighty acres of corn, hay and grain fields, now fallow and snow

45

covered, surrounded the white two-story house. A porch ran the length of the home on the north side, and in back stood a small orchard of perfectly aligned, stubby trees, pruned short and hunkered down until spring. A low root cellar stood hard against the eastern end of the building's stone foundation.

The barn, bigger than the house, had a rounded roof with a distinctive turned-up edge. It stood across the road and to the west, flanked on the right by several rows of low sheds with fenced runs attached. On the left sat two snow-covered humps, fifteen-foot-high haystacks, one nearly half gone and cut square on the end like a loaf of bread, the hay saw leaning against the vertical face. Signs of a third haystack, now a well-stomped memory, witnessed how much had been used during the first six weeks of winter. A low stone foundation of some sort, unfinished, stood across the road from the house, and a bit east. A very careful and meticulous man had apparently laid out the farm. Paul and Simon trudged past the old foundation, walked up to the house, and mounted the porch.

Paul knocked, dreading it as he did, but Simon appeared eager to get inside. Ruth always had milk and sweets for the kids. He knocked again, this time a little harder. He could feel the veins in his neck had already started to swell. "He saw us coming when he walked from the barn to the house," Paul muttered.

One more time, Paul raised his hand, but before he could hit the frame, the door opened and there stood David, Matt's son.

"Hello," he said, and just stood there.

"Is your father home?" Paul tried to keep the irritation out of his voice.

"Yeah, just a minute." David turned to go.

"Is he in the house?" Paul stopped David in mid-stride with his tone.

"Well . . . yeah."

"Then invite us in, you young pup," Paul shot, and immediately wished he hadn't said it.

David turned just as Ruth Steele came out of the kitchen. "Good grief, David, ask your uncle Paul and Simon in. Where are your manners?" she sputtered, obviously more than a bit irritated. "Come in, you two. How's Ana doing? Are the kids well? Come in, come in."

Grandpa Steele had been a cabinetmaker in the finest tradition, and the inside of the farmhouse showed it. Warm wood furniture filled the living room: bookstands, a coatrack, shelves on the walls. Paul counted six oil lamps, and those in the front room alone. They went into the kitchen, the heat suffocating compared to being outside. Matt sat at the table, his hands wrapped around a coffee mug, his eyes bleary and his nose running.

"What brings you out here?" Matt sniffed and barely glanced up.

"Got a problem I want to talk to you about," Paul said. "Thought you might see your way to help."

"Of course we'll help," Ruth said. "What is it?" Her brow knitted and she tilted her head.

"Go into the front room, Ruth." Matt scowled. "I'll talk to Paul."

"But —"

"Now!" Matt said as he half rose in his chair. Paul clenched his hands, then consciously relaxed them.

Ruth took Simon by the arm. "You come with me. When the men are through, we'll get some apple bread and milk. Would you like that?" She hustled the boy out of the room.

"Well, what kinda crack you got your ass caught in now?" Matt asked. He pulled a handkerchief out of his shirt pocket and snorted into it. He didn't invite Paul to sit.

"The winter has hit us hard, Matt, we —"

48

"Same as everybody else." Matt cut him off.

Paul's jaw muscles tensed. "I'm going to ask you once, Matt, and only once. I need some meat for the kids and Ana. She's expecting a baby an—"

"Judas Priest, Paul. Again?" Matt scoffed, the smirk on his face had now settled in. "Can't you control yourself?" Matt had been married longer than Paul, and had only David.

"Ana's expecting, and she needs something more than beans and spuds," Paul continued. "Surely you can spare a pig, or a beef. Even a half would help."

"And what is my family supposed to eat? We're in no better shape than anybody else."

Paul knew there were at least three dozen pigs in the sheds, and eight or ten beeves, not counting the six milking cows in the barn. He could feel his anger start to rise. "I know this is not the way Pa would have seen it."

"Pa ain't here, I am," Matt shot back. "And what I say, goes."

"I said I'd ask once. I heard your answer without you sayin' it." Paul turned and walked into the parlor. "Come on, Simon, we best be leaving."

Ruth stood by the front door, hands on

hips. "You are not leaving without some meat. Matt, you can't do this to your own blood, and I certainly won't do it to mine. You go pick out an animal." Paul could see she was getting angrier by the second, and Matt had not yet come out of the kitchen. "Do you hear me?" she demanded.

Matt came into the front room, his face was sullen and mean-looking. "I hear you, woman. How in hell can I miss it?" He jammed his handkerchief into his back pocket.

"I won't have you cussing in front of the boys, either, Matthew Steele," she threatened, her normal meek manner long gone. "You go find an animal, or I will." She turned to David. "David and I."

Matt grabbed his hat and coat and silently put them on as he scowled at his wife, his eyes flat and ugly. He pushed past her, yanked the door open and turned, "You two gonna stand there, or come with me?" He stomped across the porch and down the steps.

Paul checked to see where David was and turned to Ruth. "You going to be all right when I leave, sis?" Paul asked, nearly inaudibly.

David moved closer to them.

Ruth stepped near to hug him and whispered, "Don't you worry, Paul. I've been married to him long enough to know where I'm at." She did not look at all sure. Peering at Simon, she knelt down. "You go home and take good care of your mama, and tell her Auntie Ruth loves her, okay?" She gave him a long hug, her eyes shut. Paul imagined her feeling Simon and thinking Ana.

Paul and Simon went out the door in time to see Matt round the corner of the barn. When they reached it, Matt stood by one of the low sheds, looking in.

"Come over here," he grumbled.

Paul went over, Simon right behind. They bent down and peered through the low door into the gloomy interior. Inside, a full-grown hog lay stretched out on its belly, breathing laboriously. Paul stooped under the lintel and moved closer. An abnormal heat radiated off the animal, and the smell inside was not the usual swine stink. By the look of a large open wound on its neck, Paul reckoned the animal had been tusked by another or a coyote had been at it. The wound, surrounded by a crusty fringe of dried body fluid, seeped even more with every breath the pig took.

"Good Lord, Matt, there ain't nothin' I can do for that poor thing. You ought to shoot it."

"I'm giving you that one. Take it or leave it."

"What?" Paul shouted. "Are you completely gone mad?"

"Take it or leave it." Matt's voice took on a nasty edge. "More than you deserve."

Paul bolted out of the shed. "Go back to the house, Simon. Now!"

Simon turned and ran toward the barn.

Paul turned on his brother, his face hot with anger. "I've half a notion to put you and that pig out of your misery."

Matt stepped back a pace.

Paul's breath came in ragged gasps. "How in God's name can you even suggest such a thing? How can you let that animal suffer? Have you forgotten everything Pa taught us?"

Matt would not look him in the eye. "I don't owe you a damn thing," Matt answered back, sullen now. "Nothin'."

"Where do you get this evil that's in you, Matt? Lord knows you weren't abused. Pa left you the whole farm. You got a good wife. I don't understand it."

"And always you mention Ruth. Why is that?" Matt demanded, his mouth twisting. "Always got to bring her into it."

"What you talking about?"

"Think I don't know?" Spit formed in the

corners of his mouth. "I ain't blind, or stupid." Matt was now shouting.

Paul hesitated, unable to speak, or make any sense of what his brother was saying.

Matt sneered. "Now get your lazy ass off my farm, and take that skinny whelp with you."

Matt had not retreated far enough, and Paul's balled fist slowed little as it hit his brother's face. Matt's nose crunched, snot sprayed, and he staggered back against the shed's lintel. With a grunt, he folded at the waist like a closing book, and landed inside. He didn't move. Paul stood for a minute rubbing his knuckles, and stared at the shed opening. Then, he turned and walked slowly to the house.

Ruth must have seen him coming and met him at the door. "Was there trouble?" She stepped back to let him in.

"He wanted to give me a sick pig," Paul said flatly, still not believing it. He looked past her for Simon.

"The one with the sore on its neck? Surely not that one? Oh, Paul."

"Come on, Simon," Paul shouted. "We gotta go."

Simon came out of the kitchen, a huge chunk of brown bread in one hand, and a glass of milk in the other. David rushed out the door and ran toward the barn.

Ruth pointed at the dining table. "I put some things in the sack for Ana and there's a bag of flour too. I wish it could be more, but I haven't been keeping up with the store because of the cold. I wish I had some money."

"Bless you, sis. We'll be all right. Don't worry," Paul said. "And if he lays a hand on you, I'll know, and I'll be back. You tell him that. C'mon, Simon." Paul picked up the sack and bag, and Ruth opened the door for them. Paul followed Simon onto the porch.

Ruth, hand to her mouth, followed them outside. "I'm sorry. I'm so sorry. Hug Ana for me, Paul." She turned quickly, her head down, and went into the house.

Paul walked into the road and looked past the barn to see David struggling to drag his father out of the pig shed. Matt, half-crawling, half-walking on his knees, held a bloodied handkerchief to his face with one hand and savagely lashed out at David with the other. Paul felt a terrible sense of loss as he recognized the look that Matt cast across the barnyard. He turned Simon by the shoulder, and together they headed down the road toward town.

It had to have been a very confusing and

frightening experience for Simon, and Paul regretted that. His son had seen him completely lose his temper, and he regretted that too. But most of all, he regretted the loss of his brother.

When Paul entered the house, Ana stood busy at the stove. She looked at him, and his face must have answered the question on her lips, because she didn't say a word. He shut the door and put the two bags on the table. "Ruth sent some things." Simon dragged a chair closer to the stove, and sat. Paul took a seat at the table.

Ana untied the cord that held the smaller bag closed, and turned the sides down. She unloaded several brown paper packages, all neatly tied with yarn, and four or five glass jars, treasures Ruth had sent: coffee, several sugar cones, salt, raisins and dried apples, lard, a small tin of cinnamon, and some soda. In the very bottom, wrapped in colored paper, she found an apron with spring flowers embroidered around the edge. She gasped, then sat on the bench and stared at the gifts, her hand pressed against her trembling lips. There wasn't a lot of any one thing, but Paul could see his sister-in-law knew what they needed and had sent what she could. The feeling of gratitude overwhelmed him, but he knew this could cause Ruth a lot of grief. Ana looked at him, and then came over to lay her hands on his shoulders, kneading the tense muscles.

"You did what you could," she murmured. "Don't punish yourself."

"He offered me a sick pig, a fevered, poisoned animal that needed to be shot. I lost my head and smacked him." Paul looked up at his wife. She bit the inside of her clenched lips as her eyes suddenly brimmed with tears. He swallowed hard to keep his own in check, but one blink, and they flowed down his whiskered cheeks. Hunched over his knees, he covered his face with his hands, and fought to control the urge to sob. He felt Ana's hand on his back, the other on his arm, fingers gently patting. After a minute or so, he looked up at the children, now quietly sitting by the table, their eyes wide at the sight of their tearful father. He nodded at his wife and sniffed.

Ana went to her stove and lifted the heavy skillet lid. Sliding a broad wooden spatula under a steaming pile of sliced potatoes, she flipped them bottom up; a golden brown, they glistened with butterfat. She hurried to sprinkle on a bit of the salt he had brought home, knowing the spuds would taste much better tonight.

Sleep did not come easy that night. Paul knew the largesse would not last very long, and the problem of meat was still very real. His dreams that night were vivid images of his family, cold and hungry, standing outside Matt's home while Matt stood at the window and laughed at them. Only it wasn't Matt's home, it was the home he'd grown up in, and where somehow, he was no longer welcome. What had gone wrong, so dreadfully wrong?

CHAPTER 5

Ana knew the effect the smell of the coffee would have, and smiled when she heard Paul stir behind the curtain. A few minutes later, he walked up behind her, put his arms around her waist and nuzzled her neck gently. "You feel like a porcupine, you know that?" She giggled.

He pulled his face out of her hair.

"No, don't stop. I didn't say I didn't like it."

Paul went back, and this time he buried his face in her neck and huffed a mouth full of air through his pursed lips, shaking his head.

Ana scrunched her shoulders with pleasure. "Now quit that. I've got work to do." She glanced over her shoulder at the sleeping children.

Paul slapped her lightly on her behind. "I'm going to hold off on the coffee till I've taken care of the cow. I want to really enjoy that cup." He put his coat on and went out the door.

Ana gathered the ingredients and mixed a piecrust. Half of the dough she rolled and laid in a pan, then she flattened the rest before she went to the stove. A wisp of steam followed the lifted lid as she tested the plumping dried apples. She'd decided on this treat earlier that morning when Paul's soft moans and thrashing had roused her. She'd gotten up, set the apples to soak on the stove and gone back to bed. Now they were ready and she carried the pan to the table and dumped the fruit into a bowl. After adding a scant cup of crushed sugar, a handful of flour, and a teaspoon of cinnamon, she mixed the fragrant ingredients thoroughly.

In a few minutes, she'd finished and pushed the pie away from her, into the middle of the table. Beautiful, she thought proudly, just what we need today. Along with the pie-dough scraps, arranged in the bottom of a skillet and sprinkled with sugar and cinnamon, she put the pie in the oven. "Good job," she said with a sigh, and rubbed her floury hands on her new apron. She felt eyes, and looked up to meet Simon's as they peered over the edge of his bed. A contented smile wreathed his face, and she felt a rush of love for her oldest boy.

Paul came in with the milk bucket and set it down by the door. He carefully took off his coat and hung it on a peg, then took four eggs out of each pocket and presented them to Ana, one at a time.

"Things are looking up." He chuckled. "Leastwise, the chickens seem to be happy." He sniffed the air. "Smelled them apples when I got up. Could it be we're having pie this evening?"

"If you're good and don't stay underfoot all day, you just might," Ana said. "With the sun shining and good weather facing us, I thought I might get the children in the tub today."

Bathing wasn't bad in the summer when she could put the children in the sun to dry off and stay warm. In winter, it turned into a real chore. She put her washtub on the stove and looked at Simon. His scowl had told her what he thought of the idea when she'd mentioned it, and she didn't blame him. At least they were able to get well water now and not have to melt snow. Simon started out the door with the bucket.

Simon was her appointed dryer. When Ana finished with the squirming Abbey, she draped the towel around the baby's back, and pairing the ends together in front, lifted her from the tub. Then she swung her in the improvised sling, and after a couple of turns around and several squeals of delight, she deposited the tiny girl in Simon's lap, to giggle and squirm some more. Ana figured they all did it because they thought it irritated him, and that was the way Simon played the game. He hollered, threatened and rubbed, until Abbey, pink, warm, and dry, sat on the bunk bed wrapped in a blanket; her turn to sit and watch the next victim. Ana pointed at Abe.

Simon came last, which meant the water, now a light-gray color, would be cool, almost cold. Starting over with fresh water was too much to consider, so he climbed into the tub, settled down with his knees poked out and submitted to her scrub brush. He acted like it was torture, plain and simple. But, finally, thoroughly scrubbed, Simon stood up in anticipation of his turn in the towel swing. *He's so skinny with his ribs sticking out.* He rested his hands on his bony hips. Shaking her head, she took a deep breath, and threw the now-soggy towel around his back and just under his butt. She gathered the ends for a good grip, and when Simon leaned back, Ana lifted.

The piercing stab to her belly jerked her

body stiff with one violent spasm. She let loose of the towel, powerless to catch Simon as he crashed to the floor. Gritting her teeth against the pain, she looked down to see him half in and half out of the tub. Water flew everywhere as the frightened boy bolted across the space to the bunk bed. The walls of the soddy spun around her and she fell. Struggling to remain conscious, she pushed herself partially upright on the muddy floor, and the children started to wail, all at the same time.

Small hands gripped her shoulders, and then she was sitting upright on the floor. She tried to get up and another dagger of pain shot through her belly. Rolling to her knees, her hands slipped on the muddy floor. Simon stood to help her to her feet. "I need to sit down," she said and moved the three steps to the table where Simon pulled out a chair. Gingerly, she took a seat, fully expecting another assault on her body. "Get dressed and go find your father. I think he's with Mr. Mace."

Simon frantically scrambled to get his wet feet into his pants. Not pausing to put on socks, he stamped his feet into his shoes, grabbed his coat, and ran out.

Ana sat at the table and anxiously watched the door while the children sat quietly on the bunk beds and watched. Several minutes passed, and then Ana was startled by a knock on the door. Expecting Paul or Simon, she was unsure what to do.

The knock came again. "Hello? Mrs. Steele? It's Irene Kingsley."

"Come in. Please come in."

The door opened and Irene Kingsley stepped into the room. Ana knew who she was, the judge's wife, and had spoken briefly to her a time or two at the store, and seen her at church. Comely and well-dressed, but not pretentious, she looked old enough to make Ana wonder why she had a daughter as young as Sarah. Ana liked her. "Hello, Mrs. Kingsley."

Mrs. Kingsley came to the table. "What's wrong? Simon told me you fell and were hurt."

"I didn't mean for him to trouble neighbors. I told him to go get his father." Ana attempted to get to her feet.

"Don't you get up." Mrs. Kingsley moved to Ana's side. "You sit still. I saw Simon coming up the road like the devil himself was after him. I made him stop and tell me what the matter was." She took off a long woolen overcoat and draped it over the back of a chair.

"I'm not sure what happened," Ana said.

"I was bathing the children when I suddenly felt weak as a kitten. Then a most awful pain came to my belly, and I couldn't stand. Simon helped me into this chair and went for his father."

"Have you had another pain?"

"No, I seem to be okay. It just kinda give me a fright. I'm sorry Simon troubled you, Mrs. Kingsley." Ana glanced down at the half-empty tub of gray water.

"Please call me Irene, Mrs. Steele. Can I call you Ana?"

"Of course, Mrs. Kingsley."

"Irene." The judge's wife smiled. "I'm not surprised you were frightened." She paused for a moment. "Can I ask you something a little personal, woman to woman? Please say no if you don't want to talk about this."

"Yes, I'm expecting."

"Oh, dear. Are you far along?"

"About four months."

"Are you still feeling all right? Is there anything I can get you?"

"I seem to be all right, not even light-headed now. I think I'll be okay. Just a spell." Ana grasped the back of the chair and stood. "It was very nice of you to come see what was happening. That's a long walk."

"Are you sure you're okay?"

"No, really, I think I'll be all right." Ana let go of the chair. "I think I'll be fine."

"Please, let me do something." Irene looked at the four children. "Can I dress the smaller ones?"

"You can get them the cinnamon treats. They're in the warmer."

Irene went to the stove and removed the skillet. The treats, gold-colored with puffy spots all over, glistened with a glaze of melted sugar. The smell and the sight of them had the children's full attention, and Axel and Abel made a move to climb off the bed.

"You two stay right there," Ana ordered. "I have to get clothes on you before you start running around." She walked over to the bed.

The door banged open and Paul rushed in, his face contorted with worry. "Ana?" he gasped, obviously out of breath. He rushed past Mrs. Kingsley. "What happened?"

"I seem to have had a little spell or something. I'm okay now. Mrs. Kingsley came over to see if she could help."

Ana looked past Paul at the door. "Where's Simon?"

"I'm afraid . . . I kinda left him . . . behind a bit. He's coming."

"Hello, Mr. Steele, I hope I'm not intruding," Mrs. Kingsley said as she returned the skillet to the stove.

"Not at all, Mrs. Kingsley . . . it's very good of you," Paul said, still breathing heavily. "Are you sure you're . . . okay, Ana?" Paul asked.

For the first time she noticed the mud on her hands and skirt. "Other than being a little muddy, I'm all right." Then she looked again at the tub of water, and winced at the mess around it. Suddenly, she became acutely aware of the judge's wife's presence and the state of her house. She felt her face flush, and that triggered another emotion, the shame of being ashamed. She turned quickly and started to dress Axel.

"Can I do anything else?" Irene offered.

"No, Mrs. Kingsley, we're all right now," Paul said. "Thank you again, very much. It's nice to know we have such a good neighbor."

"Very well, then, I'll be going. I am so glad you're okay, Ana. It's nice to see you at the store. We should get to know one another better." Irene gathered her coat from the chair.

Ana could only nod, still feeling the effects of her embarrassment. Paul opened the door for Mrs. Kingsley and Simon charged in, looked around frantically for his mother, then hurried over, and grabbed her waist.

"Ma, are you all right?" Simon asked, his face pinched with worry. "I was scared."

"I'm just fine. I had a spell. Don't worry, sweetheart, I'm okay now."

"Oh, Ma," Simon gasped, his voice cracking. He buried his face in her side and clutched her tightly.

Ana stroked his hair for a moment, then patted him on the head before seeing Irene Kingsley out.

As she closed the door, another shot of pain started in her back, gripped ferociously, and then subsided. She took several small panting breaths, turned back to her family, and forced a smile.

Ana drifted on the edge of consciousness in the late afternoon. She wasn't used to sleeping in the day, but the episode of that morning had tired her more than she thought it could. Paul had taken the children down to the river and told her to rest. Her eyes kept popping open as the thought of what the pain meant kept creeping into her mind. She'd seen many miscarriages, and knew it was just a matter of time. *Thy will be done,* she prayed silently to ease her fear and closed her eyes again. Then the contractions came, sharp and savage, until what could not be, was. She did not even try suppressing the tears, and let her grief fill the small space. Afterwards, she sat on the edge of her bed and sobbed until her gaze fell on the small bed where her youngest slept at night. Then, with one last shuddering gasp, she forced her mind to accept her loss, and she slept.

As soon as Paul and the children returned, the sorrow she tried to hide could not be denied. He hugged her while she whispered reassurance in his ear and the children watched; simple smiles on the faces of the younger ones and a worried look on Simon's. The trauma of the morning had to be put behind them, and Ana's gaze settled on the apple pie in the middle of the table, uncut, beautifully brown, with streaks of caramel where the sugar juice had leaked out of the cuts in the crust.

"Paul, I want you to go to the cowshed and get that chicken," Ana said. He'd left the hen there when he'd moved the rest back into the coop about two weeks earlier and seen yolk on her beak — an egg eater. Paul headed outside, Axel hot on his heels.

Chicken, mashed spuds and gravy, biscuits, candied parsnips, milk, and apple pie with cream. Ana grabbed the water bucket and handed it to Simon. "Go fill that about three-fourths full, and put it on the stove. Then go to the cellar and get about seven big spuds, and a few parsnips."

She went to the storage shelf and got the bag of flour Ruth had sent. A loaf of sour-dough bread would have been better, but that was an all-day job. *Tomorrow maybe.* She started to make soda bread.

Simon came in with the water, and she pushed another piece of sycamore into the firebox before setting the bucket on the stove. Simon went out again. Ana mixed four cups of flour, four tablespoons of sugar, a teaspoon and a bit of soda and some salt, then cut in half a cup of butter and a gener-ous cup of buttermilk for the soda to work on. Kneaded a dozen times, she flattened it out in a greased skillet, cut the traditional "X" in the top, and put it in the oven.

Next, she prepared the chicken. After plunging the headless bird into the hot water, she stripped the feathers off. That stank. Plucked, the fine downy fuzz had to be burned off in the flame of a cornhusk torch. And that stank. Then, a slice around the bottom of the breastbone and all the way down to the legs opened the body. Reaching inside, she carefully grasped the innards and pulled them out. And that stank most of all. Ana did not like doing a bird.

For the next two hours, she busied herself with the special meal, and filled the sod house with a heavenly aroma. She'd done the chicken the way Paul liked it best, flour-coated with some salt and pepper, and cooked slow in the heavy covered frying pan. The skillet now held the perfectly smooth gravy she'd whisked together. Axel, Abel, and Abbey all perched on the bench against the wall, their eyes fixed on the plate of chicken in front of them. With everything ready, Ana put the gravy on the table, and after removing the bread, put the pie in the warmer.

She called Paul in from outside, and he sat down to give the children his bless-this-food look. Down went five heads, three with furtive sideways glances at their neighbor while Eric busily worried a nicely browned wing tip.

"Lord," Paul began, "we invite You to our home as we share Your bountiful gifts. We give all thanks to You for our health, our safety, and this food. Bless this to our bodies. For all things we are grateful. We ask Your blessing in —"

A loud, firm knock on the door inter-rupted him. Everybody looked up, first at him, and then at the door, before he deliberately bowed his head and finished. "We ask Your blessing in Jesus's name, Amen."

He got up and opened the door to a very tall, slim, older man dressed in a long, black coat, matching pants, a black, short-brimmed felt hat and dusty black boots — quality clothes.

CHAPTER 6

Paul stepped back to make way. "Come in, John. What a nice surprise."

"Evening, Paul," the man said, a big smile spread across his narrow face. He stepped into the room and removed his hat, setting the children twittering like sparrows in a lilac bush. John Lindstrom's visits compared well with Father Christmas coming; he always had goodies of some sort in his overcoat's big pockets. The children's eyes searched their visitor up and down. The right-hand pocket of his coat bulged suspiciously.

"Let me have your coat, John," Paul said.

John turned and started to take off his coat. With John's back to her, Paul read Ana's silent, but urgent, signal. *"Do not encourage him to stay,"* her eyes said emphatically. *"Do not!"* Ana insisted there was more to this man than might meet the eye.

Paul read her message and understood

completely. John had earned the reputation of town drunk, and more than once he and John had shared a bottle of whiskey, in amounts that Ana thought unhealthy. In fact, she considered John a bad influence, and more or less worthless. Based on several long talks with John, Paul had a different opinion. John was obviously an extremely well-read and traveled man, and Paul neither wondered nor cared where he came from, or what caused his social decline. Paul liked John, and vice versa.

He took John's coat. "Would you join us for supper?"

If cold looks were stone, the message Ana's eyes conveyed could have stunned an ox.

"Are you sure you have enough for the children?" John held up his hand. "I didn't intend to intrude on your evening meal."

"We had just finished thanking God for our blessings," Paul said, looking at John, but speaking to Ana. "We have plenty."

John slightly bowed to Ana. "I appreciate your hospitality, Ana, I truly do."

Paul pointed to a space on the bench by Abbey. "Please, sit down."

Ana poured gravy over everything except the chicken; the spuds, biscuits and parsnips all slathered. As was customary, no one at the table spoke much during the meal, but the frequent soft moans told Paul everyone was enjoying the results of Ana's hard work. Ana apparently noticed John's pleasure in particular, and most of the objection had disappeared from her face. When Ana got up to clear the dishes, Paul's mouth watered; the pie came next. Eager hands accepted the small plates as Ana divvied up the single dish. John and Paul got lion's shares, and the thick cream she spooned on top soon streamed off the warm pie and onto the plate. The sweet and tangy treat, though savored, didn't last long.

"If you big boys help with the dishes, you can visit with Uncle John that much sooner," Ana said.

The *visit* part wasn't lost on the boys, and Simon and Axel grabbed the dessert dishes and tableware and put them in the wash pan on top of the supper plates. Ana helped with the pots and skillet, and in fifteen minutes they were all done, the dishes stacked back on the shelf.

John stood and went to the door to get his long coat. He fumbled around in the breast pocket for a bit, and then, as mock concern grew on his face, the left pocket. "Humph, I thought I had my pipe with me. Guess I'm getting forgetful." He dug his hand into his right pocket, and a wide smile spread over his face. The children stood up straight — miniature soldiers — as they watched his every move, eyes riveted on his right hand. Slowly, he pulled out one long red-and-white-striped stick of candy.

Simon breathed almost silently to Axel, "Peppermint."

Abel could not contain himself. He squatted halfway to the floor, then straightened his legs, and jumped, frog-like, half a hop forward. "I'm so happy," he squealed, then stood, heels together, both hands in front of his belly, one hand trying to tie the other in a knot.

"So, I guess you're first, huh?" John grinned and handed Abel the peppermint stick.

Abel and Abbey scampered across the room like two young chicks after the same grasshopper to stand in front of John, hands held tightly by their sides. Out of his pocket came stick after stick of candy. Two each! After Simon had gotten his second one, John hung his coat back up and turned around, palms out. "You've cleaned me out. Can't understand how that candy got there instead of my pipe."

He was greeted with a loud chorus of "Thank you, Uncle John," somewhat orchestrated by Ana.

Paul, Ana and John sat at the table, the children asleep, and the small house quiet. John cleared his throat. "I really appreciate you having me in your home. I don't get to see much of normal people." His eyes misted slightly. John didn't have a permanent home, instead staying in homes that invited boarders, but usually not for very long. A month or two would pass, and it would be made known by the householder that John would probably be more comfortable somewhere else. There was never an argument. He'd simply put what he owned in a duffel bag, and go ask Paisley Mace for a bunk in the stable until another room could be located.

"I saw you coming through town the other day," John said. "You looked some upset." He paused. "I heard later you'd had a run-in with Matt." He held his hand up as Paul started to say something. "I'll admit right now that this is probably not any of my business, and I wouldn't mention it unless I thought I could help. You folks are the only ones, other than Paisley Mace, who will even acknowledge my presence. In a situation like mine that does not go unnoticed."

John's eyes were now more than misty, and then John blinked. Tears coursed down the sides of his nose to disappear into his mustache. He paused again for several seconds. "I want to do something for you folks." A raised hand stopped Paul from speaking, and John reached into his vest pocket to take out a small roll of soft leather. He unwrapped it, and spilled twelve coins onto the table. Ana gasped. John stacked the money in two piles and pushed them across the table toward Paul. "I want you to use this. Please, for me."

Simon almost fell out of his bed when the coins spilled into the light. Even in the glow of the single oil lamp, the glitter of gold was unmistakable. He'd listened and watched, and the sight of Uncle John wiping tears from his cheeks had disturbed him. *How did Mr. Lindstrom know that Pa had punched Uncle Matt?* He was having a hard time with that experience himself, and had decided to keep it private if he could. Now it seems others knew. No sooner did he have one problem figured out than another popped up.

"I can't take that," Paul said emphatically. "I know you mean well, but I can't take money I haven't yet earned." He felt shaken.

"Is earning it the important aspect, or is the chronology more so?"

"Aspect? Chronology? I'm not getting what you mean." Paul wasn't sure he hadn't been insulted.

"I mean, would you take payment for something in advance, like an order for a cord or two of wood?"

"Well sure, I've done that. But this is different."

"How so? I expect you'll repay me."

"I can see what you're doin', and I don't think I can agree. You giving and not really expecting me to repay it, is the same as just giving it."

"Are you saying you wouldn't repay a loan made fair and right? You'd intentionally default?"

"I'll always pull my own weight." Paul felt his face heat up. "You can bet your bottom dollar on it." He leaned across the table, and nearly spilled his coffee, now gone cold. "Bet your very last dollar!" Paul glanced at Ana and she was smiling. *What's that all about? Damn it!*

"That's exactly what I'd expect from you," John continued, "and not a sliver less. It's my intention to make you this loan so you can undertake something I'd like to do, but don't have resources to support."

"You've lost me again," Paul said quietly, feeling confused and frustrated. Ana continued to smile.

"We'll soon be coming into the wagon-train season, and I want to set up a small operation to sell something these people miss, but can't transport in the wagons."

"And what might that be?" Paul said.

"Chickens and eggs," Ana said. "And feathers, or ticks, or pillows." Her eyes started to sparkle. "We have just experienced not having fresh meat to eat, Paul. These people do the same, just for a different reason. Most of those women will be overcome with joy to see a fresh chicken."

Paul looked at John. "You could have said that in the first place." The frustration of a moment before dissipated.

"No, I don't think I could have. Somehow you had to say it yourself to make it right." John rose from his chair and faced Ana. "I appreciate you more every time we meet." Then he turned to Paul. "You have a prize there, a real prize."

"Pshaw," Ana said, and busied her hands in her apron, blushing furiously.

John walked to the door, got his long coat and shrugged into it. "Now that is a loan," he said and emphasized the *is*. "We'll get together in a week or so to talk about increasing your flock and adding to the coop." He opened the door. "Good night, good folks. You too, Simon." John stepped through the door and disappeared into the night.

"Simon?" Paul said, looking first at Ana, and then at the sleeping boy in the top bunk. Puzzled, Paul went back to the table and sat down. Gleaming despite the weak light of the lamp, the twin stacks of their salvation winked back at him: twelve five-dollar gold pieces. Paul had just started to absorb what had transpired and smiled at his wife. *Patient, faithful Ana.* "Can you believe this, Ma? Can you really believe this?"

"And I thought angels were supposed to wear white," she stammered, relief plain on her face. "I'm tired, Paul. Let's just go to bed now and enjoy this in the morning." She stood to carry the coffee cups to the wash table. Paul, walking softly, followed her, and when she turned back, he caught her in a bear hug. They stood and embraced each other and all the good things they felt at the moment. With Ana's face pressed to his chest and his cheek touching the top of head, they swayed slightly as though to some melody only they could hear, gently moving — slow and waltz-like.

Chapter 7

The seed money that John supplied was all Paul and Ana needed to thrive. In the five years following that eventful day and evening, what John envisioned did indeed come to pass, and this year, 1864, was turning out to be another good one. The wagon trains continued to lumber off the plains south of town to form huge campsites. They would stay for three to five days to refresh and tend their stock, repair wagons, and buy things they'd discovered they couldn't do without on the hard trail west. And they bought chickens: live chickens, dressed chickens, and even fully prepared, ready-to-eat, let's-celebrate-Molly's-birthday chickens.

And as Ana had thought, the feathers were sold too, as pillows and wagon seats, thin mattresses and chair cushions. When the wagons were not in town, unusual during the four-month rush, Ana sold to the town folks every egg the chickens laid. Though dogged hard work, all the children pitched in, and among them, they managed to get it done, the family back on an even keel.

Ana stood packing egg baskets one afternoon when she felt the tremor of a large wagon pulling up beside the house. She went out the open door and walked around the side to find a wagon, loaded with sawn lumber, tarpaper rolls and nail kegs. Up by the driver sat Paul, a fox-sly grin on his face. "Got this load of boards, lady. Could you make use of it?" He laughed as he climbed down the wheel.

"What on earth are you going to do with all that wood? From the looks of it, you've got enough to build another three coops, which we don't need right now."

"Got something else in mind. Something I've wanted to do for years. We're going to finish the inside of the house."

For years she'd suffered dirt in everything: in the beds, in the food, in their hair — dirt everywhere. The mud and straw-plastered walls held up for about a year, but one winter-spring thaw, and the cracks appeared, then pieces fell out, and the falling dirt was back; a battle lost from the start. She'd been in the Pierson soddy, just a half mile down the road. Mrs. Pierson had papered over the plaster, an expensive solution, but still short term — the dirt held at bay for an extra year or so. But wood-paneled walls? And most glorious of all, a wood floor? She could hardly believe it. Then Paul said that the wood could be reused when they built a real house. She didn't dare to dream that wildly.

Over the course of the next two weeks, Ana would occasionally stop what she was doing and watch her man work. Using two different wooden planes, he cut a tongue on one side of the long boards, and a matching groove on the other. She enjoyed looking at his broad powerful back and the short, hard muscles that rippled in his arms and chest as he pushed the plane through the wood. And though he knew she watched, she could not still the sensuous thrill of excitement when he'd give his biceps an extra tweak at the end of a stroke.

The new house felt almost luxurious. She scrubbed the floor with lye and soap to bleach it a bit. New shelves on the wall gave her the much-needed room for the things that until then had been left on the dirt floor. But most wonderful of all, Paul built two wooden partitions, one with a door, to create a separate bedroom for them. Even in Spartan conditions, a person needed some privacy, and Ana had missed that the most.

CHAPTER 8

Miss Fritz married Mr. Waldon, the town tanner. The wagon trains that flowed through always needed new traces and reins and other leather things, and Mr. Waldon had all they wanted. This made Mr. Waldon fairly well-to-do. The gist of this was, Miss Fritz no longer needed the twenty-seven dollars a month the town paid her to teach school, and she quit. The children were ecstatic, especially Simon. And Jake. And Gus. And David. All of whom had had regular altercations with Miss Fritz. The new teacher was an unknown quantity. She would be there the first day of school, and the first day was today.

Simon hurried to Sarah's house for two reasons, to get ahead of Axel and Abel, and because he simply wanted to see Sarah. The two of them, walking to and from school, had become a familiar sight on the road over the past six years. Simon would have loved to continue the liaison during recesses, but the ramifications he would suffer at the hands of the other boys made that delicious-sounding idea impossible. He had to make do with slow walks before and after school. Gus and David watched even that with suspicion. Gus, because he still thought he had a chance with Sarah, but David's interest had to be different because at school he made it very clear that he did not like Sarah Kingsley. Simon had not yet deduced David's intention, but he was working on it.

Mrs. Kingsley liked Simon. He didn't know why exactly, but concluded it was better if Sarah's mother liked him rather than not, so he suffered the warm smiles and touches on the arm she bestowed at every opportunity. "Good morning, Mrs. Kingsley," he greeted from the porch. As always, Mrs. Kingsley waited at the door.

"Good morning to you, Simon," she replied. "How is your mother?"

"Real good, ma'am. She said to tell you hello."

"I'm pleased to hear that. Tell her I'm so happy for her new home."

"I will. Is Sarah ready?" Sarah always dressed nice, but especially the first day of school when everybody had new things. Eager to see how she looked, he peered around Mrs. Kingsley. Secretly, he also wanted to show off what he was wearing. Ma had gone all out at the store, and Simon knew he looked good. She had allowed him to go with her, and he'd chosen some of the clothes. And she'd also got him some hair oil.

"Hi, Simon," Sarah said cheerfully.

Lost in his reverie, Simon had not seen her come downstairs. "Oh, Sarah, you look real nice," he blurted, instantly embarrassed at the smile his compliment brought from Mrs. Kingsley.

"How nice of you to say so. Isn't that right, Sarah?" Mrs. Kingsley added, and a warm, soft, slightly damp, hand settled on Simon's shoulder. Her thumb touched the bare skin on his neck, and his eyes widened.

"Thank you, Simon," Sarah said obediently, and then added, "And you look nice too."

Simon was quite willing to endure Mrs. Kingsley's touch to bask in Sarah's warm gaze. He wished for an eternity, and got another three seconds.

"We better go," Sarah said, breaking the spell.

"Ah . . . right . . . better get going. See

you, Mrs. Kingsley." His discomfiture made him stammer and he hated it, but it always happened, Sarah, cool as a buttermilk crock, while he stumbled around like a new colt.

Everything Miss Fritz was, Miss Everett was not, except they were both girls. Simon loved her at first sight. Dressed in soft brown, her hair loose, she exhibited a relaxed pleasantness that would make a condemned chicken quit flapping. And Miss Everett liked Simon. Actually, she seemed to like everybody in the school; though Simon was convinced she paid more attention to him than to the others. It was apparent that she liked to teach. To tell and show and demonstrate seemed to thrill her, and best of all, she lent books to students who showed a particular interest in reading, and Simon showed an interest in everything. She swamped him with literature, and he read everything she suggested.

All was not school and work. Occasionally Simon found time to go into town and find Buell. To observe the two of them at school you would think they were total strangers and wanted to keep it that way. The truth be known, they were best friends. Whenever Simon managed some time off from his chicken chores, he was at the livery with

Buell. Simon was Buell's only friend. Buell didn't dislike the other kids; he just treated them as if they weren't there, and other than his father, he avoided adults. His mother had died giving him life. He was polite to Miss Everett, but only polite, spoke only when spoken to, and then only the very minimum.

Around Simon though, and in private, Buell was a different person. He would quiz Simon on things Simon had read, or analyze a discussion that Simon and Paisley Mace had about doctoring horses or forging tools and horseshoes. These blacksmithing discussions always included Buell, but it was as if he trusted Simon to tell him some more, and Simon was always ready to oblige. Because of this, he and Buell spent many hours together, and they talked and planned about all the things that twelve-year-old boys talk and dream about. Especially they talked about the mountains. Being raised on the plains and having never even seen anything higher that the low bluffs by the river, the boys were fascinated by stories of the mountain men and trappers, the gold prospectors, and the trailblazers: Jedediah Smith, John Fremont and Kit Carson.

At the livery stable one afternoon they listened to an older man who had dropped by to see Mace. Over several hours he related the story of the famous trapper, Jedediah Smith, whom he said he knew personally. Their imaginations ran to living off the land where the mountains disappeared into the sky, and struggling against the elements and the Indians. They would describe to each other their personal solutions to supposed obstacles, insurmountable to normal men, yet easily handled in a boy's imagination. They resolved that one day they would follow the footsteps of these men and journey to the white clouds that hid the high mountains.

CHAPTER 9

Paul and Ana's chicken farm had continued to expand. With four large coops and a feed storage shed bigger than the original hen-house, they finally had an income sufficient to allow them to not worry about their next meal. But Paul still felt obligated to supply his old customers with their firewood, so along with Simon and Axel, he'd spent four days in the river bottoms felling, trimming, and sizing cottonwood. Though the species didn't make the best firewood, and proved a real chore to split, it was plentiful, so that's what they took. Now they had to deliver it.

Paul walked into Mace's livery. "I need a rig for a day. Got a load of firewood for Ellis Sievers."

"The big dray is available, and the Belgiums need a workout." The smithy stepped away from his work, and swiped a forearm across his forehead.

"Okay if I take them home tonight and

get an early start?"

"No problem. Now, or do you have some other things to do?"

"I'll come by in an hour or so if that's not too late."

"I'll be here. Got no place else to be." Mace chuckled. "Expect I'll be buried under this anvil." He reached into the forge with his tongs, and extracted a red-hot horseshoe and returned to shaping it. He raised his hammer slightly and bounced it on the anvil to start, then the steel head and the anvil began singing their duet. Mace hit three staccato taps, then raised the hammer high and brought it down hard on the horseshoe. With a ringing clang, a trio was formed: hammer, anvil and shoe. Mace's easy rhythm with the heavy hammer belied the difficulty of the task. Paul watched and admired the craftsmanship for a minute or so, then turned to leave.

As he stepped through the door, he nearly ran into his brother. "Sorry, Matt, almost run over you," Paul said in surprise. He had only spoken to Matt three or four times since their problem over the sick pig, and Matt and Ruth had not been to the house at all since then. He hated the estrangement, especially for what it did to the two sisters, and he wanted to patch it up.

Though he'd tried a couple of times, Matt still had his jaws tight and seemed to want it that way.

"Not likely," Matt said brusquely. He started to push past.

"Just a minute." Paul took hold of his brother's arm. "We really should talk."

"Nothing to say." Matt looked down at Paul's hand. "One Christian does not strike another like that. Not my rules you broke, and you know it." He shook loose of Paul's grasp.

"I'm sorry, Matt. I've said it before and I'm saying it again. I wish I could take it back. You're right and I'm dead wrong. Okay?" Paul put his hand out.

"Stay out of my way. It won't be so easy next time. Try it again and we'll see who winds up in the shit."

Matt walked around Paul, the significance he found in the detour apparent in his scowl.

"But —" Paul started, but Matt had already disappeared into the livery.

"Paisley!" Matt shouted. "Paisley, I want to talk to you."

Paul turned and walked toward the main street, past the livery's north end. There stood Mace, leaning against the wall, smoking. He met Paul's eyes and he shook his head slowly, the gesture saying all that needed to be said. Paul nodded and continued on his way to the trading store.

Ana hurried across the room when Ruth surprised her by stepping through the open door. "Good heavens, sis, what a wonderful sight you are." They gathered in a hug, putting simultaneous kisses to each other's cheeks. Ana stepped back. "Come, sit . . . oh dear, I'm all light-headed." She put her hand on the back of a chair. "Come and sit down." She glanced at the door. "Did Matt come?"

"No, I'm afraid that'll never happen again." Ruth lowered her gaze to the floor.

"Well then, how did you get here? Surely you didn't walk?" Ana knew how hot it was outside.

"I did. I had to come talk to you." Ruth looked ready to burst into tears and slumped into a chair. "First, I want to tell you how happy I am for your home. I have so much wanted to see this happen." She looked around the room. "Paul did a beautiful job. You've made it so nice."

"Paul has worked hard with our chicken farm. We have John Lindstrom to thank for the help he gave us to get started. And we are thankful," Ana said sincerely. "Now let

95

me get us a cup of coffee, and we can sit for a while. It's been so long since you were here."

She went to the shelf by the stove, got another cup, and grabbed the coffeepot. At the table, she poured the two cups full. "Now, what would make you walk over two miles in the heat of the day?" She tried to look stern. "I'm a little upset with you, happy as I am to see you. What is it?"

"Matt said he ran into Paul yesterday."

"So Paul said. Didn't go well again, either. I wish they could patch things up."

"That's why I'm here. Matt said next time Paul lays a hand on him, for any reason, he's going to shoot him." Ruth's words rushed out. "And Ana, he went to Mr. Swartz and bought a pistol. I've seen it." She reached over the corner of the table and found Ana's hand to squeeze it tightly. "I'm scared to death."

A clammy cold rippled over Ana's body. It was the same feeling that comes when the air goes still during a springtime thunderstorm as a whirlwind starts to build, gathering the power to rip the land apart. And the same sense of helplessness gripped her for a moment. "When did you see it?"

"Yesterday, he got it yesterday. He laid it on the kitchen table when he came home.

I'm sure he wanted me to see it."

"Where is it now? Does he carry it? Where does he keep it at night?" Ana searched blindly for a solution.

"I think he keeps it by his bed."

"His bed? What do you mean, *his* bed? Ruth?"

Ruth would not meet Ana's question with a direct look. She let go of Ana's hand and her own started to move in a circle on the table, as if she were trying to smooth out the perfectly flat surface. "We don't share a bed." She almost whispered it. "He hasn't been a man to me for years." Ruth covered her face for a moment, and then she groped for Ana's hands. Grasping one, she buried her face in it and started to cry.

Unable to find consoling words, Ana stroked the back of her sister's bowed head and waited while Ruth sobbed out her grief on their clasped hands. They sat at the table, silent, and waited for Ruth to slowly regain her composure.

Finally, Ruth looked up. "Please don't ask me any more. Matt would be furious if he knew I was here to begin with."

"I'm your sister. I will do whatever you need me to do. Let me get some fresh water in the basin and you can freshen up. You just sit still."

The cool water made the signs of Ruth's distress less apparent. After Ana stepped outside a moment to check on the children, she and Ruth talked for a while longer and then Ruth got ready to go. As she fitted her bonnet she said, "I didn't mean to burden you with the problem between Matt and me. But I do feel much better now that I've shared it with someone. Please don't discuss that part with Paul. I'd just as soon keep it between us."

"I'm glad you said something. Paul and I don't keep secrets, but in this case . . . well, this is different. I won't say anything."

"What are we going to do about the pistol? I got so involved in my own problem that we never did finish talking about that." She squared her shoulders. "I'm going to bring it up again. Matt has to listen to me whether he does as I ask or not."

"Be careful. Sometimes these things have a way of getting out of control. Maybe you better not say anything until I see what Paul thinks."

Ruth's shoulders slumped. "Sometimes I wish I was a man." Opening her arms, she embraced Ana. "I don't think I could keep my sanity if you weren't here."

Ana held her sister tightly. "I love you,

Ruth. Please be careful, and come again soon."

"I love you too." Ruth stepped outside and Ana followed to watch her sister for several minutes, exchanging waves until Ruth did not turn back again. Ana returned to the house.

When Paul came home later that afternoon they sat outside in the shade of the house. The children had all gone to the river for a romp in the water, maybe, in September, for the last time that year. All except Eric, who busily chased chickens around the yard. Ana told Paul about Ruth's visit.

"He said what?" Paul shouted. Eric stopped and looked at his father.

"Matt told her next time you lay a hand on him, for any reason, he's going to shoot you."

"I'm having a hard time believing that. Judas Priest, he's my brother." Paul came as close to swearing in front of her as he ever did. "I guess I'll have to avoid him for a while, if I can, but I'm certainly not going to hide from him." Paul frowned. "Sure ruins a good day, hearing stuff like that." They sat silent for a few minutes and watched Eric.

"Let's go down to the river and see how the kids are gettin' on," Ana said finally,

anxious to clear the air. They started off on
the quarter-mile walk to the Platte.

CHAPTER 10

Simon sat at the table, head down and enthralled, and followed the account of the travels of Lewis and Clark in another of Miss Everett's books. It was by a man named Gass who had been on the voyage, and Simon was to the part where they were trying to cross the mountains, and in danger of starving to death. It brought to mind his walk as a six-year-old to the west side of town one Sunday. He'd hoped to get a look at the mountains described in the geography book Miss Fritz had shown them. He also recalled the sting of the willow switch when his father had finally found him.

He struggled with some of the words, and those he wrote down on slips of paper as he read; he already had a dozen or so, and Miss Everett would be busy tomorrow. Many of the books he read gave him the same trouble. He had one by a Greek named Cicero that made no sense at all. He could read the words all right; they just didn't seem to mean anything. Miss Everett said many of the Greeks wrote that way. She called the stories parables, and said he would understand them one day, and that reading them now was not a waste of time. She said it was like planting daisy seeds. They sometimes didn't sprout for years she said, but then, one day, he would suddenly find himself in a garden of enlightenment. He didn't understand that either, but had long since learned to smile and nod. Miss Everett had another story by a fellow named Plato, which Simon had declined when she offered it. He didn't figure it would get any better because both writers only had one name and he found that suspicious. She said if he enjoyed Lewis and Clark, he would really like one by Homer — another one-name author. Simon wasn't sure about it, but he loved to read, so he more or less resigned himself to struggle through it — later.

It being Saturday, Simon and Buell were at the livery to help Buell's father make rings for harnesses. Made of brass, Mr. Waldon paid Simon and Buell up to a nickel for every one they polished. Mr. Mace had three kinds of powder, that when used in order, would take all the roughness off the rings and make the metal shine like a new gold piece. Simon thought it was a good job because it was inside, out of the cold November air, and he and Buell were together. After they put some grease on the polishing paddles — flat sticks of oak with a linen pad glued to them — they would sprinkle on some powder and scrub away.

"So boys, how's it going?" Paul had slipped up on the boys, and both of them jumped.

"Dang, Pa, about made me choke." Simon grinned at his father. "About to wear our fingers off, but we've done three each and only got four to go. They're the big ones, so I reckon we should get about fifteen cents each." Simon could visualize the shiny three-cent coins.

"Phew, what you going to do with all that money, Buell?" Paul asked. Simon could tell he was teasing.

"I'm saving for something, sir." Buell didn't look up.

"Simon's got his eye on a Barlow knife over at Swartz's store," Paul said. "Been eyeing it for a year. So what you got in mind?"

"A gun. A pistol."

"What's this about a gun?" Mace had walked up just then. "I thought we talked about this, Buell. Decided you didn't need one."

Buell stopped rubbing the brass and sat still, looking at his hands.

"Well, did we or didn't we?" Mace's voice sounded sharp.

Simon stopped his work also. He looked at Buell and could see his discomfort with all the attention. "Buell and me talked about getting a twenty-two. Mr. Swartz has two."

He and Buell had *not* talked about a pistol and Simon had assumed Buell meant a rifle. He wished then that he had talked to his pa about it before. He now felt he was defending something he didn't want to defend, and he wasn't used to that with his parents. Buell had still not looked up.

"Well, I don't know about you, Paul, but I ain't having Buell fooling around with no pistol. Can't be nothin' but trouble coming there." The firmness in Mace's voice was unmistakable.

"I agree completely." Paul squatted down on the dirt in front of Simon and Buell. "Now listen careful. Just get it out of your heads. No pistol. I might see a shotgun if your mind's set on something like that, but no pistol. Understand, Simon?"

"Yes, sir," he replied quietly.

"And you?" Mace said as he stepped in

front of Buell.

Buell sat silently and tapped his polish paddle on his foot.

"Well?"

"I guess so."

"No guessing. Look at me."

"I understand, Pa. No pistol." Buell finally looked up at his father.

"All right, then. Let's walk over to Luger's and get a sandwich, Paul. You hungry? How about you, boys?" Mace reached down and squeezed Buell's shoulder. "Sorry, sprout, I hope you ain't mad at me." He and Paul walked toward the front of the livery. When they got to the door Mace stopped. "You guys coming?"

"We'll be over in a bit. I want to finish this ring," Buell said.

Paul and Mace stepped out into the cold afternoon.

"I knew I should have kept my stupid mouth shut," Buell said. "I knew he'd say no if he found out. See what you get when you talk to older folks."

"I think they're just lookin' out for us. I know they don't have to," Simon added hurriedly. "We could take care of a pistol without getting in trouble. I would've had to tell Pa anyway before I went in with you, so it ain't like you goosed the goat. Besides that, Mr. Swartz would have said something."

Furiously, Buell buffed the brass ring he held. "Next time I decide to do something, I'm just going to do it, and let everybody go to hell."

Simon nearly dropped his ring, and stared at his friend. An odd feeling of fear and excitement ran through him. That was why he liked Buell — he didn't back away from anything. Buell continued to rub the brass while Simon stared.

Buell looked up. "What?"

"Ye cats, Buell, you can't be talking like that, or your pa will skin your hide." Simon felt obligated to protest.

"Only if someone tells him."

At that moment, Simon saw something in Buell's face that he had never seen before. It wasn't a threat, but it wasn't friendly or joking either. Confused, Simon started to polish again as he tried to understand. Then it came to him. Buell had decided to do something he was not going to share with anyone, and his expression was one of excitement, fear and confusion all mixed together, each emotion fighting for primacy. Simon felt totally excluded for a moment, and it hurt his feelings. When he glanced up at Buell again, the strange look was gone, and he wondered if he had actually seen it in the first place. It was the same as Buell's attitude toward Sarah. Simon knew he didn't dislike her, but when Sarah was around, Buell was not — he made a point of it. He looked at his friend again.

Buell grinned. "Let's go get a sandwich. I think Pa meant he was going to pay for us."

Simon followed Buell out the door, and they walked side by side up the street.

Paul opened the saloon door and followed Mace in. He hurried to shut off the blast of cold air that followed them when most of the fifteen or so people looked up. The spicy aroma of zesty sausages and pickled eggs mixed with the smoky smell of cured ham made Paul's mouth water. The three delectable offerings lay on a huge wood platter, along with two big wedges of cheese. Stacked on the bar alongside, thick slices of bread beckoned. The men headed for the food.

"Howdy, Mace, Paul." Greetings came from several of the customers, most seated at one of the dozen tables in the room.

Fred Luger, the owner, stood behind the bar. His enormous size never ceased to amaze Paul. If Paul was big, Fred was huge. Mace always teased about coming to get him if one of his draft horses took sick. "What can I get ya, fellas?"

"Pull me a beer, Fred," Paul replied.

"Same here," Mace said.

Paul eyed the sandwich fixings, then selected a couple pieces of bread and smeared both with mustard sauce. It was the German kind that Fred's wife made up at home. That and the ham were the main reason most folks came to Luger's place. Mace took the wooden paddle and did the same, and in a couple of minutes they had sandwiches that weighed near half a pound apiece. Balancing the food on one hand, Paul grabbed his mug of beer and turned around to locate a place to sit. As his eyes swept the room, he saw Matt, sitting in the far corner with Avery Singer. Slim and dapper — Ana referred to him as oily — Avery was the town's de facto banker. He didn't own a real bank. His vault, actually a strongbox bolted to the floor of his office, used two big padlocks to secure the heavy lid. But he had the knowledge and the resources that allowed him to make a very good living handling other people's money.

Paul nodded. "Matt, Avery."

"Hello, Paul," Avery said. "Things still working out for you?"

"Finally hit a run of good luck, looks like."

Paul's eyes went back to Matt. "How's Ruth, Matt?" A flash lit Matt's eyes a fraction of a second before Paul wished he hadn't asked. "And David?" Paul added, lamely. "Ana asked me to see so I . . ." The look on Matt's face told Paul he'd just as well go sit down. He walked around a table and took the chair opposite Mace, his back to Matt.

"Why is it I say or do the wrong thing every time I get around him?" Paul asked, both frustrated and a little embarrassed.

Mace snorted. "It's not you, so don't think for a minute it is. He's that way with everybody in town. Always has been and probably always will. Eat your sandwich."

The door opened and Simon and Buell stood for a second, half in, half out of the room.

"Close the dang door," someone near the bar bawled.

The boys spotted them, and Paul gave the boys a slight nod, permission to come in. Forbidden territory unless they were with either Paul or Mace. Ana did not approve of the place, even for lunch. Simon took a quick look around and his gaze stopped on Matt.

"Hello, Uncle Matt," Simon said.

Paul fumed at the nasty look Matt gave Simon.

"Humph," was all Matt could muster before he dismissed Simon and turned back to Avery Singer.

"Go make yourselves a sandwich, Buell," Mace said.

The boys attacked the pile of food like a pair of prairie wolves. Neither boy used a top piece of bread, they just stacked ham, cheese, half a pickle, and a boiled egg on top of one slice and headed for the table. Simon's egg promptly rolled off the top and bounced as it hit the floor.

Buell laughed and sat by his father. "One bounce don't catch no dirt."

Simon set his meal down and turned to look for the errant egg just as Jake's dog, at a half trot, scooped it up, turned around, and disappeared into the back room.

"Here, Simon," Fred said. "Take another egg and follow the dog. Jake's back there having his lunch. Got him working so he's feeling a bit put on today, and he'll be glad to see you two."

Simon turned to Buell, and Paul saw the look of relief on Simon's face when Buell, with a sideways nod and a shoulder shrug, grinned back and stood. Together, the boys headed for the back room.

A few minutes later, the front door opened again and John Lindstrom stepped in. He immediately saw Mace and Paul and headed straight for them. "Hello, Paul, Mace," he said as he pulled out a chair. He waved his hand at Fred, pointed at Paul's beer mug, and then held up three fingers.

Fred took a mug from the pyramid of glass on the counter.

"I've been meaning to have a word with you, Paul," John said. "Been thinking about another project."

Since that night several years ago when John had offered Paul and Ana some help, his drinking and gambling had been severely curtailed, and he was now regarded as just another member of the community. He could be found most days in Lancer's Saloon with a couple of books and the latest newspaper he could find. There he sat and read, took notes, and wrote in a journal. He didn't like to be disturbed, and most people honored that.

"If it works out as good as the last one, I'm all ears," Paul replied and chuckled.

"Timing is what we need for this one, and I haven't gotten it quite figured out yet, but I'm working on it." John looked directly at him. "You up for some more work?"

"I'm hoping you mean for the spring.

We're about run out of weather this year."

"For sure, not any sooner than that. And maybe even as late as summer, but that could cause some problems."

John had Paul's full attention. Mace fidgeted in his chair and cleared his throat.

"Nothing here that you can't be privy to, Mace," John said.

Mace settled back in his chair.

Across the room, Avery Singer got up and started for the back door.

John watched him for a second and then said, "Excuse me for a minute, I gotta go lose a couple cups of coffee."

John followed Avery out the door and across the lot toward the outhouse at the back. Avery paused for a few seconds at the door, so John stopped and waited. Avery scowled at him, then yanked open the door, stepped in and attempted to close it when John caught the latch.

"It's a two-holer, Avery. If you don't look, I won't." John stepped in after him.

A half-high partition split the bench in two, providing a little privacy for each station.

"I've been trying to catch you for a week, Singer. You been avoiding me?"

"Hell, no. I've been busy."

"I might need to draw on my account shortly."

"How much, and when?"

"Between four and seven thousand." The sharp intake of breath made John look across the partition. "I'm trusting that's not a problem."

Avery, looking down, his lips pursed and his eyes squinted shut, did not look comfortable. "No. No — I can have that for you if you give me a week or ten days. I certainly can't do it immediately."

"That's reasonable. I just want to make sure we're still all right with our arrangement."

"Certainly, Mr. Lindstrom, certainly."

"As long as we understand each other." John buttoned his trousers and pushed the door open. "I'll get back to you come the spring." He stepped out. "You can go ahead now and do what you had to do Avery, didn't mean to hold that up."

Paul saw John reenter the saloon, and Matt looked up as he came in, his head going back down immediately.

John walked over and sat. "As I was saying before nature jabbed me, we might want to look at getting into the cow business. Not real big, and not long-term, but I think there's an opportunity coming that we could be in position to take advantage of. Know anything about cows, the steak-on-the-hoof kind?"

"Beef cattle?" Paul asked.

"That's what I mean."

"Don't suppose they're any different than a milk cow except you don't have to milk 'em twice a day. How many we talking about?"

"Three to five hundred."

"Good Lord, John. Where in tarnation would we keep that many animals? There's not enough ground on the old home place for a fifth that many even if Matt would agree, which he won't. And to feed them over the winter? I've learned to trust your judgment but this is —"

John held up his hand. "Whoa, hold on a minute. They aren't waiting outside."

"Five hundred cows?" Mace's mouth hung open. "They're gonna need a lot of room."

Avery came back in just then, and as he headed for the corner table where Matt waited, Paul caught Avery's glance at John. As soon as Avery sat down, Matt leaned forward, and with his head down, started an animated conversation which, apparently, Avery Singer didn't enjoy much. Paul turned his attention back to John and Mace.

"We've got the room," John said. "More than we need for five hundred or five thousand." He looked intently at Paul, his eyebrows forming a question.

"The prairie!" exclaimed Paul.

"Exactly, Paul, exactly."

"But we don't own the ground."

"Who does?"

"I hadn't thought about it, to be honest." The ramifications that the entire prairie stood open for grabs dawned on Paul. John was right, thousands of cows.

"I'll arrange for the land if you think you can arrange to keep track of five hundred cattle for one summer," John said. "But not now, and not positively. I'm still working on the details, and I'll have a better idea in a couple months. New law I've read about says we just might be able to claim the land we need, maybe just temporary, maybe not."

Paul puffed his cheeks. "Phew. Sometimes you knock the wind out of me. And folks say you waste your time reading and studying over at Lancer's place. Little do they know."

"Keep this under your hat, and I'll continue to work on it. Could be a real opportunity. I got to go see Blake Waldon. I'll see you gentlemen later." John got up to leave.

"You fellas need another beer?" Fred called.

"Not me, thanks," John said. "You guys?"

"I got to get back to work. I'll pass," Mace said.

"Me too," Paul said. "Really got me thinking, John. We'll talk to you later."

John walked out of the saloon, nodding to half a dozen faces as he went.

"Well, don't that beat all?" Mace said as he stood. "I'll go round up Buell and Simon."

CHAPTER 11

Buell headed for school and his breath condensed into billows of white. Sunday had brought the colder air and when he squinted his eyes, he could feel his cold skin wrinkle. It felt kind of funny, so he did it again. And if he breathed sharply through his nose, the hairs inside his nose froze and that also felt kind of funny, so he did that again. Squint. Breathe. Thus, simply entertained, he trudged on to school.

Miss Everett announced they were going to devote the entire morning to Lewis and Clark's *Voyage of Discovery.* Buell knew Simon had been looking forward to this for a week because he'd read someone else's account of the adventure, a fellow named Gass, and had repeated most of it to Buell. He'd never admit it to anyone if asked, but he'd enjoyed the discussion between Simon and Miss Everett.

The rest of the class were also content to

just listen, all except David, who, Buell noticed, didn't like his cousin getting all the attention. Miss Everett saw it as well and asked David several good questions which he reliably got wrong and glared at everyone when the giggles erupted. The morning shot by, and they were out for noon recess before he knew it. Based on the morning's events, he wasn't surprised when David took a position outside the privy door when Simon had gone in. From the look on Simon's face when he came out, he'd rather expected to see David too.

"You got one real sassy mouth, Simon."

Resignation showed all over his friend's face. "There's nothing I can say that will make you feel any better, David," Simon said.

"You're right. And Pa says that talk is all you and your pa do." David's eyes took on a glassy gleam, and his breath quickened.

"I don't want trouble with you. I've been told to mind my own business."

Both Buell and Simon had received the lecture about avoiding David, but he'd thought at the time that David probably hadn't gotten the same advice. Simon was expecting the worst because his right hand closed into a fist.

"My pa says your pa and that drunk your

family sucks off was getting polluted in the saloon Saturday," David said. "Pa says that if it weren't for John the Drunk, your pa would be shoveling shit with Paisley Mace."

A thrill shot up Buell's spine, and he pushed away from his spot by the school to stride over to the privy. He pointed his finger at David's face. "Watch whose name comes out of your mouth, asshole."

David's head jerked back. "This don't concern you, Buell."

"Does when I hear my name. You want me out of it, keep me out of it."

David sniffed and faced Simon again. "Same as your pa. Always got to have somebody there to wipe your nose."

Simon's fist didn't land perfectly, but it was good enough. David's lip split, his eyes flooded full of tears, and he staggered back two steps. Then Simon lowered his head and charged full tilt into David's belly. The gasping sound of David's lungs forcibly deflating lasted until drowned out by the splintering crash of the boys slamming into the privy. They bounced backwards off the door, and crashed to the ground with David on top of the heap. Simon, gasping for air, struggled to push the heavier David off.

David pushed down on Simon's shoulders and sat astride him. After wiping his eyes with the back of his left hand, he raised the right one, bunched in a fist, and slammed it down. At the last instant, Simon jerked his head to one side and a hollow pop sound made Buell wince. David screamed and held up his right hand, its little finger bent back at an impossible angle, and the knuckle swelling fast. His face twisted in a grimace as he lowered it and start slapping Simon's face with his left hand, screaming all the while. Simon did his best to fend off the beating and managed to dodge some blows, but not many. Then he caught a flurry of long skirts out the corner of his eye.

It was Miss Everett. "Stop it, David! Stop it this instant!" She reached to grab his arm but he bunched his fist and punched her in the hip. With a gasp, she staggered and fell to her knees. "Run and tell someone," she ordered to no one and everyone. "Now!" she shouted when no one moved. Two younger boys took off at a dead run across the schoolyard, toward the main street.

David half stood and roughly flipped Simon over to his belly. Then, he sat down, slipped his left arm under Simon's chin, and reared back. Simon, gritted teeth bared and eyes squeezed shut, looked pretty much helpless. Just then his eyes opened and looked directly at Buell. Buell studied his friend's face for some sign of fear or panic and when he didn't see any decided to do nothing. It wasn't his fight.

Then David leaned forward for an instant and adjusted his grip, further around Simon's neck this time. Simon sucked in a deep breath and again his eyes found Buell's. Only this time he saw panic and Simon's eyes filled with tears. With his teeth jammed together, what Simon's lips were trying to say proved hard to read. The grimace, pursed lips parting and closing, finally produced something Buell recognized, and he heard the silent sound of the letter P. Help! Buell took two steps forward, and kicked David in the ear as hard as he could.

"Buell!" Miss Everett hollered, her hands fluttering like two scrapping sparrows and she hurried first to touch Simon's neck, and then to inspect the steady flow of blood coming from David's head. Across the schoolyard a half dozen men hurried toward them, Sheriff Staker's long stride keeping him in front of the group.

When the sheriff arrived, he knelt beside Simon. "What's going on over here? These youngsters said someone was gettin' killed." He moved to David. "They're both breathing. What happened?" He looked around at

Miss Everett and the crowd of children.

"I'm afraid David was trying to really hurt Simon," Miss Everett replied. "He had his head bent back and was sitting on him. I heard cracking. I hope he's not broken his back."

The sheriff glanced down at the boys. "And what happened to David here? Looks like someone chewed off half his ear. Simon bite him?"

One of the kids pointed at Buell. "He kicked 'im. Darn near took his head off."

"Buell?" The question seemed apparent.

"Thought David was gonna break his back. Figgered a kick was the best way to stop him."

Simon groaned and started to stir. David remained immobile.

"You hear me, boy?" Staker shook Simon's shoulder. "Open your eyes."

Simon made a choking sound as his hand went to his face, then he took a deep breath and started to pant. After a few seconds, he pushed his chest off the ground and turned to sit up. Miss Everett daubed at the side of David's head and mouth with a kerchief. His head flopped away from her hand and back, and then he opened his eyes and lay still for a few seconds.

David let out a howl, "My hand. Oh, it

hurts . . . bad." He rolled onto his left side and got to his knees. Cradling his right arm, he stood and faced Miss Everett. The blood from his smashed ear ran down his cheek and neck, and blended with the blood and spit from his mashed lip. Mixed with the playground dirt, it made an ugly sight, and he had a crazy look in his eyes as he searched out Simon. "You'll pay for this," he said through clenched teeth. Shoulders hunched, he pulled his injured hand tight against his belly. Miss Everett reached for his arm, but he shook her off and headed across the schoolyard.

Simon got to his feet and stood unsteadily. "You gonna be okay?" Buell asked.

Simon nodded. "I think so. I thought he was going to break my back."

"I want you to tell your folks about this," Sheriff Staker said. "Both of you. Hear me? Simon, Buell?" Both nodded. Then he turned to Miss Everett. "What kicked all this off, anyway?" She held her hand up and turned to the children. "Go in and gather your things. There will be no more school today. You can all go home." The cheering children stampeded toward the school as she turned back to the sheriff. "I really don't know. I heard the commotion and came out to see David on top of Simon." Both shaking their heads, they headed toward the schoolhouse.

Simon put both hands beside his head and twisted his neck from side to side; it made crunching sounds. "What took you so long, Buell? I thought you were going to stand there and let him finish me." He fingered a spot high up on his forehead, pushed on it and winced.

"Wasn't my fight. Not until you asked for some help. Besides that, I've wondered how much a fella's neck would take before it broke. Quite a bit, looks like." Buell grinned at Simon's slack jaw and stunned expression. Together, they walked back to the schoolhouse.

Simon watched in horror next morning as a stream of red arced through the air and into the toilet. His back had prevented sleep for most of the night, and his neck still hurt every time he moved it from side to side. He'd told his folks that he'd had a tussle with David and had seen no need to elaborate. No damage showed other than a bruise high above his right eye — but now this. It didn't hurt to pee, but it was obviously bloody. He didn't know quite what to do. He certainly couldn't tell his mother. And his pa wasn't a much better choice. Simon decided to go to school and tell no one for the time being. He worried as the last few red drops fell away.

David wasn't at school, which pleased Simon. Jake met Simon in the coatroom, full of questions because he'd missed the whole thing, and now had to have all the details. Simon filled him in.

Jake seemed satisfied. "You don't look too bad." Then he grinned. "Way I hear it David has a plaster on his ear big as my fist."

"Ever peed bloody?" Simon blurted out.

"What? Pee blood?" Jake looked perplexed, but not puzzled. "Is that what you're doing?"

"Yeah, this morning."

"Comes from getting whacked in the side. I've heard Pa talk about it after some of the scraps at the saloon. Said some of them fellers will do it for a week." Jake sounded very matter-of-fact.

His directness eased some of Simon's angst. "Can you die from it?"

"Don't think so. Leastwise I ain't never heard of it. Mostly it just goes away. I'll ask Pa when I go home for noon. Why don't you come along? He won't tell anyone."

Buell walked into the coatroom. "Along where?"

"David must of busted something in my

guts. I had red in my pee when I went this morning. Jake says it comes from getting whacked in the side. We're going to go ask his pa if I can die from it." Simon felt like an expert. He wondered how come he could ask Jake's pa when asking his own was out of the question. Somehow, it just seemed to be all right this way. He probed once more with his fingers, winced and then grinned at his friends.

"Have you gone again this morning?" Mr. Luger asked.

"Yeah, once."

"Still as red?"

"Seems about the same."

"Not any redder?"

"Don't think so."

"Is your side painful?"

"Only if I push on it and a little when I sit. Not bad . . . I can stand it okay."

"I want you to tell your folks."

Simon looked at Jake and scowled.

"Best let Doc take a look at you. Sometimes they want you to stay off your feet for a couple days. I really don't know enough except to tell you to see the doc. I ain't never heard of anyone dying from it, though. Jake's right about that. Now the three of you go make a sandwich, unless ya brung

126

something else."

All three hurried for the lunch platter. Simon was especially eager to get out of sight in the back room.

Paul and Simon had gone to see Dr. Princher, and they now sat at the kitchen table where Paul explained the prognosis to Ana.

"Oh, Simon, you should have said something," she said.

"Doc Princher says he'll be fine in a few days," Paul assured her. "Just bruised his kidneys."

What Paul didn't say was what Doc Princher had told him out of Simon's earshot. He had told Paul it took tremendous pressure to bruise a kidney that way, the kind that breaks backs. Paul determined to go see Matt the next day.

Paul rode up in front of what he had always thought of as the home place. He sat in his saddle and looked around at the well-kept buildings. A swift wave of nostalgia washed over him. The ridge beam, sticking out the front of the barn's high roof, the attached pulley and rope tied back, all reminded him of the day he had nearly fallen from there. His father had grabbed a handful of Paul's shirt, and a fair amount of skin, and hauled him back to the safety of the loft. He relived the whack his father had dealt him on the back of his head for not being more careful. He now understood that the smack was not his father meting out punishment; it was his father expressing relief. He chuckled at the memory. His horse shifted balance, breaking into his brief daydream. He dismounted, looped the reins over the porch rail, and then walked up to the front door. He hesitated, and then knocked.

Ruth opened the door and her face radiated a welcome. "Paul, come in."

He stepped into the parlor, and glanced around the room and then looked at the kitchen door. "Hello, Ruth. Is my brother here?" Paul mentally winced. *Now why did I say brother, instead of Matt?* Ruth hadn't missed it either. "How's David's ear?" he added hastily.

Ruth folded her arms across her chest and looked at him, head half-cocked sideways. Ana could assume that same pose. "It looks a lot worse than it is. It's not the cut that bothers him most, it's the ringing. He says it won't stop. Matt was supposed to be out in the barn. I'm surprised he didn't hear you ride up."

"It's David and Simon I want to talk

about. We have to stop whatever is brewing from taking hold. I'm at a loss to understand the conflict between them."

"Matt and I talked last night and we agree."

Her response surprised him. Matt, being reasonable? Her arms remained folded. "Well, good. I'll go out and see if I can find him, then. Ana sends her love. Everything's fine at home. Simon's back is a little tender, but he'll be okay." Paul did not feel it necessary to tell her of the visit to the doctor. He wanted to get outside. The heat in the house and Ruth's attitude, along with all the clothes he was wearing, had started to make him sweat. "I'll stop and say good-bye before I leave," he said as he opened the door.

She unfolded her arms and held the door for him, then she touched his shoulder as he walked out.

When Paul got to the barn, he stepped into the spacious interior. "Matt?" A saddle horse shifted in a stall and turned to look at him. Paul walked toward the back of the barn. "Matt, you in here?"

A door opened and Matt stepped out halfway. "I'm in here." He paused and then stepped back into the room.

Paul crossed the stable to the tack room,

walked in and shut the door. Matt sat at a bench, a bridle before him and an awl in his hand. Concentration plain on his face, he punched through the leather, eyed the next stitch hole and pierced the strap again. The spacing of the holes was perfect; Matt had always been an excellent leather worker. The room smelled like work, a delicious aroma of leather, treated deliberately with oil, and incidentally with horse sweat. The faint scent of liniment brought back memories of many exceptionally hard days. The last couple of days had been like those, only not in the physical sense. The mental strain of deciding to try one more time with Matt had kept Paul awake for two nights running, and he was feeling the effects.

Paul, as usual, lost the who-speaks-first contest. "I think we need to talk about our boys."

Matt stopped working and raised his head, a faintly satisfied look blinked across his face. "I think so too."

"First, you should know I took Simon to see Doc Princher. He said we almost had ourselves a broken back. Just that close." Paul measured the expression with his thumb and index finger a sixteenth of an inch apart.

"Who punched who first?"

Paul saw his attempt to point out the seriousness of the fight ignored. Matt had never liked to take the blame for anything, and Paul saw he was setting the ground rules early. He sighed. "Simon did."

"And who has a cut lip, a broken tooth, a smashed ear, and a finger that may never be any good?" Matt's nostrils flared for an instant and the litany seemed to make him feel better. "So, yeah, let's talk about how you can get Simon to control his temper." He looked like a man who'd just turned up a third ace in a game of five-card stud and Paul knew he'd come unprepared. "Sit down," Matt said. "You make me tired just looking at ya."

Paul took off his hat and heavy coat and hung them on a nail. He dragged a heavy tall stool over to the bench and sat. "I'm glad we can at least talk about this, Matt. I really am. Maybe we can sort some other things out while we're at it. Okay?" Matt's expression didn't change and Paul felt a tinge of hope. "I don't remember when we first started to butt heads, but I know we can't let it carry on through our boys."

Matt nodded and still said nothing.

"I asked Simon what started this whole thing Monday, and he says there was nothing particular. That's worrying, don't ya think?"

"David says Simon made a snotty remark about Ruth." Matt jutted his chin.

"Come on, Matt, my kids love Ruth like their own mother." Matt's eyes narrowed for an instant and ever so slightly. "I mean, Simon would not say anything bad about Ruth. Are you sure?"

"Why would David make it up? First he gets the snot knocked out of him, and now you accuse him of lying. Is this your idea of discussing the problem?"

"I'm not accusing him of anything. I'm just asking if you heard him right."

"What's to misunderstand? David says Simon was smarting off about Ruth. That's good enough for me."

"All right, if he needs to apologize to Ruth, he will. But even if he had something smart to say, I think David's reaction was dangerous." Matt sniffed, making Paul even more determined to make his point. "I'm serious. Doc Princher said he could have broken Simon's back so easy it ain't funny." He slipped off his stool and stood.

A faint smile crossed Matt's face. "I've thought about it and I think if David had wanted to, he could have really hurt Simon. The fact that he didn't tells me he was in control, and just teaching your boy a little lesson. You going to shield him all his life, or let him grow up?"

"It's our job to protect our kids from some things, and brutality is one of them. I've talked to Miss Everett and she thinks David lost control. She said if Buell Mace hadn't taken David off Simon, it could have been bad. Do you know that David hit her also?"

"David has apologized to her already. He said she stepped in the way. Her getting hit was an accident. And I don't take kindly to your describing David as brutal. We're talking about boys here, and if anyone got beat up, it was David." Matt stood and moved away from his stool to face Paul directly. "I didn't want to bring it up, but David has never seen me hit a person or an animal in his life. Can Simon say the same thing about you?"

Paul realized everything Matt said was the truth and had Paul at a distinct disadvantage. So Paul was a bit surprised Matt wasn't being nasty about it, rubbing his nose in it. "It looks like I'm the one who has to be making the amends. I hadn't thought this out as well as I should have. I'm sorry for jumping on you."

"We all make mistakes, Paul. Let's let this

one end right here." Matt stuck his hand out.

Paul could hardly believe his eyes. He shook Matt's hand, his heart thumping. "I'm glad we can talk, Matt. I've missed not having a brother." He didn't want to let go of his hand.

"Let's go see if Ruth has a cup of coffee," Matt said. He took his coat off a nail on the wall and headed for the door. Paul followed him.

Matt went to the door after they'd shared a piece of Ruth's cake and shook his brother's hand again. Matt felt quite pleased with himself. Avery Singer had told him that Paul and John were working on something that would probably make someone a lot of money. Avery had also told him John needed about five thousand dollars come spring, and that Paul was going to handle whatever it was the money bought.

Matt needed to know what that something was because he was overextended — and his lien holder was Avery Singer. If he could find out what Paul was up to in the next few months, he might just take the deal away. Having Paul relaxed and vulnerable was exactly what Matt needed, and his brother was that now.

■ ■ ■ ■

His son bristled when Paul told him what he needed to do. "What do you mean apologize? That's the same as admitting I said something bad about her, and I didn't. How can that be fair?"

"And if you don't and she believes what David is saying, what's she going to think of you? This is what I meant when I told you to try to mind your own business. I'm sorry, but when you punched David you brought yourself down to his level. That's just the way it works."

"But, he was saying some really bad things about you. I couldn't just stand there and let him do that. You didn't let Uncle Matt. I saw you knock him on his butt."

Paul sighed. *I knew this day would come. As soon as I smacked Matt, satisfying as it was, I knew.* He reached out and touched his son on the shoulder. "What I did to Matt was just as wrong as what you did to David. I apologized any number of times for it, and will try for all I'm worth not to let it happen again. You have to do the same, at least to David. I believe you didn't say anything bad about Ruth."

"He started it, and I have to say I'm sorry.

I just don't understand." Simon, elbows propped on the table, held his head in his hands. "All right, I'll apologize to David, but Ma, please explain to Aunt Ruth that I would never say anything bad about her, okay?"

"I'll try, Simon, but you have to remember she has as much faith in David as I have in you. But I'll try."

CHAPTER 12

Ana was looking forward to Thanksgiving Day this year. With Paul and Matt reconciled, Simon and David avoiding each other, another good summer of selling poultry behind them, they had a lot to be thankful for. Her excitement doubled when Ruth invited them all to the home place for the meal.

"Welcome," Ruth greeted them when they arrived, and her face seemed to glow with happiness. She hugged Ana tightly and then held the door open while the Paul Steele family, seven strong, marched into the house. The younger ones had never been there and were all eyes, Eric particularly interested in Ruth's cat. After the coats, scarves, and hats had been gathered and hauled to the bedroom off the kitchen, Ruth invited them to sit at the combined tables set up in the dining room. Matt and David had moved the kitchen table in so they all could sit down together. Normally, the children sat separately.

The table, a testament to prosperity, held a ham, two roast chickens and a beef roast that led a parade of food that seemed endless. Potatoes, mashed parsnips, baked squash, yeast bread, rice pudding with currants, apple and pumpkin pie, and a cake. All the dinnerware on the extended table matched, as did the tablecloths and napkins. Matt sat at one end and Paul the other, the rest lined up on either side.

Matt settled the children with a righteous clearing of the throat, and they all bowed their heads as he led them in a prayer of thanksgiving. And led them . . . and led them . . . and led them. He droned on and on about family, friends, neighbors, the nation, the war, the Indian problems, the mild winter, the animals, the crops . . . and their inequities, their faults and failures, shortcomings and disappointments. With a final plea for forgiveness of aggressive behavior, he ended. Ana saw David look over his plate at Simon on the other side of the table and sneer. *So much for reconciliation. Poor Simon.*

The mothers started to serve the meat and vegetables with a lot of decisions coming from the children: beef, ham, or chicken, one or the other, or all three? Parsnips or potatoes? Do you want gravy on that? Plates loaded, the group settled into eating, satisfied to simply enjoy all the good food, and quiet settled over the table. Except for Eric. He needed more butter, and was determined to get some. Ruth had pressed the butter into cubes, which she'd kept in the stone cool-house just off the back door. Eric reached with his butter knife, and attempted to take a slice of the top of the cube. As opposed to summer butter, this cube was solid as butter can get and as a consequence, all he could do was chase the butter dish back and forth across the table. Matt watched this with a stern scowl on his face while the rest of the family looked on in amusement.

"Let me show you how it's done properly," Matt said. He furrowed his brow, drew the dish close to his plate and squared his knife over one end of the cube. Carefully, he attempted to cut a piece off, and when the butter resisted, Matt bore down harder. The butter resisted further and Matt pushed even harder while the family watched with rapt attention. Matt, lips pursed in a thin line, gave one final push, and the butter shot off the dish, bounced off the pot roast to skitter off the table, and across the wood floor with Ruth's house cat in hot pursuit. The children howled with laughter, soon followed by Paul, and finally Ruth. They all rocked back and forth in their chairs, tears starting to stream, their self-control lost to spasms of laughter. Matt, red-faced and stern, tried to scowl them into submission — and failed.

With dinner over, the smaller children were set to play in a corner of the kitchen. David and Simon had gone to the barn to start feeding the stock, and Ana and Ruth were cleaning up the dishes.

Matt and Paul were in the parlor to have a whiskey. "I hear you and John Lindstrom are working on some kind of deal," Matt said. "What's that all about?"

"Where'd you hear that?"

"I saw you, Mace and John last Saturday in Luger's. Avery Singer said John might have something in mind, something this spring. I was just wondering."

"Not a lot to say. John said something about maybe getting some cows. He asked me to kinda keep it under my hat so I can't say much, and I really don't have a lot of details."

"No idea where he's getting them? I'm feeding about twenty. Is he considering something like that?"

"I really don't know, but I think he means

more than that. I'm just not comfortable saying a lot because I don't know that much for sure."

"Okay. So how's the poultry business going? Seems like you have a pretty good hold on all the feed there is. I tried to buy a sack for our few, and Mace said he had consigned the whole shipment to you. You gonna starve my chickens out?"

Paul apparently missed Matt's attempt at humor. "No. If you need some I'll make sure you get some. I've tried to make my orders match what I need so as not to keep the rest of you without. Sure didn't mean to cut anybody off. I'll tell Mace to set a sack or two aside."

With what Avery Singer had told him and what Paul had just said, Matt had learned some more of what he needed to know. Five thousand dollars' worth of cattle is a lot of beef. Where was John going to get them and where was he going to keep them? Maybe he already has them sold and is just going to be the broker for them; if so, to whom?

Matt switched the conversation to the war and the Indian problems. They sat talking for over an hour, and he found he actually enjoyed the conversation. When Paul's family was loaded and gone, it dawned on him that the visit had ended on a high note. That

141

was something that had not happened for a very long time, and he realized he'd benefited from it in several ways.

Winter gone and the muddy spring that followed a memory, John Lindstrom stirred up the dust as he pounded down the street. He had heard the news he'd been waiting for, and hurried to get to Avery's office. He walked in as Avery finished up a conversation with Art Lancer. Lancer owned one of the saloons in town, and was a frequent visitor at Avery's offices.

"Art, how are you?" John asked.

"Fit." In fact, Art Lancer was anything but fit. He had consumption so bad he rarely spoke more than two or three words in a row for fear he'd start a coughing spell. He preferred a response just like the one he'd given John. He breathed in short, shallow breaths that he let out real slow. It made it appear like all he ever did was exhale. "Come by?" Art said.

John was familiar with Art's way of speaking. "Don't get by the place as often as I used to, Art. Nothing personal, you understand. I just don't have the need for your services like I once did."

"Right." Art headed for the wide open door. "See you," he said to both Avery and

John. He gave a little cough and his eyes went wide for a moment, but then he relaxed when nothing developed. He walked out the door and into the street.

John found it hard to conceal his distaste for Avery Singer. It could have been Avery's personal appearance; a dandy, his black hair slicked flat with pomade that smelled like a basket of overripe fruit. Two gold teeth flashed from a row of perfectly good ones, making a person wonder if he'd replaced them just for show. Worst of all were his hands, woman's hands, a woman of leisure's hands.

"As promised, it's spring and we need to talk. I want you to have five thousand in gold ready in about three weeks. If you can't raise five thousand, then twenty-five hundred in gold and the rest in a letter of credit from our friends in Saint Louis will do."

"When do you need it?"

"I don't need it. I said I want you to have it available."

"I'm afraid I don't understand, Mr. Lindstrom."

"You are going to make Paul Steele a loan on my behalf. He will put his poultry enterprise up as collateral, collateral that you will not encumber. The mortgage agreement will cite the farm, but you will not formally put a lien on it. The term of the loan will be two years from June first at three percent. I have drawn a separate agreement between you and me wherein I lend to you the five thousand at two percent per annum interest. You have my word the interest will be refunded. For these services I will pay you a twenty-five dollar initiation fee." John laid two gold coins, a promissory note, and a signed draft demand on top of the paper Avery had been writing on.

Avery leaned back in his chair and looked at John intently. "I usually don't inquire into a person's personal affairs, but you have me stumped."

"A reasonable and appropriate approach, Singer. If you don't inquire, I won't have to embarrass you by reminding you whose business it isn't."

"I just can't understand why a man with your education and talent would give money away. Hell, man, I could easily make you five or six percent on all that cash you have lying around in the Saint Louis bank."

John noticed Avery didn't mention the two percent he'd make on the same deals. He didn't have to; John was more aware of it than Avery. "Just say I have something I need to do before I leave this place. You will take care of this matter?"

"Sure. I'll have the money, and when Paul comes to see me he'll have no problem arranging a loan." Avery read the short promissory note, signed it and handed it to John. Then he turned his chair around and pulled open the third drawer of a tall oak cabinet. Inside were several string-tied folders. He took out one labeled "Steele & Co." He untied the string bow on top and dropped the written instructions inside. "There, all set. I'll arrange for the money to be sent from Saint Louis. Anything else, Mr. Lindstrom?"

"No. Thank you, Mr. Singer." John turned and left, angling across the street to Luger's Saloon.

"Hello, you two," John said as he entered.

"Hello yourself. You look pleased about something," Paul said. It looked to John like Paul and Mace were halfway through their usual ham and cheese sandwiches.

"Hello, John," Mace said.

John waved at Fred. "I'd drink a beer unless you're still grudging for me withholding business." He pulled back a chair and as he nodded several quick greetings to other customers, sat down.

"Gonna eat?" Paul asked and reduced a large pickle by a third with one crunchy chomp. Garlic dill pickles were another of

Fred's wife's specialties.

"Too excited. I just got a telegraph from some business associates of mine in Kansas. The potential cattle deal I told you about last fall seems to be bearing fruit. Are you ready to herd cows all summer, Paul?"

Paul stopped chewing. Mace stopped the sandwich halfway to his mouth, and put it back on the plate.

"Here's your beer, John, leastwise half of one, I'm still holding half a grudge." Fred grinned at him and set a full mug of beer on the table. "Something wrong with the meat, Mace?" He must have seen Mace's aborted bite.

"No. No, it's fine. Just letting my gut catch up a little, that's all."

"Okay. 'Nother beer?" Fred glanced at the half-empty mugs.

"Not just yet. We'll holler," Paul said.

John waited until Paul and Mace looked at him. "I found out last year that there were lots of cattle up from Texas that could not get across the Mississippi River. The Union army has pretty much controlled its length, and obviously they aren't going to let supplies get to the Confederate army. I have acquaintances in Kansas with whom I've worked to procure part of one of those herds. They've been fed all winter and are now on the way here with the Texans who originally brought them up." John took a long pull on his beer and sat back, grinning from ear to ear.

Paul looked at Mace. Mace shrugged his shoulders.

"How many?" Paul gulped.

"Six hundred, give or take five percent, at four dollars a head," John said, slightly deflated by their reactions. He had expected a full celebration, and they just sat there and looked at him.

"How in blazes am I going to take care of six hundred animals?" Paul finally managed to speak. "That's two or three square miles of cows."

"I thought you'd been thinking about this."

"Well, I did, a little."

"Do you have anyone in mind who might be willing to hire on for a summer of herding?" John asked. He couldn't keep his concern from creeping into his voice. "Surely, you've looked into that?"

"Frankly, John, there aren't too many who relish traveling from here to the fort and back, much less camping out all summer. The Sioux have been raising Cain all up and down the river and people are nervous."

John could see Paul felt slightly guilty.

"I'll go for sure," Paul said. "And Simon. How about Buell, Mace?"

"Buell would jump at the chance. How dangerous do you think it might be?"

Paul hesitated for a moment. "Indians are mostly west and down along the Republican. I haven't heard of any trouble within a hundred miles of here."

"I've got six hundred cattle that'll be here in less than a month, and *we* have to be ready to do something with them," John said. He couldn't help but emphasize the *we*. "I need to rent a horse tomorrow, Mace." He got up, dug in his pocket, and dropped a quarter on the table. "I've got to go do some thinking. I'll see you guys tomorrow, in here, for lunch . . . maybe." He walked across the room and out the door, nodding at Fred as he left.

Paul watched until John was out the door. "Looks like I might have bit off something I can't swallow."

"I don't think so. You just haven't had time to think about it," Mace said.

His friend's concern was apparent and Paul felt a flush of appreciation for the husky man. "Judas Priest, six hundred. It'll take at least ten men to keep track of that many. Where am I going to get ten men for

148

the summer or the money to pay them?" Paul pushed his half-eaten sandwich to the middle of the table. "I'm going to go home and talk to Ana." He got up and reached in his pocket.

Mace held up his hand. "My turn, I'll get it."

"Okay, I'll see ya tomorrow. Do you think I can count Buell in?"

"I'm sure of it. And I don't have a lot of worry about Indians. I've not seen one in years. See you tomorrow, and don't fret, it'll work out."

Paul had noted the weak smile and knew Mace was no more convinced than he was. He left the saloon and rode home deep in thought.

Ana looked at the husband who'd come home looking worried and confused. Now his eyes sparkled and his mouth opened in amazement and relief.

"You never cease to amaze me, woman. 'Use the Texans.' Why didn't three grown men think of something as obvious as that?"

She sat and looked at Paul, a wide smile on her slightly damp face. It could not do justice to the pleasure she felt at taking the cloud of gloom that Paul walked in with and blowing it back out the door.

"I'm going to ride right back to town and tell John. I can't thank you enough, Ma. You are a jewel."

He hustled out the door, and Ana heard him ride away about three minutes later. She went back to her bread making.

John had roomed at Mrs. Bray's for several years and felt right at home, but he was surprised when Paul stepped into the parlor.

"Mrs. Bray said you were in here. Didn't mean to interrupt your reading."

"Anything wrong?" Paul had never visited him here.

"Nothing, absolutely nothing." Paul broke out a broad grin. "Matter of fact, everything is right again."

"How so?"

"I went home with my tail between my legs, and Ana come up with a solution to our herder problem in about five minutes. We ask the Texans to stay through the summer. It's not like they have anything else to do. Ana thinks they will be plumb tickled to have a steady job. I think she's right." Paul stopped and took a deep breath.

"I'll be damned." John put down his book, a slight smile on his face. "Every time I deal with that woman of yours I come away feeling like a fool." John got out of his chair.

"Let's go tell Mace. I want to pass something else by him." Paul said.

They went to the front door and John spoke toward the back of the house. "I'm going out, Mrs. Bray. I'll be back for dinner."

"Fine, thank you, John," she replied from the kitchen.

A short walk later they entered the livery and found Mace. Paul went to the workbench, leaned against it and told Mace what Ana had said.

"Texans. I'll be jacked. Good idea." Mace's hammer rested on a partially formed hoe. "How many you reckon will come with the herd, John?"

"Ten to fifteen men are normal for a three-thousand-cow herd plus a cook, horse handler and foreman. They're heading this way with about a quarter that amount, so I suppose about eight, just guessing. Now that's as many as will be coming. Doesn't mean they'll all want to stay for the summer."

"A quarter? I thought we were talking about six hundred," Paul said.

"I asked the people in Kansas to hold seven hundred over the winter and to come here with whatever they managed to keep. I'm not sure, but if the winter and spring was as mild there as it was here, we could be seeing most of that seven hundred."

Paul glanced at Mace, a slight sense of uneasiness coming over him.

Mace shrugged. "Like John said last fall, Paul, five hundred or five thousand, we have the room."

"Who are we going to sell seven hundred cattle to?" Paul looked back and forth between the two men. "That's a lot of beef."

"That part we work on this coming Monday," John said. "I've set up an appointment with Captain Atkins at Fort Hartwell. We're way early, so I'm sure we'll be the first to approach him with an offer of beef cattle. It'll just be a matter of getting an agreement on price. We'll find out then how many they can use."

"Looks like you've done all the planning," Paul said. "Now, how about grazing?"

"I've ridden up and down the river for twenty miles in each direction, and I've found two ideal places to graze cattle. I think the best one is about five miles east of here. You know that low bluff the river skirts to the north?"

"Where those two wagons burned a couple years back?" Mace asked.

"That's it. The river forms a natural barrier that surrounds three or four square miles of river bottom and bluff on three sides. Seven or eight men could range the south side of that area without raising a sweat. Best part is nobody wants to farm it because the bluffs don't hold the water, but it's perfect for grazing . . . the cows can go to the water."

"The more you talk, the better I feel," Paul said. "I thought I'd really let you down by not rustling up some herders. I don't know what I was thinking. I'm real lucky the other half is a lot smarter than the half standing here." He still felt embarrassed at how quickly Ana had come up with a solution to his problem.

"It was a typical female response, I'm afraid to admit." John laughed. "We always try to make the solutions too complicated. I think it's just to show everybody how smart we are."

Mace shook his head. "I don't know if I'd go that far."

"Could you fashion some sort of camping wagon for us, Mace?" John asked. "I hate to think of those guys out there all summer without someplace to shelter during a rainy spell. I remember too well once getting stuck in the wet for four days, and I don't wish that on anyone. Took me a week to get warm and dry again." He shook his shoulders in an exaggerated shiver. "Ooff!"

Paul looked for a place to sit, and pulled a bench away from the wall. He motioned for John to join him. Mace threw one leg over the flat of his anvil.

"No problem," Mace said. "I have two or three largish sheets of canvas I keep for replacing burned wagon tops and such. I think I could come up with something real snug if I thought about it for a bit. Maybe I could ask Ana." Mace gave Paul a mock bow with his head.

"Smart as you are, it probably might be a good idea."

"Okay, I think we have all the most pressing considerations in hand, except for one other thing." John looked at Paul. "Money."

Paul paused in thought for a moment. "There are only three people I know of who have that kind of money, or stand a chance of getting their hands on it. Werner Swartz, Avery Singer, and maybe Art Lancer. And I think only Avery could do it on short notice. What did you have in mind, John, some sort of partnership like we did with the chickens?"

"No, I think you can get what you need from Singer by yourself. Your holdings are now sufficient to provide the collateral, and anybody can see that you and Ana know

154

how to run a business. I'm still on the papers that established Steele and Company, but now only as a cofounder. I'll take a broker fee for arranging delivery, and I'll want compensation for my expenses of last winter, and of course the cost of the cattle. But further than that, I see no need for my involvement."

"But surely you've done more than just arrange for some cattle to appear? If it weren't for you paying attention and spending a lot of time studying the situation, none of this would have come about," Paul said. "And you took an awful risk buying a herd you hadn't seen."

"Let's just say I needed to do this to keep the rust off."

"Rust?"

"Maybe the wrong word. I needed something to do, and I found this venture interesting. We'll just leave it at that."

Paul, feeling perplexed, could only shrug. "Okay."

"Looks like you're gonna be the money man." Mace grinned at Paul. "Is Mister Cattle Baron still gonna go to Luger's with us common folks?"

"Maybe . . . after a good look inside to see if you're there."

John shook his head. "All right, looks like

we're set. Let me know what Singer says, Paul." He got up. "Should be an interesting couple of weeks." He brushed off the seat of his pants, walked into the livery section, and left.

"That is a busy man," Mace said. "I think there's a lot more to him than most would ever imagine. What was that about rusting?"

"I caught that too. All I know is he sure keeps his eye out for me and Ana." Paul pushed the bench back against the wall. "I'm gonna get out of here. I'll see you tomorrow at Luger's. Should know what Avery has to say by then. Makes me nervous just thinking about that much money. John never did say how much, did he?"

"Not that I remember. Seven hundred cows ain't gonna come cheap. Can't be much under, let's see . . . three thousand, maybe a little more? About that." Mace shook his head. "Too rich for my liking."

"Anything to make me feel better, right?" Paul punched Mace lightly on the shoulder. "I'll see ya tomorrow, friend."

CHAPTER 13

Avery caught sight of Paul angling across the street. He swung his feet off the desk, put a dossier away in the cabinet behind him, and slid the drawer shut. He turned and got his feet back up and chair tilted back just as Paul stepped through the open door.

"Morning, Avery," Paul said. "Got a little business proposition I want to discuss with you. Can I take a few minutes?"

"Sure. If there's some money to be made, Avery Singer always has a minute. Sit down and tell me what you have in mind."

"I've got upwards to seven hundred cattle coming up the trail that'll be here in about three weeks."

Avery nearly overbalanced his chair. *I'll be a son of a bitch. Cattle. Army posts getting more troops for the Indian problem, and more troops means more beef. Slick as willow bark.* Scrambling to keep from tipping over, he kicked a stack of papers halfway across the room. He managed to get all four legs of his chair grounded and waved at the papers lying on the floor as Paul made a move to pick up the mess. "I'll get 'em later, don't bother." He settled in his chair. "Where you going to sell seven hundred beef cows?"

"Fort Hartwell. Got an appointment Monday to discuss the price."

"How did seven hundred cattle get into Nebraska Territory this time of the year? They teach Texas cows how to fly?"

"They've wintered over in southeast Kansas."

"Can't be much of a cow left after a winter in Kansas."

"Probably not, but I intend to graze 'em here until the fall. With the spring we've had, and the mild winter, they'll get healthy in a hurry. The buffalo grass is nearly four inches high already, and it's as thick and full as I've ever seen. You might not know it, but buffalo grass as fodder is just as good dry as it is green."

"Huh, you're right, didn't know that. Until fall? Where you going keep them until then? Not enough room on all the farms combined for a herd that size, even if you could arrange it. Unless you have that little problem solved, you might have come up holding a polecat with no place to chuck him." Avery struggled to hide his irritation. *Shit. Here sits a chicken farmer about to dictate terms he could never get if not for that damned drunk interfering. I'd have this feather merchant's shirt if I didn't have Lindstrom looking over my shoulder. Feather merchant — ha, that's a good one. No place to put all those cows. I still might get a piece of this.*

"Got about four square miles of water and grass located," Paul said.

He's kinda smug about it.

"And half a dozen or so herders lined up to tend them for the summer."

"Well, sounds like someone has been looking over the options. My congratulations, Paul. Now, how do I fit in here?" Avery tried to sound pleased.

"Money. I need about thirty-two hundred dollars, and I'm willing to put up my home place and the chicken operation as my bond. You come up with a reasonable interest rate, and agree to take repayment in one chunk when I sell the cattle in the fall. Is that agreeable?" Paul knew the eleven adjoining acres he had bought two years ago and all the new buildings made his place worth every bit of that.

"I'll write that up. I know as well as anyone what your place is worth, and can't see any reason not to let you have what you need," Avery stated the obvious. It still rankled him to see an opportunity to pluck a chicken go by the way. He stood up and extended his hand. "Again, congratulations. I think you're on to a good deal here." Avery meant it when he stated the fact, but he didn't feel quite so sincere about the compliment. He couldn't help but wonder how many more of these Lindstrom interventions were in the works. He hoped not many. The well held only so much water, and he didn't like standing around without a bucket ready.

Paul pushed open the door of Luger's. Still too early for the lunch bunch, as Fred called the regulars, so Paul walked up to the bar where Fred's wife Freda worked laying out the usual spread. "Good morning."

"I'd be willing to argue that if I had time," she replied.

Paul got the impression she found it an effort just to say it. Freda went through life harried, not in a hurry, or hustling along, but truly harried. She had the look of a chased fox. What's best? Go over or under, around or through, turn right or left, stop or keep running? She snatched up the twenty-inch-long wooden platter she'd used to transport the food, marched down the bar, and into the back room. "Fred! Paul's here."

A couple seconds later, the back door slammed and Paul imagined the cloud of dust Freda raised as she cut diagonally across the back lot and into the house she kept for Frederick Luger, proprietor. He smiled to himself. He liked her no-nonsense approach.

"Morning, Paul." Fred walked into the room wiping his ham-size hands on his apron.

"Fred. Gotta cup of coffee?"

"Sure, not very hot, but you'll taste it." He poured a cup out of a white-speckled, blue-enamel pot.

Paul noticed the last half would require a little teeth straining, the grounds dark brown and soggy-looking. He took a sip and winced. "Thanks. I think."

"Mace was in for a while last night." Fred leaned his elbows on the bar. "He was worked up about something but wouldn't say much. You gonna play button-button too?"

"I can't think of a reason not to tell you. We got a herd of cows coming up from Kansas. Be here in about three weeks. Mace is gonna build us a camp wagon."

"Be damned."

Paul picked up his coffee cup, studied it for a moment, and set it back down.

"Get ya some more?" Fred pushed away from the bar.

"No, I'm still good. Got the latest paper?"

Carlisle now had a weekly paper; one folded broadsheet, printed front and back, but a welcomed addition to the town. The week-old papers they received from Lincoln and Omaha contained little about the events and issues important to people this far west. The occasional Chicago or Saint Louis paper seemed to contain even less, but John Lindstrom devoured them, and a few others read some, but most folks used them to start kitchen fires.

Fred handed him a couple. "Here ya go. I've got a couple other things to do before lunch, so if you need any more coffee, help yourself." He disappeared into the back room.

Paul sat for about twenty minutes waiting for Mace to come in. Meanwhile several of the other regulars had arrived and were tucking into sandwiches. The emphatic punctuation of a domino being clacked down in play announced lunch hour was in session at Luger's.

"Hey, Paul." Mace greeted him when he

strode through the door and headed straight for the ham and cheese.

Paul got up and followed him.

"So, how'd it go with Avery?" Mace asked.

"It was like he'd been expecting me. And I think a bit miffed about something, but I don't know what. I've given up trying to figure out what Avery's thinking." Paul reached for the bread.

"But he agreed to let you have the money?" Mace slathered his bread slice with mustard.

"Oh yeah, like I said, he didn't really make much of an issue of it. I think he was surprised I had all the angles worked out though. You could just see the wheels spinning in his head."

Mace handed him the wooden paddle.

Fred walked up behind the bar. "Heard about the Texas deal, Mace. Gonna build a mobile castle I understand." He set a crock of Freda's pickles on the bar and the customers who saw the late addition got up from their tables and hurried over.

"Got a rough design. Pull us a couple of beers and I'll show it to you."

Mace picked up his sandwich and headed for the table where Paul had been sitting. The other customers, fishing six-inch, knobbly, sage-green pickles out of the crock, held

Paul up for a bit and he got to the table just as Fred set their beers down.

Mace pulled a sheet of paper out of his shirt pocket and unfolded it to reveal a scale drawing of a modified prairie wagon. "Just a rough concept."

"Some rough concept. Stay up all night?" Paul asked, and then bit into his sandwich.

"Wasn't that hard. I bought the wagon used two years ago. It's a standard four-by-ten-foot bed made of oak and poplar. Solid as the day it left Pennsylvania. Let me show ya." Mace spread out and smoothed the paper.

Four corner posts supported a canvas-covered frame six feet above the wagon bed. Draped awnings covered the ends and one side, with another that extended out from the top on four slender ten-foot-long poles with the ends supported by a three-foot-high rail. The trailing edge of the canvas draped over the rail and to the ground to form a low wall. A foldable trestle table was depicted standing alongside the wagon.

Fred put his finger on the table. "Ain't no self-respecting cowboy gonna set down at a table to eat. Betcha it winds up as firewood."

"You might be surprised," Paul said. "Everyone can sleep out of the weather, and that much shade will be wonderful come the middle of August." He took a big bite of sandwich.

"So, ya want me to rig it up?" Mace refolded the paper and put it back in his pocket.

Paul switched the wad of meat and bread to his cheek. "Let's get 'er going."

CHAPTER 14

Three weeks and two days after Paul had arranged his loan, John rode out to see him. Paul was replacing the rope on the well windlass as John rode up.

"You got yourself a herd of cows, Paul. They're settling down right now about three miles east of town. Can you free yourself from what you're doing and go meet my Mr. Greene?"

"Sure. I'll have Simon and Axel finish this."

"Hello, John, nice to see you," Ana said from the doorway of the house.

"And hello to you too, madam." John tipped his black hat. "I'm going to abscond with your husband if that's okay. Looks like your herd has arrived."

"Oh, how exciting. I wish I could go see." She wiped her hands on her apron.

"What's stopping you?"

"Mercy, I don't have time to go running

around the country looking at cows. I'll wait till Paul gets back and he can tell me."

Paul stepped away from the well. "When the boys get back from delivering eggs, have them string this rope out and then wind it nice and even on the crank. And tell them if they lose another rope and bucket I'm liable to throw one of them in after it."

Ana sniffed at his threat. "I'll tell them. See you when you get back." She waved to John and went back into the house.

Paul had never seen so many cattle, a shifting mass of brown, black, and white moving somewhat aimlessly under a cloud of dust. Four horsemen rode on the periphery, each lazily swinging a slack loop of rope back and forth on the herd side of their horses. The cattle randomly stopped to browse every three or four steps. The two riders closest to Paul were obviously turning the herd slowly toward the river to the north. As he watched, another rider came into view on the south side of the herd. That made five. This rider raised a hand in recognition, and rode directly toward them.

"Howdy again, Mr. Lindstrom," the dusty rider said.

Paul couldn't see the eyes under the brim of a huge gray felt hat, but the dust clinging to the man's whiskers and mustache was apparent and copious. He sat straight in the saddle, his lean legs curved around the barrel of the horse's belly.

"I'd like you to meet Paul Steele, Mr. Greene. Paul, this is Nathan Greene of Texas."

The Texan took off his hat and swatted the side of his leg. The gray hat turned black. He puffed at the dust cloud, settled the big hat on the back of his head, and tugged the glove off his right hand. Leaning over his horse's neck, he reached out to Paul. "My pleasure, Mr. Steele." His eyes met Paul's with the easy look of confidence.

"Welcome to Carlisle," Paul said, and looked past the man at the milling herd and couldn't think of anything to say. "Sure a lot of cows."

"When you get these animals settled down, come in to town and we'll get acquainted," John said. "How many men do you have with you?"

"Got six left. Kilt two just after we crossed the Republican. Herd took a beating too. I'll tell y'all about it later."

"Ooff, I hate to hear news like that. Sorry," Paul said.

"Sometimes it just happens. I reckon them

boys knew it when they signed on." Nathan Greene rubbed the palm of his hand over his chin. "Be glad to get out from under all this here dirt. Got a bathhouse som'ers?"

"Absolutely," John said. "I've arranged a night for each of you at Luger's. He has rooms upstairs and a place to get a bath. His wife, Freda, is without a doubt one of the best cooks around here. Cornmeal, salt pork and coffee will not be on the menu for those who come in tonight. And those that have to stay with the herd will get theirs tomorrow. It's our pleasure to treat you." John turned to Paul. "Will you join us to-night?"

"Indeed," Paul said, pleased John had handled the social aspects. He would never have thought about it until Ana pointed it out, which she would have.

"Good, then. We'll see you at Luger's. His place is the first two-story on the left as you're heading west through town. Come when you're ready. How many will you leave with the herd?" John asked.

"Three," Nathan Greene said, pulling on his glove. "I appreciate the invite. Neigh-borly of ya. We shouldn't be mor'n an hour or so." He turned the reins against his horse's neck and leaned slightly to his right. The animal was suddenly headed east.

"Friendly enough fella, that's for sure," Paul said. "And that horse acts like it's part of him. Did you see it turn? It didn't go ahead one step, it just turned. Amazing."

"I like the man. He'd taken a great financial risk based simply on a telegram from me. Not the kind of man I'd like to see taken advantage of. Not that I'd suggest it. Did you get a look at that pistol he had strapped to his saddle?"

Greene rode up to the closest outrider and they talked for a minute, then the rider turned and disappeared east into the dust.

Word spread around town like a swarm of gnats: Paul Steele has three thousand head of cattle just outside town, and about a dozen Texans plus half that many Mexicans were going to ride in at dusk. Most of the adult male population of Carlisle stood around in clusters at various locations. Lancer's, Luger's and the trading store were all packed with people, each with an eyewitness account of some Texan's malfeasance, passed on to them by their neighbor who had heard it from a cousin. Everybody had an opinion on the subject.

"I understand them Texans are meaner than snakes."

"Heard of a man that got shot for just

shoving a Texan's horse over to get on his own. Shot the feller in the foot, and then turned his horse loose."

"I think I heard that one too."

"There was one who walked twenty miles to get his horse back. Drug the man who stolt it all the way back to town, and then drowned him in a trough. Swear that one happened."

"I think I'm a gonna keep my head down a little bit."

Through the groups of men went the tales of lore, fantasies and outright lies. John, Mace and Paul waited at a table near the back-room door.

"Here they come!" someone outside shouted.

Nathan Greene and his men rode into Carlisle from the east. As they passed the school, he could see a couple of dozen people standing in front of a two-story building, just up a little and on the left, exactly where John Lindstrom had told him he would find the hotel-saloon he was looking for. The presence of this many people, obviously looking at him and his three drovers, made him uneasy. The four riders instinctively spread out to fill the street from side to side.

When he heard someone in front of the saloon shout, he eased the Colt Walker pistol loose in its holster. True of most long-distance riders, he found the five-pound weapon a terrible nuisance when worn on the hip, so he carried it strapped to his saddle. He glanced at the other three men riding on his left, each alert as he was. As they approached Luger's, he looked for somewhere to tie up the horses. Over the heads of the small crowd he saw a rail on the west side of the building and headed for it. Three or four men moved out of the way as the Texans swung their mounts around the corner and dismounted, looping reins around the hitching rail.

Nathan looked up to make eye contact with one of the onlookers. "This here Luger's Saloon?" he asked as he reached for his pistol. He stuck it in his waistband and shifted his suspenders to lie over the handle.

The towny's eyes fixed on the massive gun. "It is." He gulped. "You the fellas with the herd of cows from Texas?"

"That's right. Supposed to meet a Mr. Lindstrom and a Mr. Steele here for supper."

"They're right inside. Where's the rest of your bunch?"

"Who needs to know?" Nathan peered

intently at the towny.

"Uh, nobody, I guess. I just heard there was about thirty of you fellas coming to town."

"Ain't likely," Nathan said with a snort.

The cowboys walked around the corner and to the steps leading to the porch in front of the door. Nathan glanced at the crowd. *These fellers are backing off like I were a shit-rolled dog. We can't smell that bad.* He stepped up on the porch to see John standing in the door.

"Welcome, Mr. Greene. This is Luger's place, and it looks like you found us." He stuck out his hand and Nathan took it.

"Reckon we did. Some welcomin' party. Y'all meet ever body like this here or jist Texans?"

"Truth be told, these good folks were expecting a lot more of you, and I think they expected you to come into town in a slightly more boisterous way." John stepped back and motioned the cowboys in.

"Well, we try not to murder no women 'r kids on the first day. Right now I reckon these fellers are more in'erested in a bath than any hell-raisin'. I know I am."

Nathan stuck his hand out to Paul. "Nice to see ya again, Mr. Steele."

"And you too. Come over and have a

seat." Paul pointed at the table where a short stocky man stood.

"Do y'all reckon we could get our horses looked to before we set?"

The stocky man came over and stuck out his hand. "I'm Paisley Mace, I own the livery. My boy's in back, and he can take your horses right over."

Nathan shook the outstretched hand. "No doubt you got a smithy's grip there, Paisley. Pleased to meetcha and we're obliged."

"Everybody calls me Mace," Mace said smiling. "Buell," he hollered over his shoulder.

"Yes, sir." A boy hurried through a door in the back. "We'll take 'em over and get the saddles off." Two other boys lined up by the bar; they had obviously been listening.

"Mr. Greene, our boys. Simon, Paul's; Jake, Fred's; and Buell, he's mine." Mace pointed to the three boys in turn and nodded to Fred behind the bar.

"Pleased to meet you, boys."

"These boys're Randall Quigg." A short thickset man of about forty years stepped away from the bar and started shaking hands. Nathan then nodded at a younger man: "And Pat Sweeney — we call him Sweeney." And then to another, "And this is Pat Lacey and he's called Lacey." Handshakes and introductions went all around.

"Watch the roan," Lacey said to the boy named Buell. "He bites."

"Thanks. I will." Buell and the other two boys walked down the bar and went out the back door.

"What'll it be first, Mr. Greene, supper, whiskey or a bath? I'm Fred Luger, and you're my guest for the night." Fred reached his hand across the top of the bar.

"Randall's been fussing about that hot bath since yesterday. Y'all got mor'n one tub?"

"Got three, and they're all ready. Werner Swartz has stayed at his store if you want to get you some new britches and a shirt. He'll be some disappointed there's only four of you, but he'll live."

"Randall, you and the boys go git what you need. Tell Mr. Swetrz I'll get square tomorrow." The three cowboys headed across the room and went out the door.

John pointed at a chair. "Sit down, Mr. Greene." John, Paul, and Mace pulled out chairs and sat. "Tell us about your trip. You said you had some trouble."

"Had a couple bad spells. We was about three days out from Hatcher where we stayed the winter, when Lacey saw four or five nighthawks followin' us. That night I heard 'em messin' round the edges of the herd, and we kept 'em away by circlin' all night, but it took the nine of us. We was dog tired next day. They kept followin', and late that afternoon Lacey laid back and got several shots at 'em with his pistol. Hit one feller's horse in the front leg but the rider doubled up with another one and they took off. Lacey rode over and kilt the horse. Never seen 'em agin."

"Did you hear that? I told you these fellers was mean as snakes," someone whispered.

"I wouldn't be saying that too loud if I were you," another one whispered back.

There'd been mostly silence as Nathan had related the experience, the onlookers obviously fascinated by the tale.

"How did you lose your two men?" Paul asked.

A buzz started up instantly. "Two men dead? I ain't heard about that," someone said. The crowd pressed in.

"The herd cut and run one night. Couldn't of picked a worst place fer it neither. We was in some real tore up country. Arroyos ever where. Them're washes and gullies. We gets us a real ripping lightnin' storm right after sunset, and weren't no keepin' 'em down. They headed east away from the storm and we went after 'em. Got 'em to turn about two miles out, and they come right back over camp. My cook, Gilly, didn't stand a chance. They was on him 'fore he could figger out which way to scat. Stomped his wagon to smithereens and him too. They kept a goin' and Lord knows how we managed to get 'em stopped. Come light, we rode back over the trail and . . . make a man sick. There were busted cows ever where. Horns broke off, bones a'stickin' out, some busted plumb open and still bellerin'. And then we found Jose. Skinny Mex, about fifteen year old. He only had two horses and that'll git you hurt. You only got two, you just plumb wear 'em out. It must've went down with 'im. They was out in the open, both of 'em all wadded up together. God, it were a right mess. We didn't have enough shots between us to do any good on them hurtin' critters, so we buried them two fellers, gathered up much as we could find of the vittles, and pushed on. Seemed like we could hear them poor cows bellerin' and fussin' for hours as we headed north."

Breathless silence followed until John spoke softly: "That's incredible." He shook his head. "Absolutely amazing."

A deafening din flooded the room when

his comment turned loose a simultaneous flood of commentary from every man in the saloon. Nathan looked at Mace, puzzled.

"These folks ain't heard nothing that exciting in their whole lives. I expect that story will be told to grandkids for years."

Randall and the other two Texans returned to the saloon, stood for a few seconds listening to the racket, and then spotted Fred, waving them over. They each carried two or three parcels and walked up to the bar. "Where's these baths y'alls been talkin' about?" Randall asked. The room had quieted as they walked across it.

Fred pointed at the stairs. "Up there. I'll show you to your rooms and where the bathroom is. I got two razors you're welcome to use. Left 'em in the bathroom by the mirror. Hot water on the stove and warm water beside it. If you want, my wife will wash what you're wearing, and have it ready tomorrow afternoon. Just leave 'em in the bathroom. She'll charge you for that." Fred headed for the stairs and the men followed.

"You have my utmost admiration, Mr. Greene," John said. "That is a hard way to make a living."

"Never done nothin' else. I reckon I was born on a horse in the middle of a herd.

Same's the rest of the boys."

"Are you ready to eat, or do you want to wait for a bath?" Paul asked.

"I reckon I'll wait. I could drink a whiskey though."

"I'll get it." Mace got up and walked behind the bar. He came back with four glasses in one hand, and a full bottle in the other. Paul's eyebrows went up when Mace set a labeled bottle on the table and then poured four drinks.

"Your good health and a profitable trip," John proposed. He tipped the glass and sipped.

Mace knocked back the whole two shots.

Nathan shut his eyes and let the contents of the small glass trickle down his throat. "Ahhhhh," he breathed out slowly, "that there is good whiskey. What kind is it?"

"It's called bourbon," Mace replied. "A family in Kentucky named Shawhan makes it. Good, huh?" He licked his lips. "Another?" He looked hopeful.

"Better not jist now. Best be gettin' somethin' in my gut before I set 'er on fire."

"I'd say you have another treat coming," John said. "Fred's wife Freda has made her delicious chicken and dumplings for you. Unless you want beef or pork."

"No, chicken'd be fine. And dumplin'?

Don't reckon I heard of that."

"It's like biscuits that she bakes and cooks right on top of chicken in gravy. I have to agree with John, it's delicious," Paul said.

Fred came back down the stairs and as he walked past to the bar, he spotted the bottle of whiskey sitting on the table and scowled at Mace.

"Supper sounds good, bring 'er on," Nathan said. "I'll git a bath later."

"I'll go tell my wife," Fred said, and then shot another glance at the whiskey bottle before cocking his head at Mace. The smithy winked at him mischievously.

Paul raised his head off the pillow and immediately put it right back down. The light in the room told him it was well into morning and Ana was not in bed. And then he remembered — Luger's. And whiskey. And smoking. And one story after another. The three cowboys had come down, clean-shaven and dressed in new striped shirts and cotton pants. Randall Quigg had nearly foundered on Freda's dumplings, and the saloon had stayed open until after two. It had been a hell of a party. He'd been so drunk he had to walk his horse home, hanging onto the stirrup. Now he had to get up and face Ana, not something he looked forward to. She had been in bed when he got home, but hadn't stirred as he'd clumped around like his legs were asleep. Hanging on the stirrup! Good lord, did I forget my horse last night? He ignored the pain, dressed as fast as his head would allow, and stepped through the bedroom door.

"Morning, Pa," Ana said cheerfully. "I've got corn cakes and eggs ready to go. Do you want milk?"

"Uh. Um." Paul, caught flatfooted, edged toward the door.

"Must have been a humdinger in town last night. You no more than lay down before you were snoring to wake the dead." Ana looked over her shoulder.

"Uh, I . . . yeah, it was quite a night. Those Texans are a fun bunch to be around."

"Milk?"

"Huh?"

"Milk. Do you want a glass of milk with breakfast?" She turned around and faced him.

"Oh, yeah. That would be good." He started toward the door.

"I took care of your horse last night." She turned back to the stove, grasped the skillet handle, and gave it a shake.

"You did?" Paul rubbed his forehead with

his hand. "Got any coffee?"

"Sit down and I'll get it." She took a cup off the shelf and poured it full. Setting it on the table, she stirred in two spoons full of sugar.

"I'll be right back, Ma," he said and went out.

A few minutes later, he gingerly picked up his cup and took a sip of coffee. "How come you ain't mad?" Paul asked, exasperated.

"Why should I be mad? You deserve a night out like that once in a while." She came over to the table, gently touched the side of his face, and then went back to the stove.

Paul looked at her back and sighed. "Women," he muttered.

"What'd you say?"

"Nothin'."

Paul's head hurt and Ana had done it to him again. Better to be yelled at than to be sweet-talked knowing you'd been an ass. He sipped his coffee as his head throbbed with each heartbeat and knew the pounding would last for hours. "The Texans agreed to stay the summer, all of them, and that turned into a reason to celebrate."

"That's wonderful."

He finished his breakfast and stood. "I'm gonna git. Nathan's going to meet me at

Luger's to settle on a price for the cattle." He gave Ana a peck on the cheek and headed for the door.

"Make sure you tell Simon to come home when you see him. I don't like him being gone this long. I'll see you when you get home tonight."

Over Ana's protests, Simon had been allowed to go see the Texans. And Mace, after some discussion, had gone along with Buell's assertion that if Simon was there, Buell should be allowed too. For the first time, Simon had spent the night with Buell.

CHAPTER 15

Simon was paying dearly for the privilege of coming along on the eighteen-mile trip to Fort Hartwell. Paul and John rode on the spring seat of the buckboard, while he and Buell rode in the bed behind. There was no way to make it a comfortable ride. Seated across from each other, the boys felt every rut and hole in the road as the shock passed from tailbone to skull. As a result, Simon had developed a bad headache. About two miles west of the fort, they entered a place called Adobe. It couldn't be called a town because it contained no individual houses or retail businesses like a bank or trading store or livery; more a motley collection of sod and adobe structures lined up on either side of the road. The lack of color was striking. Everything blended monotonously with the dusty brown color of the road.

Simon had heard them described as whiskey parlors and dance halls and they were approaching one that had to be a hundred and twenty feet long and thirty feet deep. Located on the south side of the road, it obviously contained something of interest to the soldiers at the nearby fort because of the twenty or so horses tied up in front, all but one or two displayed the US brand on their rumps. A scantily dressed woman greeted them from one of the three doors set in front of the building, her abbreviated frock, the color of sunflowers, making her hard to overlook.

"Hey, boys, stop by for an hour or so. We can have some fun."

Buell immediately moved to the right side of the wagon to kneel beside Simon and both draped their arms over the edge of the bed.

"Sit back down and mind your business," Simon's father said.

"Come on, fellas. Nobody needs to be in such a hurry." The woman stepped into the road and approached the moving buckboard. Walking alongside, within reach of the front wheel, she reached into the top of her dress and lifted out a breast. "Wanta see a sample?" She laughed.

Simon's mouth fell open. He leaned out over the low side of the buckboard, his face not more than a few feet from the woman.

"Sit back down, Simon, and keep your eyes to yourself. You too, Buell!"

Simon glanced at his father who didn't return the look, because his eyes, too, were apparently fixed on the woman.

"Paul, you're going to put us off the road," John shouted.

Again Simon tore his gaze off the woman, and looked to the front of the wagon. John, with a firm grip on the seat, doubled over with laughter.

"You two young fellas come back when you ain't got your folks with you," the woman hollered. She stopped in the middle of the road, her hands on her hips, and her breast drooping over her corset top, laughing like a lunatic.

For Simon, the naked white breast filled the entire landscape. The rig accelerated as the horses took up a canter and pulled away. Simon and Buell spilled onto the bed where they struggled against the bouncing wagon to regain control. Finally, they got to their knees, and scrambled to the rear of the wagon to kneel and stare until the woman disappeared in the dust.

Paul spotted Fort Hartwell from two miles away. Set on a low rise, the honey-gold color of the fresh-sawed timbers attested to its newness. A large fort by any standard, nearly two hundred men had labored for a year to build it. As they approached, gunfire, more a crackling rattle, reached them.

"Volley fire. Target practice, I'd guess," John said. "Or there's an Indian attack underway on the east side of the fort."

Paul glanced back at his son.

Simon grinned. "Sure, half the Sioux nation is over there waiting for us to get here."

This was Paul's first visit to the fort, and he took in every sight and sound as they rode through the opening in the low wall. They were not really walls, but more like the backs of buildings arrayed around a huge parade ground. On the east side, opposite the entrance, stood a two-story building with a porch at the ground level and a verandah above. An open building to the right of the two-story one looked to be a blacksmith shop. Along the right side, a long building with a door every ten feet had leather gear hung by each door — stables. He counted twenty such doors, and noticed the same arrangement on the opposite side of the yard. Inside the gate on the left, a storefront festooned with washtubs and other tin goods identified the mercantile store.

More low buildings with extra-high back

walls made up the rest of the enclosure and Paul assumed those were where the soldiers stayed. In front of most of the buildings, except the stables, cottonwood trees had been planted. He judged the entire area to cover about four acres. Dozens of people moved helter-skelter: officers in all-blue uniforms, yellow trim marking them as cavalry; soldiers in dark-blue pants, light colored shirts and knee-high black boots; and civilians, lots of civilians. Paul swung the buckboard around to the left and stopped in front of the trading store.

"Jump down, boys, and see if your legs still work," he said. He and John climbed down the wheels, and he handed each of the boys a heavy iron weight. He and John stepped up onto the porch and waited. The boys dropped the iron anchors on the ground in front of the team, attached the tethers to the horse's halters, and then hurried to catch up.

The interior of the store was just like Mr. Swartz's place only much bigger. The unmistakable aroma of a general store had already seeped into the new building: cinnamon's snap and lamp oil's acrid bite combined to produce the dominant smell. Then the mellow scent of ground coffee in the bright-red grinder greeted them, followed by an invitation from something that reminded Paul of Ana's baking, maybe maple sugar or dried apples — it was hard to tell. The total effect made him feel welcome.

He made his way to a low counter where, behind it, two men and a woman worked serving several people at once. He waited for a couple of minutes, and finally caught the eye of the older man who stood wrapping a package.

"Howdy," Paul said. "I'm here to talk to the army about some beef. Could you point me in the right direction?"

"Beef. Pickled, dried, or fresh? Barrels, packaged, or slabs?" the man asked without pausing.

"Fresh." Any other way had not occurred to Paul.

"On the hoof or dressed?" The man reached for another sheet of brown paper.

"Alive. We'll herd them in." Paul started to feel ill prepared.

"Now or later and how many? There you go, Mrs. Winder. Pleased for your custom." The lady picked up her three parcels and nodded a greeting to Paul as she passed.

"Uh. Ma'am," Paul mumbled as he touched the brim of his hat. *Why do I get so flap-tongued when I have to talk to someone? Does this fella need to know all this? Judas*

189

Priest, he ain't buyin' them. Paul took a slow breath and looked at the storekeeper, who now had an expectant look on his face.

"I have about six hundred grazing now that I will have ready to sell in September or October."

"Does all of it have to go to the army?"

"I hadn't thought about it." Paul had to admit. *Fine, something else I hadn't considered. And from the look on John's face, you'd think he's watching a puppet show. Wish he'd say something.*

"Sounds to me like we should have a little talk," the man said, then looked at the young man working with him. "Nate, I'm going to leave the store to you two for a few minutes." He motioned Paul toward the right and walked down the counter.

Paul turned to Simon. "You and Buell see if you can find a stick of candy or some dried fruit. And mind your manners."

Paul and John followed the storekeeper into a back stockroom. Inside and to the left stood a desk, and off to one side, two chairs. The storekeeper motioned for Paul to sit at one and John another. He leaned against the desk and stretched his shoulders back. "Gets so busy sometimes I can't take time to be civil. I apologize. I'm Trevor Ledbetter, I'm the sutler." He stuck out his hand.

"I'm Paul Steele. I'm from Carlisle, just west of here. And this is John Lindstrom." They both shook the sutler's hand.

"Pleased to meet both of you. Been to Carlisle a few times. Growing town. I know Werner Swartz." He leaned back against the desk again. "So, you got a herd of cattle, a rather large herd. Interesting."

"Strikes most people that way. John here come up with an idea that got us a herd several months ahead of what you'd normally expect." Paul explained to the sutler about the Kansas wintering.

The sutler gave a low whistle. "Mighty clever of you, Mr. Lindstrom. It's the kind of deal that determines on which side of the desk you sit. Now, you'll want to talk to Captain Atkins. Nice enough fella, if you show the proper deference. Some of these army types take their station real serious. Captain Atkins is one of them. Good thing about him though, he's as honest as they come."

"That puts him well ahead of many as far as I'm concerned," John said.

"You're right. I think the same way. I've met some who think the army is their own private enterprise, and conduct business

191

that way. I found that if I'm fair and honest, I get to stay in business. I was in Oklahoma with Colonel Sharp, the fort commander, and was offered the store here when they decided to build Hartwell."

"So how does it work?" Paul asked. "I contract with the army and they pay me cash when I deliver the herd? Is it a paper contract?"

"Close enough. Captain Atkins will determine how many of your cows he can use and make a fair offer. You agree, they use a simple contract, similar to a bill of sale, to firm things up. He signs on one side of the paper for the army now and you sign the other when you deliver. His signature is the army's agreement to take delivery, and yours vouches that they're yours to sell."

"Sounds like I came to the right man without even knowing it."

"I more or less sell everything that gets sold here in the fort. The army has been authorized to sell at cost to immigrants heading west. Your herd won't be all that hard to dispose of. Matter of fact I wouldn't mind taking a few off your hands if the army doesn't need them all, though I expect they will. They provision the other two forts in the area as well."

"So how do I get to meet with this Captain

Atkins? John contacted him last year, and was told to just come on over."

"If you don't mind, I'll take you over there myself. He's going to ask me about the cattle anyway, and we can clear up any questions right on the spot."

"Can't thank you enough, Mr. Ledbetter. You're being real helpful."

"It's not just for you. I get a percentage of everything I distribute for the army. If I don't have it, I can't sell it, and four percent of nothing is nothing. So, helping you out makes me feel good about myself, and I consider that a bonus. Let's go find the good captain."

The trip back to Carlisle finished in the dark. Paul dropped Simon off at home as they went by, the boy so tired he could hardly walk. A few minutes later, he pulled the team up to the water trough alongside the livery. He waited for Mace to come out and tell him where he wanted the wagon left. The horses started to drink deeply.

"Thought you'd been carried off by the Indians," Mace said.

Buell jumped down from the wagon and started to dance around, a pained expression on his face.

"Makes it sting don't it, sprout?" Mace

chuckled.

"Ain't funny, Pa. I can barely feel my feet." He walked gingerly over to the end of the water trough and sat on the edge, his elbows leaning on his knees.

"Well, I'm not surprised. You been on them or bouncing along on your knees and butt for fourteen hours." Mace walked over and squeezed his shoulder. "Go on in and have some bread and milk, and then go to bed. I'll take care of the harness and the animals."

"Thanks, Pa." Buell limped into the livery.

"Where do you want the wagon, Mace?"

"Leave it right there. It's rented in the morning."

Paul and John climbed down stiffly, then stood quietly, and watched the horses finish drinking. Their muzzles barely touched the surface, and they made no noise at all, silently sucking in the water, hardly creating a ripple. When the horses raised their heads, Paul backed them away from the trough a couple of steps. He unpinned the singletree on his side while John did the same on the other. Mace released the tongue, and Paul clucked the horses free of the wagon. Both animals chuffed in relief. The three men soon had all the straps let loose and the harness off, warm and damp with sweat. Once in their stalls, the tired animals snuffled through a half gallon of oats, contented tails swishing back and forth as Paul and Mace started to wipe them down with sacking to remove the sweat.

"I'm bushed," John said. "Getting too old for that kind of ride. I'm going to go home and go to bed. Interesting trip though, wouldn't you say?"

"It was that," Paul said. "I'll probably see you tomorrow. Good night, John."

John raised his hand and said, "Goodnight, Mace," and shuffled stiff-legged into the dark.

"In'eresting trip, as Nathan would say," Mace said trying to mimic the Texan's twang.

"It was. Found out you don't really deal with the army, you deal through the storekeeper at the post, the sutler. Real helpful guy name of Ledbetter."

Mace huffed over the horse's back. "So, are you gonna tell me about your trip or what?"

"Oh, yeah. The army will take up to five hundred for delivery the last week in September. And they'll probably do the same or more next year." Paul stopped and gave Mace a half smile.

"And?" Mace held both hands out in supplication.

"And what?"

"The price? What did they agree to pay? What do you mean, what?"

Paul made a couple more long passes down the horse's back. "Sixteen."

Mace's jaw dropped. "Sixteen dollars a head? Good Lord, man, you've really done it up right this time. How did you get them to give you sixteen?"

Paul leaned back on the stall. "I didn't ask for it, they offered. When I explained that these animals had wintered over in Kansas and would graze here all summer, the captain figured with what they pay for a trailed animal, mine would be cheaper per pound even at sixteen dollars."

"I guess ol' John knows what he's doin', that's for sure."

"Got to agree. My family owes him quite a debt. The kind that's hard to pay off."

"Somehow I don't think John sees it that way. You were the only family in town that would even allow him around their kids, much less into their homes. John has said as much to me. He thinks Simon is a special kind of boy."

"It always makes a man feel good to hear others think highly of his family. I'm no different. I'm very proud of them."

Mace stopped to fold his piece of burlap. "So, you gonna spend the summer on the prairie?"

"I talked to Nathan about that, and he said it all depends on how much room the cows have to roam. These are Texas cows, and they've learned to stay near the water. He said they won't stray far if the browse is good, and I think the place John ferreted out has a lot of grass."

"Buell's chomping at the bit. Simon too," Mace said. "Buell rode out Saturday to see where they were camped, and came back wanting to go out Sunday and spend the day. Only your taking him with you today could have changed his mind. That is one stubborn boy."

"Simon's much the same." Paul pushed away from the wall and went back to grooming. "They see it as a river picnic. We'll see how they feel after they ride their first eighteen-hour day gathering up a storm-scattered bunch."

"I got that camp wagon about ready to go. Homer Jenkins is sewing up the last couple of end flaps. Should be done tomorrow. When do you want to take it out?"

Paul thought about it for a few seconds. "Ain't so sense waiting. When it's ready, we'll hook a team and go. How much do you have in it?"

"Money? A little over forty dollars. Time? I got about fourteen and Homer will have upwards to eight. I'm gonna assume I get the wagon back when you're done with it this year, so I'll just rent it to you." Mace patted his horse on the back and stepped out of the stall.

"I'm thinkin' maybe I ought to just buy it outright. The captain said the army would be interested in doing the same thing next year. That being the case, I'm gonna need it again. Work out what you have to have for it and let me know."

"Good enough. I suppose you're about to drop. I'll put the saddle on your horse."

"Appreciate that. You're right, I need something to eat, and a good night's sleep."

Mace saddled Paul's mare and watched him ride up the street and around the corner. He went into the living area and found Buell asleep in an easy chair. He woke him enough to get him on his feet and led him to his bed.

Simon and Sarah sat in the swing on Kingsley's front porch. "When will we ever get to see each other?" Sarah asked. "I thought we could spend some time together like last year." Head slightly bowed, she peered at him, her lips forming a half pout.

"Either I spend the summer out there or Pa has to, and that's not possible." *I wish I dared tell her I'm looking forward to spending the summer on the prairie with Buell, but somehow I don't think she'd see it my way.*

"Will you at least come back once in a while?"

"Sure, I'll come see you as much as I can, but I really don't know how much work it's going to take to keep the cows where they're supposed to be. I'll know more about it by next week."

"I guess I'll just have to wait," she said plaintively. She took Simon's hand and laid it in her lap.

Simon looked at his hand, and as he did so the slight swell in Sarah's bodice drew his attention. The vision of what he'd seen in dusty Adobe flooded back in all its fleshy whiteness. He swallowed hard and could feel the color rise above his collar. "I'll go out tomorrow with the new wagon and come back Friday. We'll see how it goes then."

Simon felt someone watching, and looked at the oval glass in the front door. Mrs. Kingsley waved and he snatched his hand out of Sarah's lap. He knew both Sarah and her mother could see the heat of his embarrassment, and that only added fuel to his plight. They continued to sit in the gliding swing and talk until Simon had to leave to do chores. As usual, he felt a slight emptiness as he rode his father's horse away from Sarah's house, but for the first time ever, he felt a little relief as well.

Chapter 16

Paul found the Texans camped about a hundred yards from the river; far enough to keep out of the mosquitoes and gnats, but close enough to the water to make it handy. Four men sat in the shade of a mature cottonwood tree. Nathan Greene got up as the wagon rolled to a stop.

"Good ta see y'all," he drawled. "Reckon you can set that wagon right up agin those trees on the right." He pointed to a small group a hundred feet downstream.

Paul urged the team ahead and turned slightly to the right as he did so. He stopped when he was abreast of the first tree. It looked like an ideal spot. He climbed down and walked back to the camp.

"If you think that's where you want it, we can take the team back to town with us. If not, we can leave the horses for a couple days. What do you think?"

"I think where she sets'll be fine."

"Simon, Buell. Unhook the team and leave the singletrees under the wagon. I'll lead the horses back to town."

The boys unhooked the heavy leather straps from the oak and iron bar that delivered the power from the horse's shoulders to the wagon's front axle. Then they fastened the ends of the traces to hooks on the harness straps that went over the animal's rumps.

Paul nodded. "The boys want to stay a while and watch the herd with you. I know we talked about it, but I'm gonna give you a chance to change your mind."

Simon and Buell had ridden out on two of Mace's horses, and they now stood next to Paul, waiting to hear Nathan's answer.

"I've had a good look at the place you picked out here, and I gotta tell you, you done real good. I reckon the six riders I got is all I'm gonna need to sit on this here herd."

Buell appeared visibly shaken, and Paul knew the boys had talked about little else for several days.

Nathan shot them a glance. "But we can always use another waddy or two. I suspect we could teach 'em a mite about cowboyin'. Mind you, I cain't pay 'em what I pay Lacey there, but then I won't be expectin' 'em to be a diggin' in like Lacey either."

"Sounds fair to me. You pay 'em what you think they're earning," Paul said. He turned to Buell and Simon. "Okay with you boys?"

"Yes, sir," Simon said.

Buell nodded at Paul, then looked at Pat Lacey and grinned.

"Guess that's settled, then," Paul said. "I brought enough canned food and the usual dry stuff to keep both boys going. It's in a box in the wagon. Might be you could teach 'em both a bit about camp cooking." He was pleased the boys could stay and knew Nathan was doing them a favor. He hoped the boys would see it the same way. "Well, we'll leave it at that. Much obliged, Nathan. I'll be getting back to town." He shook the Texan's hand, then turned to Simon and Buell. "You boys pay close attention and do as you're told. We'll see you again soon."

Paul untied his horse from the rear of the wagon, climbed on, and then, leading the two draft animals, he rode out of camp.

Matt walked into Luger's and looked for Paul. He didn't see him, but found Mace sitting at the usual table by the bar and approached. "Hello, Mace."

Mace looked over his shoulder and his eyebrows rose in surprise. "Hello, Matt.

Come for lunch?"

"Well, yes and no. I come to see Paul, and you can usually find him here around noon."

"He'll be along. He was by my place about two hours ago and said he'd see me here. Sit down."

"Thanks, I will. So, what do you think of all the commotion with the Texas herd? That was some deal."

The back door swung open and Fred hustled in with the daily food offering. He hooked the door with his heel and banged it shut. "Well, hello, Matthew. What brings the rich farmer to Luger's?" Fred walked down the bar toward Mace's table.

There was no love lost between Fred and himself. "Come by to see if I could catch Paul." Matt tried on a smile.

"Ain't here yet. Expect he'll be along. Get you a beer or something?"

"I'll wait till he gets here, and then I will, thanks." He gave up on the smile.

"Okay." Fred set the platter down and started to arrange the food. Freda came through the back door, a crock of pickles held by the rim in one hand, and a large glass jar of pickled eggs balanced on the opposite arm. She huffed down the bar without a word, set the load down and huffed right back out, slamming the door. "Thank you, love," Fred said to the closed door. He turned and gave Mace a wide grin. "Woman loves her work," he said as he levered the glass stopper off the egg jar.

"So, what do you think about the Texans?" Matt asked.

"I think John Lindstrom is a planning genius," Mace replied.

"I agree. I understand now how he did it. I'm just not sure why he started to think along those lines in the first place. What prompts a man to come up with stuff like that?"

"Some people just take to that naturally. Me, I pound on things and sometimes they turn into something useful and sometimes not. I can figure out how to make most anything if someone comes to me with a plan, but I've come to accept the fact I ain't an idea man."

"But how did he know who to contact in Kansas?"

"I think John knows a lot of people, and not just around here. Old Prosser over at the telegraph is always flagging John down with two or three scraps of message paper."

"Is that how he contacted the people in Kansas? The telegraph?"

"Far as I know. That's what he showed us the afternoon he told us the herd was on the way. I remember, cuz I thought at the time a message that long must've cost someone a pretty penny."

"Hmm." Matt glanced at his watch. "I just remembered something. I've got to go see Avery for a few minutes. I'll try to get back." He got up and hurried out the door.

"I don't like that man and never will," Fred said as he walked up to the table.

"Tried to sell him a beer though, didn't you?" Mace teased.

"Well, business is business, and I still don't like him. You ready yet? Food is."

"Sure." Mace hustled to the bar and as his mouth watered heavily, built his usual one-pound sandwich. Today Freda had supplied smoked venison and sausages.

CHAPTER 17

The trembling came through the blanket, penetrated the wadded-up coat Simon used as a pillow, and vibrated into his brain. Slowly he left the realm of deep sleep, and moved into the semiconsciousness of morning denial. *Cold.* His back felt like ice, and he groped to catch the blanket's edge and found it. His tug resulted in exposed feet, and he scrunched deeper into his fetal position. *Was it dark?* He blinked open his eyes for the briefest glimpse and saw a flicker of light, but his senses denied anything else. *Need more sleep.*

Smoke! His eyes popped open and he raised his head to look toward his feet. The flicker of light he'd seen under the draped edge of the awning turned out to be a campfire, and it wasn't as dark as he thought. Then the tremble came again, more pronounced this time, and he heard the lip-flapping flutter of an exhaling horse.

The creak of leather told him someone was leaving a saddle, and then he heard the faint clink of a spur.

"Hello, Sweeney." Simon recognized Randall Quigg's voice.

"Mornin'."

"Ever'thing quiet?"

"Yup."

"Coffee's up."

Someone cleaned a cup by rapping it against their leg, Simon guessed Sweeny. The coffeepot bail clanked against the side several times as Simon imagined Sweeney trying to stand it upright, and failing. Silence. Then, "Sumbitch!"

"Hot?" Randall.

"Humpf."

The sound of pouring coffee followed by the pot being set back on a rock made Simon sit up. The awning kept him from seeing the eastern sky, but he guessed it to be near seven, and Randall had coffee made so it had to be time to get up. He pulled on his shoes and laced them. Standing, he grabbed his coat and put it on; his hand slid past a disgustingly cold wet spot inside one sleeve — drool. He stepped around the awning to see Sweeney standing by a low glowing fire, and Randall hunkered on his heels beside it.

"Morning, Simon," Sweeney said.

"Good morning, Mr. Sweeney, Mr. Quigg."

Randall pointed to a white enamel-covered cup next to the coffeepot. "Y'all drink coffee?"

"Yes'ir." Simon went over to the fire and was looking around for the stick when he saw Randall watching him.

Sweeney stooped to pick up a piece of kindling on his side of the fire. "Let me git it. Damn thing can be hot." He glanced toward Randall, who looked cheated, until he grinned. "Expect you heard me check it out. You learn quick." He poured Simon a full cup.

"What time is it?"

"About seven, half past maybe. I have a pretty good sense of the time."

Randall snorted. "Bullshit, he smelled the coffee . . . always does."

"Buell and Lacey still out, then?"

"Yep. They'll be along as soon as Morgan and Griz find 'em."

"They already been up and gone? I didn't hear 'em."

"Weren't supposed to." Randall winked. "You'll learn to be quiet too, first time a boot catches you upside the head for clomping 'round camp in the morning. Not like

209

Sweeney. Hell fire, you'd think a buffalo was beddin' down."

Simon now understood why they were both speaking so softly. Somewhere in the darkness, Nathan and the cowboy named Lester must be sleeping. He imagined a boot, looping through the darkness, aimed for his noisy mouth. He had a sip of coffee. "Oh," he said quietly.

"Like it?" Sweeney asked.

"Strong." Simon wished he hadn't been so quick. "Strong, but good." He looked around for the sugar, or maybe some canned milk.

"We kin never tell when we'll get another cup, so we make the one we got worth it," Sweeney said.

Simon heard a metallic clink in the low morning light, then the sound of a hoof kicking a rock. A minute later Lacey and Buell rode into the firelight. Buell looked pleased as a weasel in a chicken coop as they both climbed down. Lacey dropped his reins on the ground and headed for the coffeepot while Buell led his horse to a low bush and tied it up.

Lacey rubbed his rear with both hands. "My butt's tired. Morgan and Griz kin have 'em for eight hours." He grabbed a cup and filled it.

Simon saw that the bail kept on the side away from the fire stayed cool enough to handle. "You guys stay out for eight hours?"

"Yep. Don't seem long thinkin' 'bout it, but sit straddle a horse with no place t' go and you'll see different." Lacey's grin had a knowing quality.

"So those guys that just went out will be back this afternoon."

"And yer askin' yerself what yer doin' up so early," Lacey said over to top of his cup.

Simon felt sheepish. "Uh, I heard Sweeney come into camp."

Lacey shot Sweeney a dirty look, and Randall snickered under his breath.

"Next time chuck a rock at him," Lacey said.

"Yes, sir." Simon didn't think that likely at all.

Lacey turned to Randall. "What you fixing for breakfast?"

"You ain't a gonna believe it. Fried cackleberries and real bacon."

"Eggs? Chicken eggs?" Lacey stared at the cook.

"Yup. Simon's pa sent a small barrel of 'em, packed in oats. Don't rightly know how many for sure, but they's plenty."

"That right, Simon?" Lacey asked.

"Well, I guess so. That's the way we pack

'em for the wagon trains, but only in the spring when it's cool. The folks eat the eggs, and the oxen eat the oats. You can drop a barrel and not break one egg." Simon felt pleased to provide something useful to know.

"Be damned," Lacey said. "Boy, am I going to enjoy this." He squatted as Randall selected a brown egg from a small basket. Simon recognized it from his younger days as a collection basket and shuddered unconsciously.

"Ain't that purdy?" Randall held the egg high for a moment, then put it back and proceeded to lay slice after slice of streaked bacon into the huge skillet set over the fiery bed of coals. The pan had three attached legs that held it above the heat. Simon guessed a whole pound of bacon sizzled as it shrank, and the men watched in fascination; everyone unconsciously licked their lips.

Matt sat across the desk from Avery Singer. "You think you can get Prosser to tell you who Lindstrom was talking to in Kansas?" Matt asked.

Avery shuffled some papers, set them down, and picked up another stack.

"Well?"

"I suppose I could push him a bit. It's a risky thing to be doing. He takes his piddly job real serious, and should he decide not to tell, all he has to do is talk to John and I'm fried." He set the stack of papers down abruptly, and frowned.

Matt leaned forward in his chair. "One day I'm going to find out what John Lindstrom holds over you and when I do . . . well, just say you're not going to like it."

"He and I have a business arrangement, just like you and I do. He expects me to keep my word, and you don't expect any less. Just remember —" Avery stopped in mid sentence.

"Remember what?" Matt stared at Avery, unblinking.

"I'm not saying . . . uh . . . just remember that I do know what John's doing, and I've told you what I can without betraying a trust." Avery had gone white around the corners of his mouth. His gaze shifted wildly from Matt's shirtfront, to the clock, and back to his desk.

"You don't want to know what I'm thinking, Avery." Matt half rose from his chair and leaned across the desk, both hands flat on the papers in front of him. "Don't even dream it."

"Damn, Matt, what do you take me for?

We've been friends for years. I'm not gonna do something to ruin that." He still wouldn't meet Matt's eyes.

"You get to Prosser and find out what I need to know. You never use a short stick to tease a rattlesnake, Avery, and your stick ain't very long." Matt got up and left.

Avery held a past-due note on Prosser, and he knew the skinny telegrapher was late with several others as well. He hated using one of his hole cards for something that didn't directly benefit himself, but the look in Matt's eye had been absolutely venomous. Avery leaned forward and held his head with both hands.

He shut his eyes for a moment, and remembered back to the good days in Saint Louis, the women, the card games and the easy life, but most of all, the card games. With a sigh of resignation, he got up to walk over to the telegraph office. "Shit!" he said as he pulled the door closed.

Simon waited in the shade of the wagon, stripping long thin pieces of fiber from the chunk of cottonwood bark he held. Lacey had told him and Buell that they could shoot his pistol when the night-watch crew got up from their nap. That had been six hours ago, and Simon craned his neck to see if anyone might be stirring under the awning.

Nathan walked up, the ever-present coffee cup in his hand. "Looks like yer doin' some nest buildin'. Bored?" He went to his knee, and then to his butt, legs sticking straight out in from of him. He shifted his shoulder blades to find a tolerable spot on the wagon wheel.

"Waiting on Lacey and Buell to get up. Lacey says he's gonna let us shoot his gun."

"Got a hankerin' to feel 'er buck, do you? Ever touched off a full-sized pistola?"

"Haven't even shot a thirty-two. Shot a twenty-two rifle plenty though."

"Big difference. Kicks like a mule and smokes like to never see. You in a big hurry?"

"Kinda been thinking about it a while. I suppose I can wait."

"Naw, c'mon. I cain't hardly abide sittin' on the ground. We'll sneak down by the river, and you kin shoot mine." Nathan peered around Simon and into the shade of the awning, then grunted to his feet and shuffled over to his saddle. After undoing a couple of buckles, he took the holster and enormous pistol off the rig. "This here's a Colt Walker. Enough sauce in 'er to knock down a Mexican mule." He headed toward

215

the river, Simon a half step behind. "You reckon your pa ain't a gonna object?"

"He lets me shoot Jake's twenty-two. I know how to be careful." Simon could not keep his eyes off the now-exposed pistol. The bore looked big enough to stick his finger in.

When they got to the riverbank, Nathan handed him the gun. "Here, just hold on to 'er, and feel the weight."

Simon knew he was going to have a hard time holding it at arm's length. "It's a lot heavier than I thought it would be."

"About five pounds. Here, poke 'er out in front of ya."

Simon raised the massive pistol to shoulder height and immediately put his other hand up to help support it.

"That's it. Use two if'n ya have to. Can you hold 'er?" Nathan got behind Simon. "Now I'm gonna cock 'er back." He reached around and put one hand under the trigger guard and with his other hand, ratcheted back the hammer. Simon watched the cylinder turn. "You see that there plop right next to the water?" He pointed the muzzle in the general direction of a pile of cow dung about twenty feet away.

Simon nodded, his breath coming faster.

"Line yer sights up jist like on yer twenty-two, and when yer ready, haul back on that trigger. Now mind, she'll buck."

The end of barrel described wild circles around the cow pie. Simon could keep the front blade lined up with the narrow notch cut in the hammer, but together they never lined up on the target and he desperately wanted to shoot the pistol. Then the dung heap appeared just over the top of the muzzle, and Simon jerked the trigger. With a shocking clap of noise, the pistol twisted back in his hand, nearly coming loose as the gun rose above his head. Nathan wrapped his hand around it and steadied Simon's grip. Just over the top of the pile, a twelve-foot plume of river water rose straight into the air.

"Damn," Simon muttered. "Hot damn."

"What'n hell's goin' on?" Lacey, in his underwear and barefooted, stormed around the end of the prairie wagon, naked pistol at the ready. He stopped, half crouched, turning his head from side to side.

Chapter 18

June fifth was Sarah's fifteenth birthday, and she and Simon had been given permission to celebrate it with a picnic by the river. Sarah had planned the whole thing, and all Simon had to do was stop by the house at noon and pick her up. Paul needed the horse, so Simon made the half-mile trip to Sarah's on foot, and now, within shouting distance of her house, he could see her sitting on the porch, picnic hamper next to the steps.

"Hi, Sarah." Simon climbed the four steps and stopped at the edge of the porch.

"Hello, Simon." She got up and adjusted her hat, a wide-brimmed straw arrangement with a yellow bow that hung down the back.

Simon thought she looked splendid. "Got everything we need?"

"Hopefully. I insisted Mother let me do it all, and I was real careful. I'll tell her you're here." Sarah made for the door.

"Can't we just take off?"

"Don't be silly." She opened the front door and called, "Simon's here, Mother. We're ready to go."

A moment later Mrs. Kingsley joined them on the porch. "How are you today, Simon? I've heard you're turning into quite a ruffian out there on the prairie with those awful Texas people."

Mrs. Kingsley had made it clear that she was not impressed by the cowboys.

"Not really, ma'am. It's as boring as anything you can think of. Mostly we just sit around camp, or sit on our horse on the prairie, hopefully in the shade of a tree. About the only excitement we get is if a few cows decide to wander south. Usually they just stay by the river in the shade." Simon was amazed with himself. He hadn't said that many words to Mrs. Kingsley in a year.

"I heard they were teaching you and Buell how to use weapons."

The word "weapons" had the snap of a whip when she said it, and her frown told Simon more than what she said; the conversation appeared to be headed in the wrong direction. "Not really teaching us how to use them. More like how dangerous they are, and how much we have to be careful around them. Mr. Greene says civilized people shouldn't even have to carry them."

"Did he indeed? Well, maybe I've misjudged Mr. Greene a little." She looked pensive for a moment. "And he said that? Well, good."

And soon's we've covered all them uncivilized bastards with dirt I'll give up mine. Simon repeated Nathan's words to himself in his best Texas accent and smiled behind his eyes.

"So, gather up your picnic things and go enjoy the afternoon." Mrs. Kingsley waved her hand toward the basket. "I have to tell you that Sarah packed that herself. Wouldn't let me touch a thing." She reached out and laid her hands on both their shoulders.

Simon tensed. There! Her thumb caressed the side of his neck. "Yes, ma'am. We'll be back early afternoon. We're going to be almost straight away from here." He pointed due north, then reached down and picked up the basket. Its weight surprised him.

Half an hour later they found a level bench covered with soft green grass at the bottom of a low bluff. Several full-grown cottonwood trees, now near leafed-out, provided dappled shade. They'd carried the basket between them nearly all the way, and they set it on the ground. Sarah waved him away from it, lifted the lids on both ends, and extracted a medium-sized blanket and a tablecloth. With both spread, she unloaded two cloth-bound sandwiches, a quart jar of applesauce, a small jar of cream, two bowls, a tin containing raisin cookies, four bottles of root beer and some sugar. Now he understood the weight. He caught the aroma of smoked ham and knew where it came from — Mrs. Luger's. He had eaten lightly at breakfast, and the long walk had raised a good appetite.

"Here, the big one's yours." Sarah handed it to him. Unwrapped, it overflowed with ham and the special cheese containing seeds of some kind that Mrs. Luger served in the saloon.

"Thank you, and happy birthday again, Sarah." Simon took a bite to be rewarded by the tang of spicy mustard. More Luger's, and it tasted wonderful. He attacked the huge sandwich, taking bite after bite, chewing and swallowing without pause.

"I guess when you eat that's all you do," Sarah finally said.

Simon looked at her and blinked. "What do you mean?" He savored the lingering taste of the meat and cheese.

"I thought you'd gone into a trance. I've never seen anyone concentrate on their food that way."

Thinking back a few minutes, he realized what he had done, and felt slightly embarrassed. "You make a wonderful sandwich." He shrugged. "That one is my favorite. I'm always glad when Freda, er, Mrs. Luger has ham and cheese for lunch."

Sarah arched her eyebrows. "You eat in the saloon?"

"Not all the time." He added quickly, "And when I do, it's with Buell and his pa . . . and mine."

"Well, I should think so." She paused a moment, and then cocked her head slightly. "What's in there?"

"I don't know. A bar, some tables and chairs. It's smoky."

"Are there low women in there?"

"Low women? Low . . . Sarah!" The image of one of the women that served beer at Lancer's appeared. "Of course not."

"Well, it is a saloon," she said huffily. "Mother says anyone who frequents those places will be damned in the end."

"My ma doesn't like them either, but she says we have to live in the world as it is, and learn to handle our affairs accordingly. I think I agree with her. I go in there to see Jake and get something to eat. Sure, there's a lot of cussing and such going on, but that doesn't mean I have to do the same." Simon realized this was their first serious disagreement.

"Isn't it better to stay out of places like that all together? You can get a sandwich at Swartz's just as easy. If my mother asked me to stay out of a place I would."

"But the food is better at Luger's. I know where the mustard on that sandwich came from . . . and the ham and cheese too." Simon's heart beat faster and he realized he'd raised his voice. "You'll eat Mrs. Luger's food, but you won't associate with her. How can that be right?"

Sarah glared at him. "It's not her or Jake. It's the place they run."

"But that's Luger's. If I want to see Jake, I have to go where he is, and that's the saloon. You sayin' I can't see him just because his folks run the place?" He stood and walked a few feet away to stand with his back to Sarah.

"I didn't mean to make you angry. I just don't like the idea of you going to places like that. Mother really likes you, so does my father. He thinks you'll turn out to be a very successful man one day if you can avoid the wrong company. And mother thinks people who go to saloons and gambling halls are the wrong people."

Simon took a deep breath and let it out

slowly. "I like you a lot, Sarah, you know that, and mostly because you're always the same. But I like Buell and Jake and Armand too . . . and even Gus, I guess. But Armand is big, slow, and rude, Jake is kinda messy and swears a lot, and you know most people think Buell is strange and a bit dangerous. And I like them the way they are. I can't expect them to change just because I think they could be better. Maybe I wouldn't like them that way." He turned to see if she was understanding. "And maybe you'd like them better."

Apparently not. Simon breathed deeply again. "In one of those books your father let me read, and, I might add, says will teach me a lot of things, it said, 'We give up three fourths of ourselves just to be like other people.' I didn't understand it when I read it, but now I do. What you just said made me understand." He felt a flush of fear as he realized the depth of their disagreement.

"What you read in those books is not always right. My father says a fool can also know how to write."

She took on the stubborn look he'd learned to respect: head down, brow furrowed, lips set in a straight line.

Simon said, "Mr. Lindstrom said our conscience lets us find our way, and that making a mistake teaches us how not to do something. I think you made a mistake telling me to stop doing something I don't see as wrong, and I made one by telling you my reasons, and not listening to yours."

"Sometimes I can't keep up with what you say, Simon. Do you have to talk like a book?"

"I don't mean to. What I meant was, don't ask me to change something just because you've been taught it's wrong. And I'll try to listen to your reasons for asking." The festive mood of the picnic had dissipated, and Sarah sat silently on the blanket and looked away at the river, her arms folded across her chest. He knelt beside her and touched her arm. She looked at his hand for only a moment, and then returned her gaze to the water.

"I suppose we just as well gather up and go back to town," he said.

"I suppose." She got up and started to fold the blanket. Simon reached for the tin of cookies and she took it out of his hand and put it back on the ground. "I'll do it." Her curt words felt like a slap.

The walk back to town was long and silent and uncomfortable. Sarah had not offered to share the basket handles, so Simon's legs were thoroughly banged up by the time they reached the porch.

Mrs. Kingsley sat on the swing doing needlework. "You've been gone less than two hours," she said as they walked up the steps.

"It got too hot," Sarah said. She took the basket from Simon, turned, and walked into the house.

Simon, left standing on the porch with Mrs. Kingsley, felt the questions streaming from her eyes. Her raised eyebrows demanded answers. "I think we had an argument, ma'am."

She patted the seat beside her. "Come and sit."

Simon saw no way to escape and did as she said.

"Tell me what happened." Mrs. Kingsley spoke softly and quietly.

"She doesn't like my friends or the places we go."

"Surely she didn't say that in those words."

"Not those exact words, but that is exactly what she meant." Simon paused and looked at his hands.

"Go on. What else?"

"I mentioned that I went to Luger's once in a while to have lunch and she said that only damned people go there. My father and Mr. Mace go there for lunch nearly every day. So do a lot of people. I've seen the Reverend Bray in there. I tried to explain they weren't bad, but she wouldn't listen. I like my friends for who they are, not where they are. We just decided to come home."

She turned to face him, and her face relaxed before she spoke. "I don't approve of saloons and such, and won't let the judge frequent them. It's simply not seemly. I suppose Sarah has heard me say as much, and has taken it to heart. I have to abide with my beliefs, Simon, and express them as I see fit, but I also know others can do as they see right as well. I accept that, and accept those who disagree with me. Sometimes a young person doesn't see that last part. I'll talk with her, and explain that. I'm sorry your day ended badly, but I'm sure she'll think about it, and maybe try to be more tolerant." She reached over and put her hand on his arm.

Simon couldn't stop the flinch.

She chuckled. "I suppose it's time I stopped doing that too. It's just that I've always seen you as the boy I never had."

"It's not that bad, er, I mean, I don't care if . . . I really don't —" He stopped and took a deep breath. "I mean, thank you, ma'am. I've always liked you and Judge Kingsley, and you've always been good to my family and me. But I've never gotten used to that, and it always makes me blush." Simon could feel the color rising even as he spoke.

"I understand completely. We'll let this afternoon fade into memory, and tomorrow Sarah will be Sarah again, mark my words." Her hand started to go for his arm and then she stopped, giving him a warm smile instead. "It's lovely to talk to you, Simon. You are so, ah, what's the word? Worldly. Sometimes I wonder where you've gotten some of the wisdom you show. So much for such a young man."

Simon got up. "I'm going to go home. I have to go back to the cow camp in the morning. Tell Sarah I'm not sure when I'll be back in. Good-bye, Mrs. Kingsley."

"Good-bye, Simon, and say hello to your mother for me."

He walked down the steps and started down the dusty road toward home, putting together in his mind how he was going to explain his early arrival.

CHAPTER 19

Simon and Buell, along with Nathan, Sweeny and Lacey assembled by the river. Since Simon's trial with Nathan's big pistol, Buell had wanted to shoot it, and Nathan finally relented. Buell's experience turned out more or less the same as Simon's, only dirt instead of water had shot into the air, the empty peach can undisturbed. Nathan stuffed the pistol back into its holster and put it down.

After some discussion, the older men agreed the boys would have a better time if they shot pistols that weren't loaded with so much powder. Randall filled three more fruit cans and three root beer bottles with water, and stood them on the laid-down sycamore trunk. Buell and Simon stood side by side fifteen feet away, Simon with Sweeney's Remington, and Buell with Pat Lacey's Colt. The cowboys referred to both as the army model and both shot a forty-four-caliber bullet.

Everyone stepped back as the boys raised their pistols and took aim. The cowboy's guns weighed a lot less than did the Walker, and Simon had no trouble holding his up and fairly steady.

"Far when yer ready," Nathan said.

Both pistols went off together. A cloud of white smoke obscured the targets for a moment, and then whisked away on the breeze. All six targets stood, dumbly waiting. Buell looked past Simon, at Lacey, both eyebrows raised in question.

"Went over quite a bit, Buell," Lacey said. "Aim a little lower, say the bottom of the can. Same for you, Simon."

Simon went first this time. He raised his pistol, steadied a moment, and fired. A tiny rainbow formed and disappeared in the mist created by the spray of the exploding can of water.

"Ya-hoo!" hollered Nathan. "Good shot."

Simon pointed his pistol at the ground and moved back a step. Buell cocked the Colt, peered along the barrel for what seemed a long time, and pulled the trigger. The pistol bucked when he fired, but the five targets still stood.

Lacey smiled encouragement. "Little too tight. Ya hit about four inches low. Windage is perfect, just gotta git 'er up a twitch."

Buell gritted his teeth and shook his head. "Your turn, Simon."

"No, go get it, I'll wait."

"I said it's your shot, Simon. I don't need anybody waiting for me to get it right."

Simon stepped up, cocked the pistol, and using both hands, aimed. After a short pause, he fired and a second can exploded in a mist of river water, the can blown flat from the shock of the bullet.

Buell took a deep breath, and stepped up. He stared intently at the targets, and then let his breath out slowly.

"Slow and steady, Buell," Lacey said quietly. "Don't yank on the trigger."

The other onlookers stood silent, not moving at all. Buell raised his pistol and aimed. He, too, used both hands and for what seemed like forever, he waited. Then he fired. Five targets stood. "Damn it!"

"Use Sweeney's pistol," Nathan said.

Simon turned the butt to Buell and they traded guns.

"Now, same thing. The Remington has better sights, or some say. Git the front blade and rear sight notch lined up. Then, look fer your target. Don't be a'tryin' to see all three things at the same time. Eyes cain't do it."

231

Buell looked at Simon. Simon shrugged. Nathan's tone didn't leave much open for discussion. Buell raised the Remington, aimed and fired. Water sprayed everywhere.

"Good shot," shouted Simon as he thumped him on the back. "It was the smallest can and ya hit it dead center. Ain't nothing left."

"Reckon ya found another Remington man, Sweeney," Nathan said. He looked at Buell. "Some fellers jist cain't line up with a Colt. Plain don't fit. Simon, try that Colt of Lacey's."

Simon cocked back the hammer and sighted down the barrel. Nathan was right; he had to concentrate on the tiny notch in the top of the hammer that made up the rear sight and adjust quite a bit to get everything lined up. He swung over to the last can, centered on the middle, and squeezed the trigger. The fourth can took off skyward like a flushed partridge, trailing a spray of water. His shot had hit just below the base of the can. He stepped back and Buell moved forward again.

Buell raised the cocked pistol, steadied for a moment and fired. A brown bottle splattered in a flash. He looked at Lacey. Lacey winked.

"You boys kin shoot till you cain't pay fer

it," Nathan said. "Tomorrow you learn to make them slugs yer sendin' into the dirt. We bought ours, you git ta buy yers." He patted both boys on the shoulder. "Gits in yer blood, don' it. Jist remember, them's cans. They won't shoot back."

The boys took turns and shot for over two hours.

Paul rode into camp and tied his mare to the rope corral that held the Texans' horses. The shade of several spreading trees sheltered about a dozen of them. They stood hip-shot, side by side, nose to rump, their constantly moving tails swishing flies off of each other. Two lay on their sides, sound asleep. Paul smiled to himself. He walked over to the prairie camper and found Nathan alone, braiding horsehair around the handle of a short whip. "Looks peaceful enough," he said as he squatted down.

"The night boys took their bedrolls down't the river. Cooler. Left me with my thoughts and the damned deerflies. Nice and quiet. Days like this here makes life worth living." Nathan gave the strands of hair he was working on several twists then wrapped the excess around the handle and secured it with a strip of soft buckskin. He stuffed the work into the saddlebag that lay beside him.

"Let me git you a cuppa coffee?" He grunted as he rolled one leg across the other and stood. "Ground gits harder ever time I sit on it." He ambled over to the fire ring and picked up the pot. Shaking it, he nodded questionably. "Maybe." After knocking two cups clean on his pants leg, he poured the black liquid into them.

Paul didn't see any steam when Nathan handed him a cup and the Texan eyed him over the rim before taking a sip. Paul slurped his mouth full of the tepid brew and swallowed. He couldn't keep a straight face. "No offense, Nathan, but do you guys go out of your way to make it taste this bad?"

"Ah, hell, that's purdy good brew, you ask me." Nathan's eyes twinkled mischievously, and then he took another small sip and sloshed the rest on the ground. "Gone cold though. Cain't abide cold coffee."

Paul set his cup on the rim of the wagon wheel. "So, how are Simon and Buell working out?"

"Couple of fine boys. Me and the fellers has took a real shine to 'em. Ain't nothing they ain't willin' to try, especially yours. Raised up right, he is." Nathan reached into his shirt pocket and pulled out his cigarette papers. He flipped open the flat packet and blew gently on the edge of the stack. The papers ruffled, and he caught the corner of a single sheet with his fingertips and freed it. He offered the papers to Paul.

"No, thanks, never took it up. Thanks for the good words about Simon. I'll tell his mother. She's the one's got 'im this far. She'll be pleased to know it shows."

Nathan stuffed the papers into his shirt pocket. "Much as I hate to admit, I think my original guess were a good'n. The spot you picked here keeps 'em cows nice and bunched up. Two men workin' easy kin keep track of 'em. So, if'n ya need them boys som'ers else, you kin have 'em. Quite frankly, I'd hate to see Simon turn out to be jist a cowhand anyhow. And Buell? That boy's got a restless streak in 'im that ain't gonna be satisfied sitting on no horse all day." He creased the paper down the middle, laid it between his first and second fingers and held one corner with the tip of the thumb. Pulling a small cloth pouch of tobacco out of his pocket, he used his free hand and his teeth to open the top.

"It wasn't the only reason I came out, but it was one of the things I wanted to ask you. Fact is, Mace could use some help, and Simon has a chance to put some of his schooling to work, so I appreciate you being straight out with it. I think it's best they both come back to town. So, how are the cows looking? Gettin' fat?"

"Oh, yeah, this here grass, shade and water is a longhorn's heaven. I expect you kin see some twelve-hundred-pound critters come September."

"That good? Our Captain Atkins will be happy. And a happy customer comes back again."

Nathan shook some tobacco onto the creased paper, and then closed the bag using his teeth. He put the pouch back into his pocket. With his thumb, he closed the sides of the paper over the tobacco not quite evenly, and licked the overlapping edge. His thumb rolled the paper and tobacco into a rough cylinder and he then twisted one end and stuck the other in his mouth. The whole process took less than a minute. "Reckon this might be one of them rare deals were ever body gets done good," Nathan said as he reached for a match. He scratched it on the wheel rim, and lit his smoke in the flare. One deep drag consumed almost a fourth of the smoke. "Sure purdy cow country here."

Both men stood silent for a few moments, gazing out over the river bottoms and the low rolling hills to the north. "The boys'll be back about noon for a spell if yer wantin' to see 'em." Nathan broke the silence. "Otherwise, I can tell 'em."

"I'd better be getting back. They can stay the night and come back tomorrow. I know from talking to Simon they've learned a lot in the five weeks they've been out here. It's been real good of you guys to take 'em in. They'll not forget it." Paul stuck out his hand.

"Ain't been no bother 'tall. Like I said, them's both of 'em fine young fellers and we wuz pleased to have 'em. I'll send 'em home in the mornin'." Nathan shook Paul's hand, and they walked to the horses.

"See you in a couple of weeks, Nathan," Paul said as he swung into the saddle. He reined his horse around and headed back toward town.

CHAPTER 20

Simon and Buell sat on the ground with their backs against the wall of the livery. When they had ridden into camp the day before yesterday, Nathan had told them they had to go back to town. Now they sat here, both more or less silent in their own thoughts, and feeling strangely alone.

Simon felt that the few weeks away from his folks had slightly loosened the strings that held him so tightly to his family. He was of two minds about not being out with the herd. The eight hours spent in the saddle, or at least out on the prairie with the cows, had been mind-numbing dull. On the other hand, the time at camp with Buell, Lacey, Mr. Greene, and the others had been some of the most enjoyable he could remember. With the exception of some Mormons who had stopped by the farm for chickens, it was his first exposure to something really different.

He had grown to like Mr. Greene and Pat Lacey especially, but in their campfire stories they had both admitted to killing three men, Mr. Greene one and Lacey two. Mr. Greene's seemed to be an accident, more or less. Someone came sneaking around the camp one night, and Mr. Greene had come up on him. He heard what he thought was a pistol being cocked so he had cut loose with his own. The cowboys found a young Mexican man the next morning about a half mile from the camp with a belly wound. Apparently, he'd run off and bled to death in the night. A gun was never found and Mr. Greene impressed on the boys how miserable he'd felt about it. But in their part of the country, it was accepted that you protected what was yours with as much force as you saw fit. There had never been any question about him being held legally responsible for the death. In fact, the law never heard about it, because in the remote parts of Texas at that time, there was no law.

Lacey's story was not so ambiguous. He had hired on with a cattle rancher outside Abilene. One of the other hands who'd been with the ranch for a long time simply took a dislike for Lacey, and harassed him constantly with snakes in his bedroll, sand in his food, and off-color remarks about his masculinity. It came to a head one evening when Lacey came off the range to find his string of horses gone from the picket line. After taking care of his mount, he'd stormed into camp, and when he asked where his horses were, the cook had nodded at Lacey's tormentor. When he confronted him, the man started to swear and called Lacey a coward and a liar for accusing him without the proof. The other herders scattered away from the two men, and wisely so.

The troublemaker pulled his gun from his waistband and aimed at Lacey, who dove out of sight behind the cook wagon. From there, he drew his pistol, and with a poorly aimed shot, hit the man in the shin, knocking him to one knee. A second bullet, a more deliberately aimed, two-handed shot, hit the man right in the top of his bowed head, the bullet first passing through the hand he held up to ward off the attack. Again, the law didn't hold Lacey responsible for the man's death because all the other hands vouched that the dead man had goaded Lacey into a fight.

The sheriff had told Lacey he had better keep a cool head the next time he was in town. The rancher hadn't been so understanding, firing Lacey and telling him to leave the area or suffer the consequences. Lacey had ridden east to the Red River area. The second killing was never discussed; Lacey simply saying it was something he wished to forget.

"Sure miss banging away at the cans," Simon said.

Buell was drawing geometric patterns in the dust with a stick. "I miss the talking, and breakfast."

"That too. I was just thinking about the story Lacey told. The one where he blasted the feller in the head. Could you do that, Buell?"

"Yup." Buell wiped out his work with a quick flick of the stick.

"Just aim and shoot him. Like Lacey did?" Simon looked at Buell.

"Yup." Another design started, a precisely rendered circle drawn in the dust.

"I don't think I could. I reckon the feller getting shot in the legs like that was enough. He wasn't gonna shoot anymore."

"Maybe." The first circle now had another one drawn inside.

"C'mon Buell. He had his hands up."

"He drew first. Lacey had the sense to just get out of the way. Way I figger it, either Lacey killed him then or later. The fella wanted to shoot Lacey, and he was gonna do it." The third circle, smaller yet, joined the first two.

"But . . ." Simon paused and looked at the design in the dirt. The fourth and fifth rings had been added, the smallest about the size of a dollar.

Buell suddenly stabbed the stick into the center of the dollar. "No buts. You just do it." Buell hissed the words between clenched teeth and then dropped the stick and faced Simon, his eyes flat and distant for a moment. Then he blinked a few times, and kicked the design back into dust. The out-of-focus look gone, he grinned, and started to get up.

Simon sat motionless for a couple of seconds as he recalled seeing that odd look before — the fight with David. His groin tingled, and his testicles drew closer to his body. He rose to stand by Buell. "I hate it when you look like that."

"Like what."

"Like you're looking at something in your imagination and can't quite make it out . . . or . . . something. I don't know. I just don't like it. It's kinda scary." He'd just blurted out something he had not intended to discuss with Buell.

"Scared? Of me?" Buell stepped away and looked him up and down. "Like I'd take a poke at you?"

"Not exactly. I can't even get my mind to say what it is, much less tell it in words. It's like when we were kids, and slept in the hay up there." Simon pointed to the roof of the livery. "We talked about it then. There was nothing we could see or hear, it was just something we knew was there."

"I kinda went away for a minute when you were talking about Lacey shooting that fella. I could almost smell the gun smoke. I imagined it was me with that Remington." Buell paused and then shook his head. "I don't want to talk about it. I get confused about what I think sometimes. And it's kinda scary for me too." He looked down at the ground.

"It's all right. You're my best friend, and I didn't mean I was scared of you, just kinda scared for you, if you know what I mean." He leaned against the wall.

"You'll never have to be afraid of me, Simon. I've had that strange stuff go on in my head before, and I know I couldn't raise a hand against you. I know it." Buell looked directly at Simon. His face held an expression of hard determination, a sincerity that seemed almost desperate.

A thrill of recognition shot through Simon's chest, and he felt an overpowering sense of gratitude for Buell's commitment. And then, an equally powerful sense of dread descended when he realized that Buell's sincerity could be directed just as fervently and maliciously at an enemy. He sought to dispel the mood. "I guess you're stuck with me. And me with you." He punched his friend hard on the point of the shoulder.

"Sumbitch!" Buell clapped his hand over his mouth and glanced toward the door. "Sorry, been around Lacey too much, but that hurt." He made a face and rubbed his shoulder vigorously.

"Meant it to. You get to moping too much." Simon dodged a retaliatory jab. "Your pa's gonna catch you swearing and kick your butt."

"Not unless he can stop swearing at the horses. You ought to hear him talk to 'em when he's trying to put a hot shoe on. They don't like the smoke stink, and will lean on 'im. Phew, you think cussin'."

Both boys headed toward the street, Simon wary of the punch he knew he had coming.

"Guess you start at Swartz's in the morning, huh?" Buell asked.

"Yup. Miss Everett told him I could easily do his accounts, and maybe set up some better way of keeping track of where he lets credit. She says it will do me good."

"Storekeeper Simon. I never thought I'd see the day. Wait till I tell the boys at camp."

Simon knew Buell had every intention of visiting the Texans often. "No need to spread that around. It's not something I'm gonna do all my life. Miss Everett told Pa that I should work a commission deal with Mr. Swartz. For every dollar I save him, I get five percent. Then we'll see who gets to jingle his pockets." Simon grinned at Buell as they reached the street. "Anyway, I'll see you tomorrow at Luger's. Pa said a working man gets to visit a working man's saloon for lunch."

"I'll tell Pa that. Maybe he'll see it the same. Shoveling shit is as working man as you can get." Buell had been recruited to clean the stables from top to bottom.

"See you tomorrow, then?"

"I reckon." Buell nodded toward the general store and Simon's gaze followed.

Simon saw the jab coming a split second too late, and the full force of the punch instantly rendered his right arm numb. His mouth opened in a silent cry of pain as he grasped his shoulder. "You asshole," he hissed at a retreating back, and Buell chuckled without looking back. Through the pain,

Simon silently admired the accuracy and stealth of the attack, and then headed for home, holding his arm across his chest.

CHAPTER 21

Simon stood facing Werner Swartz in the general store. "Just help Gus clean up and unpack shipments and stock da shelves," the grumpy German said. He sat at a paper-cluttered table, slouched back in an armchair, his feet nestled in the mess on the tabletop. "And when you haff that done, we will see if smart you are as that school-teacher say."

His German accent grated on Simon's nerves. "Yes'ir."

"And Gustav says you like to be some lazy, yes? Every time I find you not work I take fifteen minutes from you. Ya?" The question was obviously not a question. "And that five percent you look for, you don't get until in my pocket I have what you safe me, ya?"

"Yes'ir."

"So. Get to work with Gustav. Is full of new goods, the back of store. I can't sell if the shelves not have it." He smiled condescendingly as though he had just imparted to the village idiot the secret to running a mercantile store.

"Yes'ir." Simon turned to find Gus standing in the doorway. "Morning, Gus." He said it more cheerfully than he felt.

"Let me show you what we have to do today." Gus turned and disappeared, Simon's greeting left to hang in the musty air, unattended.

Simon followed Gus into the store, and there Gus stopped and showed him a sheet of paper. "Here's a list of all the shit that came on the wagon last Wednesday. You're lucky you weren't here to help unload it. But, seeing as how I was, you get to unpack it. I'll watch and make sure you get it right." Gus hiked his ample butt up on a barrel labeled "CRACKERS."

Simon looked at the chaos of the large room. "If this was here last Wednesday, why are we unpacking it on Monday?"

"You were hired to work, not ask stupid questions." Gus scowled at him.

Gus's sharp reply surprised Simon for a moment, and then surprise turned to irritation. Barrels, wooden boxes, cloth and burlap bags, and paper-wrapped packages were stacked and strewn all over. "Where do we start?"

"First thing, not we, you. Hand me those papers on top of that biggest box." Gus pointed to a three-square-foot box that stood about four feet high. On top lay a folded sheaf of papers. Simon handed them to Gus.

"Says here there are thirty-one items in this shipment, so look for stuff with a number dash thirty-one on it."

Simon saw many such items. He pointed at 13-31. "That one okay?"

"Sure." Gus riffled the papers. "Says it's yard goods. Know what that is?"

"Cloth and thread and such?" Simon knew exactly what yard goods were.

"Very good, schoolboy. Knock the top off and see if you can take down the sides without spilling shit everywhere. There." He pointed a pudgy finger at an iron bar. One end had been flattened and the other given a slight bend. "Pry it loose with that."

The top of the box came off easily and inside were rolls of cloth, over a dozen of them. It looked to Simon that if he took the sides down everything would fall over. He grabbed the first roll and started to lift it out of the box.

"Knock the sides down," Gus said from his perch.

"Everything will fall over. I can —"

"Knock it down."

Simon pried one side away and it flopped down on the floor. Followed immediately by half of the cloth bolts. He looked at Gus.

"You get the cloth dirty, Pa will make you pay for it." The smirk on his face showed he'd achieved the desired outcome.

Simon picked up the bolts and leaned them against those remaining in the box. "Where do these go when I have them out?"

"Some go into the store, some go on the storage shelves behind me, and some go to the shelves by the door. Those are special order, and whoever ordered it will pick it up in the next few days."

"Am I supposed to guess which is which?"

"Don't get a smart mouth. I'll tell you what goes where. You just unpack it."

By the end of the day, Simon had managed to get through about half of the shipment. Gus spent the entire day either parked on the barrel, or following Simon about the store, pointing and criticizing. Simon decided at the end of the second day that the alternate Wednesdays, freight days, were not going to be the highlight of that week.

Simon stood on a small step stool stacking

cans of fruit on a shelf. "A-hem." The sound of a female gently clearing her throat turned his head. There stood Sarah. "Well, hi," he said, climbing down. *Boy, does she look nice today.* He wiped his hands self-consciously on his pants. "Nice to see you. What you doin' in here?"

"What do you think I'm doing in a store, in the middle of the morning, with a shopping basket on my arm?" She fluttered her eyelashes at him.

"Okay, I'll be the storekeeper. Can I help you find something, ma'am?"

"Why, yes'ir, you can. I need sixteen oyster-shell buttons, about quarter-inch size."

"Right this way, ma'am." Simon led her to a large double-door cabinet, which he opened. He pulled out a drawer, and inside, segregated in dozens of small boxed sections, were hundreds of buttons of all sizes and colors. "Do you see what you want, madame?" Simon motioned to the selection with a sweep of his arm and the tiniest hint of a bow.

Sarah giggled. "Why Mr. Storekeeper, you have such a complete collection of buttons. You do run a fine store." She looked at the open drawer for a moment, and then turned to face him. "I've missed talking to you,

Simon. Do you think we can try the picnic again Sunday?" She put her hand on his arm, her giggly mood gone, and her gaze direct and intense.

Simon swallowed hard. "I've been meaning to ask, but I wasn't sure if you had gotten over our last trip." Which was more than just the truth. He'd been thinking about it daily, but hadn't been able to figure out how to approach her.

"I was being thickheaded that day. I will never interfere with your choice of friends again." Sarah blurted out the promise. "Can we go then?"

"I'd really like that. Do you want to go at the same time as we did last time?" He suddenly felt light as a feather.

"Perfect." With the color rising in her face, she quickly turned her attention to the button drawer. She pointed. "Give me sixteen of those pink ones."

Simon pinched out a few and counted the number into her hand. "Anything else?"

"I need a spool of white thread and . . . just a minute, I have a list." She pulled a slip of paper from her cloth bag and handed it to Simon. He quickly gathered up all the items and set them on the counter in front of Mr. Swartz.

"That is it all, Miss Kingsley?" the shopkeeper said, peering up from his arithmetic.

"Yes, thank you." Sarah spoke to Mr. Swartz but her eyes were on Simon.

"You pay now or want it for your fadder's account?" Swartz scowled at Simon.

Sarah finally looked at Swartz and smiled. "Please, write it down."

"Ya." He laid the few items on a sheet of brown paper, wrapped them, and put the package in Sarah's basket. "Tank you for your business."

"You're welcome. Good-bye, Mr. Swartz." Sarah headed for the door.

Simon hurried to open it for her. "See you Sunday then, noon?"

"Yes. We'll have a good time. I promise." She swept by him, and the smell of lavender wafted past his nose.

"And is fifteen more minutes I don't pay for you," Swartz grumbled from the counter. "On your own time your picnics you arrange. Ya?"

Simon barely heard the admonition. It had become a regular event, at least four times a day and always as warranted as this one. Right now, Simon could not have cared less. Sarah had forgiven him for his rudeness at the river, and Sunday could not come soon enough. He went back to stocking the canned goods, the task now much lighter.

■ ■ ■ ■

Sheriff Staker sat at his desk and stared out into the street. He liked this small town — quiet, friendly and law-abiding. He knew everybody, and everybody's business, and he liked it that way. He had expected that maybe some trouble might blow in with the Texas herders, but that hadn't materialized. They'd been to town three times since that first raucous night, but no trouble had ensued. One pair favored Luger's; the others seemed to like Lancer's place. Only two of them carried pistols, and only one of them, the one named Lacey, wore a holster. Yep, nice and quiet.

His mind wandered back six years to Cincinnati. His work as a detective had been interesting, but the brutality some men, and women, were capable of, had eventually soured him. In a particularly nasty case, he had caught a murder suspect in the act of cutting and wrapping his three young victims into neat packages. It had been the final straw. He left, headed west, and stopped when he reached Carlisle. A conversation with Judge Kingsley had convinced him this was going to be a good place to live. And he was glad they'd had that conversation.

He rearranged his bottom in the chair. Across the street, Matt Steele strode into the telegraph office. *Again? That's about a dozen times in the last six weeks. Nobody sends that many telegrams.* A few minutes later, Matt came out again, and stopped to study a piece of paper he held in his hand. He flicked one corner of it with his finger, creased it twice, and put it in his coat pocket. Then he stepped off the boardwalk and angled across the street. *Looks like he's going to Lancer's again and that's strange too. Matt's never been a drinker, but now he seems to be in Lancer's nearly every day.*

Matt stepped up on the boardwalk and as he passed the jailhouse door, Staker caught his eye. The faint smile Matt was wearing vanished and his eyes snapped away. Staker heard his pace quicken. *Now, that was the look of a downright guilty man.*

A door closed across the street — Prosser at the telegraph office. He took his key out of the lock, and disappeared around the side of the building. *Going home? Too early for lunch. He leaves at twelve, sharp, returns at one, sharp.* Staker pulled out his watch and looked at it. *Odd.*

Staker had always thought Alex Prosser a

bit strange and his wife was without a doubt the shyest creature the sheriff had ever met. They mostly kept to themselves. Staker thought the skinny telegrapher, always punctual and correct, would sooner choke than cheat someone. To look at him as he scurried about his business, sleeves rolled down and collar buttoned up tight on the hottest day, Staker could not imagine him having a deceitful bone in his body. He smiled as he visualized the little puffs of dust Alex kicked up as he hurried home. For all that, Staker liked Alex Prosser.

He adjusted his butt again, but it didn't do any good. Swinging his feet off the desk, he stood and stretched. *Might as well take a little walk. Yessir, nice quiet town. Few strange people, but still . . .* He stepped out into the warm July morning.

CHAPTER 22

Mace watched David Steele swing the spring wagon in a sliding U-turn in front of the livery and pull back hard on the reins when the rig came even with the wide doors. The horse snorted and stamped her feet, protesting the bite of the bit in her mouth.

"You handle that horse like that when your father sees it and you'll wish you hadn't, David," his mother said. Ruth glared at her son. "And you needn't turn us over just because you didn't want to come with me."

Mace stepped away from the livery door. "Hello, Ruth." He walked over to the horse and ran his hand down its neck, talking softly to it. "Easy girl. Stand easy." He stroked the damp shoulder until the animal stopped fidgeting. Then he stared long and hard at David. "In a hurry are we?" He moved to the front of the carriage.

"Hello, Paisley," Ruth said in a familiar tone. They'd known each other for many years, and she'd been a good friend of his wife, Pearl, before she'd died. "I have a rim coming loose and wanted you to look at it while I go to the store. That is, if David hasn't torn it off with his terrible driving." She glared at her son again, then stood and held out her hand to Mace.

He helped her make the step down. "Glad to. Which one?"

"This side on the rear." She pointed.

Mace inspected the wheel, flexing it out with both hands pulling on top. The mare turned her head to watch. "Not bad, but you're right, a little loose. I'll take a better look in a bit. Got a horse with something stuck in a hoof just now. How long you going to be?"

"About an hour."

David rolled his eyes back and heaved an overly audible sigh.

"That'll be fine," Mace said. "I'll see you then."

Ruth glanced up at David, and walked toward the main street. David climbed down and started out to follow.

"Unhook that horse and put it in the shade, David. Won't take you a minute," Mace said.

David stopped and turned around. "What?"

Ruth heard him and stopped also.

"I said unhook your horse and put her in the shade. No need for her to stand there in the sun for an hour." Mace watched as David decided whether or not to challenge.

"You know better than to leave your horse unattended," Ruth said.

"Shit."

"One more word like that, and you'll take a bath right there." Mace pointed to the water trough. David hesitated. *Sizing me up?* The thought amused Mace. He stood and waited, ready.

David returned to the horse and dropped the shafts. Then he unwrapped the reins from the footboard, folded them, and threw them across the mare's back. She jumped. David, still holding the loop of reins, viciously jerked the horse's head sideways, and when she reared, he jerked down. His free arm drew back with the looped rein, his head up and looking at the horse's muzzle, his target obvious.

Mace's hand shot out and took hold of the back of David's collar. He yanked down and David slammed into the dirt, flat on his back. His amazed look turned to one of rage.

He rolled over and got to his feet. "You sonuvabitch!" He spat the words, and charged straight at Mace, head down, both fists bunched.

Mace pushed down on the back of David's head and sent him sprawling, headlong into the dirt again.

"David, you stop it!" Ruth shouted as she started toward him.

Mace motioned her to stop. He grabbed David's arm and pulled him to his feet. Stepping behind him, he trapped the young man's arms to his side in a bear hug. "I told you to watch your dirty mouth, boy."

"You bastard, you sonuvabitchinbastard," David screamed. He tried to slam the back of his head into Mace's face.

Mace picked him up off his feet, walked deliberately to the trough, then, flipping David's feet high over the algae-tinged water, he let go. David went back-first into the trough and Mace shoved his head under. Kicking his feet furiously and flailing his arms against the side of the trough, David tried to resurface. As soon as the furious boy sucked in a mouthful of the tepid water, Mace let go and stepped away. David sat up, coughing and choking, then hung onto the sides of the trough and looked for Mace, his eyes ablaze.

"Want some more, or are you ready to cool off?" Mace took a step closer to the trough.

David opened his mouth to say something, and then shut it. He heaved himself upright and his clothes, covered all over with clots of slimy green algae, streamed water. Breathing heavily, he stepped out of the trough, stood for a moment, then turned and strode away to look back only once, his face seething with rage. Several people stood at the corner of the main street, talking and pointing.

"I'm sorry for that, Ruth, but I can't abide someone abusing an animal. And I won't let anybody talk like that around you." Mace walked to the horse and picked up the reins. The horse shied, so Mace laid his hand on her shoulder and patted it gently until the animal stood still. "Really, Ruth, I'm sorry."

"He had it coming. Matt has had to take a strap to him several times the last few months. I don't know what gets into him. He'll get over it." She looked to where the people stood on the corner. "I suppose I'll be explaining this for the rest of the afternoon."

He nodded toward the knot of people. "I know at least two of them saw him go for the horse. Let it go at that. Not the first time they've seen a feller get a lesson."

"I suppose you're right. I'll go do what I have to do, and then drive myself home. Will the wheel be all right?"

"I think so. I'll look it over, and if not, you can take one of my rigs."

"Thank you, Paisley. I've always been able to count on you." She gathered her skirt, and headed toward the group of onlookers on the corner.

Mace watched as she passed them; a short nod of her head seemed to dismiss any questions. He led the mare into the shade of the open shelter beside the livery, and threw the reins over the hitch rail. He shook his head as he went inside to care for the tender-hoofed horse.

Mace was not surprised the next day when Sheriff Staker stepped into the livery.

"Hello, Mace."

He looked up from the sheet of iron he was marking. "Hey, Loren, whatcha need?" he asked, nonchalant.

"Matt came by this morning and said you and David had a run-in. Want to tell me your side?" He leaned against the big anvil.

"Not a lot to tell. He was going to slap that bay mare of Matt's, and I stopped him. He objected, and started cussing like a

262

trooper in front of his mother. I warned him once. Didn't hurt him none . . . I mean, I didn't really punch him, just kinda dropped him in the trough to cool off. Could of stung his pride a mite, but he needed pulling up."

"Not exactly the way I heard it from Matt, but that comes a lot closer to what a couple of others have to say who watched the whole thing from up the street. They said young David went crazy."

"I think he was surprised how quick he wound up on the ground. The young ones always are. Figger if they make a lot of noise and puff up, the rest of us will move over. Well, he found out different. I reckon he got a cheap lesson."

"I tend to agree. If Matt wants to force the issue, I can reasonably point out your action was self-defense." The sheriff paused a moment. "Got a little itch though, that needs scratching."

"So scratch."

"Remember that blow-up Matt and Paul had several years back? And the whipping Matt's boy laid on Paul's boy, Simon? Well, I was there when David did that to Simon, and there was something wild about him. Gave me the creepers. Anyway, Matt told me something that kinda set my teeth on edge. To use his exact words, 'Me and the boy keep score real good, and looks like we have three to settle now.' "

"Meaning what?" Mace mentally repeated what he had just heard.

"Well, right after the Matt and Paul thing, I got word that Matt had bought a gun, a hideout Smith and Wesson. I caught up with him the next day and told him I knew about it, and that if anything went amiss I knew exactly where to come. He was some upset. Considered it a personal affair, and said buying a gun was his business. I let it go at that. I found soon after that he had gotten rid of the gun."

"And?"

"And now this. Checked with Swartz this morning and Matt bought another one. Had David with him when he did it. Don't like it, but there's nothin' I can do about it, but let you know."

"Phew. So now I have to look out for someone taking a potshot at me?"

"I don't honestly know. Had to tell you though." Staker pushed away from the anvil.

"Appreciate it, Loren." Mace stuck his hand out.

The sheriff shook it and left.

"Damn."

■ ■ ■ ■

Buell quietly moved away from the door to the stables and walked quickly to the back exit. Stepping into the sun, he watched the sheriff move up the street. His heart pounded hard in his chest.

Pat Lacey half dozed in his saddle under some trees that cut off most of the midday sun. His horse raised its head, snorted and looked toward the west. A horse and rider, half a mile away, loped in his direction. At a quarter mile, he recognized Buell. He smiled to himself, and prodded his horse out of the shade and into full sunlight. Buell altered his direction and soon jammed his horse to a stop in front of the Texan.

"Howdy, town boy." Lacey eased his horse back into the shade. "Git tarred of a soft bed?"

Buell pushed his hat back and grinned. "What's it to you? You own the prairie?"

"Nope, jist cain't imagine someone comin' out here on purpose." Lacey slipped a stirrup and cocked his leg around the saddle horn.

"Kinda miss being out here with the cows, though I can't say the same for the human company. Cows sure gotta smell better."

"Whatcha git used to, I reckon. So, yer pa cut ya loose fer an afternoon?"

"Kinda. Actually, I left him a note saying I was gonna ride out for a couple hours. He won't mind. Let's get off these horses." Buell swung his leg over the back of his saddle and stepped down.

Lacey kicked his left foot free and slid off his horse. Dropping the reins, he walked a ways away from the horses, and then hunkered down on his heels. With his eyes, he invited Buell to do the same. "Looks like ya got something on yer mind."

"I guess I do." Buell sat down and sighed. "What would you do if you knew someone was gonna shoot you if they got the chance?"

"Whoa, whatcha talkin' there? You ain't got nobody gunnin' fer you do ya? Hell fire, ya ain't old enough to have that kind o' enemy." Lacey examined Buell's face closely.

"Well, it ain't exactly me they're looking for. It's someone I have to protect."

"That there makes a lot of difference. Most times though, a feller likes to take care of his own business. Who's this here feller . . . is a feller ain't it?"

"It's my pa." Buell's eyebrows twitched

with concern.

"Different yet. He's kin. That's same as your own self." Lacey rocked to one side and sat on the ground. "Now tell me what'n hell yer talkin' about."

Buell told him what he'd overheard in the livery. He also told him about how vicious the fight between Simon and David had been.

"I can see yer problem, Buell. Don't rightly know what to tell ya." Lacey took his hat off and scratched his head as he thought.

Buell watched, and waited.

After a couple of minutes of silence, Lacey continued. "Man sticks a smoke pole in yer kisser, ain't a lot a thinkin' to do, you jist do what you have to. Now, this here looks like a threat, but you cain't be sure, and shooting a feller when ya ain't sure has gotta be dead wrong. I reckon what I'd do is to ask the feller straight out, and be ready to ride 'im if'n he bucks."

"Just tell him I think he's up to no good?"

"Yep. And another thing. Do it where ya ain't got to account to nobody."

"You mean no witnesses?"

"That's what I said. And if'n it comes to it, best not to be hauling out no pistol. The hub end of half a wagon spoke will gener'ly get their attention, and it ain't so perm'nent." Lacey settled his hat back on his head.

"Thanks, Lacey. I figgered you'd probably seen something like this before. But I thought you would be more likely to, well, you know, show 'em your gun."

"Guns only gonna git you more trouble. Don't never think this here Colt will fix yer problem. It won't. Have it handy, and know how to use it, but you only draw 'er out when you're sure, and cain't see no other way." Lacey looked directly into Buell's eyes. Satisfied he'd made his point, he reached into his pocket and hauled out his tobacco and papers. They spent the next couple of hours talking about Texas and all the country in between. Buell headed back to town when Lacey's relief showed up.

CHAPTER 23

Sunday turned out a glorious day. Simon picked up Sarah at one o'clock sharp, and they retraced the steps they'd taken weeks before. Same spot, same kind of sandwiches, same blanket. Only this time, they talked like they had not seen each other in months: about the Texans, and Buell and the herd; and Simon's new job at the store; and Miss Everett; and what they wanted to do when they were older; and why dandelions grew where flowers wouldn't; and how to take an egg from a chicken without getting pecked. Completely talked out, they ended lying together, on the blanket, with Sarah's head on Simon's arm, both sound asleep.

The ache in Simon's arm finally woke him. His eyes popped open to look right into Sarah's face. Her lips slightly parted, a wisp of damp hair stuck to her forehead. The look of contentment and peace on her face made Simon's breath catch in his throat — she was beautiful. He lay still and admired up close every feature of her familiar face. As he did, it occurred to him that it was not that familiar. He had never had the chance to look this carefully without being embarrassed.

He so wanted to touch her smooth and flawless skin; instead, he marveled at the shape of her eyelashes. Evenly spaced, they tapered from the eyelid where they glistened with oil, curving upward to almost disappear in an incredibly fine tip. Her lips had tiny lines all through them, stopping in a perfectly formed arc where lip turned to skin. Tiny beads of sweat formed in the shallow furrow under her nose. His gaze moved down her chin and onto her throat. The graceful arch of her jawline met her neck, and the creamy expanse of flesh disappeared under her collar. His eyes continued down past her shoulder and stopped on the swell of her breasts. They rose and fell with the measured rhythm of her breathing. The image of a large white breast, held up for view, came into his head. His testicles contracted and he realized he was getting hard. And then he felt eyes. He looked up and into Sarah's soft hazel gaze, a half smile on her lips.

"What are you looking at?" she whispered.

Simon's heart went to full race. His eyes involuntarily slipped back to her breast, his mind screaming that it was the last thing he should do. He paused for a split second on the forbidden view, and then looked again into her eyes. He felt the horrible rush of blood to his face, and knew he was blushing furiously. "I . . . I'm sorry."

Nothing else would come to his lips, and his eyes begged hers to look away. She held her gaze, and then slowly she leaned closer and kissed him full on the mouth. It seemed to last forever, and Simon was unable to recognize any sensation but the touch of her lips on his as he shot into heaven, conscious only of the softness of her mouth, the barely perceptible quiver of her lips as they sought to bond with his.

And then he fell back to earth, Sarah again lying on her back, eyes shut, her breathing slow and even. His heart beat so hard, he could feel it in his neck and the ache he had felt in his arm wasn't even a vague memory. Still savoring the kiss, Simon wished he could roll over and lie on his stomach, or failing that, hoped Sarah would keep her eyes closed for a few more minutes.

"What you mean too much I pay?" Werner Swartz's eyes grew wide and he planted his hands on his hips.

Simon sat at the table in the storeroom, surrounded by pieces of paper. "When I compared the bill with the freight inventory on that last shipment I found they had itemized thirty-three articles shipped, but we only unpacked thirty-one. There's a box of canned peaches and a fifty-pound sack of rice they're asking payment for that we didn't get."

After spending two days unpacking a shipment, he had wondered how Mr. Swartz kept track of it all. Gus hadn't paid much attention, content to simply stack and shelve stuff as they came to it. Miss Everett had suggested doing what he'd done. Now nearly noon, he had sorted papers and written down figures all morning.

"But each one they ship has number, ya?" Mr. Swartz looked skeptical.

"The freighter puts the number on, not the supplier. The freighter gets paid by what he moves, not what the shipper sells." Simon pointed to the freight ticket.

"And more than once this happened?" Swartz's apprehensive face showed clearly in his voice.

"I've looked through nearly a year's worth of bills and freight tickets. If I understand right and you get a shipment every other

272

week, then quite a few bills and freight tickets are missing. Nearly every one I've looked at has at least one item charged that you didn't get." He held up the piece of paper. "Some more than one. It seems to depend on the size of the load."

"And you on purpose think this is?" The scowl on his face expressed anger beginning to build. "I will get the law for them. You are sure what you see?"

"I can see more items billed for than you received. I don't know whether or not the shortage comes because your supplier doesn't send it, or because the freighter removes an item or two, and then numbers them after that. I really can't prove who's cheating. I just know someone is."

"And you know how much cheated I am?" The storekeeper leaned forward anticipating the answer.

"So far I have found ninety-six dollars and eighty-five cents."

"Mein Gott!" Swartz's face turned crimson and he pounded on the desk.

Simon slid his chair back and after a full minute of what Simon assumed was cursing, Swartz stopped in mid sentence and looked at him.

"And you think I pay you five percent for finding this?"

Simon felt like a weevil in a cracker barrel for the look Swartz gave him. "I hadn't even thought about that."

"Well, I think don't you should. I was cheated. You did not save me money. It is gone." He continued to bore into Simon with his dark eyes, his brow furrowed and his hands planted squarely on his hips.

"But I think you will save money in the future if —" Simon stopped as the blood started to rise again in the storekeeper's face. "No, sir. I see what you're saying."

"Good, two times cheated I don't want. This is good job you do. I will tell your papa." Swartz, visibly relieved, stared down at the papers. "And why is missing tickets and bills? I show Gustav how to put papers away. You are sure it was good you look?"

"I used what was in the box here," Simon said. "It was not very well organized."

"I will talk to Gustav and see why papers missing." Swartz shook his head and walked out of the storeroom, muttering to himself.

Simon put the papers back in the box. *I wonder where Gus put the rest?*

Matt stepped into Avery's office and shut the door.

"Do you really have to shut the door, Matt? It's hotter'n hell in here," Avery said.

"I want to talk to you in private. Can you lock this door from the inside?"

"Sure, but I —"

"Then lock it!" Matt pulled a chair away from the desk and sat.

Avery stood, went to the door, stuck his key in the lock and turned it. *What's so damn secret I have to lock up in the middle of the day?* "There, it's locked."

"I need some money, quite a bit of money."

"Okay, that's what I do. How much and what for?" Avery always got to the point when it came to money.

"I'm going to turn the tables on someone, and I have just the plan to do it."

"You found out how to get your hands on some cows, didn't you?" Avery watched Matt's eyes closely and saw the look of chagrin flit past.

"How in hell did you know that?"

"Didn't, till just now. I suspected you had gotten what you needed from Prosser. He ain't been too cheerful lately. Guilty conscience I think." Avery loved it when he anticipated someone.

"Well, if you know, you know. Doesn't change what I'm going to do. I just need to fix the financing right now so I can arrange something down south."

"All right. I know what for. How much?"

"About five thousand."

"Damn, Matt, either you're going to buy twice as many as Paul did, or you're expecting me to finance you one hundred percent. Either way, I can't risk it." Avery knew Matt only had about four hundred dollars in the bank. He also knew Matt never kept much around the house; Matt and David's father-son relationship didn't breed a lot of trust.

"I'll put the farm up," Matt said.

"I . . . you know I . . . I'm not sure you should." The heat in the room could not completely account for the sudden flush that Avery felt.

"What are you talking about? What do you mean, I shouldn't?" Matt moved to the edge of his chair. "I told you once about short sticks and rattlesnakes."

Avery cleared his throat. "I'm aware of only two people who know about the farm. You and me. That's what I know. But, I can't be sure there's not someone else. And not knowing makes that farm risky collateral." His own audacity surprised him.

"You sniveling little bastard. You were well paid for your trivial piece of work. If you, for one instant, think you can hold that over me, you are sorely mistaken." Matt's face had turned dark and he glared at Avery.

"When only two people know something, it's one word against another, and if you think my word won't hold up to yours, you're crazy. I'll warn you one more time: don't even dream about bringing that up." Matt's breath came hard, the veins in his forehead bulging. He blinked quickly a couple of times and suddenly sat back down.

"I can't do it, Matt," Avery said quietly but firmly. "There are people in Saint Louis I fear a lot more than anyone around here. If I asked them to lend that much money and it fell through, I wouldn't last a month." He mentally steeled himself for Matt's inevitable tirade, but Matt was suddenly very calm.

"You did get rid of all the paperwork, didn't you?"

"Of course," Avery snorted. He met Matt eye to eye.

"Then you have nothing to worry about. Nobody knows, or will ever know." Matt paused.

Avery broke off the eye contact and looked at the clock.

"I'll tell you what," Matt said finally. "I'll let you in on the deal."

"That makes it a little easier," Avery said. He put a tone of interest in his voice. "What kind of a split are you talking about?"

"Let's go fifty-fifty. I'm not in it for the money. There's the trust that my father set up. I can access that, can't I?"

"Legally, yes." Avery nodded his head, sagely, he thought. "You can borrow against it if the collateral is ironclad. Your wife must agree, though. That's the way the old man set it up. But I can do that, yes. I'm the administrator of that trust," Avery said and then paused. *I can sell my part of this to Lancer, and maybe get Blake Waldon in on it too. They're always whining about missing all the money deals. Maybe, just maybe, float the whole thing and not risk anything myself. Uncle Sylvan never needs to know. Yeah, this feels better by the second. 'You protect your own ass best by risking someone else's.' Who told me that? Doesn't matter, it's true. And my snake-playing stick just got longer.*

"Yeah," Avery continued. "We can work something out. You said five thousand? You sure that's going to be enough?"

They worked over a few figures, and then Avery unlocked the door. He watched Matt head across the street for Lancer's. "Going to be a lively place come spring," Avery said to no one. He went back to his desk and sat down. Turning, he pulled open a drawer in the cabinet behind him and pulled out a binder. He opened it, checked its contents for a moment, and put it back. After closing the drawer, he leaned back in his chair and let out a satisfied sign. "Yup, lively."

CHAPTER 24

Simon reined up his horse at the livery and hollered, "Hey, Buell."

A moment later, Buell stepped through the door. "Ready to go I see."

"You said about eight o'clock. Can't be much before that now," Simon said.

"I'm saddled. Just gotta get my hat." Buell disappeared into the livery.

Back outside, he climbed into the saddle and together they rode north out of town, in silence — usual when riding with Buell. The horses seemed to sense the easy mood and walked with a lazy gait, heads down and relaxed. About fifteen minutes later, they arrived on the low banks of the river, and Buell guided his horse in among the trees that stood along the bank, then stopped in an open space. They dismounted, and while Simon tied up the animals, Buell untied his saddlebags and pulled them off his horse.

"Got something to show you," Buell said and headed toward the river. At the river's edge, he sat and unbuckled one bag. Simon sat beside him, his curiosity making him crowd Buell.

"Damn, Simon, give a fella some room." Buell elbowed him in the ribs.

Simon scooted back a little, still staring at the bag.

With a sly smile on his face, Buell stuck his hand in the bag and withdrew a long-barreled pistol.

"Shit," Simon chirped, "where'd you get that?"

"Adobe, kind of."

"Who knows you have this?" Simon's eyes could not leave the gun with its dark-blue steel, bright brass trigger guard, and red-brown wooden grips.

"Pat Lacey, you and me. Here, take a hold of it." Butt first, he handed the gun to Simon. "It's loaded."

"It's a beauty. Looks a lot like Sweeney's, but it's not as heavy."

"It's not as big. Thirty-six caliber instead of forty-four. Same gun almost, a Remington." Buell's face beamed. "I wanted you to be the first to see it."

"How'd you know where to find one in Adobe?"

"I didn't exactly get it in Adobe. Lacey won it in a card game there. He said I could have it for what he had bet on it, six dollars. It's worth more than that, but he said he wasn't that fond of a thirty-six."

"What's your pa gonna say?"

"He ain't gonna like it, but I'm nearly fourteen and plenty of guys our age have pistols. Hell, some of them are already out on their own. I don't care what he says, it's mine, and I'm gonna keep it."

As Buell's voice rose, the color came up in his face.

"Are you going to tell him you have it?"

"Nope."

The silence that fell between them held for several minutes as both stared at the gun in Simon's hand, Simon's mind a blizzard of concerns. *Ma and Pa are going to find out. How can I keep it from them? Maybe they won't ask. Yeah, no reason for them to ask. I'll just avoid any talk about guns and stuff. Simple. Boy, that's a beauty. Wonder how it shoots?*

Buell looked directly into Simon's eyes for a moment, and then asked, "Wanna shoot it?"

"Oh, yeah," Simon replied instantly.

"Didn't take you long to decide. What if someone asks you about it?"

282

"Why should they ask? Let me go set something up." He handed the pistol to Buell and went looking for a couple of targets. It didn't take him long to find a can and two bottles. Remembering the first time they had shot in the Texans' camp, he went to the river and filled the targets with water. Lining them up on a downed cottonwood bough, he hustled expectantly back to Buell.

"You first." Buell offered the pistol to Simon.

"Have you shot it yet?"

"Nope, just got it Wednesday."

"Wednesday? And you could wait till today to try it out?"

"With you working at the store till six or later, we couldn't get down here without having to explain what we were going to do. And I wanted you to see it first."

"Then you shoot first. You ought to." Simon held his hand up in refusal.

"All right, but you can go first if you want to."

Simon made no move to accept the pistol and Buell looked at the targets. "Did you load it or was it loaded when you got it?" Simon asked.

"It was loaded." Buell looked at him and then down at the pistol. "I see what you're gettin' at. Mr. Greene said a man loads his

own gun or suffers a fool's consequence."
He frowned. "Shit. Now what do we do?"

"Do the balls all seem to be set in about
the same?"

Buell looked at the muzzle end of the
cylinder. "Yeah."

"Run the ram against 'em."

Buell worked the rod against each ball in
turn. "They all feel right. So what could go
wrong?"

"Mr. Greene said no powder was the most
common mistake, and too much powder
would just scare the beans out of you. I
think we've checked it all." Simon thought
hard about what the Texans had told them.
"The damn things can kill from both ends," he
visualized Nathan Greene telling them,
gimlet-eyed and intense. *"You gotta be careful."* Simon gave Buell a quick half nod and
shrugged his shoulders.

"All right, let's do it." Buell turned to face
the targets, twenty feet away.

Instinctively, Simon's hands went to his
ears, and he stepped behind Buell to watch.
Using only one hand, Buell cocked the
hammer and sighted only briefly before
pulling the trigger. The pistol cracked
sharply, belched a cloud of smoke, and the
first bottle exploded in a flash of water and
shattered glass. Buell took one long step to

284

the right and Simon had barely focused on the targets when the pistol barked once more. The other bottle splattered into bits. Startled, Simon looked directly at his friend's gun hand as Buell moved again. In one fluid move, he cocked the pistol, aimed, and fired in less than a couple of heartbeats, sending the can spinning off the log.

"Shit . . . I mean, holy shit, Buell, where'd you learn to shoot like that?" Simon's mouth hung open and he stared at where the targets had been, all three now gone in seconds.

Buell turned around and pointed the pistol at the ground. A wisp of smoke lingered near the muzzle in the dead calm air. "Been practicing . . . with Lacey."

Buell's satisfied grin and the slight squint of his eyes seemed to reflect his mood. "I've finally found something I can do better'n most, and it feels good."

Simon's plan to simply not discuss guns or shooting came apart less than twelve hours later. Ana had asked Paul to invite John Lindstrom to supper, and all now sat around the table to enjoy a dessert of warm apricot cobbler. Simon was savoring his favorite dish when John spoke.

"How'd your target shooting go this

morning, Simon?"

Simon spit a mouthful of half-chewed pastry all over Abel.

"Hey!" Abel stared at his food-speckled arm. "You spit on me."

Simon covered his mouth as his face heated up and he looked from his mother, to his father, to John, and back again, deciding who was safest to address. He chose John, and in the same instant, made another decision. "Wasn't me." His eyes held John's gaze for only a moment, after which he turned his attention to Abel. "Sorry Abe, guess I choked." He made a perfunctory effort to flick some crumbs off of his brother.

"Humph, Sheriff Staker said he was fishing this morning and heard quite a bit of pistol fire, and then about ten o'clock, saw you and Buell heading back to town. Guess it must have been someone else." John took another bite of cobbler and chewed slowly, watching Simon.

"We were down at the river and I heard some shooting, but it wasn't us. We just fooled around for a couple hours, and then rode back to town." Simon could feel his ears flaming and his father exchanged a confused look with John.

Paul cleared his throat and tugged on his earlobe.

"So, how is the herd coming, Paul?" John asked.

"I was out there on Thursday, and Nathan said he's never seen cattle gain so much weight in his life. I'm no cattleman, but even to my poor eye they look sleek as any barn-raised cow. They really look that good." Paul glanced at Simon.

"Are you going to do the same thing next year?" John asked.

"I don't see why not. The army will need another supply of meat, and I think if we deliver prime stock this year, they'll consider us favorably for next."

"Precisely as I see it." John handed him a piece of paper. "Here's the name of a broker in Kansas. You two can take care of all the details yourself this time." He smiled at Ana.

"Well, I appreciate your confidence, but I'd like to count on your help when it comes to dealing prices and such," Paul said.

"No problem, I'll be happy to do that, but I'm sure you can do nearly all of it on your own. You don't realize it, but you and Ana have handled most of the details thus far. All I did was arrange to get the herd here, and Nathan did that."

Simon listened intently as the adults discussed financing and delivery schedules. He was grateful his deceit had not been discovered, but he felt horrible about what he'd done. Every time one of the adults glanced his way he could feel his guilt glow around him like an aura. He thought the evening would never end.

Monday morning was pure misery for Simon. He hadn't slept well and felt grateful to get to the store and away from the seemingly furtive looks his mother gave him over breakfast. His father had left early and spared Simon the discomfort of facing him. Even with the ever-critical Mr. Swartz, the store seemed more like a sanctuary.

"So, what seems to bother you this morning, hey?" Mr. Swartz asked and waved the feather duster in Simon's direction.

"Just didn't sleep well, sir."

"Well, you are sure not for sleeping here. You pay attention good to customer or I get half hour or so for your time, I think." He snorted and returned to busily rearrange some of the dust on a row of cans.

Simon went through the morning in a daze and picked the most physical tasks to keep himself alert. He looked forward to his lunch hour, which he fully intended to spend with a quiet nap in the storeroom. The long awaited hour of noon came, and John Lindstrom walked into the store.

"Good morning, Werner," he greeted them, "and you too, Simon."

"Good morning, Mr. Lindstrom. What you see I get you?"

"Not looking to buy anything today, thank you. I just wanted to see if Simon would join me for a stroll at lunch." He smiled at Simon.

Simon hoped the disappointment he felt didn't show on his face.

"Ya, that is good. It is dinner now, and he can go."

Simon untied the heavy apron he wore, folded it neatly, and laid it on the shelf under the counter. Mr. Swartz nodded his approval.

Simon and John Lindstrom stepped into the warm August air. As they did so, a surge of panic caused Simon to inhale sharply. *Had Buell been caught by his pa? What if John asks me again if I was shooting? Why didn't I tell them last night?*

"Are you coming?"

Simon looked up to find he'd fallen a couple of steps behind and he hurried up. "Yeah, I guess I was kinda lost there for a minute. Where we going?" Simon asked as nonchalantly as he could.

"I asked Mrs. Bray to fix us a lunch. She makes the best shredded-chicken sandwich

I have ever eaten. She has a recipe for some kind of sauce that would make turkey feathers taste good. I think you'll like it."

They soon covered the two blocks to the boardinghouse where Mrs. Bray stood waiting for them. She ushered them into the kitchen. "I've got to go see Mrs. Frank at the dress shop, Mr. Lindstrom. You know where everything is, so help yourself. I expect to be gone an hour or so." She swished her ample body across the kitchen and left.

When the kitchen door shut, Simon thought he knew how one of Sheriff Staker's prisoners felt.

"Help yourself to one of the sandwiches." John pointed to a plate that held four.

Dutifully, he put one on his plate, and sat down. He had yet to meet John's eyes.

"Go ahead, take a bite," John said as he sat. "You'll see."

Simon picked up the sandwich and bit into it. "This *is* good!"

"See. The sauce is eggs, oil, vinegar and spices of some kind. She whips it until it's nice and smooth like that. Goes on anything." John took a huge bite of his own and chewed contentedly.

Simon waited and watched while nibbling at his meal.

Finally, John spoke again. "So, how's the store job going? I hear from Werner that you've saved him considerable money. I knew you'd do a good job."

Simon's relief left him slightly faint. "It was nothing, really, just comparing simple lists of numbers and seeing they didn't add up. I haven't been paid in full yet. Mr. Swartz says I don't need the money all at once, and I'll get it after all the trekkers are done coming through. That shouldn't be long. If I don't get it soon though, he'll find a way to get some of it back. Seems I can't get through a day without him finding something to take out of my pay. Broke a crock this morning. Just happened to move a sack it was leaning on, and off the shelf it came. Cost me twenty-five cents, and when I said it . . ." Simon's voice trailed off into silence as tears welled up in his eyes. He bowed his head. His sandwich swam out of focus. The room remained quiet for a while.

"Hurts, doesn't it?" John said.

Another period of silence pressed down on him, then: "How can I ever make it up to them?" Simon finally muttered.

"That's the sad part, Simon. You can't completely. I wish I could tell you otherwise, but once a trust is broken, the seed of doubt is planted. It may never flourish, or even sprout for that matter, but it will always be there. You know it, and so do they. I talked to your father this morning, and asked his permission to have this chat with you. I consider it an honor that he allowed it."

"It was so easy, Mr. Lindstrom. It just came out. I didn't have time to think about it."

"That's probably not true. I think you'd determined ahead of time that you were going to lie if you were ever asked. That's why it seems you didn't have to think about it. You'd probably convinced yourself the question wouldn't come up. But it did, and you didn't need to think, your predisposition to deceive took over. As is often the case when you lie, the first person you fail is yourself. You created a situation where a lie could seem the easy way out. Do you see what I'm saying? You were ready to lie."

How could he know that? I knew it was wrong to fool around with a pistol and went ahead and did it. And he's right, I was ready to lie. How can that be? I'm not a liar. Confusion still reigned. "I think I understand, sir."

"And your problem is compounded yet. Your father didn't confront you Sunday because he wasn't sure. He went to see Mr. Mace this morning, and Buell was asked to account for his actions. Buell admitted he

292

had shot the pistol. Mr. Mace didn't tell him Sheriff Staker was the source of the information. Buell may assume it was you who told."

Simon's heart sank. "But I didn't," he stammered. "It just looks that way. Oh, Uncle John, I've really made a mess of it haven't I?"

"I have to agree. And you're the one who has to make amends as best you can. It will cause you some embarrassment and shame, but the sooner you proceed, the better."

John had both arms on the table and leaned forward, his face serious, almost stern. Simon saw those emotions, but he also saw the look of concern that John's eyes couldn't hide.

"I'm glad we had this talk," Simon said. "I didn't know what I was going to say to Pa and Ma. I still don't, really, but knowing they know everything makes it easier somehow. But Buell. I don't expect he'll talk to me at all." Simon shook his head in dismay. He could picture Buell's face in his mind, and the image made his stomach tighten.

"Try to understand how your folks feel, son. I won't presume to speak for them. The same goes for Buell. We'll leave it at that." John leaned back in his chair.

"I'm sorry," Simon said.

"And I accept that, but it's not I to whom you need to apologize."

"Yes, sir, I understand."

Early evening finally arrived, and Simon put his apron away and left the store. Walking slowly along the boardwalk, he came to the corner and looked toward the livery. He felt a surge of relief when the front doors were closed, and with a deep sigh, he continued toward home.

"Hey, Simon!"

He turned to see Buell, waving at him from the now-open door. Simon headed toward the livery.

Inside, Buell leaned his fork against a stall and took off his gloves. "I've had enough for today."

"Yeah, me too."

"Have you heard we got caught?" A slight smirk formed Buell's face.

"Uh, yeah. Mr. Lindstrom had a talk with me at noon."

"Mr. Lindstrom?"

"Yeah, I haven't figgered that out yet. He was nice about it, but there's no doubt my folks aren't very happy."

"Wonder how they found out." Buell absently dug a finger in one ear.

"You don't know?"

"Nope. Someone told yer pa, and he told mine."

"It was Sheriff Staker. He was fishing and heard us. Saw who it was when we rode back to town."

"Can't never put nothin' over on him. Old fart seems to know everything."

"I was afraid you might have thought it was me," Simon said quietly.

"Huh? You? You're joking?"

Simon, now suddenly ashamed, looked at his friend.

Buell's eyebrows shot up. "You're not joking." He snorted. "Damn, Simon, I'd never think that."

"You can see why I might think it, can't you?"

"I guess." Then Buell grinned widely. "But I'm saving my lies for something important. Shit, Simon, don't look so beat up. Got time to go see Jake?"

"I think so. Yeah, let's do it." Simon grinned at Buell and they walked, side by side, up the street to find Jake.

CHAPTER 25

Mace heard the spring wagon pull up and stop in front of the livery. He put down his hammer and walked out into the road.

"Hello, Paisley," Ruth said from the seat.

"Hi, Ruth, what brings you over here?"

"I think the horse may have picked up a pebble." She pointed to the front of the animal. "Right side. She seems to favor it."

He noticed she hadn't looked at him while she spoke. "Let me help you down and I'll take a look. Won't take a minute." He reached up to her, grasping her arm as she placed her foot on the single step. As she came down she cringed and he heard her groan. "I'm sorry," he said, "I can be such a clumsy oaf."

"No, it's not you. I fell and bruised my arm. It's not that bad." She stared at the ground.

He waited for her to look up. Then he gasped. "And bruised your neck at the same time? How did you get that terrible mark on your neck?" He stared at the blue-purple blotch.

Ruth's hand went to her throat and when she tried to push the collar higher, she winced.

"How, Ruth?" Mace wanted to reach over and move her collar.

"I . . . I fell."

Two horsemen rode by, tipped their hats and greeted them both.

"Let's get out of the street." Mace took her elbow and guided her toward the livery. She resisted only for a moment, and then walked into the building.

"Who did this?" Mace demanded.

"Please, Paisley, it will only make matters worse if you interfere. I don't want you to get involved."

"Ruth. We've been good friends for years. I can see there's nothing wrong with the mare just by the way she's standing. You need help, and I'm glad you came here. Now, tell me what's going on."

"It's David."

"How in hell can that be? What's Matt know about it? Sorry for swearing but, good Lord, Ruth, how can Matt let this happen?"

"He doesn't know." Suddenly Ruth turned for the door. "I must go. I wasn't thinking when I came here."

Mace grabbed her forearm. "Does Ana know? Or Paul?"

"Please, this was a mistake. Don't say anything. Please, I'm begging you."

The pain in her eyes both infuriated and crushed Mace. "Ruth, I've got to do something. I can't stand by and let you get hurt like this."

"If you think anything of me, let this go. I'll get through it. You'll only make it worse. I shouldn't have come. I don't know what I was thinking. Promise me, Paisley. Don't say anything. Not now. Promise?"

"Damn it, Ruth." Mace faced her, his heavy fists clenched, and slowly shook his head back and forth like an agitated bull. "Damn it."

"Thank you. Don't worry, I'll be all right." She reached out and touched his hand. "Thank you for being my friend." She turned and walked out to her wagon.

He helped her into the seat and she tongue-clicked the horse into motion. He watched until she turned the corner, heading west. Reentering the livery, he picked up his hammer and swung it with all his might, shattering the oak planking of the bench top. Trembling with rage, he stared at the damage, imagining.

Now what the hell do I do? That little son of a bitch is abusing his mother, and that worthless bastard Matt is so . . . so, gawdammit. She came here for help, anybody can see that. Does she want me to break my promise?

"Damn it to hell!" Mace sat down on a bench and held his head.

Paul and John had been at Luger's for over fifteen minutes before Mace arrived for their daily noon get-together. Instead of going to the bar to get a sandwich as he usually did, he came directly to the table.

"I've got a real problem, guys." Mace looked completely lost.

"I can see that," Paul said. "You look like a whipped pup."

"Can I get you a beer, Mace?" Fred called from behind the bar.

"Not just yet." Mace dragged back a chair and sagged into it. He put his elbows on the table and rested his cheeks on his knuckles.

"Well, you came in, so you're obviously ready to share what it is that's bothering you," John said.

"Hard one. A woman came by the livery yesterday afternoon and it was plain that someone had knocked her around a bit. Of course, I couldn't see a lot, but when I

299

helped her down from the wagon, my hand on her arm hurt her enough to make her wince. And even though she tried to keep her collar high, I could see her neck was bruised real bad. Made me sick to see it."

"Well, who was it?" Paul asked.

"That's the hard part. She begged me not to say anything, and I more or less promised. Damn it. I can't get those black marks on her neck out of my mind."

"It's Ruth, isn't it?" Paul said.

Mace couldn't keep the surprised look off his face. "I can't say, Paul, I promised."

"You don't have to. I've been wondering if something was going on there for a couple or three months now. Ruth, Ana, and Irene Kingsley have been getting together at least once a week for a long time, and about a month ago, Ana mentioned that Ruth had been missing a lot. She has only seen her about three times since summer set in. I put it down to Matt being on an ornery streak, but the longer it went, the more I wondered. You just confirmed my fears. Looks like I'd better pay Matt a personal visit."

"Don't jump to conclusions. I ain't said it was Matt." Mace's mouth clicked shut. He pursed his lips and shook his head in resignation. "Shit . . . it's David."

"David!" Paul studied Mace's face intently. "David?"

"That's what she said. She also said Matt doesn't know. I can't hardly believe that. I mean, they're husband and wife, for hell sakes."

"Well, we have a mess here. I can't stand around and let her get beat up, and I can't go barging into another man's home, even if he is my brother. I need to talk to Ana about this. I can understand your problem, Mace, I really can."

"I can see this is a family matter, Paul, but I feel compelled to say something," John said. "I'm not even sure I should have been privy to any of this, but now that I am . . . well, I have to say what I think."

"It's not my family either, John," Mace said. "But I'm in it up to my teeth. I have a lot of faith in your judgment. You seem to be able to see some things that others completely ignore . . . deliberate or otherwise."

"I agree with him," Paul said. "Tell us what you think."

"I realize a man's supposed to handle his own family affairs, but that same man owes his family fair treatment. If David, a minor, is abusing his mother, Matt has a duty, both legal and moral, to do something about it.

If Matt, however, is the perpetrator, then civil law comes into play. Wife or not, a man cannot batter a woman with impunity. The problem confronting you is how to abide by Ruth's wishes that Mace stay out of it."

"Perpetrator?" Mace said, "I gather that means he's doing it?"

"I'm sorry. Sometimes the books come out without me thinking. But you got the gist of it. Anyway, how do we convey our suspicions to Matt without letting on that Ruth told you? And what if it is David, and Matt doesn't know? I say that, even though I agree with Mace, it's hard to believe."

"I think I can work out a way to get the point across to Matt. Ana and I will pay a visit soon. Matt and I usually find ourselves alone when we do and I'll think of something. David is another matter. Maybe my talk with Matt will get passed on. We'll just have to hope and watch."

"Got to do something," Mace said. "I'm not sure I can see another bruise like that and not do something about it." Dogged determination etched his face.

Ana lay on her side in bed, facing Paul. "There are some things about Ruth and Matt that you don't know," she said quietly. "Some time back she told me they were having problems. Not beatings or anything like that, just problems. The kind that might make it possible that Matt would not see bruises on Ruth."

"Do you mean they're not sharing a bed?"

"They don't even share a bedroom."

"Why?" Paul plainly could not imagine such a thing.

"I promised I wouldn't discuss it. Enough to know that what she said could be true. Matt may not know David is hurting her." Saying it made tears sting her eyes.

"Well, I'm going to do something about it. I will not have her getting beat up."

"Of course, but let me talk to her first. I think we should go see them this Saturday. I'll find out what's going on, and then we'll decide what to do." She reached out and placed her hand on his face. "Hold me, Paul. I need you to hold me tight."

CHAPTER 26

Mace looked up from his work when David walked through the door. He had been expecting him, because Matt had told him yesterday he was going to send his horse in to have a shoe refitted. He laid his tongs down on the hearth.

"I left Pa's mare under the shed." David looked at him sullenly.

"I want to talk to you for a minute, David." He leaned back against his workbench.

David glanced suspiciously around the stable. "What do you want?"

"Got something I need to get off my chest, and I think you can help." Mace held his hands up, palms out, in a gesture of nonaggression. "I know you'd just as soon spit in my hand as shake it, but I want you to listen for a minute. Please."

David cocked his head to one side, like a chicken surveying a bug. Mace could see curiosity start to get the better of David's uneasiness.

"So, what do you want with me?" He hooked his thumbs in his front pockets and turned his head just barely aside. Then he spit on the dirt floor, his insolence deliberate and calculated.

"Remember our talk out front, by the water trough?"

David's cocky expression disappeared instantly. "Yeah, I ain't about to forget that."

"Well, that discussion was about abusing your horse. And all you got for that was a little wet." Mace pushed away from the bench and stood upright, stepping toward the door as he did. David moved away and farther into the stable.

"Now I want to talk to you about abuse of another kind. Something a lot more serious."

"I don't have to listen to you." David glanced at the front door and licked his lips.

"I think you better, boy."

"I don't know what you're getting at. I ain't abusing nobody."

Mace watched David measure the distance to the front door and judge it too far. Two saddles on stands blocked the side-door exit.

"I'm not sayin' you are. I'm just saying the grief you could suffer if you were, would make you wish you'd stayed in the horse

305

trough."

David's face flushed. "Then what are you saying?"

"Simple. If I ever see another bruise on your mother, I'll come for you with a bullwhip, and I'll take you apart." Mace moved toward David as he finished speaking, and David retreated until his back met a stall gate. Standing toe to toe with David, Mace continued calmly. "I know you're only seventeen, but that's old enough to know you take your medicine when you need it."

David stood as tall as Mace, if not taller, and Mace's calm voice seemed to give him courage. "You can't threaten me. I ain't beating nobody, and you ain't gonna find it so easy to get me down again."

"I ain't threatening you. I'm telling you what will happen. You got a mean streak in you that's gonna cause you some serious pain, and I'm telling you, your mother gets hurt again, I'll be the one to deal it to you."

"What's going on?"

Mace turned to see Buell standing in the door to their private rooms.

"I'm having a talk with David. Go back into the kitchen, and shut the door."

"I'm stayin'."

"Do as I say." Mace glowered at him.

Buell leaned back against the wall and

folded his arms.

Mace turned back to David. "Don't forget what I've told you, David. I mean every word of it." He stepped back to allow him room to leave.

David shifted toward the safety of the door, and then stopped, the insolent look reestablished. "And I'm telling you, old man, you keep sticking your face in where it ain't been asked, and somebody's gonna shoot it off."

Before Mace could get his eyes on him, Buell had shot away from the wall and across the open space. Charging, head down, his shoulder caught David in the lower ribs; a clearly audible crack snapped through the air. David gasped. Both of them crashed into the door frame and collapsed in a heap on the floor; Buell's fists pummeling David's face. Mace finally reacted, and pulled Buell off, but Buell got in one final kick as Mace dragged him across the dirt floor.

"Get up and get out of here, David." Mace pushed Buell away.

David got up, gasped again and gripped his left side. "You'll pay for that, Buell. Both of you will pay." His face had lost its color, making the murderous look on it almost unearthly. "You bastards." He stepped out the door and into the street.

Mace's emotions ran amok. "Damn it, Buell, that was none of your business." He felt concern for his son's condition and angry that he had heard the discussion about Ruth, but he was also immensely proud that Buell had instantly come to his defense. "Are you all right?" He looked closely at him.

"I'm fine. He had no right to say that to you. He goes for you, he goes for me. You're my pa, and we're all we got."

Mace couldn't find his voice. That was more than Buell had ever said to him in one piece in his entire life. And what he had said was worth more than Mace could express. He didn't know how to react. "The boy has a mean streak," he said as brusquely as he could muster. "Someday he'll pay for it. I want you to stay away from him." He put his hand on Buell's shoulder.

"Ain't afraid of 'im." Buell said it matter-of-factly.

"I can see that, but I still think you should stay out of his way if you can. I hate to brand someone, but I think he's crazy."

"Lacey says the crazy ones are the easiest to handle." Buell smiled. "I'll watch out, Pa." He touched his father's arm and walked out of the livery.

Mace shook his head as he tried to grasp just how old his son seemed at times. He missed his wife deeply at that moment.

Saturday found Paul and Ana sitting on the brocade sofa in Ruth's parlor. "What do you mean they attacked him?" Paul looked across the room at Matt and Ruth. "That isn't like Mace. He's hard to provoke, and certainly wouldn't attack a boy."

"Well, he did. He held David while Buell hit him in the ribs with something. They broke one and bruised several. He's in terrible pain." Matt was plainly speaking the truth as he knew it. "I've told Sheriff Staker about it, and I'm going to see something done. This is the third time either Buell or Paisley Mace have attacked David, and I'm not going to let this go on."

"I don't know what to say, Matt. Mace is my friend, but I can see why you're upset. Is David here? I'd like to talk to him."

"He's not. When I got back to the house this afternoon, he was gone."

Matt looked at Ruth. "Did he tell you where?"

"He didn't, but I know he took a horse."

Paul had been unable to catch Ruth's eye since they had arrived a half hour earlier.

Ruth got out of her chair. "Let's go in the

309

kitchen and make some coffee, Ana."

Paul watched closely to see if Ruth limped or showed any sign of pain. He saw none. The two sisters left the room, and Paul was dismayed to find Matt watching him just as closely. He cussed himself for not being — what? Careful, aware?

"I'm sorry about David. I hate to see anybody come to grief," Paul said.

"I think Mace has a mean streak in him, and I think that little rooster of a son has the same thing. I can easily imagine Paisley allowing his son to take advantage of David while he held him. I may be a bit rough on animals once in a while, but you don't abuse another human."

The sharp look Matt gave Paul spoke volumes. Matt had obviously not forgotten, nor forgiven him for, the incident with the pig. It also made Paul think that maybe Matt didn't know what was going on in his own house.

"You don't know how much I wish I could take that back, Matt. I've said I'm sorry, but I'll say it again. I'm sorry. I just lost my temper."

"I accept that as I did the first time. Don't fret about it." Matt said the words, but the expression on his face said something completely different; Matt would never forget that day.

Paul and Ana left a couple of hours later. The visit had been an uneasy one, both tiptoeing around the issue of Ruth's abuse; the three of them well aware of it, while Matt appeared to be clueless. And they left knowing David was guilty of abuse, and Matt guilty of contempt.

Mace looked up from his work to find Sheriff Staker leaning against the open door of the livery. Mace quit pounding.

"Seems you and Matt's boy can't be in the same room together," Staker said laconically.

"You know as well as I do, he's a liar and a bully." Mace couldn't keep the irritation out of his voice. "He said something that Buell took as a threat, and Buell jumped him. Simple as that. Two boys having a go at it. Don't tell me you didn't do the same when you were a youngster. Hell, David outweighs Buell by thirty pounds." He put his hammer on the anvil and placed both hands on his hips. Trying to explain something when he couldn't completely divulge everything vexed him. *Loren's just doing what he has to do but damn it, this whole thing is completely ass-backwards. He ought to be rousting Matt and David, and it's Buell that gets hauled up short every time there's any trouble. Shit!*

"David says you held him while Buell whacked him with a wagon spoke."

"And you believe that? C'mon, Loren."

"You saying that ain't what happened?"

"Of course that ain't what happened. Damn it, sometimes I wonder why I vote for you. You know good and well I wouldn't do a —"

"Whoa there, hoss," Staker said. "I'm just asking, and you're telling me what I need to hear. I already had a talk with Doc Princher, and he said that rib wasn't cracked by no wagon spoke. Probably not even a fist. It was a pressure fracture, like what a man gets when a horse falls on him. I know David's lying. I just have to ask the question. I did and you answered."

"Well dammit, why do you let me get all worked up? You seem to get a kick out of it." Mace's jaw muscles tensed.

"I'm sorry. I don't get a kick out of it, but I do it on purpose."

"See, that's what I mean. You do it on purpose. Damn it."

"I found out a long time ago, if I can get a person riled up enough, they'll say what they mean for the most part. They don't even think about lying. Works real good on you." Staker's eyes smiled.

"Well, it ain't good for a man's heart," Mace said half joking, and his muscles relaxed. "So now what do we do?"

"Same thing a lawman always does: wait, watch, and clean up the mess after." The truth of his words was plain on his face. "Ain't been no real crime, nobody has complained, leastwise nobody with a legal interest, and I can't arrest someone simply cuz they're a hard case."

"So that's it? We just have to wait until someone gets hurt bad. That doesn't seem right."

"It isn't right, Mace. It's legal. Tell Buell to steer clear of David. I'll give David the evil eye when I see him, but that hasn't done much good in the past." Sheriff Staker stuck out his hand. "Sorry for the hard questions."

Mace shook his hand. "You're a good man, Loren. Knew it when you come to town. We're lucky to have you. No hard feelings."

Staker stepped out of the livery and surveyed the street, checking windows, doors and openings between the buildings, all done in an instant and instinctively. The same instincts that warned him of trouble

313

coming. He could feel it and hated the fact that all he could do was wait for it, like a live goat in a bear trap.

Buell strode across the stable floor toward the doors.

"What you doing with that pistol strapped to your leg?" his father asked.

Buell stopped.

Mace put his tongs down and leaned against the forge. "C'mere. I want to talk to you."

Buell sauntered over to him. "I got it, so I might as well wear it."

"When I said you could keep it, I didn't mean you should wear it wherever you went. You don't need a pistol to go to Luger's."

"I'm not going to listen to one more threat by David Steele."

"And that's just what I'm afraid of. You think that pistol's gonna stop 'im?"

"He's a bully who picks on animals, smaller people and women. Only time he'll take on a fair fight is if he's riled, and I ain't gonna rile him. But he's gonna know I won't back off an inch either."

"But there's always hard cases coming through here that will press you just cuz you're young. Do you know that?"

"I'm not that young, Pa, and I know how

to use this. I can use it real good. I know what it will do, and I won't ever use it if I can help it. I made someone else that promise, and I'm making it to you now."

"Dammit, Buell, it scares the hell outta me."

"I'm not smart like Simon, or strong like you, or big like Mr. Steele. And I don't have a lot to say even if people would listen. But this pistol changes that. I'm equal. I feel better with it."

"It don't make you better, Buell."

"I didn't say *I'm* better, I said it makes me *feel* better. I'm calm with it. I feel like I can do things now I couldn't before. I'm not afraid to look up."

"You mean you're more confident?"

"Yeah, that's the word. I'm confident."

"I'll take your promise, then. But never provoke someone just cuz you're wearing it. Okay?"

"That's the way I thought anyhow."

Mace gave Buell a wan smile and nodded his head. "We'll see you later, then."

CHAPTER 27

It was only six thirty in the morning, and Simon and Buell were already dust-covered and cotton-mouthed. September first, delivery day for the herd of cattle to Fort Hartwell, had arrived, and for five long days prior, Simon, Buell, and the Texans searched the draws and secluded copses along the river for the cattle. They now had five hundred animals up on the prairie and headed east, with another hundred and forty-four in the corrals just outside Carlisle.

It had been a hot, dusty and frustrating job, but the boys had jumped at the chance to go when Paul and Mace had offered. Nathan Greene figured they could be at the fort by early afternoon if they kept the herd moving steadily, but they were finding that easier said than done. The cattle had meandered all summer, and didn't take kindly to being hurried; the cowboys constantly riding out to angle a stray back into the herd. Sweat-soaked and tired, Simon and Buell exchanged knowing glances as the squalid settlement of Adobe came into view.

By two o'clock, they circled the herd to a stop just south of the fort and near four huge corrals, now empty except for a few sad-looking horses in one of them. The cowboys held the cattle in a tight group while Paul and John rode off to the fort. They soon returned with Captain Atkins, Mr. Ledbetter, and four soldiers. They approached Nathan Greene.

"Captain Atkins, Mr. Ledbetter, I'd like you to meet Nathan Greene of Texas," Paul said. Nathan jockeyed his horse between the mounts of the two men, and extended his hand to each in turn.

"My pleasure, I'm sure," he said.

"Mighty fine-looking herd of cattle, Mr. Greene. My compliments. Mr. Steele told me they were fat and sound, but I didn't expect anything near as prime as these. I'm pleased, very pleased indeed."

"Yer good Nebraska river bottom gits most of the credit. Like I told Paul here, that there's gotta be a longhorn's heaven."

"Well, if you would be so kind as to direct your drovers to put one hundred and twenty-five in each of the four corrals we can finish this transaction." Captain Atkins turned to address a three-striped older soldier. "Sergeant, have your men move those horses back to the fort."

"Yes'ir." The sergeant saluted and the four men rode to the farthest corral and hustled the half dozen horses out, and herded them away.

"Mr. Ledbetter and I will tally. Please don't move them too quickly."

The two men moved their horses to either side of the now-open gate and took out small notepads and short pencils. Poised, they waited for the first of the cattle to move between them.

The equine ballet that followed displayed the experience and skill of the Texans. Cutting left and right, spinning on the spot, and moving back and forth with apparent ease, the silent, serious men never allowed more than two cows at a time through the gates. They ran the prescribed numbers past the tallymen in an uninterrupted stream and soon had the five hundred cattle in the corrals. It was three thirty.

"I count exactly five hundred, Mr. Ledbetter. What does your book say?" the captain asked.

"The same, five hundred. Never quite had such an easy time of it. Your hands are very expert at that Mr. Greene. I'm impressed,"

Ledbetter said. He moved his horse closer to the Texan and stuck out his hand. "Pleasure doing business with you."

"Reckon the same. And thanks. Them's a good bunch o' boys."

"Excellent maneuver, Mr. Greene. I, too, offer my appreciation for a job well done. Now, Mr. Steele, if you will accompany me back to my office, we can conclude this." Captain Atkins swung his horse around and waited for Paul to fall in beside.

Nathan turned to the men. "If'n ya wanna, y'all kin head out fer that Soldier's Roost place in Adobe. I'll swing by and pick up the two young'ns when Simon's pappy gits done. I asked your pa, Simon, and he figgered it weren't any harm in you boys seeing that place up close."

He barely had the words out of his mouth before the whole crew wheeled their horses and set off at full gallop, headed west in a cloud of brown dust.

"I'm a little surprised that Paul let Simon and Buell visit that place," John said as he looked at the quickly vanishing riders. "Just from the one look we had this spring, it didn't impress me as all that sophisticated."

"Fact is, he weren't all that quick to agree. Chewed on it fer most of the mornin'. Don't exactly know what turned him, but about noon he rode up to me and said it were okay."

"Hmm. I suppose they have to see it eventually, and they are getting to be men. Especially Buell. I get the distinct impression that boy is much older than his years."

"I read 'im the same way. Him and Lacey hit 'er off real good, and Lacey's always walked a mite on the wild side. Good man, jist a bit touchy."

"No sense sitting out here like a couple of prairie dogs. Let's go up to the trading post and wait there for Paul. I've about had enough of this sun."

Nathan nodded agreement and they rode toward the fort.

John rode thinking about the perfectly executed business deal they were about to finish up.

Nathan's thoughts were about how good a cool beer and a shot of whiskey would have tasted had he gone with the boys to the Soldier's Roost in Adobe.

Simon rode hard beside Buell as the crew whooped it into Adobe, Randall Quigg out in front, deference given to his age. Skidding to a stop, they all dismounted in front of the Roost and tied their horses to one of the many rails. Simon paused as Buell undid the flap on one saddlebag and took out his pistol, now secured in a holster and wrapped in a belt. He unwound the leather and buckled the rig around his waist.

Lacey stepped up beside Buell. "Whoa, there. I ain't a gonna say you cain't, but I gotta say you shouldn't."

The rest of the crew stopped short of the door and watched as Buell tied the bottom of his holster to his leg. Sweeney looked at Quigg and both shook their heads.

"I gotta agree with Lacey," Sweeney said. "You don't need that in there. Hell, they might make you take it off anyhow."

Buell turned to Simon, the challenge plain on his face.

Simon shrugged. "There isn't any sense in my saying anything, so I won't." He gestured toward the door of the saloon and waited for Buell to start toward it and then, exhaling through puffed-out cheeks, he followed.

Kerosene lamps hung from the ceiling and blazed alongside and in between the mirrors behind the bar. The street-side wall had them as well, placed in sconces set four or five feet apart. The bar, located opposite the doors, ran the sixty-foot length of the room. Five men behind the counter served the twenty-five or so customers lined up against it, mostly soldiers. Tables, set six or eight feet apart and in two lines roughly paralleling the bar, served even more people; some playing cards or dominos, some just talking among themselves, and some actively engaged in ribald exchanges with half a dozen women. Simon looked for, but didn't see, the woman who'd bared her breast. Everybody, without exception, had a beer mug or a whiskey glass either in hand or nearby.

Quigg led the cowboys across the plank floor to a vacant spot at the left end of the bar where he hailed a bartender. "We're from Texas and we're thirsty," he said when the man reached them.

"What's your pleasure, gents?"

"I'd like a whiskey and a beer," Quigg said. "How about you boys?"

"Yup," Sweeney said.

"Me too," Lacey said.

The other two cowboys ordered the same.

Simon looked at Buell, and then at the bartender. "I guess I'll not have anything." The heat of embarrassment climbed toward his ears.

Sweeney snorted. "Hell, you say." He gave Simon a friendly cuff on the back of the head. "Gotta have a drink with us. Least have a small beer."

"I'll have a beer then, thank you."

The bartender grinned at him and clucked his tongue, then looked at Buell.

"I'll have a beer . . . and a whiskey." He looked back at Simon with a slight smile. "Can't kill me."

"Your pa might though." He instantly regretted saying it when Buell's eyes sparked and the muscles in his jaw flexed. Simon had seen that sign many times; Buell had just been challenged and he didn't like it.

"Coming right up," the barkeeper said. He moved to the tall handles of the beer pumps and soon returned, scooting six empty shot glasses down the bar with the full beer mugs. With the beer divvied up, he expertly aligned the six glasses and reached under the bar to retrieve a half-empty bottle of whiskey. He pulled the cork, and without pausing, poured all six glasses full in one continuous motion.

"That'll be one dollar and fifty-five cents, or two bits each if you're plowing your own row. A nickel for the kid's beer." He nodded at Simon.

Six Liberty quarters clattered on the bar. The barkeep looked at Simon for his nickel. The flame of embarrassment that began when he'd ordered, fed on the fresh fuel of the bartender's gaze. *I'm flat broke. Nobody said we'd be visiting any place where I'd need money. It's all at home.*

Sweeney must have seen his problem. "Let me be the one to buy yer first beer. 'Tis yer first, ain't it?"

"Yes'ir. I've had a taste or two in Luger's storeroom, but I've never had one to myself." He felt like hugging Sweeney as the nickel lit on the bar and spun for a second.

All eyes had followed the flipped coin and watched as the bartender's hand slapped it still. "Thank you, gents. Gimme a holler when you're ready for another." He scooped the coins off the polished wood and headed for a customer who beckoned farther down the bar.

"Here's to a great summer's work," Quigg said. "I think Nathan and Mr. Steele are mor'n happy with us." He raised his whiskey glass to the rest, and then tossed the contents down his throat. He gritted his teeth, then quickly took a long pull on the beer before setting it down with a grunt. "Ooff, that's some kinda raw skunk piss they're pushin' here."

Buell followed suit with his whiskey. A look of shock took over his face, his eyes went wide and he swallowed hard, twice. Then, he shuddered like he had a bad chill, and tears started to flow furiously.

Lacey slapped him on the back. "What's

the matter Buell, reckon that's a little strong fer ya?"

The Texans were grinning at him and winking at each other.

"Damn." He managed only the one word, then coughed once, shook his head, and coughed again.

"Take a pull o' yer beer," Sweeney offered.

Buell wiped the tears from his eyes and reached for the mug.

"Looks to me like he's still a little wet fer this." A young soldier in dusty blue trousers and a light-blue shirt stood chuckling at Buell's discomfort. He didn't look to be much older than either Buell or Simon.

"He'll do just fine, Blue," Lacey said.

The other Texans turned to stare at the soldier and the word "Blue" apparently caught the attention of four or five other soldiers standing by the younger one.

"I got my doubts," Blue said. He smiled at the other soldiers and nodded.

"Can't even talk," another one said, chuckling.

"Leave it alone, Blue," Lacey said. He was watching Buell, now clearheaded and eyeing the young soldier coldly.

"Just messing him a bit. Can't he take up his own?" Blue winked at the man next to him.

"I can and I will." Buell stepped away from the bar and faced the young trooper, his jaw muscles working.

For the first time, the soldier got a look at the Remington riding in the tied-down holster. He gave his friends a nervous glance. Passive, their faces showed nothing as they watched the little drama. All the soldiers were armed, their pistols in holsters with flaps that covered them completely.

"Take 'er easy Buell, he was just a funnin' you a little. Didn't mean no sass, did you?" Lacey asked the soldier.

"Ain't saying I did, and ain't saying I didn't." The soldier looked Buell up and down.

"Can't step in here, Blue," Lacey said, "but I'll shine some daylight on somethin'. I wouldn't mess around. He looks young, but that there can get you hurt."

Buell's eyes never left the soldier whose hands hung down loosely.

"I can mind my own here, Lacey," Buell said. "This here fella seems to want a fight, and I can give it to 'im."

The other soldiers moved out of the way and the Texans followed suit.

"I ain't picking no fight," Blue said, "but I ain't never run either. I was just funnin' you a little. You want to make a big pile out o' that, I reckon we can." The soldier's tongue flicked across his lips.

Buell's cold stare continued. "I didn't find it funny."

Simon's heart started to race when Buell's jaw muscles stopped flexing, his face perfectly relaxed, like he was about to take a shot at a water-filled soda bottle.

Lacey must have seen the same thing. "Let me tell you somethin' Blue. I've see'd this feller put two balls in a flushed prairie chicken at thirty feet. You ain't no thirty feet."

Buell's eyes remained fixed on the face of the young soldier whose brow now shone wet with sweat. "Still think it's funny?" he said quietly.

By now the entire bar watched intently, quietly, and his whispered words carried the length of the room.

"Well?" Buell asked.

The harsh metallic crackle of twin hammers being ratcheted back to full cock brought with it several audible intakes of breath around the saloon.

"I ain't no thirty feet away either, and I got the right medicine for cocky prairie roosters." The barkeeper pointed a short double-barrel shotgun straight at Buell. "Uh-uh. Don't even think it," he said, as

Buell started to turn his head. "Ain't no-body that quick. Unbuckle the belt, son, and let the holster fall." A slight sideways gesture with the shotgun emphasized his request.

Buell reached across, undid the buckle, and let the holster fall away. The tie-down on his leg turned the holster upside down and the Remington clattered to the floor.

"Now step back a couple." Again, a twitch of the shotgun helped make his point. "Please, put his gun here on the bar," he said to Sweeney.

Sweeney reached down, picked up the pistol, and laid it by the beer mugs.

"Good. Now, you soldier boys take your youngster down't the other end, and you boys stay right here." The barkeeper glanced at Lacey, then picked up the pistol, and put it under the bar. "He can have that back when you're ready to leave." He uncocked the shotgun as he walked away.

As the soldiers started down the bar with their drinks, Blue made a move to turn around. Another soldier, this one with two stripes, grabbed him roughly by the arm and steered him along. "Consider yourself lucky, stupid. That boy's a killer. I can see it," he said in a harsh whisper.

Buell eyed Sweeney coldly and Lacey saw

the look.

"Don't be a lookin' evil eye at Sweeney, Buell. I'd have picked 'er up if'n he hadn't. Shit fire, that boy was jist pokin' at you a bit, and ya cain't be bracin' a feller for smilin' atcha. I thought it were funny too. Thought you was gonna choke fer sure."

Simon's breathing slowed as the tenseness in Buell's face left like it was being poured out.

He turned to Simon and grinned. "That was some nasty shit. You were smart to have the beer." He picked up his mug, and Lacey's frown stopped him short. He chuckled. "I wasn't gonna do nothing, Lacey. Just seeing how far he'd go."

The cowboys crowded back to the bar, retrieved their beer mugs, and, to a man, drained them, then looked up the bar for the barman. The incident just past seemed to be forgotten, or maybe conveniently ignored, but it was obvious to Simon that all the men, except Lacey, kept just a tiny fraction of extra space between themselves and Buell.

John and Paul arrived about an hour later and, as a group again, they headed for Carlisle. The cowboys seemed pleased to have the job behind them, a payday coming up tomorrow, and with eight thousand dollars in US Army gold safely tucked in his saddlebags, Paul's lively chatter with them showed his buoyant spirits. John, satisfied to see his friend take a monumental step toward economic freedom, smiled to himself, and the happy crew rode into town just before midnight.

CHAPTER 28

Paul chased the dollar figures around on the paper lying on the kitchen table. He owed Avery Singer thirty-two hundred plus three percent interest for ninety days. The herders had earned twenty dollars a month each for three months and he was going to give Nathan a hundred-dollar bonus on top of his monthly thirty-five dollars. Mace had two hundred and ninety dollars coming for the prairie camper, and the boys were going to get fifteen dollars each for their help in the spring and on the drive to the fort. And last, John needed a broker's fee for arranging the cattle in the first place. He resolved to talk to him later that day.

All told, Paul had over four thousand dollars clear and still owned one hundred and forty-four head of prime beef. Several people had approached him with offers, and Ledbetter, the sutler, had said if he couldn't get sixteen dollars a head in Carlisle, he'd be happy to take them. He had contemplated these figures before, but as he sat and stared at two money pouches, he realized that for the first time in his life he could provide for his family the way he wanted to. His throat grew tight and it ached to swallow as he looked across the table at Ana. She smiled at him, and her face seemed to glow.

Paul, Mace and John sat at their regular table in Luger's, the place alive with activity. Twice the usual number of people milled around, talking, laughing and generally having a good time. Word of the sale of the herd had spread like the news of a fallen preacher, and everybody gathered to congratulate Paul, and drink the free beer he was buying. Most were genuinely pleased that Paul's long years of hard work and honest dealings had finally paid off.

"How's it feel to be famous, Mr. Cattle Baron?" Mace teased. "Reckon he'll still have time for us now, John?" He took a big bite of his sandwich.

Even John had ordered a beer and sipped it slowly. Paul didn't think his stomach would handle food, much less alcohol, so he drank a root beer.

Avery Singer came through the door, and

immediately made his way to their table. "Congratulations, Paul. The whole town is buzzing about your deal. I'm glad to be a part of it." He stuck his hand out and Paul shook it. "Mind if I join you?"

"Not at all. Can I buy you a beer?" Paul felt slightly ill at ease, but curious, because Avery had never attempted to socialize and here he was doing it publicly.

"No, never touch the stuff, and it's way too early for a whiskey. Thanks anyway."

"I guess I should come by and settle up," Paul said. "Gonna be in your office after noon?"

"Sure. No hurry though, I'm making interest, so the longer you keep it, the less you get to keep." He let out four or five short, high, nasal, coughing barks that ended with a stuttering intake of breath. That was Avery's laugh. He looked around to see who else had appreciated it, and his wide smile faded a little at the neutral faces looking back. He cleared his throat, and scooted his chair closer to the table. "Gonna do this again?"

"I really don't know," Paul replied. "Obviously, it turned out this time, but there are a lot of things that can go foul. With the South whipped, the army will no doubt move from the state militias to the regular army for manning the forts out here. The politics that could come with the change make dealing next year an iffy situation. I got along real good with the captain I dealt with at Fort Hartwell, but there's no sayin' he'll still be there."

Avery nodded, his eyes full of interest.

"And then there's the blockade. With that gone, will there still be cattle available in Kansas and along the Mississippi? And can I get as good a man as Nathan Greene to trail a herd up here for me, and take the care that he did? Lot of things to consider. And if I can —" Out of the corner of his eye, Paul finally noticed an exasperated John, who quickly put his forefinger to his lips and then down again.

"I can see a lot of thinking before I do anything," Paul finished lamely.

"Rightly so, Paul, rightly so." Avery glanced at John. "Well, if you decide to do something, let me know. Your credit is sterling. Better be getting back. Just wanted to offer congratulations."

Avery got up and left the saloon.

"What in hell did he want?" Mace asked. "He wouldn't give you the time of day this spring unless you rented the clock."

"Money," John said, "always the money. And Avery is an expert at wheedling information. It's his stock in trade. The sooner he knows which way a deal might be going, the sooner he can influence the players. A word of advice to both of you. Avery is smart as a whip, and completely devoid of character or integrity."

"Can't be anybody completely without character, can there?" Paul said. "I have a hard time believing that. Surely some things affect him."

"Only if it interferes with what he has planned. Mark my word, he's ruthless. I know this for a fact. Terrible indictment, but true just the same."

Paul saw the seriousness on John's face and it took some of the pace off the celebration.

"I better get going too," Mace said. "Got two horses that need shoes all around. Gonna be a busy afternoon for me. I'll see you two later." He stood and covered a thunderous burp with his hand.

"Don't work too hard." Paul nodded as Mace left, then turned back to John. "And speaking of work, have you thought about your broker's fee? I'd like to get that settled. Wouldn't any of this have happened without your thinking. I expect you can name your price," Paul said seriously.

An odd look came over John's face. Indecision, and something that could be seen as slight panic, changed his whole demeanor. He leaned across the table and looked at Paul intently. "I have something I want you to do for me. Do it, and we'll call us square."

"Anything, John, anything at all," Paul said, slightly shaken by the lost and confused look that suddenly clouded his friend's face.

"I simply want you to listen to a story. My story," John said, his face almost glum.

"Sure. What is it?"

"Don't be too quick. I'm going to share a burden that nearly killed me and you may think it more than you want to carry. I wouldn't think less of you if you decided not to."

"You're my friend, and I want to help."

"All right, but not here. Can you come by after supper . . . come by the Brays'?"

"Sure, John. That would be fine. Any particular time?"

"Make it eight. Thanks, Paul. I'm going to leave now. I have some thinking to do. I'll see you tonight."

John rose slowly and headed out of the saloon. When he got to the door, he turned and gave Paul a half smile and a slight nod.

"Good job, Paul." Alex Prosser, the telegrapher, stood by the table.

Paul started. "Why, thank you. Took a lot of good people." His eyes glanced upward. "And more than a little help from Him."

Prosser took a half step away, and then hesitated ever so slightly, as though he wanted to say something else. "Yeah, good job," he said, almost absently. Then he clapped Paul on the shoulder, and crossed to the bar where Fred stood pumping beer as fast as he could.

Paul stayed another hour or so and then went across the street to settle with Avery. John's warning rang in his head as he entered the office.

Shortly after the hour, Mrs. Bray answered Paul's knock. "Good evening Mr. Steele. My, aren't you the talk of the town?"

Mrs. Bray was always cheerful and had a kind word for everybody. Paul liked her, as did most people. He took off his hat. "It's nice to see you. Ana and I are blessed, no doubt. Is John in?"

"Yes. He said to expect you, and asked you to come up to his room. You know where it is." She stepped back and nodded an invitation to enter.

"Thank you." He climbed the stairs and knocked on John's door, which opened almost instantly.

"Hello, Paul. Thank you for coming."

The room, tidy and comfortable-looking, held, besides the large bed, a wardrobe cabinet, a writing desk near the window, and set across from the bed, two stuffed chairs with a small table between. John indicated one of the chairs. "Please, sit down."

Paul put his hat down beside the chair and sat.

John took the other chair, and without making eye contact, inhaled deeply and started to speak. "I'm a lawyer. Leastwise I was. I practiced in New York and New Jersey with a very successful office. We were three partners and five associates. We did work primarily for the federal government. At times, we took on private cases as well, when we felt it appropriate. There was, at the time I'm speaking of, a rather celebrated case, at least locally. It involved a question of slave ownership." John closed his eyes for a moment and took another deep breath. When he opened his eyes he looked right at Paul and continued. "The plaintiff, a farmer from Delaware, was having a hard time enforcing his right to a family of seven slaves who had found their way to New Jersey. This was about fifteen years ago, right after the Fugitive Act was signed into law. Apparently, the owner was well-connected, because a state judge in New Jersey had me appointed to present his case. I am not an advocate of slavery. I think it's wrong in every respect, but I was also devoted to the law, and this farmer had been denied due process. I traveled to the small town of Busey to present his case."

Again John stopped. His hands trembled slightly and he took them off the table and folded them in his lap. "It's hard to tell this story, Paul. I'm not sure I can."

"Then, don't. If you've changed your mind and want to keep it private, I'd understand."

"It's not what I want to do. It's what I have to do. I need to purge this demon, and this is the only way left. I've tried alcohol, hiding, prayer, and denial. So far nothing has done it. I've looked a long time for someone I can trust, and it's time I had it out. You can still opt out. It's not a pretty story."

Paul shook his head and folded his arms across his chest.

"The trial was very straightforward. The judge knew the law, and I simply presented the facts. The defendant was a Methodist minister who had allowed the runaway slave family to stay in the rectory. His appeal was to common decency and charity. He wasn't even represented by counsel. He produced the seven people, a man and his wife, four children and a grandmother, the woman's mother. They were not allowed to bear testimony. They just stood huddled in front of the judge, terrified. The judge asked one question of the reverend. *Were the slaves his?* He asked the farmer the same question. When the farmer produced a bill of sale from Charleston, the judgment was immediate, and for the farmer. He ordered the marshal to escort the farmer and the family back to Delaware."

"You did what you saw as your duty. Nothing wrong with that. I don't hold with slavery, either."

"If that was all I felt responsible for, it would be a lot easier. There's more."

John's eyes glazed over with tears. He shut them and bowed his head. Paul felt the urge to reach across the small table and touch him, but sat still. John looked up, wiped his eyes with the back of his hand and then breathed slowly and deliberately for a few seconds.

"The farmer asked that I make the short trip with him across the river to Delaware. He said he wanted me to see that the lives of the slaves were not as portrayed by the

good reverend. I was also interested in seeing the conditions, because even with that
brief encounter in the courtroom, I felt a
bond with that unfortunate family. So I
agreed. We left immediately, ferried across
the river, and arrived at the plantation about
five that evening. He had fifty or more
slaves, living in rows of . . . well, you
couldn't call them houses. They were more
like sheds, no door or windows, one against
the next, all the same, except one toward
the end. It had been smashed flat. He told
me that was where the runaways had lived,
and he had destroyed it and everything they
called home with it. The slaves were taken
to what looked to be the smokehouse where
he said they would stay until he could make
other arrangements. He admitted it had
been foolish to destroy the property, but it
had been the overseer who had actually
done it. I was invited to stay the night with
the suggestion that we could maybe get to
know each other a little better. I saw no
harm. He seemed a reasonable man, and I
thought I might learn something about the
pro-slavery point of view."

He paused again and Paul could see that
he was reliving a painful event. His creased
brow twitched, and the muscles in his jaw
flexed as he clenched his teeth.

"We did, in fact, have a rather pleasant meal. His wife joined us. Neither of us had the least influence on the other's attitude regarding slavery. He saw it as a property issue, the same as owning a herd of dairy cows. Several times, he stressed his point about the need for lessons to be learned from 'unfortunate incidents like runaways,' as he put it. I thought he was talking about the legal issue. I went to bed about eleven."

John got up and walked to the window. He stood there and stared out into the darkness, his hand clasped behind his back. Paul watched the even rise and fall of his shoulders as he breathed slowly and deliberately. When John turned around, his eyes held no focus.

"I went to bed about eleven," he repeated, his voice flat and monotone. "I woke to shouting, lots of shouting, and then an incredibly high-pitched scream. I couldn't imagine it was human. I bolted out of bed, and ran to the open window. Across the yard burned a huge fire and lots of people were running around, some carrying buckets."

He stopped. Slowly his legs gave way, and his back slid down the wall, to leave him sitting on the floor.

"I put on my trousers and boots and ran downstairs, out into the night. The owner stood on the verandah, watching. I hollered at him to help, but he just looked at me with a smile. 'Lessons, my Yankee friend, lessons. And more to come.' Then he went back into the house. I ran over to help and could get only close enough to see the door was chained shut. The screaming from within was beyond imagination. I will never forget it. Mercifully, it lasted only a short time. I found my horse and left in my nightshirt."

His head sank to his chest and he started to cry. Sagging sideways, he buried his face in the crook of his arm and sobbed, his chest heaving as he drew deep gasps of air. Paul knelt beside him and laid his hand on his shoulder. Slowly the quaking subsided.

"Leave me now, Paul. I'll be all right. I just need to be alone."

"You sure?"

"I'm sure. The devil is beaten. I'll be okay."

Paul stood, paused for a moment, and then said, "I'm sorry, John. I can't find anything to say. I'll go." He picked up his hat, opened the door and when he turned to look once more, John sat up and leaned his head against the wall. His face, now calm and relaxed, offered Paul a half smile, and he nodded. Paul stepped through the door and closed it softly.

CHAPTER 29

"I've decided to do it again, Ma," Paul said. They were sitting outside on the bench by the house having a late cup of coffee. The children were in the soddy, Simon tutoring the younger ones in their schoolwork.

"I don't see any reason why not," Ana said. "From what you told me, that officer at the fort — Captain Atkinson? — said you'd have no problem selling another herd."

"Atkins. And you're right, he was really pleased. Nathan and his men are still in town. He said he'd be happy to go back to Kansas and arrange another herd for me. All the guys except Sweeney are willing to stay there through the winter. But I have to let 'em know in the next couple days. Big difference between traveling back to Kansas and traveling to Texas."

"I think we should do it. Last time we took the risk of losing this place, but now you can finance the whole thing yourself. I think we were meant to have this, I really do."

"Okay, that's settled. I was hoping you'd see it that way. Now, I have something else I want you to help me with." Paul grinned at her. "Thinking about a surprise."

"Sometimes your surprises are real surprises. I remember that huge load of lumber you dropped off in front of the house one year."

"Well, it ain't far from that. Ana, let's build a proper house."

Her hands went to her mouth as her eyes filled with tears. "Oh, Paul, do you think so? Do you really think so?"

She got up from the bench, and moved to stand in front of him for a few seconds. Then, smiling through her tears, she wrapped her arms around his neck and sat on his lap. Weeping quietly on his shoulder, she thoroughly wet his neck with her joy.

Paul rocked her gently and patted her back. "I think so, Ma. You've had it coming for a long time, and now I can provide it. I'll go see Lincoln Pratt and find out how much of what I need he has on hand. It's possible we could be well on our way before winter sets in."

■ ■ ■ ■

As soon as Paul and Ana had decided to build the house, Ana got in touch with Ruth and Irene Kingsley. It took them only a week to come up with a plan. The shaped-stone foundation of the new house was set west of the soddy, upwind of the chicken farm.

Ana, Ruth, and Irene busily poured over dozens of catalogs Mr. Swartz had lent them. They looked at pictures and descriptions of furniture, lamps, rugs, drapery and curtains, wallpaper and paint, and stoves. They examined the pictures in minute detail, discarding items for deficiencies that a male could not fathom, while choosing others for reasons even more obscure.

Paul hired three men to work full-time framing and sheathing the walls and building the roof. With the window glass due in two weeks, and the shingles shortly thereafter, they stood a good chance of having the house enclosed before the snow flew. This would allow Paul to work all winter on the interior. Everything seemed to be going their way.

Mace faced his son across the supper table.

"You got to let me know when you're comin' and goin' Buell. I heard you come in last night and it must've been two o'clock."

"I know, Pa. I didn't mean to be out that late. I got out in the prairie and kinda lost track of everything."

"Well, whatcha doing out there anyway?" Mace hoped this might be one of those rare times his son would talk to him.

"I was sat on a low rise west of town looking and wondering what was going on in all the houses. It's so quiet out there." Buell offered a sad smile. "I can let my mind do what it wants."

"So, what exactly do you think about?" Mace felt both encouraged and surprised at the flow of conversation.

"Depends on what I see. I watched two soldiers ride back toward Fort Hartwell. I saw a lady on horseback west of town heading toward the river. A while later, a feller east of town rode off in the same direction. They come back about two hours later, only this time they switched ends of town, and again, about fifteen minutes apart. So I try to imagine what they're doing, what their lives are like. Why are they sneaking around? I wonder where the soldiers are from. Stuff like that."

"Are you lonely, Buell?"

His son looked past him for a few seconds before answering. "I don't think lonely is the right word. I feel alone, but not lonely, and I hate God for what he did to my mother."

Mace's scalp contracted. It had been years since he'd mentioned Pearl, remembering the pain he'd seen in the boy's face last time he had.

"Sure, I see Simon's ma and I wish I had someone like her, but you're ever bit as good a pa as Simon's, so I consider myself lucky."

They looked at each other, and Mace, for the first time ever, saw love in his son's eyes. "Why haven't you talked to me like this before? I didn't know you had this many words in you."

"Just cuz I don't talk much don't mean I don't think about things, or I don't care about you. I have a lot of talks in my head. That's what I do on the prairie and down by the river. Sometimes Simon and I spend a whole afternoon down there and don't say two dozen words to each other. But that don't mean we ain't talking. See what I mean?"

"I can't really say I do. I'm the kinda feller that has to talk all the time. I'd go nuts if I didn't have people comin' and goin' all day. But I see that you can get along without it. You and Simon get on fine, and that Texan, Lacey, he took to you right off. Sometimes I worry that I'm not doin' all I can for you, and I want you to know it ain't cuz I don't care. Sometimes, I just don't know how."

"I know, Pa. I'll try to let you know when I'm going off, but if I don't, don't worry too much. I ain't gone far. And I want you to know I really appreciate you not hounding me about my pistol. Somehow, it makes me feel less alone."

"Didn't see no point. You've growed faster than I could keep up with. You know a lot more than I did at your age, and I feel somehow you'll sort things out. Just remember, you always have me, and you have a real friend in Simon. And let me tell you, Buell, friends, real friends, are rare, and if you take them for granted, you'll lose them for sure." He paused and studied his son. "So." Mace suddenly ran out of words and reached across the table to lay his rough hand on Buell's. He gave it a squeeze. "I love you, son, never forget that."

"Thanks, Pa."

The comfortable hush settled around them, a feeling of security brought by understanding, and Mace realized that anything else said at the moment would destroy a connection only rarely made between him and his son. The supper meal lay cold and forgotten, but Mace felt completely satisfied, and for the first time in his life drew strength from the silence.

CHAPTER 30

Carlisle finally shook off winter's grip, and though April seventh of 1866 dawned clear and cold, the morning sky promised a warmer day. A few patches of snow could still be found in sheltered spots on the river bluffs, but you had to search for them. The sight of completely bare earth rejuvenated Paul, and he paused on his way to the soddy, the fresh milk in the bucket wafting wisps of steam into the still air.

He studied the low roof and weathered boards of the sod house and smiled. He and Ana had raised five children in that tiny place and now, soon, they would move everything in there to the new house across the field. Paul couldn't see all of it for the chicken coops, but there it stood, overlooking the Platte River, clear wood still awaiting the first coat of paint, but finished. He and another man had worked all winter on it. He continued on to the house and pushed the door open.

"Gonna be a beauty today," he said cheerfully.

Ana stood by the stove, scooping cooked oatmeal into bowls. The children all sat around the table watching their mother get breakfast. Simon, typical for a morning, browsed a book.

"I hear school will be out for the summer in two weeks, Simon. Ready to go back to work?" Paul asked.

School lasted as long as the children were not needed for working in the spring. As soon as the local farmers could get on the ground, school was adjourned by consensus.

"Not really," Simon said. "I do nothing all day but help teach this rabble and their friends." He punched Axel on the arm but missed Abel when his brother scooted away.

Miss Everett had told Paul that Simon was a natural teacher, and she relied on him to teach the older children while she helped the young ones get started. She had high hopes for him, and had finally convinced Judge Kingsley to allow Simon to use some of his books and references. Paul knew Simon had already spent several limited sessions in the judge's library. Limited, because Mr. Swartz still demanded most of Simon's free time. The judge had set up a small table

352

and a comfortable chair for him, and had told Simon he required only three things: to put everything back where he found it, to leave when the judge was there, and to write down the title of the books he used. The judge kept the list.

Alex Prosser looked up as Matt entered the telegraph office.

"You have anything for me?" Matt demanded brusquely.

"Yes'ir. Got it about an hour ago." Alex shuffled through six or seven sheets of paper. "Here it is." Matt took the telegram and Alex watched him read the short message. He didn't miss the sharp look Matt gave him.

"I needn't tell you to keep this to yourself," Matt said.

Alex saw the pleased look on Matt's face and averted his eyes, fully aware of the color rising in his face.

"Good." Matt left, slamming the door.

Simon strode along the road toward the Kingsleys'. The judge had read Simon a short piece out of a book and suggested if Simon had found it interesting, he might want to read it next. Simon had indeed found it interesting. Written by a man named Goethe, he'd told Mr. Swartz about it that morning, and the storekeeper told Simon he could take off early and go read some of it. It seemed Mr. Swartz was very fond of the same author.

Mrs. Kingsley answered his knock on the door. "Hello, Simon. Come to visit, or have you come to read?"

He noticed right off that she smelled wonderful, violet he guessed. "I want to use the library, if that's all right, ma'am." Dampness started to form under his arms.

"Of course. The judge is out, playing cards, so you have full and free access. You know where it is." She stepped back to let him in, but not quite enough, her bosom lightly brushing his shoulder as he slid by. Mortified, his ears on fire, the walk across the parlor to the library took forever, and he felt her eyes bore into his back.

"Thank you, ma'am," he said as he opened the door and escaped into the wonderful smell of the room. The judge had left the copy of *Faust* on the table. Simon picked it up, sat down in his chair and began to read.

Simon's thoughts swirled like a dust devil. Every time he thought he understood what he'd read, another few lines would force him to reassess what he'd just learned. Why had the judge given him this book to read?

The short passage he had heard the other night had been simple to understand: "What you don't feel, you will not grasp by art, unless it wells out of your soul." He thought that meant you can't fake what or who you truly are. But what he read today simple confused him. He began to wonder if this might be like the Greeks Miss Everett had helped him read. Maybe the meanings would come later. He marked the page and rested the closed book on his chest.

The door opened and Mrs. Kingsley halfway entered the room. "I'm going over to Mrs. Bray's for a couple of hours, Simon. Feel free to stay." And she was gone as quickly as she had appeared.

The front door closed, and he relaxed in the silence of the library; the steady tock-tock of the tall-cased clock rippled the stillness of the room. The steady cadence encouraged his mind to wander, and he sat quietly in the chair, completely disengaged. Until he felt nature's urge.

"Damn it," he thought. And then: *"Damn it, I'm swearing more and more. Dern it!"*

He got out of the chair, laid the book on the table where he'd found it, then opened the door and listened. Hearing nothing, he stepped out of the library and headed across the room toward the kitchen and the back door leading to the privy.

The sight of naked skin jerked him to a halt, mouth open and heart hammering in his chest. Sarah, in the warmth of the kitchen, reclined in a big copper tub, eyes closed, arms extended beside her, giving him a full frontal view through the door that stood a quarter open. The waterline crossed just over the tops of her nipples, and the cloudy water masked everything below. Swallowing hard, he fought to do what he knew was right, but he wanted so badly to stay. The fear-of-getting-caught puritan fought a fierce battle with the desire-to-gaze-at-her rogue, and the rogue won. With the kitchen lamps turned full bright and the parlor in semidarkness, he felt sure she couldn't see him. So he watched, fascinated.

The back of her neck must have itched because she lifted one hand from the water to scratch and — there! A full breast, but so unlike the one at Adobe. Firm and small, the nipple reacted instantly to being taken from the warm water. The jaw-dropping image lasted but a moment. Her hand slowly descended into the water again, along with that gorgeous breast. Without knowing it, Simon had risen on the tips of his toes, craning his neck, willing that pink-brown wonder to stay exposed, but as it sank, so did his heels. How long did he dare stand there? Mrs. Kingsley could return early. He remembered his last look at the clock, it wasn't quite seven. "She'll be a while yet," his gazing rogue argued.

Then Sarah's eyes popped open and she took a long, deep breath, stretching her arms over her head. Both breasts burst into full view and each seemed to compete for elevation. Simon groaned, and then slapped his hand over his mouth, frantically looking to see if she had heard. She hadn't, because she reached over the side of the tub and caught the edge of a towel. Knowing what must come next, Simon shot a glance at the front door and steeled himself for the grand prize. Sarah stood.

Simon could not compare the sheen of her body to anything he'd ever seen before as the water sought to return to the tub. He'd passed into a new realm, crossed a frontier. The warm yellow cast of the lamplight made her skin the color of honey. Nipples erect in the cooler air, she stood for a moment and ran her hands down her body, wiping off the excess water. Then she looked toward the door and directly at Simon. He stopped breathing, and his eyes opened so wide they stung as he waited for the flash of recognition. It never came.

He inhaled a quivering gasp of air and a cold sweat crept over his scalp. She looked away, and with her gaze on the floor, stepped out of the tub and stood on a small rug, the towel held against her side. She raised a leg to place a foot on the short stool sitting at the end of the tub, and dried; first her foot, then her calf, and finally, putting her leg down again, her thigh. The towel flashed between her legs, and he tried to imagine what he couldn't see. She repeated the ballet for her other leg, then, towel slung over her shoulders, she used the ends to dry her belly and chest. Shrugging the towel off, she dried her rear and then, with a flourish, she launched the towel out of sight. Turning her back to him, she reached to the left and retrieved a large fluffy ball and daubed her body with it, powder puffing into the air.

Simon's gaze moved to the curve of her hips. On the left one, a scarlet, teardrop-shaped birthmark, the narrow end pointed down, beckoned to him, and he had the insane urge to rush in and kiss it. His hard got even harder and he suppressed a groan. Suddenly, Sarah took two quick steps forward and disappeared. With a whimper, Simon turned, and as fast as he dared move, scurried out of the house.

■ ■ ■ ■

Simon sat in Mace's chair. He'd been studying Buell's relaxed face for several minutes,
and couldn't decide if he was sleeping or
not. He decided not. "Have you ever seen it
up close," he asked.

"Sure." Buell wrinkled his nose, and then
rubbed it. His eyes never opened.

"Well . . . where?"

"Adobe. Last year."

"Well, did you just look?" Simon couldn't
keep the irritation out of his voice. *Can't he
construct a sentence over three words long?*

Buell opened his eyes and grinned at him.
"Nope. Lacey said I ought to do it just to
see if I liked it. He reckoned it was like trying one of them new mixed drinks at the
saloon. Ya pay yer money, and if it don't
suit yer fancy, ya don't have to order it
again." Buell's eyes shut again.

"And?" Simon waited. "Well, you gonna
tell me or not? Shit, it's not a big secret."

"Then why you askin'?" The quick smile
and the crinkled eyes said Buell was having
a good time.

"I saw Sarah . . . last week when I was at
the Kingsleys' reading. I can't get it out of
my mind. It was the most beautiful thing

359

I've ever seen."

"Whoa." Buell sat up from his slouched position in his chair. "Naked?"

"Yup. Bathing. I wanted to touch her so bad." Simon looked at his friend, slightly embarrassed, but still at ease telling Buell about Sarah. "She has a birthmark on her butt." Simon felt himself blush. "Looks like a teardrop."

"Boy, you got a case of it. I suppose I can see someone gettin' a little worked up about it, but from what I've experienced, it ain't worth much. Now, not sayin' anything against Sarah, I like her a lot. She's yer girlfriend and that makes 'er special to me. But I don't see myself getting all wrapped up in it. Pa gets along fine without a woman, so I expect I will too."

"Well, what's it like? Even if you don't want anyone special."

"Just like your hand, only it costs you three dollars. Shit, Simon, I can't describe it. You lay on her and she sticks it in for you and you wait until she makes it happen."

"But —"

"That's all there is to it, Simon." The familiar mask dropped over Buell's face.

Simon let out an exasperated puff, slumped back in his chair, and let his daydream jump back to Sarah — naked.

CHAPTER 31

Ruth struggled to control her anger. Matt's foul mood seemed worse than usual of late. He stood facing her across the kitchen table.

"I can't afford to send him anywhere. What school he needs he can get right here." Matt scoffed. "And when I need your advice, I'll ask."

"But we planned that he should go to Pennsylvania to school. What happened to the money?" Ruth demanded.

"Don't you question what I do with the money." He scowled at her. "It's mine, and I'll do with it as I please. As for that lazy pup, he can earn what he needs, either here on the farm, or he can get a job somewhere else. It's time he pulled his own weight."

"Your father explicitly set up an account to send all his grandchildren to school. I know it, you know it, and so does Avery. I wonder what Paul and Ana would think about it?" Ruth pushed her chair back and stood, glaring at him.

"You say a word, and I'll beat you till you can't see straight. Do you hear me?" He stepped around the table and stood directly in front of her. "Do you?"

She had never before felt in danger of being hit by Matt, but the murderous look in his eyes now shocked her. "Yes," she whispered.

"You keep your nose out of the money matters, that's final." He grabbed his hat and slammed out of the back door.

She heard his horse lunge into a gallop as he headed for town. *Lancer's Saloon, no doubt. Oh, Ana, what am I going to do? My life is crumbling.* She sat down and toyed nervously with her coffee cup.

Simon looked at his parents across the kitchen table. "I find it hard to believe you're taking Mr. Swartz's side." His gaze went first to his father and then his mother as he searched for support. "He promised to pay, and now he's putting me off again."

"I talked to him about it yesterday," his father said. "He says he simply can't afford it right now. He has a lot of money tied up in supplies for the upcoming wagon-train season and paying you right now would be, well — not impossible, but inconvenient.

He was very pleasant about it, more like he was asking than telling me, and I have to agree with him. You don't need the money right now."

"But I *know* how much money he has, and the sixty-seven dollars he owes me won't strain his account one bit. He owes it to me. I'm sorry, but can't you see that?"

"We can see that," Ana said, "but you have to realize that helping a neighbor is what makes having neighbors worthwhile. The help comes back one day. I know he owes it to you, and he does too. He's not denying that. He has obligations you may not know about. He's just asking you to hold off a little."

"But I know how he works. Every day he finds some way to dock my pay a little. I hate to say it, but I'm afraid he'll try to get out of paying the bonus at all."

"Don't be silly," Ana said. "He wouldn't cheat you. I've never heard of him cheating anyone. Sometimes his prices seem a little high, but never cheating."

Paul shook his head. "I still have to try to see his side. You're a youngster who has no need for that money right now. He does. I hate to deny you because I can see your point, but I have to side with Gus. He'll pay you, don't worry about that, but not until later."

"And that's exactly what he said last year, and I didn't see an extra dime." He knew the point was hard to refute.

Paul paused. "We'll compromise. Give him until the middle of June. By then, he should have sold enough to the wagons to recoup some of his costs. Sound fair?"

Simon shrugged. "Yes'ir. I'll wait."

Paul, Mace, Buell, and Simon sat eating their lunch when Alex Prosser hurried into the saloon and found them. He walked up and handed Paul a telegram. "Just came for you, and I thought you might want to see it right off."

"Why, thank you Alex. Appreciate the service." Prosser didn't personally deliver messages as they come in. His job required only that he be available to receive and send messages from eight to six and allowed him an hour for lunch at precisely twelve noon. Toward the end of the day, he'd send his helper to deliver the telegrams around town. Paul glanced at the wall clock. It read three minutes after twelve noon. Service indeed. "Can I buy you a beer?"

"Thanks, but no. I have to get on home. Beth expects me, and she'll have something fixed." He nodded at Mace and turned to go.

"Well, thanks again, Alex."

"No problem and good luck." He gave Paul a conspiratorial wink and left.

Mace stared at the folded yellow form. "Is that what I think it is?"

"Probably." Paul took another big bite of his sandwich and chewed slowly for several seconds before winking at Buell.

Mace sat quietly and looked at him, but when Paul made to take another bite, he burst out: "Well, dammit, you gonna look or not."

Paul reached for the pickle on his plate, gave Mace a wide smile and bit it.

"Shit, I'm gonna go back to work," Mace said with a snort. He got up, shoving his chair away, nearly tipping it over. But he didn't step away from the table.

Paul, still chewing, handed Mace the telegraph and nodded. "Uopemmit," he muttered around a mouthful of dill pickle.

Mace sat down, unfolded the paper and read the message, a grin spreading from ear to ear. "It's for you." His face colored as everyone's eyebrows rose. "Nathan's on his way. Six hundred and twenty-seven cows. Greetings to John and me."

"Well, that was worth waiting for, wasn't

it, Mace?" Paul smiled at his friend.

"Always gotta play the clown. I shoulda just took the damn thing and left. That woulda fixed ya."

"But you didn't. Opened it like a schoolgirl with a valentine."

"To hell with you." Mace's grumpiness did not follow through.

"Lacey coming?" Buell asked.

Mace looked at him. "It don't say who's with him, just that they're leaving in the morning. Hope so. You and him got to be pretty good friends. I hope they all come."

"Me too," Paul said. "They were a real good bunch. Sure took good care of those cows last year. Well, that starts the creek flooding. I better go see Avery. Simon, I want you to come along." Paul picked up the last bit of his sandwich, pushed it into his mouth, and, with a nod to Fred, he and Simon left the saloon.

Simon and his father stopped by the trading store to tell Mr. Swartz that he would be a little late coming back from lunch.

"Well, it's no pay you get for not doing the work." Swartz shook his head like Simon had just announced he was quitting. "I will manage."

"Thank you, Gus," Paul said. "I'll have

him back in short order."

Simon shot his father a see-what-I-mean look, and they left the store for Avery's office. When they walked in, they found him busy with something in his file cabinet, his back to the door.

He turned when they stepped into the room. "Paul. Kinda been expecting you. Get your message?"

"How'd you know I got a message?"

"Saw Alex Prosser hotfootin' over to Luger's about an hour ago. Figgered it might be news about your cows. From the look on your face, I think I'm right."

The smug look obviously irritated Simon's father.

Avery saw it too. "It's my business to second-guess, Paul. No offense meant. Just tickles me when I get it right." He gave Paul a golden smile.

"None taken. But most people hate it when you're right."

Simon looked at his father, astonished. Avery's jaw dropped.

"I'm sorry, Avery, that didn't sound like I meant. It's just a little unsettling when you do that."

"I see what you mean. Apology accepted. I'll try to remember not to be so direct next time." He gave Paul another grin. "So, what can we do for Simon?"

His father's eyebrows shot up. "What do you mean, for Simon?"

"I just did it again, didn't I? You brought him along deliberately. I saw you go into Swartz's. Two and two makes six." Another toothy smile.

"You're impossible," Paul said in an exasperated tone, and then he smiled. "I'd like you to show Simon the folder you have on Steele and Company. Also, the paper-work on the new house."

"No problem." Avery turned around and extracted two folders from the third drawer of his cabinet. "Steele & Co." emblazoned the front of one and "Loans, Short Term" on the other. He untied the first and looked at Simon. "Steele and Company is a firm founded by your father and John Lindstrom for the purpose of managing and directing the affairs that concern the poultry opera-tion on the family farm and, as of last year, your cattle enterprise. There are the original documents and agreements still in force, and copies of completed agreements and transactions. The originals of completed transactions are in the possession of your father. Any questions?" He looked at Paul and then Simon.

"Who can see what's in there?" Simon asked.

Avery pursed his lips, and then smiled. "Good question."

Simon had talked to Avery two or three times over the last six months about computing interest and compounding. He had suspected then that Avery thought the ideas were Mr. Swartz's. His look suggested he didn't believe that now.

"Your father, Mr. Lindstrom, and owners and operators of this bank, such as it is."

"Not my mother?"

"No. Unless your father was to die, heaven forbid, and then only by order of a probate court. Do you know what a probate court is?"

"Yes'ir. It's a court that adjudicates wills and such, or just a judge who rules when a will has not been filed."

Simon's father looked at Avery, then at him. "Where on earth did you learn that?"

His father looked proud, and that pleased Simon. "Judge Kingsley's library. Some of what he suggests I read gets tiresome, so sometimes I look at some of his law books. I just happened to know about probate."

"Well, you impressed the hell out of me," Avery said. "Excuse the cuss word. Anything else?"

Simon hesitated for a few seconds before looking at his father and then Avery. "Can we establish a proxy for Pa's interests? Something else I read. Judge Kingsley called it an attorney power or something like that."

"We can do that. Or rather I can have it done. Now, can I ask what made you think of that?"

"Ma and Pa talk a lot at night. I listen." Simon glanced at his father as a twinge of guilt flushed his conscience. "I don't mean to, but I've always used the sound of their voices to put me to sleep. I noticed Ma has lots of good ideas, but Pa is the only one who says yes or no. And it seemed to me that she should be able to do that too."

Avery's eyebrows went up as he listened, and Simon saw the look he gave his father; Avery wasn't sure how Paul was going to take this challenge to his supremacy. Simon never had a doubt.

"I think he's absolutely right," Paul said. "I hadn't given that any thought. You do what's needed to set that attorney power up."

"Dare I ask if you want to know anything else?" The wide smile was directed at Simon this time.

"No, sir. Thank you." Simon sensed Avery was not quite as thrilled as he seemed to be about giving a sixteen-year-old boy that kind of information.

"So." Avery shrugged. "Do you remember what I told you about simple and compound interest?"

"Yes'ir."

"Good. Very good. Anything else I can do for you?"

"Nope. I just thought that Simon was old enough to know about my affairs. Seems he's more than ready." Paul looked at Simon proudly. "Let's get you back to the store." They got up and Paul extended his hand. "Thank you, Avery."

"My pleasure, as always." He took Paul's hand. "And Simon, you're welcome here anytime. I'd be pleased to teach you what I know about this business."

Avery watched them cross the street and disappear into the store. He felt like a fox that had just found a hole in the chicken fence.

Matt glowered as the telegrapher shook his head. "Nothing, Mr. Steele."

"Well, dammit, Prosser, send it again," Matt shouted, gone white around the mouth.

"I can, Mr. Steele, but you're wasting your

money. They acknowledged the first message. There's no doubt they got it."

"Then why haven't I heard back?"

Prosser had already told him the answer, but he repeated it, "Receipt at the distant end does not mean delivery to the addressee." Prosser blinked once, slowly. "Maybe the person you are addressing simply hasn't picked up the message yet. But sending it over will not do —"

"I heard you the first time. I'm not deaf or stupid. Dammit!" Matt turned and stomped out of the office, slamming the door and headed in the direction of Lancer's.

Prosser watched him storm off and a satisfied smile swept over his face as he opened the drawer and took out the week-old message. Addressed to Matthew Steele, Carlisle, Nebraska Territory, it was marked "URGENT." He put it back, well under the rest of the papers in the drawer and rocked back in his chair. With his feet propped up, and his ears in listen mode, he dozed off.

CHAPTER 32

The dust from six hundred cattle could be seen five miles away. Buell kicked his horse into an easy lope and headed for the livery.

"Looks like we got Texas company." He sat in his saddle, looking down at his father.

"You sure?" Mace stood outside the barn holding a dipper of water.

"Can't be wagons — too much dust. Gotta be the herd."

"Well, it's about right time-wise. Why don't you ride out, and if it is, swing back by Paul's place and tell him. The new house ain't set up on the bluff like their old one. He might not have seen 'em yet." Mace drank the rest of his water, and then raised the dipper to Buell. "Want some? I'll get it."

"Yeah, think I will."

Mace went back inside and came back with a quart jar of water.

Buell drank deeply and handed it back. "I'll see you in a couple hours." He reined his horse away from the livery and rode off.

Nathan sat on a low rise northwest of the herd thinking it was as good-looking as the one they'd trailed in last year. The cowboys began to circle the leaders, getting ready to bring the herd to a halt. Their steady, almost leisurely, pace made handling them easy. Then he spotted a rider heading straight at them and, instinctively, he spurred his horse on an intercept course. About a quarter mile away, he recognized Buell and reined in. He nearly had a smoke rolled by the time the youngster arrived.

"Howdy there, young pardner." He flashed a wide smile through the dust on his face. "Good to see you agin."

"Same here, Nathan . . . I mean, Mr. Greene." Buell turned his horse to stand side by side with the Texan, Buell's horse heaving for air.

"Nathan's fine, Buell. See'd us comin' did you?"

"Oh, yeah, you guys raise quite a trail. Is Lacey with you?"

"Sure nuff. And Quigg and Rafe and Griz, and would you believe it, Sweeney too. Old cuss jist couldn't stand it. Showed up about Feb'ry, damn near froze to death. Dumb ass." The smile on his face said Nathan was pleased to have all the cowboys back. "So, how's yer pa and the rest?" He sucked a long drag on his cigarette and squinted through the smoke.

"Pa's fine. Simon's pa built 'em a new house. Simon still works at the store."

"Be darned. New house."

Buell looked toward the herd and studied the riders. "Where's Lacey?"

"He's eatin' dust on the tail end, his turn at drag."

Buell leaned forward slightly, as if to move.

"Why don'tcha let that cayuse blow fer a bit?"

Buell sat back in his saddle. "Yes'ir, guess I run him kinda hard. Sorry."

"Tell him, not me," Nathan replied, nodding his head toward the horse. "So, do you know if'n we're gonna set this herd in the same place as last year?"

"I don't. I'm supposed to go tell Mr. Steele when I found out for sure it was you."

"Who else would it be?" He watched for Buell's reaction, unable to resist teasing.

"Well, nobody else, I guess. Pa just said come check."

"Hell's fire, even a sodbuster kin tell a cloud of trail dust, cain't they?"

Buell flushed a little as he conceded the point with a nod. He looked past Nathan again, at the herd and riders.

Nathan helped him out. "Why'nt ya ride over to the herd real slow-like and say howdy to the boys. I'll ride over t' see Paul. Where'd he build thet new house?"

"Just west of the old one, and a little closer to the river. Can't miss it."

"Them'r famous last words, but I'll do my best." He watched Buell walk his horse, now breathing much easier, toward the herd, and then urged his own into an easy canter toward the northwest.

The attractive house, facing south with a spacious porch across the front, stood two stories tall. Tan paint with two-tone blue trim made it apparent a woman had a hand in the design and decoration. Elegant scroll-work embellished the eaves with the pattern repeated under the porch rails. Nathan spotted Paul by a small building to the right of the house and rode over.

"Howdy, Paul." Nathan swung down from his saddle. "Real good to see ya." He pulled off his glove and extended his hand.

Paul had obviously heard him coming and stood waiting. "Hello, Nathan. Good to see you too. Better trip than last year?"

"Nary a tick, not so much as a burnt biscuit, but it'll feel damn good to wake up in the same place two days in a row, I kin tell ya that." He looked at the building Paul was working on, and then at the new house. "Ain't ya had enough nail-bendin'? From the look of it, you done pounded a few. Whatcha buildin' here?"

"Well, believe it or not, Ana wants a chicken coop. Says she wants fresh eggs when she needs 'em. Chicken farm not half a mile away, and she wants a coop. Between you and me, I think she just misses the sound of 'em. And she wants a place for a cow, too, so it looks like the horses will have to adjust to living with one. Got the herd camped on the river yet?" Paul settled his butt on a sawhorse.

"Nope. Didn't know if'n we had a right to it agin. They's circled up jist south, still on the prairie." Following Paul's lead, Nathan hunkered down on his heels.

"Oh, yeah, we have the rights. John filed homestead papers for us in Omaha last fall. Luger, Mace, John, and I have all claimed a quarter section about where we grazed last year. The claims are on alternate diagonal quarters in each section so we effectively control the two square miles that the cows seemed to favor. John thought it might be a good idea to lay claim, even though nobody else wanted it. Too steep and broken up for farming, but perfect for cows. If we decide not to keep it, we simply let the claim lapse, but until then, and that's five years, we can graze on it."

"From what I've see'd, you cain't go far wrong listenin' to thet feller."

"I agree. And he has Simon starting to think just like him."

"Saw Buell. He said Simon was still working at the store. How's the missus?"

"Everyone's fine. I spent the winter on the house. Would you drink a cup of coffee?" Paul pushed himself erect and looked toward the house.

"You bet. Don't reckon I'll allow myself into the house though. I smell like a goat and carry enough dirt to muddy up a crick." He banged his gloves on his thigh and the dust flew.

"Nonsense, you —"

"Ain't no arguing. I get to Luger's and have me a haircut and shave first, then I'll feel right about it."

Paul nodded and went into the house.

"Hello, Nathan. Welcome back to Carlisle." It was Ana, standing in the doorway of her new home, her pride obvious. She held a cup in her hand, steam wafting over the edge.

"Howdy, Miz Steele. Admirin' your new

house. It is a picture." He reached for the cup.

"Double measure of sugar if I remember right."

Nathan smiled. "Cain't get enough of the sweet." He felt a blush start as the nuance occurred to him. He studied his cup of coffee.

"Well, if you won't come in, at least sit on the steps with us," Paul said as he sat, leaving room for Ana.

Nathan joined them. "So you figgerin' on the same deal as last year, then? Want us to stay?"

"If you would. Did your crew come up again?"

"Sure did. Even old Sweeney. Got us a good cook too. Boys'll be jiggered to hear they got a summer job. Couple of 'em found sweethearts here." He slurped a mouthful of coffee and shut his eyes with pleasure. "Boy, Miz Steele, that there is fine coffee."

Half an hour later, Nathan headed back to the herd and Paul went into town to have Mace ready the prairie camper. They were back in the cow business.

CHAPTER 33

Captain Atkins sat at his desk while Matt leaned over it, his face florid. "What in hell do you mean it's not open for consideration?" Matt nearly shouted. "I saw in the Carlisle newspaper that the army was accepting proposals for a supply of beef cattle. I have them, and I want to sell them to the army."

"If you will take your seat, Mr. Steele." Atkins touched his thumb to his chin, blotting a speck of moisture Matt had deposited there. "The need has been satisfied. The contract let. The offer is not open for consideration." He fixed a steady gaze on the irate farmer.

"But I spent a lot of money. I've committed all I own to that herd. It will be here in less than three weeks. It would have been here sooner if not for some incompetent prat-sitter."

The farmer's voice was now level and

controlled, but Atkins could see the rage in his face. "Your personal affairs are not the concern of the US Army, Mr. Steele. I have already contracted to buy sufficient cattle to meet our needs."

"But that's not fair! I was not given a chance to make an offer. You bought them from my brother, didn't you? You do know Paul Steele is my brother?"

Atkins detected a different tone now, maybe panic or despair. "It was not a request for bids, Mr. Steele. It was a request for goods. Those goods, sufficient to meet our needs and whose standard of quality has been proven in past transactions, have been offered, and I have accepted, contractually. I am not at liberty to divulge our contractor's name until the contract is fulfilled. And yes, I am aware of your association with Mr. Paul Steele. I think our business is concluded. Sergeant, see that Mr. Steele finds his way out."

After Matt had been escorted out, he reached for the handkerchief inside his blouse pocket, withdrew it, and wiped his face in disgust.

Half asleep, his feet propped up on the desk, the sound of breaking glass startled Sheriff Staker. His boots slammed onto the floor and he sat straight up in his chair.

Matt stood just inside the open door. "I want you to arrest that son of a bitch across the street." He pointed over his shoulder.

"Whoa, whoa, Matt." The sheriff stood to come around his desk. "Who? Across where? Settle down."

"Prosser, Alex Prosser. He kept a vital telegraph from me, and because of that I stand to lose a lot of money. I want him arrested for . . . for . . . fraud or, or . . . shit, anything. I just want him in jail where he belongs." Matt paced back and forth between the sheriff and the door.

"First, a couple of rules," Staker said. "One, I'm not going to arrest anybody just because someone says so. And two, a judge decides who belongs in jail. Now settle down and take a seat. Tell me what you think happened, and I'll look into it." He indicated a chair, walked around behind his desk and sat. "Now, tell me."

"I bought and paid for a herd of Kansas cattle last fall. I paid men there to feed them all winter and then they were to trail them here this spring. The foreman was to telegraph me when they were ready to head west. I never got that telegram until Paul's herd was already here. Now Paul has sold his herd to the army and they don't need mine. I'm stuck with it. And Prosser did it on purpose. I know it."

"You don't know it. You charge it. I forgot rule number three: I find out who did what to who. I'll go talk to Alex. I'm sure his story will be a little different. As for your getting beat in a business deal, I'm not in the financial counseling business. Go see Avery Singer."

At the mention of Avery's name the blood left Matt's face. "Why should I go see Avery? Why'd you say that?" Matt had the look of a trapped coyote.

"Figure of speech, Matt. Financial counseling? Avery. He's a banker." Matt's reaction puzzled the sheriff. "I'll go talk to Alex and work this out. I want you to go on about your business. And stay away from Alex Prosser. You have a problem with him, I settle it, not you. Understand, Matt?" The sheriff stood.

"I don't expect justice here, Loren. Everybody knows you favor Paul and Mace, and they're both in on this. I'm not stupid. I can see what you're trying to do." Matt was on his feet again. His eyes flicked from side to side and he blinked furiously, looking slightly crazed. Turning on his heel, he abruptly left the office and turned right.

Staker watched him until he went into

Lancer's Saloon. Sighing, he picked up the coal bucket from beside the stove and went to the open door to pick up the broken glass.

Prosser rocked back in his chair and looked up at the sheriff. "I simply lost it for a few days. Some days I receive as many as twenty-five telegrams. I stack them in the order received and I give them to the addressee when they call for them, or the boy delivers 'em in the afternoon. Matt's simply fell off the back of the desk. I didn't see it until later."

"But the urgent type get special handling don't they? They pay more for it."

"That's right. I'm supposed to make an extra effort to make delivery. I do that."

"But you deliver some personally, don't you, urgent or not?"

"Not usually."

"Not usually, but you have done so, haven't you?"

"On occasion."

"When was the last time?"

"I don't recall, exactly."

"Would a peek at your log improve your memory?"

Prosser looked at the sheriff for a moment. A faint smile ghosted across his face, and then drifted away as he leaned forward. "I delivered a message to Paul Steele about two weeks ago. At Luger's. He was having lunch there. I delivered it on my lunch hour. It was convenient."

"Do you go to Luger's for lunch often?"

"Not often, but on occasion."

"And what was in that telegram?"

Prosser sat up straighter in his chair. "I won't divulge that to you or anyone. The contents are private, and Western Union stakes its reputation on that. So do I."

"You won't tell anybody what's in it, or who sent it, except the addressee?"

"That's right. And if I were forced to, the ramifications could be most unpleasant for all concerned." Prosser leaned back in his chair and folded his arms across his skinny chest.

Sheriff Staker left.

Avery tilted his chair as Matt slumped into the one opposite.

"We might have a problem, Avery," Matt stated flatly.

"I try to avoid the 'we' word, Matt. It's why bankers require collateral."

Avery knew why Matt was there. He had heard several days before about the heated exchange between Captain Atkins and Matt,

385

the accusation leveled at Prosser, and the result of the sheriff's investigation. And as usual, Avery's information was precise and current.

"I have the herd about two days out, and it seems the army doesn't need any beef this year," Matt said.

His shaded truth confirmed Avery's suspicion that Matt wasn't going to level with him. "But I saw a notice in the paper saying they did." He watched Matt closely. *How did he expect me not to see it?*

"They found another source," Matt sounded dejected.

"Paul's herd?"

"Yes, dammit. He and that crooked telegraph operator kept a telegram from me until Paul could get his herd here and make a deal with the army. They cut us out."

"Another word I like to avoid, Matt, is *us.*" Avery paused. "So, what are the options?"

"I can graze them right where Paul and those Texans have theirs. I have as much right to that ground as they do. I can slaughter the herd as I need to, for sale to the wagons this summer. Blake Waldon can do some, and I'll talk to Carl at the slaughterhouse about taking some."

"But Carl already has arrangements with

several people to do the same thing. So does Blake. I'm not sure that's viable."

"Well, you suggest something, then. We, and I mean we, Avery — you're in this fifty-fifty, remember — we better come up with something or we stand to lose it all."

"Actually, Matt, I'm not exposed on this. I sold my interest to Blake Waldon and Art Lancer last fall."

"You what?" Matt nearly shouted. The color bled from his face.

"I sold my share to those two. Your farm is collateral against the loan from the trust."

"Why?" Matt's eyes blinked rapidly.

"You said you weren't doing this for the money, Matt. A statement like that makes me extremely uneasy. Unless there's money involved, there's no control, and I don't like that. Now that you know there is, things are back to the way they should be. You default on that loan, and your farm reverts to the trust fund." Avery watched as the facts slowly seeped into Matt's whiskey-soaked brain. "True ownership notwithstanding," he added pointedly, "David, and Paul and Ana's children are sole beneficiaries." Avery couldn't suppress the satisfaction he felt as he watched Matt crumble.

CHAPTER 34

"You can't graze yer critters here." Lacey sat his horse facing four dusty riders. "This here's claimed, and we already have a herd settled."

"And who claims it?" The smallest of the four seemed to be in charge.

"Who's asking?" Lacey said.

"Name's Baylor."

"Mr. Paul Steele owns this herd and this here's his range. And we're riding for him." Lacey tilted his head toward three riders scrambling out of a draw.

"I got orders to set this herd just north o' that hill there. I was told this was free range. Where I come from in Kansas that means I put 'im where I want to."

"Well, you been told wrong, and I reckon we can hold our own if'n you want to argue. Or, you can go see the sheriff in town. Your choice." Lacey turned to see Nathan, Sweeney, and Griz, pushing their horses toward him.

"We got a problem, Lacey?" Nathan asked as he pulled up alongside.

"Nope. They do. They're Kansans, and they're looking to bed down right in the middle of us. Told 'em they can't."

"Youngster's right," Nathan said, looking at the four riders. "Yer squatting on private range . . . and that means yer trespassin'."

Lacey glanced at the .44-caliber Colts strapped to the front of Nathan's saddle. They were unlashed and ready.

The skinny one leaned over and whispered something to the rider on his left. "All right. We'll go see the law. We find out yer yarnin', we'll come back and talk about it."

"Awful close to calling me a liar, fella," Lacey said. He turned slightly in his seat, exposing the butt of his Colt.

The skinny cowboy glared at him for a moment, and then turned his horse away. "C'mon, let's get to town." He spurred his horse savagely.

"Scummy sumbitch," Nathan said.

Matt stood in front of the sheriff's desk, thinking about what the sheriff had just said, but he had a hard time gathering his thoughts. "But there's no way I can keep my cattle off a single quarter section of land.

He's effectively tied up that entire two-mile piece of range."

"Looks that way," Sheriff Staker said, shaking his head.

Matt thought he saw a glimmer of sympathy in his eyes. "But Paul can't keep his cattle off of mine, either," he said hopefully. "He has the same problem."

"He would, if the ground was yours, or even filed on. It isn't. Where you're at is free range."

"But it's not free. I can't keep my cattle on there without fencing it."

"And you can't fence it, it's free range."

In that instant Matt saw the neatness of it, and at the same time the basic unfairness. *Lindstrom! Only a lawyer could come up with something like this.*

"Unless you can guarantee me you'll not trespass on Paul's ground, I'm gonna ask you to stay off that range," Staker said. "And I don't see how you can give that assurance."

"But I have to have good grazing, Loren. I'm facing financial ruin here." Matt heard himself pleading.

"I'm the sheriff, Matt." Staker looked uncomfortable. "I try to keep the peace and enforce the law. Paul is within his rights to do what he's doing. If I force him to share the range, his investment is jeopardized, just like yours. I can't do that. I'm truly sorry, but you just got beat in a business deal. Nothing I can do."

Matt turned and shuffled out of the office, his shoulders slumped. Ruth had stopped talking to him, David's insolence was getting worse by the day, Avery no longer wanted to see him, and Lancer had recently asked him to pay for his drinks as he got them. For the first time in months he got on his horse and turned west toward home; Lancer's, just a block east, ignored.

Matt had spent forty-four hundred dollars on the purchase of the herd, plus another four hundred to feed and tend them over the winter. Now the drovers were demanding payment for trailing the cattle here, and he had exactly twenty-seven dollars and fifty-five cents to his name. He owned a herd, worth nearly ten thousand dollars a month ago, now a liability.

He could trail them back east and try to sell them there, but the drovers weren't willing to trust him further. Queries to the cattle brokers in Saint Louis and Omaha had told him dozens of people had seen the same market, and were now well on their way with their own herds. His would be worthless by the time he got it there.

"We'll give you three dollars a head for the herd," Baylor said. The skinny cowboy sat at the kitchen table, across from Matt. He stank.

"I have nearly five thousand dollars invested in that herd. I can't possibly sell for less than eight dollars. That's half of what they're worth."

"They ain't worth shit around here. You just found that out, didn't ya?" Matt saw the predatory look the Kansan gave Ruth. She stood just inside the kitchen door with David. When her hand instinctively went to her bosom, Baylor grinned, and Matt's pulse rose.

"I can't do it, and I haven't arranged for your money yet. Can you wait a couple days?" Matt could not meet Ruth's eyes.

"Boys are gettin' itchy. Might consider a little trade." He leered at Ruth.

David clenched his fist, and mouthed an obscenity as he glared at Baylor.

Matt stood. "You've got a filthy mind, and you'll get your money soon enough. Now leave." He looked at David. "Show him the door."

David stepped in front of his mother.

Baylor stood, glanced at David before smiling at Matt. "We'll wait a couple days, and then maybe we'll just take the herd." He pushed roughly past David, strode across the parlor and left, leaving the front door open.

Matt slumped forward in his chair, his head in his hands.

Buell, Lacey, Sweeney, and Quigg had joined several soldiers from Fort Hartwell, a crew of buffalo skinners, and the usual group of locals for a rowdy night at Lancer's. The four friends stood at the right end of the bar throwing dice for drinks, and Buell was up. He had four fives to beat, easy. He shook the dice cup.

The screen door at the front banged open and four cowboys barged in, only to stop and look directly at him and the Texans.

"Them's the Kansans I told ya 'bout," Lacey said to Buell. "Skinny one's named Baylor."

The newcomers strode to the middle of the bar. "Gimme a beer, and put an egg in it," Baylor said, his speech slurred. He turned his back to the bar and leaned against it. "Who let the greasers in here, barkeep?" he asked the bartender who hurried over. "How you expect decent folks to keep their liquor down with them around?" He turned to face Buell and his friends.

Lancer waved the other barkeeper away, glanced at the Texans, and quickly worked the pump handle. After cracking an egg to half float in the yellow brew, he placed it on the bar. "Here, fella." He eyed the other three men. "Rest?"

"Whiskey," they replied, nearly in unison. They all looked toward the cowboys at the other end of the bar.

Lacey stepped well away from the rest. Buell fell in beside him.

"No call . . . for insults," Lancer said to the Kansans. Swallowing hard, he suppressed a cough.

"You hear 'im fellas, no insults. That means the greasers gotta go." Baylor stepped to the right, clear of his friends and looked directly at Lacey.

"I'm gonna make 'lowances fer the liquor, Kansas," Lacey said. "But don't be pushin'. You other three got a say in this?" No answer came. "Best be gettin' clear of 'im if'n ya ain't."

The trio walked away from the bar.

"Now ain't that jist like a greaser? Ya got four agin one Jayhawker. Them odds is 'bout right." Baylor, his mouth curled in an insolent smile, laughed at the Texans with his eyes.

"They ain't gonna side," Lacey said.

"Only one talkin's me and I'm askin' you to ease back a mite."

Baylor looked at them, his face smeared askew with contempt. "How about yer purdy pardner there?" His gaze shifted to Buell, and Buell felt his face stiffen with the insult. Baylor leered at him.

"He ain't in it." Buell caught Lacey's eye as Lacey glanced his way. "Step back to the bar."

Buell stared at the Kansan.

"It ain't yer fight, Buell." Lacey again.

Buell felt his teeth clench and his jaw muscles tighten, then he took a short step forward and moved a little to the left, in front of Lacey.

"Do like yer mammy says, boy," Baylor taunted. "Met anoth'ern jist like ya today. Little Steele boy. I asked for a piece of his ma and all he could do was whisper cusswords at me."

"What Steele boy?" Buell asked quietly.

The Kansan tilted his head back and looked down his nose. "What diff'rence it make? Reckon they'll all pimp their mammies for a little nipple suckin'."

"I asked, which Steele boy? I ain't askin' again." Buell suddenly felt very relaxed.

"Buell," Lacey said in a whisper, "you don't have to do this. Leave it be. Kansas?"

"He's right, boy. Leave it be. Go suck a titty some'ers." Baylor's eyes fixed on Buell's. "Snotty little shit." Then he reached for his pistol.

A small black hole appeared magically beside Baylor's nose to be filled by erupting bright red that sprayed out of his head. A small patch of scalp blew away from above his left ear and hit Lancer in the neck. Baylor took half a step back, then crashed into a chair, clutching his mouth. His eyes first expressed amazement, then flashed to terror for a moment, and then begged for help in the few seconds the light in them lasted — and then the light went out. He heaved a gasp of air through his fingers, blood and spittle bubbling between them before his hand fell away and he lay still. The smell of human waste assaulted the room. Buell stood transfixed, his Remington still leveled at where Baylor had stood.

"Damn it, Buell," Lacey cried. "Gawdammit!"

A customer bolted for the screen door, banged through it and ran out into the night.

Sheriff Staker covered the three blocks from his home to Lancer's in less than two minutes. He had dreaded this night, one that he knew was inevitable, and cursed because he'd known he couldn't prevent it.

"Put your pistol on the bar, Buell," he said as he walked into the room.

Buell stood at the bar, facing the door. He lifted his pistol carefully, and turning slightly, put it down on the wood surface.

"You . . . move," Staker said to a customer sitting with four others at a nearby table. "All of you, move." They pushed their chairs back and stepped away from the table.

"Now, go sit in that chair," he said to Buell, indicating the closest one.

"Did you see this, Mr. Lacey?"

"Yes'ir."

"Art, how about you?"

"Self-defense."

"I didn't ask your opinion, Art." The sheriff looked at the other barkeep. "You see it?" The man nodded. "How about one of you boys?" Staker asked of the three Kansans, now standing alone together, warily watching the rest of the crowd and casting glances at their fallen trail boss. No one spoke. "Well, one of you must've seen it." Staker took a quick step toward the three. Two dropped their gaze to the floor. "You." He pointed to the one who hadn't. "You come with me. And you two," he said, looking at Lacey and Lancer's bartender.

"Buell, walk in front of me to my office. The rest of you go on about your business. Leave that body alone. Doc Princher will be here shortly. Anybody not understand what I just said?" He surveyed the room, his steely gaze inviting no challenges. "Good." He stepped to the bar and retrieved Buell's pistol. "Let's go." He followed the four men out of the saloon.

Staker had sent a messenger to get Mace, who now stood in front of him. "What'n hell'd he do?" Mace asked, plainly frightened.

"Looks like he shot a man." Sheriff Staker shook his head. "I'm sorry, Mace."

"Buell, is that true?" Mace's face twitched.

Buell sat on a cot in one of the three cells at the back of the room. The door stood open. "I guess I did." He lowered his head.

Staker thought he looked very young and small.

"Dammit it, Lacey, what'd you have to teach him to shoot for? Now look at what you done." He glared at the cowboy, and the fear on Mace's face had turned to worry. "What happened, Loren?"

"I haven't figgered that out yet. I wanted you here before I questioned your boy. Take a seat. Rest of you, too, if you want."

They all sat except Lacey, who moved toward Buell.

Staker looked at Lancer's man. "I'll start with you. Exactly what did you see? Not what you think happened, what you saw."

"Jayhawker come in with his three friends. He ordered beer . . . with an egg. Art waved me off and pulled a beer, then the Jayhawker said he didn't like greasers in the bar. He was talkin' to the Texans."

"How do you know he was talking to the Texans?"

"Ah, I figgered he was talk—"

"I told you," the sheriff cut him off harshly, "what you saw, period. Is that so difficult?"

The man blushed and the Kansan looked at him with a faint smile. Staker stared at the barkeeper and waited for him to continue.

"The fella said something about greasers being in the saloon. Art told him weren't no need to insult folks. Lacey there told him the same thing. The feller said something else about greasers getting out of the place. And he was looking right at Lacey and the boys when he said it. Lacey said the fella was drunk and to back off. And the fella was drunk."

"I said, what you *know*!"

"Dammit, I'm a saloon keeper, Sheriff, I know a drunk when I see one. The fella was drunk. Anyhow, then he accused the Texans of ganging up on him. Lacey said he was the only one the Kansan had to deal with. And then the fella said something about Buell."

"Like what. Something don't tell me much."

"Called Buell, 'Lacey's pretty partner.' "

The Kansan's smile widened. Staker glanced at him. "You think that's funny?"

"I do, Sheriff, then and now."

"And then what?" Staker returned to the bartender.

"Buell stepped in front of Lacey and —"

"Stepped in front of him? How do you mean?"

"Just that. Stepped in front. Put himself between the Jayhawker and Lacey. Lacey told him to get out of the way, but Buell ignored him. And then the Jayhawker started in on Buell. Said Simon Steele's ma was a whore and Simon would let anybody use her."

Staker looked at the Kansan. The smile was gone, but the Kansan returned his cold stare.

The barkeeper continued, "And Buell asked the fella to repeat what he said and the Kansan called him a little shit and went for his gun. I saw that plain as day. He went for his pistol first. Somehow Buell managed to get off a lucky shot and hit the fella in the face."

"You, what's your name?" Staker asked the Kansan.

"Gilmore. Will Gilmore."

"What was your part in this?"

"I had no part. Baylor was drunk and on the prod. He and this feller" — he nodded at Lacey — "had a little run-in out on the prairie. Didn't set well with Baylor. We saw the Texans and this young fella in the saloon when we came in. Baylor decided to lean on 'em a little. The youngster here took exception to something Baylor said about the Steele woman. We were out to the farm west of here today. I didn't go in, but knowing Baylor, he said something nasty. He always did."

"West of town? You mean east?"

"I know how to find Wyoming, Sheriff. I mean west. Anyway, Baylor started goading the kid. And the kid was standing almost in front of your cowhand there. Took him right out of the picture. Baylor drew . . . well, he started to draw, and the kid shot him in the head."

"Did Mr. Lacey ask him to back off?"

"Yep. Twice. I remember, because I was surprised. Baylor was a little leery of the Texan. Said so. Reckon that's why he took on the youngster. Figgered the kid and the cowboy were friends and all he wanted to do was raise a little hell. Guess he miscalculated."

"You don't seem too upset about it."

"I'm not. He was going to get it one way or the other. I expected some indignant husband though, not some sodbuster's kid. Baylor was a nasty piece o' work."

"It wasn't, as you put it, some sodbuster's kid. Buell is Mr. Mace's boy and Mace is our blacksmith, not that that makes a bit of difference." Staker was getting a little tired of the man's indifference to another man's death.

"You mean the kid was standing up for the wrong woman? That's a good one. Old Baylor got killed by mistake." The Kansan chuckled. "I'll be damned."

"Lacey, did Buell step in front of you?"

"Afraid so. I reckoned the scrap was 'tween me 'n that Kansan. But when he called Buell purdy, Buell got right in front o' me. I told him to move but . . ." He shook his head in resignation. "And I asked the man ta ease up. Asked 'im twice'st. It weren't no use. Feller had his nose pointed

402

and he was goin' fer it. I saw 'im start to draw, and saw his head get busted by that slug. I didn't see Buell shoot. I was watching the other feller's eyes."

"Okay, Buell, come on out here."

Buell emerged from the jail cell and stepped up to the sheriff. Mace got up and went to his side.

"So, Buell. I'll ask you one simple question, and you don't have to answer if you don't want to. But I gotta tell you, Judge Kingsley will ask the same question if you don't, and then you *will* have to answer. Do you understand? How about you, Mace?"

"I've listened to everybody, Loren," Mace replied. "I can't see where Buell done anything but protect himself. That feller was bound to shoot someone, and I'm just glad Buell knew how to use that pistol, and it's the other fella laying over at the saloon. Sorry as I am to say it, that's God's truth." Mace laid his hand on Buell's shoulder. "I don't see any reason not to answer any questions, son. You go ahead."

"All right. Buell, was it your intention to kill that man when you stepped in front of Lacey?" Staker watched Buell's face closely.

Buell closed his eyes for a couple of seconds. "No, sir," he said, shaking his head.

"I see a clear case of self-defense. Three

eyewitnesses agree Mr. Baylor drew first and that Baylor was the aggressor. You can all go about your business. Buell, here's your pistol."

Staker stepped to the gun cabinet and picked up the Remington. Buell took it and nonchalantly dropped it into his tied-down holster. They filed out of his office and Staker followed, locking the door behind himself. The Kansan and the bartender returned to the saloon, now a beehive of activity as everyone tried to get inside to see that had happened. Lacey said a few words to Mace and Buell, and then walked away from them toward the saloon. Mace and Buell turned the corner as soon as they reached it and walked south, obviously avoiding the crowd a block farther down the street.

Sheriff Staker headed for Lancer's. He'd help Doc Princher round up some men to pack the body over to the mortuary. And he'd try to find out exactly where Mr. Baylor came from so word of his demise and any personal effects could be sent. He felt weary as he walked, as though another's death had taken a part of him too.

Simon and Buell strolled toward the river.

"Are you sorry you killed him?" Simon asked.

"I'm not sorry he's dead. You should've been there. The fella was mean."

"That's not what I asked." Simon looked directly at Buell. "Are you sorry it was you who killed him?"

"I don't really know, cuz I can't remember doing it. One second I was listening to him call your ma names, and then Lacey is telling me to put my gun away and moving me back from the guy on the floor."

"He wasn't talking about my ma, Buell. He was talking about David's."

"Would that make it all right? He was saying some awful stuff."

"I don't know what to think, but I wish it hadn't happened. Everybody looks at us like we're something to avoid."

"You mean us, or me?" Buell stopped and turned to face Simon.

"Some of them are afraid of you, Buell. I can see it in their faces."

"Then you are talking about me. Fine, but that bastard deserved what he got. Do I care if it was me that give it to him? No! Would I do it again? Yes. Scum like that needs to be taken care of, and it's scum like me that has to do it. I didn't pick the fight. It came to me. Maybe I was born to do this, Simon.

Shit, I killed my own ma, and maybe that's all I'm good for."

His friend's face took on a woodenness that Simon had never seen. Buell stood silent, hard eyes locked on his own, head cocked expectantly.

"I get so mixed up when I try to understand you. You're my best friend, even before Sarah. I've tried to make sense of what you tell me, about how you see things in your head, and how you seem to go away, right as we talk sometimes. I've tried to find out as much as I can about what's going on by reading, but I always come out with the same answer. And I don't like that answer, Buell. That answer means I don't know you, and I don't want that. Let's try not to talk about it. Let's just say you did what you did because you lost control for a couple of seconds. I can understand that, and still have you as my friend. That's what I want. Okay?" Simon's voice broke slightly, and he blinked his eyes quickly several times.

Buell looked at him for several seconds, and then stared off toward the distant river bluffs. Finally, he looked back at Simon and breathed a deep sign. "I think you're right. I lost control. Maybe that fella didn't deserve to die, but he's gone, and I can't do anything about it. You're my best friend, and I want to keep it that way too. Now let's not talk about it anymore."

Simon looked at his friend for a moment, and then they turned and started back toward town, the need that had sent them on the walk satisfied.

CHAPTER 35

Paul and Matt sat on the front porch of the new house. The warm afternoon sun felt good, but it seemed wasted on Matt. His composure had rapidly crumbled from the moment they sat down.

"I need to sell that herd at some sort of profit, Paul. I can't take the beating that the Kansans are offering."

"I'll help all I can. You, Ruth, and David will not go hungry, nor will you have to look for shelter, I can guarantee that."

"I'm not asking for charity. I'm asking for a loan. Or better, from your standpoint, I'm offering you a deal that will triple your money."

"But only if I can find buyers for another six hundred cattle, and you admit that's the problem." Paul shrugged. "Nobody needs them."

"You want to see me beg. You've worked at that for a long time, haven't you?"

"I have not. I never wanted to see you lose anything. I love Ruth as much as my sisters, and if you get hurt, so does she. I had no idea you were trailing a herd into Carlisle at the same time I was. Why on earth would you do that? You must have figured I had another herd on the way."

"Do you think you had some special right to sell that herd to the army? Why couldn't *I* do it? If you hadn't paid Prosser to keep that message from me, I would have had the herd here first, and then we'd see who'd be begging who for help." Matt's voice rose as he spit out the accusation.

"Prosser? What does he have to do with it? I haven't . . ." Paul paused. "Your herd was waiting? For word from you? Or payment?"

"You know full well I had a herd waiting in Hatcher." Matt's eyes blazed. "Waiting and ready."

"Hatcher? Why Hatcher? That's the town where I arranged for mine. Why Hatcher, Matt? How'd you know that?"

"None of your damn business."

"I think I understand now." Paul glared at his brother and then stood. "You were ready and willing to sink my family. I find it hard to believe, brother, but I can't see anything else. You were going to cost Ana her new house."

"So what?" Matt stood, shoving his chair into the wall. "You and your high and mighty, holier-than-thou attitude. You've always been that way. From the very beginning, you and Pa conspired to keep me down. Always ready to make me look bad. And Ruth. Always ready to try her again." Matt's breath came in ragged gulps, his face beet red and his fists clenched. "I know what went on between you and her. I know you were sniffing around before she chose me. But you wouldn't let it go at that." He thrust his face close to Paul's. "Even after we were married you kept at it. I saw you. Always so polite and nice and always one step away when she needed something. I know what you did!" Matt was now shouting, spit flying as he rushed to get the words out.

"My God, Matt, do you hear what you're saying? Stop it!" Paul reached a hand out to his brother.

Matt slapped at it savagely. "Why does David look exactly like Axel? Huh? Why? Because they're half brothers," he said with a sneer. "I've been living with a harlot and a bastard for eighteen years. I knew it, you knew it, and so did Pa. And I haven't touched her since I figured that out."

"Leave my home, Matt. I've never even thought such a thing. You've lost your senses. Go home and think about what you're saying, and pray for forgiveness, pray hard." So shaken he had to lean on the porch rail for support, Paul pointed at Matt's mare. "Go. Now!"

Matt scrambled off the porch and mounted his horse. "You know what you've done, and you'll burn in hell for it, Paul. You will burn." He spurred his horse away from the house and rode straight south, into the prairie.

Paul collapsed in his chair and watched his brother disappear. He was still sitting there when Ana drove the spring wagon up to the front of the house.

"Paul, what's wrong? Are the children all right?" She clambered down from the rig and hurried up the steps. "Paul! What's happened?"

He reached out to grab his wife and buried his face in her bosom. "The children are all right. It's Matt. I think he's gone crazy."

Simon sat across the desk from Avery Singer, listening intently as the banker explained financial leverage to him. Simon had brought a proposed scheme to apply an escalating interest rate to late-paying customers, and as part of the discussion, Avery was explaining leverage and how and why it worked both ways. Simon was fascinated.

Art Lancer and Blake Waldon burst into the office. Blake Waldon smelled as rank as his business, the stench of stinking hides in his skin, and in the confines of Avery's small office, the effect was overpowering. The men ignored Simon.

"Matt Steele has sold that herd for four dollars a head. Those Kansans are trailing it to Omaha as we speak."

"So," Avery said, and reached for his handkerchief.

"Own half," Lancer said.

"Correction, gentlemen, you are holders of a signature loan that you undertook, speculating Matt's herd would sell at a profit, and make you a tidy sum in the process. Is that not true? And, before you answer, I might point out that young Mr. Steele here may not need to know your private affairs."

"Private be damned," Waldon said. "You know good and well that you told us this was one of those deals that would be hard to lose on."

"That's true — hard, but not impossible,"

Avery said. "Death will come certainly, everything else can be leveraged." He smiled as Simon's eyebrows shot up.

"But four dollars doesn't even get us our money back. We'll both actually lose fifty dollars each, plus the eleven percent interest," Waldon said.

Art winced when Blake quoted the usurious figure.

"I hate to pile more bad news on your already strained bank accounts," Avery continued, "but another party has first claim on the sale proceeds."

"What? You mean we don't get the whole twenty-four hundred?" Blake mopped his sweating face with a crusty handkerchief.

Avery took the opportunity to do likewise and took a deep breath through the perfumed fabric of his own. Leaning back in his chair, he gazed passively at the two men. "You are not entitled to any of it. Your paper is secured by a signature only. No collateral is listed or mentioned."

"Blake, I, nothing? Twenty-five hundred, gone?" Lancer stated it as a fact, resignation showing on his face.

"Your calculations are as sound as your bank accounts *were*," Avery said. "There are twenty-four hundred dollars in receipts against a five-thousand-dollar loan. Twenty-

five hundred of which was secured collater-
ally, with beef cows."

"You screwed us, Avery." Blake could not
keep up with the sweat pouring down his
forehead.

"I did not. I told you of an investment opportunity. You saw fit to take advantage of
it. All investments hold risks. You are both
businessmen and know that. Had the deal
gone the other way, I doubt you'd be standing here thanking me. Now if you will
excuse me, I was tutoring young Mr.
Steele." He looked directly at both of them.
"About leverage."

Simon and Sarah sat on the picnic blanket
facing each other over the remnants of their
meal.

"I told you Buell was going to get in
trouble. Next will be Jake. People who hang
out in saloons will always come to no good."

"We've discussed this before, Sarah, and I
thought we decided to maybe agree to
disagree." Simon took her hand.

"You decided. I agreed to try to see your
point of view. I have and I can't. Simple as
that." She turned her head away and studied
the river.

"I tried to explain. That man was going to
try and kill Buell. Can't you see that? He

had no choice but to defend himself." Simon tugged on her arm to make her face him.

"If he'd not been there he wouldn't have had to make the choice. It was his company that got him in trouble, just like I said."

Simon saw the futility of his argument. "Okay. Let's leave it alone. I wished he hadn't had to do it, but it's done. He's still my best friend. Let's think about us. I won't get involved in a situation like that. I believe disagreements can always be worked out by talking and compromising. Like now. I'll stay out of those places, if that's what you want. I won't carry a gun. All right? I intend to learn the retail trade and work for Mr. Swartz, and maybe someday open a store of my own. Or maybe learn some more about banking and work for Mr. Avery. I just want us to be happy and together."

"The store? I thought you would work with your family in the cattle business. Father said your father stands a fair chance of becoming very rich and successful. Don't you want to do that?" Sarah turned to him, a quizzical look on her face.

"I think Axel and Abe want to, and I really don't care. I enjoy the bookwork and stuff like that at the store. The numbers fascinate me. Why? Would you mind if I was just a

415

storekeeper?"

"Of course not. It's just that . . . oh, I don't know, store keeping is so boring. And look at Mrs. Swartz. I don't think she's had a new dress in years." She tilted her head down and looked at him from under her eyebrows, coquettish. "How about the law? Father says you seem to have a knack for it."

"I'm not sure about that. Recently I saw how the law can be used. I don't think I want to be a part of that."

"What did you see?"

"Even though Mr. Avery didn't tell me to be quiet about it, I think what I saw was meant to be private. I'll just say the rules allowed some people to get hurt who shouldn't have been."

She let out an exasperated sigh. "Oh, Simon, you are so straight at times." She lay back on the blanket and patted the ground beside her. "Come on, let's have a nap."

CHAPTER 36

Paul's furrowed brow expressed irritation, and matched the intense stare he directed at Simon over his father's coffee cup. "Sheriff Staker wants to see you before school, and he wants me to be there. You and Buell been up to something?"

"No. Why immediately think of Buell? Everybody in town is doing that now, and because I'm his friend, I get the same thing." He glanced at his mother for support. "Used to be you trusted me. Now the sheriff wants to see me, and you think the worst. Why?"

"Don't be disrespectful of your father, Simon," Ana said. She stood by the new stove Paul had bought her.

The family sat at the round oak kitchen table, the other children quietly concentrating on their breakfast. Paul's mood did not invite further argument, so Simon said nothing.

417

"Well, let's go see what he wants." Paul slugged off his coffee and stood.

Simon noted that his father chose not to answer his question.

Twenty minutes later Simon and Paul entered Sheriff Staker's office. Mr. Swartz sat in the chair opposite Staker's desk. The storekeeper pointedly ignored them.

"What can we do for you, Loren?" Paul asked.

Simon saw his father glance at Werner.

"I'll come straight to it. Mr. Swartz says Simon is stealing." Sheriff Staker looked at Simon.

"Stealing? Stealing what?" Paul asked Mr. Swartz, but the storekeeper didn't look back at him.

"Gus says Simon has been regularly taking money from the till. He says his son has seen Simon do it."

"Simon?" Paul looked at him.

Simon tried to think of something to say but the word "stealing" flying around in his brain scrambled everything else.

"Well, what do you say?" Paul asked again.

"No! Of course not. How can you think such a thing?" Simon's body tensed as he felt anger taking control of him.

"Gus say he know where is some of this

money," the storekeeper said.

Simon looked at his father and the question he saw in his eyes horrified him. It was not if, but why.

"No! That can't be. I haven't taken anything. I've worked hard and helped him to do things better. I wouldn't steal. I wouldn't lie. Pa, I wouldn't. I never have. Have I?" Simon beseeched his father for support. "Have I?"

His father met his eyes for a moment, and then dropped his gaze. "I wish I could say that's true, Simon. But I can't."

The awful truth slammed into Simon like a perfectly aimed punch to the gut. John Lindstrom's words filled his head. The seed of doubt, he had called it. The seed of doubt. Simon's heart felt empty.

"Can you show us where the money is, Werner?" Staker asked.

"Ya sure. It is where Simon keeps the apron. He has place in back for gloves and the apron. I show."

Swartz got out of his chair, and for the first time looked at Simon. The triumphant look on his face confused him. They walked the short distance to the store and Werner unlocked the front door. In the back storeroom, he lit a lamp, and pointed to a narrow cabinet. "Is inside. On the shelf."

Staker opened the cabinet door to show the apron and gloves, and under them, a flat envelope along with several pieces of paper. Stuffed in the very back was a cloth sack. He turned and looked at Werner.

"In the bag. You will find money. My money."

Staker removed the sack, and Simon heard the unmistakable metallic sound of gold coins. The sheriff unfolded it and reached inside to withdraw three coins. Lamplight glinted off two five-dollar pieces and one tiny gold dollar. He offered his open hand for all to see. "Is this where you keep your personal items when you're here?" He looked at Simon.

Simon could only nod, the sight of his father standing there and saying nothing in his defense having taken his voice.

"Are all these things yours, then?"

"No," Simon whispered. "Not that." He pointed at the white bag.

"And these?" Staker took out the papers.

"Calculations. About shipping charges. Nearly done with them."

Staker shut the cabinet and headed for the front of the store. Approaching the counter, he dumped the contents of the bag. Dozens of coins scattered across the smooth wood.

"There, you see." Swartz pointed his stubby finger at Simon. "Thief."

The accusation sliced the air. Both the sound of the accented word, more spit out than vocalized, and the look of utter contempt on the storekeeper's face crushed Simon to silence.

"Do you deny it, Simon?"

Simon didn't answer.

"He said it wasn't his, Loren. There's got to be some explanation," Paul said lamely.

"Where's your son, Werner?" Staker asked.

"He is at the Dobe. He take wagon with supply to customer there. He is being back today."

"I'm going to keep this for the time being." Staker started picking up the loose coins. "I need to talk to young Gus. You tell him to come and see me as soon as he gets back from Adobe."

"Ya, I tell. And him." Swartz pointed at Simon. "I want him not to be in store. Never!"

"Let them out, Werner," Staker told the storekeeper. "Simon, you can go to school. Nothing will be said of this until I decide what to do about it. Nobody's saying you're guilty."

Simon felt betrayed and alone as he and his father left the store.

■ ■ ■ ■

Staker headed back to the storeroom. "I want to take another look in there, Werner." Swartz started to follow. "No need for you to bother. I know where the lamp is."

His schoolmates' glances all conveyed an accusation, and with every giggle or whisper directed at him, Simon's day turned into a matter of survival. Even Miss Everett was cool toward him, and the last lesson of the day, "Civil Government, The Justice System," deliberately selected to torment him. As he left the schoolhouse, Sarah and Buell stood waiting.

"I'm going to the store. I'll walk with you to work," Sarah said with a smile.

The sight of them scrambled his emotions. *She wants to embarrass me and has chosen this way to do it. She knows I can't go to the store anymore.* He stopped well short of them. "I'm going to go with Buell," he mumbled. "I don't have to work today." Disappointment registered in her eyes. *That's almost a lie, but so what?*

"Then you can walk me home." The smile she wore vanished, replaced by a concerned frown.

If the smile wasn't real, can the worried look be? "You go ahead, I'm going with Buell." He abruptly turned away from her.

"Simon! What's the matter with you? You've been a crab all day." She stared at him, her hands on her hips.

"Let's go, Buell." They walked away and left her standing.

"I gotta agree with Sarah. You're like a bear with a toothache," Buell said as they hurried the single block to the main street.

Simon, striding along, said nothing.

"Why ain't you going to work? Old Swartz finally fire your ass?"

Simon stopped and glared at Buell. "You my friend or not?" He turned and continued walking fast.

"Whoa. What's chewin' on you?" Buell hurried to catch up as Simon strode purposefully toward the livery. "Come on, Simon, wait up."

Simon rounded the corner of the livery and went through the big doors.

"Hello, Simon." The look on Mace's face told Simon his father had already talked to him.

"Hi, Mr. Mace. Looks like you know," Simon said as Buell came into the barn.

"Know what?" Buell almost shouted. "C'mon, Simon, what's going on?"

423

Mace put his hammer down and crossed the floor to the boys. He put his hand on Simon's shoulder and looked at Buell.

"Simon's gonna need some help, son. I'm gonna go get a cup of coffee. You two can talk." Mace went into the living area and shut the door.

"Well?" Buell's eyes locked on his own.

Simon told him about Swartz.

"That son of a bitch. Either that old fart put the money there or Gus did. One or the other." Buell eyes flashed angrily. "Dirty bastards."

"You believe me, Buell? You believe me when I say I didn't do it?"

Buell blinked twice, real quick, and his head jerked forward like he had been slapped from behind. "Believe you? Of course I do. You wouldn't steal a spud if you were starving to death. Gawd, Simon, what a stupid question."

Simon's relief was palpable, euphoric almost, when he realized his life was not in shambles, that he had an ally, a friend. And then a stab of guilt struck him. He had doubted Buell's loyalty without thinking, and he learned in that instant what a friend was. "Thanks, Buell. I knew you would, but when your own father doubts you, it makes it hard to expect much of anybody."

"Hey, I know you. You're not a thief. I just can't see why they'd do this. I mean, if he didn't want you around, all he had to do was fire you. Or just tell you he didn't need you anymore. This don't make sense."

"I think it does. It's the middle of June."

"The fourteenth, so what?" Buell looked puzzled.

"He isn't going to ask Sheriff Staker to do anything."

"But he just accused you of stealing a lot of money."

"And he has it all back. Or at least he will after Staker talks to Gus. No. What he wants is me out of there, and a reason not to pay me what he owes. I'll bet on it."

"What'n hell you talking about?"

"Remember me telling you that Pa wanted me to wait until summer for the money Mr. Swartz owed me?"

"I got it. That dirty bastard. He'd do this for a few lousy dollars."

"And get away with it. I'm in the bog, Buell. Every time I turn around there's something else that stinks. I'm going to go home. I need to talk to Pa. I got mad at him today for something I did this spring."

"What? Sometimes I have a hard time keeping up."

"Never mind. I just gotta go talk to my

folks. I'll see you later."

Simon left the livery and headed for home, the mile distance allowing him time to think and get a hold of his feelings.

Ana looked at Paul, who nodded in assent, then she hustled the younger children out of the house. She joined Paul and Simon at the table.

"Pa, I got really mad at you today for doubting me," Simon said. "And I'm the one who put the doubt there. Uncle John told me that this spring, but then I didn't appreciate what he was saying. Now I do."

"It hurt me to see you face that, knowing it had to come someday, knowing, yet unable to do anything about it," Paul said. "I just didn't think it would be as serious as this."

"Do you still think I might have done this?"

"No. It's not in you. I have to admit I was unsure at the store. Staker just dropped it on me, and I really didn't have time to think. Now that I have, some things just don't add up. But I don't know what to do about it."

"Mr. Swartz is not going to pay me what he owes," Simon said matter-of-factly. "That's the reason for this." Simon saw the truth light Paul's face.

"Just for the money? There can't have been more than sixty or seventy dollars there."

"I didn't take it. So either Gus or Mr. Swartz put it there. I don't know who, and I probably never will, but I know one of them did."

"I have to admit something too. When you lied about the pistol shooting, I didn't want to face it, so when John volunteered to talk to you, I jumped at the chance. That was wrong. Maybe, if I had talked to you then, we could have sorted it out. But John was the easy way."

"No, Pa. Uncle John was hard on me. You might not have been. I was wrong, and he let me see it for myself. I wish I could tell Axel and Abe how important this is."

"There are some things that can't be taught, Simon. Some things have to be lived."

"I see that. I'm just glad you believe me now. That was the worst part. You and Ma thinking I was lying." He looked at his folks and smiled.

"We'll have to see what Sheriff Staker has to say. He's a fair man, but he's also a very strict lawman. He'll do what he has to do, so be ready to face whatever it is, fair or not."

"I know. I can do that now knowing you and Ma believe me. And Buell. He never did doubt me. Can you believe that? Not for a minute."

Staker looked up at Werner Swartz. "So that's all you want?"

"Ya. Just he stay away from store. And I owe nothing. Maybe I get back what he take, but maybe not, I think so."

"You're not going to press charges? Just drop this?" Staker said.

"Ya. Is done now." The storekeeper turned to leave.

"Just a minute, Werner. Here's the bag, and the money." Staker opened his desk drawer and took out the white sack. "Seventy-three dollars exactly." He handed it across.

"*Danka.* Tank you." Swartz took the bag and again turned to leave.

"And something else, Werner."

"Ya?"

Staker pulled out a stack of several dozen small sheets of paper.

"Looks like invoices, freight tickets and such. And the dates match the missing entries in those calculations Simon had in that cabinet."

"Where you get this?"

"Found them stuffed behind that cabinet you showed me. I could be wrong, but I'd say someone put them there, deliberately." Staker handed him the papers. "Now you can get a proper accounting, can't you, Werner?"

Swartz took the papers and glanced at them. His eyes narrowed briefly and then he left.

Staker took a deep breath. "I don't think Simon did it. To the law, what I think doesn't matter, but what does matter is Werner's not going to press charges. All he wants is for Simon to stay clear of the store. And Simon forfeits what he has coming in wages and bonus."

"But that —"

Staker put his hand up. "I don't think you can force the issue, Paul. He has a witness to Simon's pilfering, and we found the money where Simon admitted he kept his personal items in the store. Legally, Swartz's case is fairly clear. Simon stole from his employer."

"But —"

Again, Staker put up his hand. "I'm convinced young Gus put the money there.

I'm also convinced he and the freight driver are colluding to defraud his father. I'll get to them. Gus did it just to get Simon out of there before Simon sniffed out the same facts I did. Werner saw an opportunity to lay his hands on seventy-three dollars he didn't know about, and at the same time, keep what he owed Simon. If what you say is correct, Swartz made about two hundred dollars in this little episode. I can't prove that, but I think I'm right. And I will store that away for later. Count on it."

"So what does Simon do? The whole town is going to think him a thief and a liar." Paul grimaced.

"Not justice, I know," Staker said. "But this is a small town, and I have my influence. A few well-placed words will soon have everybody knowing what actually happened. Then you might see some justice. It won't be legal, but I think we can get it right. Sometimes I'm ashamed of what I do for a living. I just hope we haven't damaged a good young man irreparably."

Paul let Simon stay with the Texans all summer. Mace did the same with Buell. As promised, the story of how Mr. Swartz had cheated Simon out of his wages ghosted into the sewing circles and domino games.

Several customers started to question his prices, and complain about the quality of the merchandise in his store, and rumors that another mercantile enterprise might start up in competition caused Mr. Swartz much more than two hundred dollars' worth of trouble. But some were content, indeed pleased, to think the worst, and they gave Simon knowing stares and whispered comments behind fans and gloved hands.

CHAPTER 37

Matt, more alone and isolated now than ever, worked hard on his farm in the day, hoping against hope that a good crop would solve his financial crisis. David helped when he had no choice, sullen and angry. And Matt, at night, every night, tried to lose his problems in the smothering haze of alcohol.

The horse slid, straight-legged, to the bottom of the draw. The spine-crushing jolt at the bottom made Simon gasp. The three cattle he had seen burst from the bushes and headed up, Simon in hot pursuit. Cresting the ridge, the cows saw the rest of the herd and placidly walked to join it.

Such had been the pattern for four days as he, Buell and the Texans rounded up the herd. The army expected them at the end of the week, and today was Wednesday. Simon spotted two more cattle below, gritted his teeth, and urged his horse to start down again. Come Friday, he wasn't disappointed at all when his father told him neither he nor Buell would be needed for the trip to Fort Hartwell.

Paul thought the drive to the fort had gone well, and Captain Atkins met them, same as last year, only a couple hours earlier. They were now headed back to Carlisle, the mood relaxed and cheerful even though there'd be no stop in Adobe this year. If they rode steady, they'd be home by dark.

"Wish't I had a couple thousand jist like 'em," Nathan said. "This here range sure puts the meat on 'em."

Paul nodded. "We'll have to talk about one more trip. John is having his doubts, with the railroad being well west of Omaha now. That's gonna make trail driving a poor proposition." He studied the gathering storm to the west as he spoke.

"No matter. Still gotta get 'em rounded up 'fore they kin ship 'em. Long's there's cows they's gonna be cowpokes. Sure gettin' nasty-lookin' yonder." Nathan nodded toward the clouds in the west. Clearly, he'd been watching them too. "I don't like the color o' them low ones. Hate to git caught out here in a thunderstorm, and thet looks like a good'n." Nathan reined in his horse

433

and waited a minute for the rest to bunch up. "Don't like the look of that. I think we oughta head fer the river. See if we kin git a bit lower. We're sore thumbs out here on the prairie. Let's go!"

Paul and Nathan turned their horses and started to lope toward the river, a mile away. The rest spread out and followed suit. Inexorably, the storm bore down on them, gaining ground rapidly. Brilliant lightning forked in a dozen places, and a few seconds later, thunder laid the horses' ears back. The animals needed little urging to slip into a gallop, the dirt flying from their pounding hooves picked up by a gusting wind. The riders yanked their hats down tight, and leaned low over their horses' necks.

Just as they reached the bluffs, the storm hit with all of nature's fury. Sliding and slipping, the men rode the frightened horses straight into a draw and dismounted. Turning the horse's heads hard against their bodies, they laid the animals down in the willows. They were no sooner prone than the hail hit. Pieces of irregular-shaped ice smashed through the thick brush, finding soft flesh. Nathan's horse struggled to get up and the Texan lay across the horse's head. Exposed, hailstones the size of chicken eggs struck him dozens of times. His hat flew off and a second later, his back arched and then he slumped down again and didn't move. Paul could do nothing but hunker in the thicket.

For several minutes the hail hammered the group while the lightning and thunder, a cacophony of sight and sound, split the air. Paul first heard, and then felt, a low rumbling through the ground under his chest. The terrorized horses fought to regain their feet, the struggling men unable to keep them down. The riders dragged on the reins to stop their mounts from running off. The rumbling sound took on an unearthly overtone, a screech, like some demented creature caught in a steel trap. The pitch rose higher and higher as the creature sought them out in their hiding places. Paul pressed his cold face into the safety of the riverbank and prayed. And then it passed, fading in a minute to a low growl, leaving, finally, blessed silence. Only a steady rain remained.

Soaked and cold, they loaded the unconscious Nathan on his horse, and worked their way out of the draw, falling on the muddy ground, and scrambling to avoid the flailing hooves of distraught horses. When they crested, the storm, now two miles away and still black and evil-looking, struck sparks of defiance as it moved, unstoppable, to spread total chaos across the prairie to the northeast.

Doc Princher put the covers back over Nathan's shoulders. "I think he's gonna be all right. Sure took a whack on the head though. His eyes react and he can feel it when I stick him. We'll just have to wait him out."

"I thought we was gonna freeze getting here," Paul said. "Longest six miles I've ever traveled."

He shuddered as he thought of the night before. They had tied Nathan to his horse and made it to Carlisle about eight thirty. The crops around town were no more; the wheat and barley fields flattened, and the few fruit trees stripped bare of both fruit and leaves.

"That was some storm," Princher said. "I'm not surprised you heard a tornado. It looked like it could produce one. Glad you fellas got out of the way. I'll check back this evening."

The doctor walked out of the hotel room and went downstairs. Paul studied the Texan, now looking very vulnerable, a huge, purple goose egg on the side of his head. Mrs. Luger had agreed to look in on him once in a while, so Paul left for home.

■ ■ ■ ■

Matt stood behind his barn, hat in hand, shaking his head. He'd spent the morning surveying the damage, but still needed to look again, unable to grasp what he'd seen all morning. Numb, he walked to the edge of the downed wheat, picked up a few of what was left of the seed heads, beaten empty of the kernels that had just the day before weighed them nearly to the ground. His oats, farther west, had suffered the same damage. Gone, completely and utterly destroyed.

Three more days. Just three and he would have had his McCormick reaper cutting and binding that beautiful crop. Three more days, and he would have had the wagonloads sold, enough to save the farm and more. But now he was ruined. He shuffled into the barn to saddle his horse, and minutes later rode out of it toward town. Matt sought the familiar haze in which to lose sight of this devastation.

Ana answered the knock on the front door to find David, stoic in the morning light. It was the first time in over two years that she's seen him there. "Why, David." She stepped back. "Come in."

"Ma wants to see you." David stared at the porch floor.

"Is anything wrong?" The damp hand of fear brushed her neck. She reached out and touched his arm.

"Pa's gone," he said simply and without emotion.

"What do you mean gone? Has he died?" Ana shook his arm harshly.

"No, he's just gone." He scowled and looked at her hand. "He left yesterday afternoon sometime and hasn't come back. Ma wants you to come over."

"Help me harness the horse."

She headed through the house for the back door. When she reached the kitchen, she turned to see David still on the porch looking at her. "David! Now! Help me with the wagon." Ana charged toward the back door.

Ana sent David to the old place to find Paul and then she drove straight to Ruth's. She found her on the sofa, her face swollen from crying, her eyes bloodshot and haggard-looking.

"He went out to look at the storm damage and a little later I heard him ride away. I expected him right back. I thought maybe he needed something in town. And he didn't come and then it got late. He always comes home for supper. Sometimes he leaves to get a drink at Lancer's, but he always comes home. Oh, Ana, where has he gone to?" Her dry eyes pleaded, long since bereft of tears.

Ana looked at her sister and saw despair dragging Ruth's features to the low level of her spirits, and she took her in her arms and held her as she would a child, cooing and patting her back. Paul arrived shortly thereafter and went to look around the farm. About half an hour later he came back to the house.

"I looked in the barn to see if his horse might have come back. The stall's empty. I'm going to go tell Loren Staker. I'll be back as soon as I can. I'm sorry, Ruth. We'll find him."

The sheriff banged on Art Lancer's door. Art opened it and peered out. "Yeah?" he asked sleepily. He glanced at Paul, and then recognized the sheriff. "Loren. Matter?"

"Was Matt in your place yesterday afternoon or evening?"

He nodded. "In one thirty. Stayed two hours." He shrugged.

"Did he leave with someone?"

Art shook his head.

"I talked to the man working the bar now. He said there was a couple of rough-looking characters in there, but they didn't leave until about four. Apparently Matt was determined to put something out of his mind. Your man said he drank probably two thirds of a bottle."

"And you let him? Not very charitable of you, Art," Paul said.

"Matt. Two thirds? Not much. I don't let . . . customers get . . . bad." He took a long, slow breath. "You know it." Art sounded insulted, and he scowled at Paul.

"He's right, Paul. Sorry, Art." Staker glanced at Paul and then looked back at Lancer. "So, he wasn't talking to those two toads? I saw them when they rode in."

Lancer shook his head. "Matt trouble?"

"Nope. Just didn't go home. Ruth hasn't seen him since yesterday afternoon. Nobody has."

"Damn."

"Well, thanks, Art. Sorry to kick you out of bed at eight thirty."

Art nodded and shut the door.

"Guess I better send someone over to Adobe. I can't imagine him riding that far, but you never know. I'll wire Sheriff Twitchell over in Kendrick and have him poke around too."

Kendrick was about seven miles west.

Matt could not be found in Adobe or Kendrick, and all day and into the evening, Staker waited in his office for some word of his whereabouts. The next morning two farmhands located Mr. Matthew Steele.

Sheriff Staker found Paul standing on Matt's porch. He dismounted, tied his horse to the hitching post, and waited for Paul to come down the steps to join him. "Couple fellas heard a horse nicker where a horse shouldn't be," he said quietly. "Matt's mare was there, and they found Matt on the riverbank. I've moved him to Doc Princher's office. His neck is broke."

Paul winced when he heard the last words. "Did he fall off his horse?"

"Don't think so. His horse was well away from the bank, tied up. No, he went off the edge and fell about twenty-five feet. I can see he lit headfirst. He'd been up on top for a while because his coat was lying on the ground, folded, and I could see where he sat. There's no sign of a struggle, and he wasn't robbed. His watch and a little money were still on him. I just don't know. For Ruth's sake, he slipped and fell."

"I'll tell her. Thanks, Loren."

A sick feeling welled up in his stomach as he climbed into his saddle. "Give her my regards, Paul. This is a tough one." He turned his horse away from the house as Paul opened the door and went in. The door had not even shut when Ruth screamed, the high piercing sound causing Staker's horse to sidestep suddenly. The closed door diminished, but could not silence, the awful sound as Ruth, facing her loss, offered up her soul in a wailing protest.

CHAPTER 38

"I want to see every piece of paper you have with the name Steele on it. Now!" John Lindstrom demanded. He hovered above Avery's desk, his six-foot, three-inch frame dressed in a dark frock coat and a black hat. The equally large Sheriff Staker stood right beside him. Together, they were an impressive sight, and Avery Singer almost did as he was told without thinking. Almost. He put on his best bluffing face.

"You only have the right to some of them, Mr. Lindstrom . . . to those of Paul Steele, and only as he has so designated. You don't have the same privilege regarding any of Matthew Steele's affairs." Avery's composure quickly slipped back in place and he stood up to gain whatever advantage that might give him. It wasn't much.

"This says I do." John laid an order from Judge Kingsley on the desk. "That says I represent the estate of Matthew Steele. It also says Sheriff Staker can have a look around. Sheriff."

"I'm looking into Matt's suspicious death," Staker said. "And I might want to look at your dealings with him, Avery."

"My dealings, as you refer to them, were and are legitimate, I can assure you."

"Good, then you have nothing to worry about, do you?"

"Please read the order, Mr. Singer," John said. He tapped his finger on the papers.

Avery picked up the papers and scanned the two pages. Suddenly he found it harder to breathe.

"See something you don't like?" Staker asked.

"No . . . of course not. It's . . . all in good order," he said, but couldn't completely control the stammer. He glanced at John. "Have you read the provisions?"

"Of course. I'm a lawyer."

Avery's eyes widened and he glanced at the sheriff.

"He knows, Mr. Singer," John said. "So does the judge. They know it all. That does not release you from your word. You will still keep my background confidential."

Avery nodded and laid the paper on the desk.

"So," John said, "knowing the provisions,

please give the sheriff your keys, and take a seat over there by the window."

"But . . . I don't see how . . . you don't really . . ." Avery, physically shaken, could not finish his thought.

"The order states in part, complete and uninhibited access to any and all records. I interpret uninhibited as you getting out of my way," John said as he stepped around the desk. "Now, the keys, if you will."

Avery opened his desk and handed the keys to the sheriff. John curtly nodded and Avery walked across the room and sat in the chair by the window. He couldn't bear to watch as Staker unlocked the strongbox and the two tall cabinets. The sheriff nodded to John, who went to the cabinets and started to methodically search through the folders and stacks of neatly ordered and labeled files.

"Why, in the name of all that's holy, would he keep something as incriminating as the original will?" Paul asked. He and John sat across the table from Sheriff Staker, in Avery's office. Avery was across the street, enjoying the sheriff's hospitality suite.

"Leverage," John said. "Avery has a character flaw that compels him to know something secret about everyone. Even the most insignificant fact will do. He's a compulsive social voyeur, if I may coin a phrase; a snoop, I think is the new word. And then he'd use that information to his advantage." He shook his head. "I know his Uncle Sylvan in Saint Louis quite well. Singer was sent here to learn a lesson. He has a gambling problem, among other vices. I agreed to keep an eye on him. Sylvan Singer is honest and aboveboard, Avery's polar opposite. He will be very disappointed, but you may rest assured that he will make good on any obligation Avery undertook, or that may be in jeopardy because of his current predicament."

"Like Waldon and Lancer?" Paul asked.

"I don't think his magnanimity will extend that far. They were charging Matt eleven percent on their loans. I think justice was done there."

"I have to agree," Staker said. "They were looking to gouge him when he was most needful. That's not right."

"And the trusts for which Avery was trustee? What about them?" Paul asked.

"I am going to ask Sylvan if I might be entrusted with them until he can arrange for someone to come out and take over Avery's affairs. This bank is actually owned by Sylvan's holding company."

"Do you mean Avery didn't actually own this?" Staker asked.

"Nope."

"Then how did he commit to loans and the like?"

"He had a limit. It looks like a thousand dollars. For anything above that, he had to ask Saint Louis for clearance."

"I'll be damned. Is there anything genuine about Avery Singer?"

"Only his charm, gentlemen, only his charm."

The judge looked at Ruth over the paper he was studying and smiled his sympathy. Ana and Paul sat beside her. "I rule the will, executed at Carl Steele's death, to be a forgery. We are here to correct that travesty. Pursuant to that, I will read the document I judge to be the true last will and testament of Carl Steele."

Judge Kingsley, slowly and deliberately, read the twelve clauses that Carl Steele had had printed in Omaha, the details clear and unambiguous. Paul was to have control of the farm with Matt sharing the labor and proceeds, the shares to be determined solely by Paul. A house was to have been built, the size already determined by a pre-laid foundation. It was precisely the same size as the home place. Trust funds had been set up for the grandchildren, the shares divided equally among as many children as were born to Paul and Matt. The trust was to be delivered to the children when they reached the age of twenty. Two unencumbered lump sums of five hundred dollars each were to be paid to Ana and Ruth, as wives of Paul and Matt. And he read on to the last detail.

"Are there any questions about what I've just read?" the judge asked.

All three slowly shook their heads.

"Very well. As this will is part of Carl Steele's property, I am giving it over to Paul." He got up, walked around his desk and handed the papers to him. Turning to Ruth, he bowed slightly and took her hand. "Once again, my condolences, Ruth. I'm very sorry."

"Thank you, Judge," she murmured.

The three got up and left the courthouse, cum law office, cum real-estate office.

Ana put her hand on her sister's arm. "Would you like to come home with us for a cup of coffee?"

"No, I want to go back to the farm and just think. I'm homeless. I have no means to support David and my —"

"Don't you even think such a thing. I will not hear it!" Ana felt her face get hot, and she closed her fingers on her sister's arm. "Do you hear me? I won't have you worrying about something like that. You must not." Ana now held Ruth by the shoulders, her face directly in her sister's.

Ruth looked down, as though she were ashamed.

"Look at me," Ana demanded.

Ruth raised her head.

Ana let go of her and turned to Paul. "You tell her she has nothing to worry about."

"Of course. There's no need for you to do anything. You must stay in your home. David is old enough to run that farm. I'll see to it that he gets it done right."

"See? Nothing," Ana said. "Absolutely nothing to worry about." She stepped close and hugged her sister. "Now go home and rest. I'll be by to see you this afternoon."

Ruth's eye's filled with tears, and she reached for both Ana and Paul, hugging them. "I love you two so much," she murmured.

Ana smiled at her sister as Paul helped Ruth into the spring wagon, then Paul's arm settled around Ana's shoulder. They watched Ruth drive down the street.

"I'll drink that cup of coffee with you," he said and boosted Ana into their wagon.

■ ■ ■ ■

Paul and Ana sat at the kitchen table. "We own the old home place, Ana. All of it. We were supposed to have it all along. I'm still having a hard time making that real." Paul picked up his cup and took a sip.

"I don't understand. Matt couldn't be satisfied with a house of his own, right there on the farm. Free and clear and built to Ruth's wishes. He had to have it all."

"Now I understand that old foundation across from the house. Pa was thinking even then about Matt and me sharing. I wish I could understand why he was so rough on me. I worked three times harder than Matt did, and Matt always got the praise. I got the blisters."

"I think your father was as wise as Solomon. Could we have survived what we had to if you were not as strong as you were? Did he know you'd need that strength?" Ana laid her hand on his arm. "He knew the quality of your heart, Pa. He was depending on you to carry Matt later. He could not have known what Matt would do, but he prepared you for the worst."

"But you could have been living in that beautiful house. That makes me angry.

Matt's pride and greed made you suffer."

"I can't say I would have preferred to live in the soddy. But what memories we have. So close to our children. Would we be so close had we not lived in each other's pockets?" Ana chuckled. "Would we have missed some of that, living in a grand house? I don't know, Paul, but I'm content with our lot. I'm truly grateful for our blessings." She got up and came around the table to stand by him. "I think it would be a sin to wish changing anything that might take away a single part of what we have." Ana kissed him full on his lips and then hugged him to her chest. "I love you." She sat back down, and wrapped her hands around the warm coffee cup.

"So, you don't want to move onto the home place?" Paul asked.

"No. My husband built me a house. We built it. And the kids built it. This is our home. No, Paul, I want to stay here."

"You have no idea how that makes me feel." His lip trembled until he bit it into submission.

"Oh, I think I do." Ana reached across the table and squeezed his hand.

"Let Ruth know this afternoon, then. I'll go have a talk with David. I'm not expecting that to go without a hitch or two. He

451

and I have never seen eye to eye, and he may not like the idea of working for me. I'm hoping we can work that out."

She could see he was no longer talking to her, but thinking out loud.

"I suppose I can find someone else to run the place for me, or run the chicken farm and I can run the home acreage. Yeah, that would work too. Wish Simon was just a little older, but then it's obvious he isn't cut out to be a farmer. Anyway, it'll all work out." He stopped talking and looked at her, his face getting red. "Won't it?" he finished lamely.

Ana smiled and got up. "Another cup? That one's gone cold."

The agreement with David had not been that hard to reach. Faced with trying to find a job in town where the general consensus granted he was a bully and an ingrate, he agreed to work for Paul. His ability to shirk his duties was severely limited because Paul hired another hand as well, this one a Missouri farmer, used to hard work and long hours and not one to brook laziness.

David soon learned how hard his father had worked. They burned the flattened grain fields after the last hay crop was cut. And paid a premium price for stock feed in

Kendrick.

Ruth accepted, finally, that she was welcome to stay in her home as long as she wished. She gave all of Matt's clothes to the Reverend Bray to do with as he saw fit. Then she, together with Ana, joined the literary club, a quilting circle, a homemaker's group, and the Women's Suffrage Movement.

Avery Singer, escorted by a stern-looking, well-dressed, and obviously wealthy gentleman from Saint Louis by the name of Sylvan Singer, met with Judge Kingsley. Folks were surprised that John Lindstrom, the former town drunk, and this well-heeled gentleman were the best of friends. Folks were also surprised that John was the only citizen in town asked to attend Avery's hearing.

Judge Kingsley ruled that Avery Singer be assessed a fine of two thousand five hundred dollars, and Judge Kingsley further advised, though he did not rule, that Mr. Singer's continued residency in Carlisle would be looked on with disfavor. Mr. Sylvan Singer agreed to escort Avery Singer out of town.

Nathan Greene regained consciousness after ten days of comatose slumber. He could not remember anything from the time they left Fort Hartwell until he woke up to see Freda Luger's huge backside. He just knew he was, as he put it: "Hungry enough to eat a goat." He and the other Texans left for Oklahoma Territory with a promise from a couple of them to keep in touch with two of the town's young ladies.

Werner Swartz could not meet Simon's eye. Young Gus showed a renewed interest in his job at the store, more or less commensurate with Sheriff Staker's interest in him. With the new system of cross-checking invoices to lading bills, the shortages mysteriously disappeared. No apology to Simon Steele was forthcoming.

The episode in the Kingsleys' kitchen had radically changed Simon's view of Sarah. He could not look at her without blushing, yet he found he hated to be apart from her for more than a couple of days. It was apparent, to anyone who cared to look, that they were always going to be a pair. Sarah enjoyed his undivided attention.

CHAPTER 39

Easter of 1867 arrived dry and cold, and for David, dark. In a foul mood, he hated getting up early for farm chores, but the Missouri Mule, as he referred to Mr. Jensen, had Sundays off, so David had cows to milk. Sometimes Mr. Jensen could be convinced to come by, but not often, today being an example.

In any event, the cows suffered his mood, and it didn't improve when he left the barn and saw a buckboard parked in front of the house. Stomping through the kitchen door, he spotted Paisley Mace sitting at the kitchen table with his mother. "What's he doing here?" David looked at his mother, his face set in an angry grimace.

"He's here to take me to the Sunrise Service at the church."

Mace stood. "We should really try to get along, David."

"I don't want you here. Get out." David

glared at him.

"There's no call for that, David. I invited Paisley here."

"Well, you didn't ask me, and I want him out." Challenged, he started to lose control and his hands clenched into fists.

"I don't need to ask you. Now you stop being rude, or you can go back out and stay with the animals."

"You can't treat me like that." He stepped toward his mother.

Mace stepped in between. "Don't." He looked David in the eyes. "You'd better cool down."

"You'll regret this." David stormed out the door.

Mace turned around and looked at Ruth, who'd gone pale around the mouth. "Phew, I thought you said things were going all right. That looked like the David I know."

"Things have been, really. I don't understand it. He has never been warm toward me, but he hasn't acted like that since Matt died."

"Do you want me to leave? I really hate to, with him in a foul mood. But I don't want to cause trouble either."

"No. This is my home. I can ask whomever I want here. We'll go as planned. Now sit down and finish your coffee. I'll get my cloak and we'll leave."

Mace finished his drink and they attended a wonderful service together. There were several, especially older, residents who remembered times past regarding Ruth and Mace and smiled. And others who fussed like old hens at what they saw as an impropriety.

Later that afternoon, Ruth did regret challenging David. No one knew it because it didn't show, and Ruth kept silent about the pain.

CHAPTER 40

Carlisle grew through 1867. Eight hundred ninety-three people now called the little town on the prairie home. And Nebraska became a state. Mace and Ruth saw more and more of each other. Simon and Sarah continued their dance. Buell was Buell. And then 1868 came, lavished twelve months of life on the folks of Carlisle, and ended.

The railroad connecting east to west was nearly a realized dream. The new station in Carlisle bustled with activity. Boxes arrived, filled with dreams only now available; and coaches left, carrying dreamers, only now able to search far and wide.

Steele and Company had acquired nearly two square miles of prime wheat-growing land and a mill to change to flour the golden grain raised on those fields. The home place, expanded by another forty acres, now prospered as a model of efficiency as David developed into a successful farmer.

Simon had finished school, and in the meantime had helped, in one way or another, several of the new businesses in town get established. Life was good in Carlisle and New Year's Eve, 1869, was going to be celebrated in style at Luger's Emporium, newly named and renovated.

The ladies settled as a group in the anteroom. Separated from the main saloon, they could enjoy a glass of sherry or wine and chat among themselves. Even Sarah and Mrs. Kingsley allowed themselves a visit on very special occasions, tonight being one, while others of the Temperance Movement stayed home. All present enjoyed the run-up to the magic hour when the New Year, full of promise and hope, would be ushered in. Freda Luger, wearing one of her rare smiles, bustled in and out with drinks and favors. She actually seemed relaxed.

With the main saloon packed, Paul, Mace, John and Alex Prosser sat at a table pushed up against the wall. Mace and Paul had to constantly lean over the table to stay out of the way of the milling throng.

"Quite a party," Mace said. "I don't recall seeing this many people in one place except for the July picnic."

"There are people here I've never seen in Luger's. Must be the free beer." Paul chuckled as he looked over at the proud saloonkeeper.

Lancer's had remodeled the year before, and Fred Luger had seen his business drop by twenty-five percent. Simon helped him put together a summary of the last three years' accounts and Fred had gone to the bank, now a genuine institution complete with a new robbery-proof vault. The manager, handpicked by the bank's Saint Louis owner, had proved a fair and honest man. The loan had been forthcoming and Luger was showing off the results tonight. He had dreams of all these people coming back, every one of them, every night. Such is the hope of a New Year's celebration.

In their back room sanctuary, Simon, Buell, and Jake sat around a table, Simon and Jake with a beer each.

Buell stood, holding a full whiskey glass, and raised it high. "Here's to freedom from worry and strife. To play when I want, 'thout askin' a wife, to drink with my friends, and stay out all night, still standing up straight when they turn out the light." With a bow, he gave Simon a huge grin.

"Where did you get that?" Simon asked,

truly amazed. Never, in all his years of talking and listening to his friend, had Buell shown the slightest interest in such an effort.

"Some of that shit's gotta rub off. I been listening to you longer than I want to remember. And most of what you had to say didn't make a lick a sense."

"Well, I hope you step in it too," Simon said as he raised his beer mug.

Buell reached over the table and clinked his glass against Simon's. Jake did the same. "To freedom," Buell said.

The three of them toasted the secret they had been discussing. Simon was going to ask Sarah to marry him when he turned nineteen in September.

David didn't want to go to Luger's but he needed a whiskey, and Ruth didn't allow it in the house. He'd tried hiding a bottle, but it always ended up missing. Even the stuff he hid in the barn disappeared, and he suspected the Missouri Mule. Opening the outside door at Luger's, he entered the foyer. As he passed the ladies' anteroom, he heard Sarah's lilting giggle.

He stood and stared at the closed door, off-limits to males. Sarah laughed again. His lip turned up in the start of a sneer, and then he noticed the scrawny man sitting in the tobacco booth, watching. He gave him a dirty look, and walked through the door, into the saloon. He'd be in Lancer's if Art Lancer would let him, but he was barred until further notice for beating the daylights out of a drummer. The salesman, drunk, had picked the fight, and Lancer couldn't get around the bar in time to stop David from pulverizing the man's nose and dislocating his jaw. David had enjoyed it. Scanning the bar, he saw a few less people at the left end and headed that way, elbowing his way through. He got several rude remarks in the process, but as soon as the jostled person saw who they were addressing, they quickly made way for the scowling farmer.

Luger waited for him at the bar. "I don't want any trouble." David's altercation at Lancer's was common knowledge.

"Not here to cause any. I just want a drink." He watched Luger for any sign of a challenge.

"What'll it be?"

"Rye, a double."

David picked up the drink and turned around to look over the crowded room. He saw many familiar faces, but no one he wanted to talk to. He tossed back his drink and gritted his teeth as the alcohol burned a path down his throat. He turned to catch Luger's attention and spotted instead Buell, Simon, and Jake coming out of the back room at the far end of the room.

The trio sauntered up to the bar and Jake stepped behind it. Three men standing next to David departed hastily, Buell's reputation still very much intact even though he wasn't wearing a gun. Fred Luger's new rules prohibited firearms. Simon and Buell walked along the bar until they were within touching distance of David.

"Hello, David," Simon said. "Glad you could come out for Luger's party."

"I didn't come for the company, so don't waste your civil manners on me."

"I'm sorry you feel that way. I wish we could let bygones be just that. We're still family."

"I'm not here to listen to you whine. I came to get a drink. Period."

"Fine. Maybe I can buy you one?"

David looked at his cousin and felt like spitting on his shoes. "I've had enough of your charity. You and your family are thieves and liars. I work like a slave so you can fiddle your books and take it all away." He looked at Buell. "And your pa, sniffing around like a dog."

Buell started to move but Simon put up

his arm and caught him in the chest. "Can't control your mouth, can you?" Buell pushed Simon's arm away.

"I don't like him, and I like you even less. And without your pistol in your belt, you ain't that big." He glared at Buell. "You wanna start something, come on."

"I told you, no trouble, David." Luger stood across the bar with Jake right beside him.

"I didn't start any. They did."

"That ain't the way I see it. I want you to leave."

"You ain't got no right. I didn't do anything." David could feel the blood rise in his face. Several people had heard the exchange and now stood, listening.

"I got the right. Now leave . . . the back way." Luger started around the end of the bar.

"You bastards." David pushed his way down the bar, spilling drinks and jostling all the way as he cleared a path through the partygoers. He got to the rear door, humiliation shoving at his back, and turned. The hatred he felt for Simon and Buell seemed to chill in his lungs. He tore the door open and left.

Ana's happiness could not be contained.

464

She got out of her chair, wrapped her arms around Simon, and squeezed with all her might.

"I am so pleased. It goes without saying that we hoped you two would one day marry, but I ho—" She stopped, superstition holding her tongue. Wish for the rain and live with the storm, she thought and smiled. "Irene and I have talked about this, and she will be thrilled." She went back to her chair and sat.

Simon took a seat on the sofa. "I haven't told anybody except Buell and Jake."

"Well, when are you going to tell Sarah?"

"I'm not sure. I've been with her since the first grade, and I should know her as well as I know anybody but . . . sometimes she really surprises me."

"That's what makes her a woman. We never want you men to really understand us. Best to keep you wondering." Ana smiled at her oldest son. "Don't you worry. Sarah is very fond of you, and if you ask her I think you'll like the answer."

"I hope so. But it'll take a bit for me to work up the courage."

"Then don't be so deliberate about it. Wait until the moment seems right and ask. If you plan it, then things you can't control will interfere at the worst possible time."

Simon looked at her and shook his head. "That's why a fella talks to his ma."

"Have you decided to go back East to school yet?" She knew Simon was getting encouragement from every quarter to apply at Harvard or Yale: The judge, John Lindstrom, Miss Everett. All believed he had the potential to excel in business. The judge thought he could very well become a successful politician. "Make a real difference for Nebraska" was the way he liked to put it.

Ana wasn't sure Simon could be a politician. The way the US Senate had changed the Nebraska Constitution to suit Washington politics had been a serious topic in the house, and Simon had been disgusted with the lot of them. The fact that John seemed to agree with Simon carried a lot of weight.

"Going to school means several years away from Sarah and Carlisle," Simon said. "Just that thought makes me feel odd. I don't know if getting an education will make it any easier to make a living or not. I just don't know."

"You don't have to decide now," Ana said. "Next year is soon enough. And let the question to Sarah come when it will. Thank you so much for telling me, though. That means a lot."

CHAPTER 41

John Lindstrom sat in his office. With Nebraska statehood granted, he had applied to the Nebraska bar and gotten his license to practice law. He'd done it primarily because he was still trustee for several trust funds he had taken over when Avery Singer had been asked to leave town.

Before him were the calculations he'd done to figure David Steele's share of the trust Carl Steele had set up years before. The original five thousand dollars set aside in 1850 had grown to over twenty-two thousand. John had been very successful at growing the fund by liquidating some real estate, and aside from the near disastrous mess caused by Matt's loan the year he died, Avery Singer had done equally well for the fund. Paul had retired Matt's loan at the eleventh hour. John shuddered as he remembered contemplating the legal ramifications of that not getting done. Paul and

Ana's children — and David Steele — were actually quite wealthy in their own right. John had pretty much decided what he wanted to say to David when, and if, he arrived.

He was surprised the young man arrived on time. David stopped just inside the door. "You wanted to see me?"

"Yes, I did. Please, sit down." John motioned to a chair across from his desk.

David hesitated for a moment, then shrugged and sat. "Why not?" He folded his arms across his chest. "What do you want?"

"On June the fifth, you gain the age of twenty years. And on that day, you are entitled to one sixth of a trust fund that your grandfather Steele set up."

David abruptly sat forward in his chair. "Money? Cash?"

"Yes, there are some bonds and two promissory notes, but for the most part, cash."

"How much?"

"As of this morning, and as close as I can calculate, thirty-six hundred ninety-one dollars. But —"

"Haw!" David slumped back in his chair and looked at him sullenly for several seconds before taking a deep breath and exhaling slowly. Leaning forward again, he shook his head, a cynical expression on his face. "And now you're gonna tell me I get screwed out of it, right? About what I ex—"

"No." His critical stare silenced David. "If I can finish. The provisions of the trust do not require that you withdraw your share. You may leave it until the last beneficiary turns twenty years of age. That would be your cousin Eric who, now eleven, would be twenty in eighteen seventy-eight."

"I'll take —"

"Please, David, let me finish. A fund worth over twenty-two thousand dollars will draw more attention than one worth thirty-seven hundred. Leaving your money to work in concert with the rest would be a wise decision. You may withdraw your share at any time after its maturity, but when you do, you have to withdraw all of it. Now think about it a minute."

"I want it now. Today."

An expression John had seen before appeared on David's face; pursed lips, jaw thrust forward and narrowed eyes, David daring him to challenge. "You've misunderstood. You may have it on June the fifth. That's a little over a month away. I'll draw up the papers," John said stonily. "You can pick up your money on your birthday."

"No bullshit? All of it? I'll be damned.

Yahooo!" David stood, his face beaming, and then he stared into John's eyes. "You ain't fooling?"

John said nothing.

David continued to study John. "You ain't," he declared, and started to laugh. "I can't believe it. I can finally get the hell out of this place." Still laughing, he turned to leave.

"David, wait a minute. The existence of the trust is confidential. You are not to tell any of the others that they have an inheritance coming. I'm asking you to keep this in confidence."

"So why did you tell me?"

"It's provided in the trust. Beneficiaries are to be told the first day of the month prior to their birth month. Today is the first of May."

"And if I don't keep quiet?"

"I'm simply asking."

David turned and left without answering.

Sarah and Simon sat together in the porch glider at Sarah's house. The early evening air hung perfectly still, and the smell of fresh-turned earth announced the real arrival of spring. Half reclining against the cushioned arms, both lost in their own thoughts, Simon kept the swing moving with one dangling foot. They were in perfect harmony, eyes closed and facing each other.

"Sarah?" Simon said quietly.

"Uh-huh."

"Have you thought about my going away to school?"

"Uh-huh."

He opened his eyes and looked at her. A familiar buoyancy, like he'd suddenly become weightless, took his breath for a moment; it happened when he saw her like this; her eyes closed and her face completely relaxed. The flat light of the evening made the peach fuzz hair on her face glow. She breathed through her mouth, her barely parted lips inviting a kiss. Lost in the curving, turning, half-conscious nether land of fantasy, he no longer saw just her; their minds and spirits had merged.

"Caught you looking again."

Simon gasped as her face snapped back into focus. "Uh . . . I . . ." He swallowed hard and wiped his face with one hand. "I was a thousand miles away." He chuckled nervously.

"Obviously." Sarah offered him a bare whisper of a smile. "And what were you thinking of?"

"Same as always when I look at you dozing. You're beautiful, and I can't believe you

471

love me."

She leaned over and kissed him gently on the cheek. "It's not hard to do," she said and then sat up straight. She lowered one foot to stop the gently moving swing. "I think I could survive your being gone all winter and spring, so long as I knew you would be back every year. But you would have to write every other day. And Father said they let students take a lengthy break at Christmas. You could come home then too."

"You have thought about it, then? I wanted to go, but decided to do what you wanted. I'm so happy you agree."

Simon stood, and after taking a deep breath and clearing his throat lightly, he faced her. His heart accelerated and a cold sweat crept down his back. "Good. That's good . . . uh . . . now Sarah . . . now I . . ." His brow furrowed and he cleared his throat again. "Now, we have to decide what school I should apply to," he finished lamely. He gave her a weak smile as his shoulders slumped.

Disappointment flooded her face, then merged seconds later with confusion, both adding to his frustration. He moved to the railing and leaned against it, staring into the gathering dusk.

■ ■ ■ ■

With her arms folded across her chest, Ruth stood between the table and the stove, and watched her son.

"I ain't gonna spend another minute looking at the ass end of a mule." David looked up at her.

"You have to. Either that or we have to find somewhere else to live. I will not stay here, as much as I love this place, if we cannot earn our keep."

"What the hell you mean *our*? I'm the one that busts his ass fourteen hours a day. You, with all your shitty meetings, and all your shitty friends. You don't work hard enough in a week to raise a sweat for a minute." David stood up with a rush, jarring the table and spilling his coffee.

She instinctively stepped back.

"I'm tired of it, sick and damned tired. That Missouri Mule that Uncle Paul sent over here? All he does is watch me work, and then go tell Paul when I sit down for five minutes."

"David, you are not being reasonable." Ruth wanted to object to his language, but decided she'd better not. She'd seen this more times than she wanted to remember, the outrage, the flared nostrils and clenched fists.

"Reasonable? We get screwed out of this farm, somebody kills Pa, and you want me to be reasonable? You make me sick. Get the hell out of here!" He took a quick step toward her.

Ruth turned and bolted for the parlor. His boot caught her at the very top of her thigh. The impact spun her around and she lost her feet. Arms flailing for something to grasp, she slammed into the dining table, the edge catching her just under her armpit. Grinding her teeth together against the pain, she first sat, then slumped prone on the floor, her lungs refusing to respond.

David didn't give her a second look. He grabbed his hat from the table, swatted the empty coffee cup against the black stove, and crashed through the screen door.

A few minutes later, Ruth clutched the front door frame and watched as David galloped across the barnyard, and then off the road, heading toward Adobe again. Hanging onto furniture and leaning on the walls for support, Ruth made it back to her bedroom to examine the damage he'd inflicted this time.

"He took off 'bout one or one thirty

yesta'day. I was fixin' to stop for a bite to eat, and saw 'im ridin' hard east. He weren't on the road, more out in the prairie. Figgered he'd be back t'day, but he never showed." Jude Jensen, the man Paul had hired to help David, looked distinctly uncomfortable.

"Does Mrs. Steele know where he went?" Paul asked. He stepped around the hay rake he was working on.

"I went to the house and asked her. She said he had biz'ness he had to take care of. Said he'd be back t'morra. Problem is, Mr. Steele, with just the two of us, we cain't be waitin' no two 'er three days to git them oats in the ground. I hate like the dickens ta be a scampin' on 'im like this, but God ain't a'gonna wait." The Missouri man sighed and turned his wide brimmed hat nervously in his hands.

"Wished he'd tell someone when he needs to take off. He knows better than that, don't you think?" Paul was exasperated. He couldn't leave what he was doing, and every hand around was busy with their own spring work.

"It ain't like 'im," the Missourian said. "That young feller's got to be the hardest workin' boy I ever met. Darn near kills me some days to keep up with 'im. I expect if we get after it in the mornin' we'll git 'er done, but if'n he don't show up, I gotta have some help." He looked down at his crushed hat, unconsciously crumpled into a gray wad of dusty felt. With a slightly disgusted snort, he snapped it against his leg, and then held it with two hands behind his back.

"I'll come by first thing in the morning. We'll figger something out."

"A'ight. I'll git back at it." Jude Jensen clapped his hat on his head, climbed on his mule and rode off.

Paul stretched his shoulders. He hated working under machinery; his wide body just didn't want to fit where it was needed. He got down on his hands and knees, retrieved a wrench from the dirt, and scowled at the rusty nut he had been threatening for the last ten minutes.

Paul rode up to the house and tied his horse to a ring. The door was closed, so he knocked.

"Come in," Ruth called.

He pushed open the door and stepped into the dimly lit parlor. The single lamp burning sat on the end table next to the sofa where she sat. The curtains were all closed. "Wanna leave it open?" Paul asked. "It's really getting nice out there."

"No, please close it." Ruth laid down the tatting she held in her hands. "How's Ana?"

"Baking bread." His eyebrows flashed appreciation with the thought.

"Your favorite. I know." Ruth smiled a half smile.

"Did David come back from his . . . uh . . . trip?"

"Yes, he's out now with Mr. Jensen, planting oats." She did not meet his eyes. "Would you like a cup of coffee?" The ritual Swedish offering was made.

"Sure." The ritual acceptance.

"I don't want to chance getting this tangled up," she said, indicating her needlework. "Would you mind getting it?" Definitely not part of the ritual.

Paul looked at her for a moment and then smiled. "You want one?"

"No, I've had mine. But you go ahead."

Paul went into the kitchen and opened the cupboard that held his mother's beautiful blue china cups. A wave of nostalgia hit him. He took out a cup and filled it. Not very hot, but hot enough. He chuffed, remembering his father sitting at that very table. Every cup of coffee his father had ever drunk, from scalding hot to barely tepid, had been greeted precisely the same way: a hissing, tentative sip, followed by a soft sigh and a satisfied grin before he'd pronounce it "Just right to drink." Paul smiled to himself and went back into the parlor.

"Did you find it all right?"

"Yeah. Just gathering wool for a minute." He took a tentative sip and chuckled.

"What?" Ruth said, smiling at him now, and her smile looked heartfelt this time.

"Nothin'. Just talking with a memory for a second." He sat on the end of the sofa and looked at her. "I know it's not my business, but where did David go?" He immediately put up his hand to stop her answer. "I admit it's none of my business and then ask anyway. That's stupid. Forget I asked."

"That's okay, he —"

"I don't have the right to ask, and I've put you on the spot by doing so. I'll go out and see him, and if he wants to tell me, he will." Paul downed the rest of his drink and got up. "I'll git now. Thanks for the coffee."

He walked into the kitchen, put the cup on the wash counter, and returned. "I'll see you later, sis," he said, as he pulled the door open.

"Leave it open, Paul. You're right, it is getting nice out."

"So, looks like you're getting it done." Paul

sat astride his horse. David stood beside the Pennock's Planter, while the two draft mules swished flies with their tails. The left mule turned its head to look at them. Apparently satisfied, it turned back and started to doze with the other mule.

"God ain'ta gonna wait," David mocked. "I hear that one more time I'm gonna punch that ol' fart in the gut." He spit into the dirt.

"He means well. He's a good man." Paul swung his leg over the saddle and got down. The left mule checked the status again, and went back to dozing.

"He sure gets in my craw. I can't seem to make 'im happy, no matter how hard I work."

"That's not exactly true. Matter of fact, he figgers you're one of the best farmers he's ever worked with."

"Yeah, sure. What else does he tell you on his daily visits?" He spit again.

"Daily visits? I don't expect I talk to him more than once a week. Sure, I see him, but that's because he lives in the old soddy. He's got his work and I've got mine. I'm there with the poultry, not to see him."

"Well, I'm getting tired of this. All I do is work."

"You're going to find that life is like that. Work."

"Yeah. We may just see about that shortly. Your friend John told me about Grandpa's trust fund. Come June, I won't be needin' to do this shit. Come June, I might just get the hell out a here."

"I'd be really sorry to see you go, David. I mean that. The last couple years you've grown up a lot. You've still got a hot head, but you'll learn to control it. There's a place for you here. And it's possible you won't be working shares forever."

"What you mean? You own this. I ain't never gonna make enough to buy anything."

"You have your share coming from that trust. I don't know exactly how much it is, but it must be something. Have you thought about buying in here?"

"Sure. And give you the money. No, thanks. I've seen how that lawyer friend of yours takes care of shit like that. You can stop thinkin' about it. You ain't gettin' your hands on it."

"I don't want your money. I'm offering something stable."

"Good, because you ain't gettin' it." David threw the reins over his shoulder and gripping the four lines in his fingers, leaned back. "Yaw mule! Git!"

The mules jerked their heads up and leaned forward in the harness. The clattering planter started off, dust flying as David pulled away, stiff legged, controlling the powerful animals expertly. Paul watched for a minute, then mounted his horse, and rode back to town.

John's office door swung open and David entered. The lawyer nodded toward one of the three chairs. "Good morning. Sit down."

David took a seat. "Got it ready?"

"Yes. But I have to ask you one more time. Please think —"

"Give it to me." David cut him off. "You said the fifth, and it's the fifth!"

John released a deep sigh. "Very well. Sign this."

"What is it?"

"Read it. It's simply your statement that you desire payment in full on this date. That terminates your participation in the trust. It's irrevocable." John leaned back in his chair and watched David glance at the document.

"Gimme a pen."

John pushed the inkwell and pen toward him. "Your full name . . . David Carl Steele."

David studiously wrote his name, and then pushed the paper away.

John slid it across the desk, glanced at the signature, blotted it, and put it aside. Opening his desk drawer, he took out a white pouch and thumped it in the middle of his desk. "I've made the amount to be thirty-seven hundred dollars, twenty-two cents. This pouch contains that in gold and US notes." He shoved the heavy bag across the desk.

David grabbed it, and with his eyes gleaming, fumbled with the thong binding the top. Finally, he pulled it open and reached inside to withdraw a bundle of notes — five-dollar bills. Grinning like an idiot, he reached in again and withdrew a paper. It had the Carlisle Mercantile Bank heading.

"If you would, please count that."

"Don't need to." David held up the bank paper. "This says thirty-seven hundred dollars and twenty-two cents, just like you said."

"Then please initial it."

David did as he was told.

John picked up the document and glanced at it. "If that's all." John looked at him, wishing there was some way to change David's mind.

"That's it." David stuffed the packet of fives back into the bag and stood.

John stepped around his desk and opened

the door. "Be careful, son. For God's sake, be careful," he said as David hurried past.

David stepped into the street, looked left toward Lancer's, and then right. Sheriff Staker stood in the doorway of the jail across the street — John nodded at them before turning to go inside. David headed for Lancer's.

Chapter 42

Sarah stopped the buggy in front of the house and looked around at the farm. She'd always liked this place, so neat and clean. She stepped down, tethered the horse, and walked up to the front door where she knocked.

"Well, hello," David said. He pushed the screen door open.

"Is your mother here?" Sarah noticed he stood a little unsteady on his feet.

"Who wanch ta know?" He blinked slowly.

"Is she here, David?" she repeated, curtly.

His eyes narrowed. "Always . . . sharp. Used ta gittin' yer way."

"You're drunk," she accused. "I'll leave."

David flushed, and more quickly than she would have thought possible, reached out and grabbed her arm.

"When I say ya can," he muttered. Nearly yanking her off her feet, he pulled her into the house. "Bitch."

Panic shocked Sarah like a gunshot. Her scalp tightened and her eyes widened. She felt her bladder about to release and turned her face away from him; not looking would make him go away.

"Always lookin' but never givin', huh, Sarah? All through school ya teased. Both Gus and me. And then scamprin' off ta that shit Simon. Well, ya ain't scamprin' t'day." He spun her around and wrapped both arms around her shoulders. Sarah kicked and screamed as he carried her across the parlor, through the kitchen, and into Ruth's bedroom.

"No!" Sarah screamed. "David! No!"

She beat at the strong hands clasped across her chest, the pain in her crushed breasts making her light-headed. She bent forward and tried to bite his arm, helpless in his powerful grip. She screamed again, and he dumped her on the bed, her skirt and petticoats flying up. Frantically, she pushed her skirts down and saw his eyes go wide as he stared at her pants. She screamed again and tried to claw his eyes, but he threw her skirts over her hands.

David fought through the tangle of cotton and lace, found her face and clamped his hand over her mouth, finally stifling her strangled protests. She slapped and clawed at the fabric that covered her head, and confused her hands. He bore down harder on her mouth with one hand while the other reached toward her belly. His fingers found the top of her bloomers, and as he slipped one side over her hip, she suddenly went slack.

He uncovered her face and felt for her breath. Smiling, he used both hands to strip off her underclothes, then stood up, undid his belt, and ogled her bare skin. The scarlet teardrop on her hip drew his attention. Stooping over the still woman, he traced the edge of the birthmark with his work-hardened finger, the contrast of his hand's coarse skin and her smooth bare hip, raw and vulgar. Chuckling, he fumbled with the bulky belt he wore under his shirt. The ties resisted him, but finally came loose and the money pouch thumped to the floor. Breathing heavily, he shrugged out of his suspenders and tore at the buttons on his pants.

Ruth and Ana had spent the afternoon as they frequently did, talking. The warm June day kept them on the back porch, out of the sun and with a view of the river bluffs.

"I'll be happy when we finish that quilt," Ana said. "I didn't like the looks of that pattern when we first saw it. And now I know why. Sometimes I have to fight sleep when we're working on it."

"You think that's monotonous, try tatting. One slip and you wind up tak— oh, dear!"

"What?" Ana said, startled.

Ruth, her hand over her mouth, had a guilty look on her face. "I was supposed to show Sarah a bit about tatting this afternoon. It completely slipped my mind. How embarrassing."

"Oh, my."

"I'll just have to stop on my way home and apologize. I'd better do that right now." She got up.

"You're right. Maybe you can . . . no, it's too late. She'll understand. Probably spent a pretty dull afternoon though."

The sisters walked around the house to Ruth's buggy. Ana waved as her sister started the short trip to the Kingsleys'.

"She's in her room," Irene Kingsley said. "She came home rather upset. Said her horse nearly ran away with the shay. Scared the daylights out of her. She looked horrible. Poor thing. I haven't bothered her for a couple of hours. I think I can go up and tell her you're here."

"Oh, no, Irene. Just tell her I'm terribly sorry I missed her. It completely slipped my mind. I'll just go home, and we'll arrange another time."

Ruth got into her buggy and took the south road home, avoiding Main Street.

Next morning David sat nursing a wicked headache. He had not slept well and the cup of coffee he stared at looked foul. He put the cup down on the table. "I don't want you to start," he grumbled when he saw his mother looking at him.

"Mr. Jensen cannot work seven days a week," Ruth said. "I told him he didn't have to be here tonight or tomorrow morning for the cows. It's up to you." She stood by the stove, a cup of coffee in her hand.

"Well, you got a problem, then, because I'm going to Adobe tonight, and I don't expect I'll be back. You still remember how to milk a cow?" He looked at her and sneered. "Maybe you can do something around here for a change."

"That's not fair. I keep your clothes clean, cook your meals and keep this house."

"And leave the buggy out front for me or the Mule to put away." He dared her to deny it.

"Where were you to see that? I thought you were gone. Did you see Sarah Kingsley then?"

"I . . . no, I wasn't here all day. I was in the barn when you come home. I saw you leave the rig out front."

"Why didn't you come in then? I didn't hear you leave. Where were you yesterday?"

David stood and deliberately walked around the table. He dwarfed his mother as he stood in front of her. Now full grown, he stood six foot three and weighed nearly two hundred fifty pounds. He saw fear steal across her face. "I don't have to tell you anything." He grabbed her arm. The coffee cup fell from her hand and bounced on the wooden floor. "What I do and where I go is none of your damn business." He shook her hard, snapping her head back and forth. "How many times am I going to have to kick your ass for you to understand that?" His voice was low and shaky.

She knew what was coming, he could see it etched in her face and reflected in her eyes. He liked what he saw as he gritted his teeth and took a deep breath. Grabbing her arm, he spun her around and pushed her away. Following her, he kicked her between the legs as hard as he could and her back arched when he heard a muffled snap. Without a sound, she sprawled face-first on the floor.

He stood over her. "Get up," he growled.

"You ain't hurt." She didn't move, so he stooped to turn her face up for a look. Her chest rose and fell as she breathed. "Get up! You've had your ass kicked before."

Since Mace had warned him, David had used his foot to mete out his version of discipline. And always, he kicked her in the butt; sometimes two or three times. No one should ever see the bruises. No one ever had. But she had never gone down like this before. If she fell, she'd always gotten up and left the room with a whipped-pup whimper, usually to her bedroom, where she'd stay a while, later to ignore him completely for a few days. She couldn't know it, but he considered the last part a bonus. He looked at her again, this time kneeling beside her. Her eyes fluttered, opened for a moment, and then shut again.

"Shit," he said. "Lay there, then, but you still got cows to milk tonight."

He took his hat off the hook and left. Ten minutes later he rode off, toward Adobe.

Ana waited in vain for Ruth to show up at church Sunday morning, and afterwards, Paul took her to the home place to see if everything was all right. As they approached, the unmistakable sound of a cow in distress greeted them. Paul hurried the horse into the barnyard.

"You go see about Ruth. I'll go see what's wrong with the stock."

Paul clambered off the buggy and hurried to the barn. Ana tied up the horse and went to the house. Opening the door, she called, "Sis? Are you home?"

"I'm in here, Ana." The voice came from the back of the house.

Ana hurried through the parlor and kitchen to Ruth's bedroom door. Her sister, pale and drawn, lay in bed. "What's wrong?" she said as she went to her side.

"I'm afraid I twisted my back. It kept me right here all day yesterday. I nearly made it up this morning, but not quite. It still hurts to bend it. I knew you'd come when I didn't make church." She looked past Ana toward the door. "Is Paul seeing to the cows? Those poor creatures. They've been bawling for hours."

"Yes. He'll see what's wrong. How did you hurt yourself?"

"I was putting a pan on the top shelf, standing on that little stool. My foot slipped and I fell right on top of it. I fear I've broken something." Ruth's eyes filled with tears.

"Don't cry now. We're here. I'll send Paul for Doc Princher, and he'll take a look."

"Ana, I've wet the bed. Can we clean up

before the doctor gets here?"

"Of course. I'll get some clean clothes and we'll change everything. Can you get up?"

"I think so, with help. I'm sure once I can get on my feet, I'll be all right. It's just rolling over and sitting up that hurts like the dickens."

"She has taken an awful blow to the coccyx," Doc Princher said. "That's the little piece of your spine right at the very end. It doesn't do anything useful, but it's like any other bone in your body, break it and you're going to know it. I expect she came as close to snapping it as you can, but got away with a bad bruise. In the long run that's best, but for now it's actually more painful than a fracture."

"So what's best for her?" Ana asked.

"Well, if the pain gets too bad, I can give her some laudanum, but knowing you girls like I do, she won't cotton much to that. No, I expect a few days of taking it real easy is the best medicine. That busted tailbone will slow her down without me telling her to. She'll be all right." He patted Ana on the arm. "Unless she gets worse, I won't have to see her again, but you know where I am." He heaved a huge sham sigh and hung his head sadly. "Everybody knows where I

492

am." He grinned and left the house.

"What do you think?" Ana asked Paul as they stood on the front porch and watched Doc Princher drive away.

"Same as you. Looks like . . . David." Paul's lips set in a hard line, and his jaw muscles twitched.

"She's going to deny it."

"I know, and there's not much we can do about it. I worry about how Mace is going to react. He told me there's a chance he and Ruth might marry one of these days."

"Really? Now that's odd. If Mace is thinking that way, he must have a reason, yet Ruth has never mentioned it. I wonder if she's afraid of what David might do."

"All I know is, the whole situation's a mess," Paul said.

Ana put her hand on Paul's arm. "I'm going to stay here tonight."

"I don't think I like that. Where has David been and what shape is he going to be in when he gets home? I don't like it at all." Paul shook his head, his lips pursed.

"I'm not leaving her. Ruth can barely get up. And someone has to milk those cows." She put her hands on her hips, knuckles down.

Paul puffed out a breath of air. "All right, I'll go home and tell the kids where you are, and come back. I'll wait till David comes home and decide if it's safe for you to stay. Axel and Abe can come milk the cows."

David saw the horse and buggy in front of the house, and recognized the roan in the traces. *Uncle Paul!* He rode into the barn and put his horse away. As he strode toward the house, he heard boys' voices in the cow barn.

"I see I have company," he said sarcastically as he barged though the front door. Paul and Ana came out of the kitchen and into the parlor. He knew he smelled of whiskey, stale tobacco and coal-oil smoke so Ana's sniff made him smile. "Staying long?"

"I might," Ana said. "Your mother fell and hurt her back quite badly."

"She's always stumbling over something. What now?" He slumped onto the sofa.

Ana's eyes widened. "What now? She can hardly walk, spent all day Saturday and Saturday night in bed, and that's all you have to say?" Her fists went onto her hips.

"Well, how am I supposed to know?" He glanced at Paul. "She all right?"

"She will be, but she can't do anything strenuous for a few days," Ana said. "That means she's not milking cows, washing, cooking or climbing stairs. I'm going to stay a day or two and take care of her. And I'm not asking, David."

"You may have dried your youngest cow. You know better than to leave milk cows," Paul said.

David saw the anger in his uncle's face. "How was I to know she let the Missour— Mr. Jensen off for the weekend?"

Ana came over to stand in front of him with Paul right behind her.

"How'd you know that?" Paul asked, his eyebrows rising. "She said you were gone all day Friday."

"I . . . she . . . you just said they hadn't been milked. Obviously, she told him not to come."

"This farm is your responsibility. Why do you have to take off on these . . . adventures, like this?" Paul stepped to Ana's side. "If you can't or won't take care of this place, I'll find someone who will. And I know it's not a matter of can't. You're a fine farmer. You just have to pay more attention."

"Ana, Paul," Ruth called from her bedroom. "Please let this go for now."

Ana turned around and went into the kitchen to stand at Ruth's door. "I know he's yours and we don't have the right to hound him, but sometimes I can't contain myself."

"You needn't stay. David will help me." She raised her voice. "David, come here."

David came to stand just inside and leaned against the wall. "What?"

"I'm going to ask Ana not to stay. You tell her we'll be all right."

"Of course we'll be all right. I'm not the best cook, but I can feed us," he said with a sniff. He crossed the kitchen to stand where he could see his mother.

"Are you sure, sis?" Ana asked. She looked back at Paul, now standing in the kitchen entry, and he nodded.

"I'm sure," Ruth said. "You go home and take care of yours. We'll be fine."

"Well, I'm coming back in the morning just the same. We'll have coffee. I won't take no for an answer." Ana stepped over the bed, kissed her sister on the forehead, and went back into the parlor. David followed. She turned to face him and spoke in a low voice. "Doc Princher left some laudanum in the kitchen. If she needs it . . . well, she'll tell you. I'll be back in the morning."

Paul and Ana left the house, and Paul went to the barn, returning a couple of minutes later.

"They're almost finished. I told them to

let David do the straining and come home. The young cow barely milked at all." Paul shook his head in disgust as he climbed into the seat. Clucking sharply, he turned the horse and headed for the south road.

Mace heard a horse stop out front, and a few seconds later Paul stepped into the peaceful silence of the stable. Paul looked around until he spotted him.

"Hi, Mace, what you fixing to whack on now?"

Mace dropped his piece of chalk on the sheet of metal he'd been marking. "Got a couple braces I need to put on a mower. What's up?" He leaned against the bench.

"Thought you should know that Ruth took a spill."

"A spill? Is she hurt?" Mace stood up straight and stepped toward Paul.

"Busted her tailbone. Doc says that hurts like all git-out. Ana went out this morning to see how she's doing. Ruth spent Saturday laid up in bed."

"How'd she do that? And where was David? Off drinking?"

"Afraid so. He didn't get back till late Sunday afternoon, more like evening, really. I had my boys milking his cows. Anyway, she said she fell on a stool . . . putting something up on a shelf and slipped." Paul looked at the floor.

"Don't look like you're convinced that's what happened."

"I can't say, Mace. I'd hate to think a boy would do that to his own mother. If I knew for sure he had, I'm afraid I'd . . . I don't know what I'd do. But I don't. It's just something about his attitude toward the whole thing. Like he didn't care. And that stool. It would be a stretch for her to reach the top of the cupboard standing on it."

"Damn it," Mace muttered. "She wanted me to go to church with her again, but I can't abide them old biddies clucking their tongues when we come in. She'd of had help a lot sooner."

"You couldn't know. What's done is done. Doc said she'll be all right, just needs to rest for a few days. I expect she'll be up tomorrow or Wednesday."

Mace reached around and untied his apron. "I'm gonna ride over and see her for a minute or two. You expect that'd be all right?"

"I'm sure it would. Ana's there, so your old hens won't have much to cluck about. Not much chance of them seeing you anyway."

"So much the better."

"Gotta git. Just thought you should know. I'll see you." Paul gave him a weak smile and left.

Mace knocked on the door and waited. He knocked again, harder, then looked over his shoulder at Ana's buggy. He waited another minute, and then walked around the house to the back door. It stood open, and he could see Ana at the stove.

"Ana, it's Mace," he called through the screen door.

"Come on in. I heard you knocking, but I'm right in the middle of egg custard, and can't leave it for a second." She swept a wooden spoon back and forth in a pot on the stove.

"Kinda gave me a shiver. Saw the buggy, and then couldn't get an answer," he said as he came into the kitchen. It smelled of vanilla. "So, how's Ruth?" He glanced at the closed bedroom door.

"Napping. I was just about ready to wake her up. Soon as this is done, I will. Won't be a minute or two more." She gave him the quick smile of a woman too busy to talk, and concentrated on the pudding. Mace leaned against the door frame and watched.

She spooned a large dollop of the rapidly boiling dessert into a bowl of three whipped eggs and stirred everything together. She did that two more times to warm up the eggs, and then she dumped the mixture into the boiling pot. This turned the contents a soft-yellow color and she let it boil for another minute before pushing the pot off to the side.

"There," she said. Reaching for a small pan, she dumped its contents of melted butter and vanilla flavor into the custard and stirred it in. "Let that set for a bit and we can have some. I'll see if Ruth's awake."

Ana went to the door and opened it slightly. "Sis, you awake? Oh, good. You've got company."

"Who?" Mace heard Ruth's voice faintly.

"Mace," Ana said.

"Oh, dear! Ana, come in and shut the door." Mace heard that more clearly. Ana turned, smiled at him and held up two fingers. "Two minutes," she mouthed the words silently.

Ruth sat propped up in bed, her hands folded in her lap. Mace felt completely out of place and swallowed hard to make his words start to flow. "Hi, Ruth. You look gr— I just . . . Are . . . phffff." He puffed out his breath in exasperation.

"I'm fine, Paisley. I feel a lot better than I

did yesterday, and I'm determined to get up and have a cup of coffee at my table tonight." She smiled brightly.

Mace, seeing the smile, felt much better. "Scared the hell . . . I'm sorry . . . Paul gave me a scare when he told me you'd fallen. What the dickens were you doing?"

"I was standing on a chair putting a pot away on top of the cupboard. Somehow my foot slipped and I fell." Her gaze faltered and she looked at her hands.

"And all you hurt was your . . . uh, your . . . you know." Mace moved closer to the bed.

"I fell, Paisley. I was not being careful and I fell. That's all."

She glanced up so briefly Mace almost missed the look, but he saw enough to know she was pleading with him to believe her. His emotions ran from pity to sorrow to anger and to rage in as many heartbeats. *Paul said she was standing on a stool.* His teeth clenched tight as the enormity of the crime unfolded in his confused brain. *How could David do this? And to someone as tender as Ruth.* His breathing came fast and shallow.

"Paisley."

Mace's mind seethed.

"Paisley!"

"Wha, what." He shook his head and looked at her.

She held out her hands. "Please don't think what you're thinking. I can't allow it. Do you understand me? I won't allow it."

"But Ruth, he —"

She cut him off. "Don't even say it. We will get through this. He's getting better. The death of his father was a terrible blow. He has to take it out somewhere."

"But for God's sake it —"

She put her hand on his lips. "He's better. I must give him a chance. Please."

Her eyes left him no choice. "I'll try, Ruth, I'll try. But this —" He nodded at her. "This is hard to take."

"I know. Just a little while. Okay?" She squeezed his hand. "Now, have a cup of coffee with me." She faced the door and raised her voice, "Ana, can we have some coffee, please?"

"I'm sorry, Simon," Mrs. Kingsley said. "She won't tell me why, she just doesn't want to see you." She felt as confused as he looked standing just inside the front door.

Simon nodded sadly and took a deep breath. "Thanks, Mrs. Kingsley."

She touched him on the face as he left. "I'll tell her you called." Irene watched him climb on his horse and turn east, toward home, and she pondered her changed daughter, a child much different from the one she'd raised. Simon told her they hadn't quarreled, but Sarah now stayed in her room all day, coming downstairs late in the evening to sit on the porch glider. Irene soon learned to leave her alone; one wrong word and Sarah would escape to her bedroom again. She'd considered talking to Doctor Princher, but to tell him what? She so hoped it was just a passing mood.

Irene Kingsley shut the door and glanced longingly up the stairs as she went back into the parlor.

CHAPTER 43

Mace led the freshly shod horse to the shelter on the west side of the stable and tied her up. Returning to the stable, he rounded the corner of the building and spotted David, riding straight at him, an insolent smirk on his face. Mace jumped to one side, and then, just as David swept past, he reached out and grabbed the bridle. David's smirk disappeared, and before he could say a word, he and his horse were in the stable.

"Get off!" Mace held the startled animal steady.

"Go to hell." David tugged savagely at the reins. "Let go of my horse."

"I said get off!" Mace stepped past the animal's head, grabbed David's belt, and heaved back. David lit in a heap on the dusty floor. Mace let go of the bridle, and the horse raced out of the barn. David scrambled to his feet and Mace faced him, a wagon spoke held tightly in his hands. "You're gonna listen, or I'm gonna brain you." Mace breathed heavily, more from pent-up anger than exertion.

"I ain't gonna listen to nothin." David's eyes flashed hatred.

"I think you will," Buell said from behind him.

David spun around.

Buell stood just inside a stall. He wore his pistol, his gaze flat and without emotion. David turned back to Mace, trapped.

"I told you what I'd do if I found out you were abusing your mother."

"I ain't abusing her." David hissed the words. His breath came more quickly and the color rose in his face. He clenched his fists.

"Shut up!" Mace half raised the piece of heavy oak. "I think you are. I can't say for sure, and your mother won't say it right out. She thinks you can't help it. And for those kind thoughts, you beat her."

"She needs her ass kicked. Always whining. Never satisfied. It was the same with Pa. Except he took it. I won't!"

He charged at Mace, head down like a bull, sure of his strength and weight. Mace stepped aside and jammed the slim end of the spoke hard into David's side as he went past. David's breath exploded out of him, and he collapsed to his knees, gasping. Mace stood over him, the heavy wooden spoke ready to strike.

"I can't be sure, boy. If I was, I'd kill you right now." Mace ground his teeth, the spoke moving back a fraction.

"Pa. Don't." Buell wrapped his hand around the heavy club and gently but firmly, pulled at it.

Mace blinked, let go of the heavy piece of wood and then looked at Buell. Still breathing heavily, he grabbed David with both hands and dragged him to the door. "Get out," he rasped.

David, gritting his teeth and holding one hand against his side, staggered to his feet.

"You sonsabitches." He stepped through the door and turned to face them. "You'll burn for this. And maybe right in this barn." He disappeared into the street.

"Has he been beating his mother?" Buell asked.

"I'd bet on it. She won't say so, and asked me to leave him alone. Then he tried to shoulder me with his horse out front and I saw red."

"How bad did he hurt her?"

"He put her in bed. Couldn't hardly move for two days. And then he rode off to Adobe

506

or Kendrick and got drunk. Left her lying there."

Buell winced slightly. "You hear what he said about burning the barn?"

"Yeah. He's all bluff and bullshit. Not the first time he's said something like that." Mace felt calmer now. "No. I'll leave him alone like she asks, but I'm gonna be watching. I catch him at it, God help him."

"Hey, grocery boy," David said as Simon walked into the barbershop.

Simon ignored the remark, and glanced at the man sitting in the chair; the man was a new face. Simon gave him a friendly nod and sat.

Mr. Moir, the barber, smiled at Simon. "Morning, Simon. What'll it be? The ears lowered, or the hair raised?" He laughed out loud, which for him was one hoot and two snorts. Most would have simply chuckled. The barber looked to see if the new man appreciated his old joke. He didn't seem to. Shirley Moir was known all over town for his sense of humor. His size and name almost guaranteed that. A skinny six footer, he resembled a bird-nest-topped fence post with an Adam's apple. So it was either laugh with them or — actually, that was the only option.

Shirley seemed glad to see Simon. "So, heard the one about the fly with no wings?" One of his bushy eyebrows shot up in anticipation of the punch line, it nearly met his hairline.

Simon smiled to himself. *And the cobbler had no shoes.*

As usual, Shirley didn't wait for the answer. "They called it a walk." He hooted and slapped his leg with his comb hand. His customer watched, wide-eyed, as the scissors flailed around his head. Settling down, Shirley returned to the haircut.

"Sorry to hear about your ma," Simon said, looking at David.

"Yeah, that was real sad," Shirley said.

The look David gave the barber caused Shirley to reflexively step behind his customer, and the exchange ended any further levity in the barbershop.

"Hear tell yer woman ain't feelin' so good, either." David gave Simon a fake smile. "Someone said she won't even talk to you." The word "woman" had come out as a slur, and his smirk said that's what he'd intended.

"That's none of your business, David."

"It's everybody's business, grocery boy. You two have been stuck together like tree sap since . . . since forever. So when she changes her mind, we all want to know

508

why." David stood and the new man gaped at what he saw.

Simon, seeing the attempt at intimidation, stood as well. "She hasn't changed her mind about anything." He leaned forward to emphasize his point.

David must have seen the gesture as a threat because he took a full step toward Simon, drawing to within a couple of feet. "And I'm telling you, she ain't gonna marry you . . . not this year or any other year." David's face had flushed completely, his sneer now had teeth.

The new man bolted from the chair, tore off the apron, and frantically dug a coin from his pocket. He slapped it on the counter, and then bolted through the open door without a backward glance.

"I can't understand you, David. Always ready to hurt. Always ready to belittle. Something's not right with you."

"Me? That's good. You're the one who's lost his woman. Don't believe me. Ask her. That's if you can ever get back in the house." David scowled at the barber, then, putting his arm across Simon's chest, walked past him and out of the shop.

Shirley Moir released a huge gasp of air and walked around the barber chair and sat in it. "Can you come back after a while,

Simon? I'm not up to doing much right now. And close the door, would you?"

Sarah entered the parlor from the kitchen. Simon looked at her, seeing all the beauty and softness that had held him for so long. And then something near panic rose up in his chest, making it hard to breathe. "Hello, Sarah."

"Hello, Simon. Mother said you were here." She stood halfway across the room.

"I need to ask you s-something, Sarah, something important."

"What is it?"

He moved closer, her scent making his throat ache, and he desperately wanted to take her in his arms and hold her tight until his panicky feeling went away. He sought to meet her soft gray eyes, but they looked everywhere but into his. His sense of frustration built, and the urge to turn on his heel and leave took hold. He fought it. *This time I have to ask. I have to.*

"Sarah . . . I —" Simon failed to finish.

"What is it, Simon? We have no secrets, never have. What is it?"

Struggling to overcome the urge to bolt, he remembered, in succession and with blinding speed, the special times, the private and tender experiences they'd share, that made her so special. *What if I've been told wrong and David was just needling me again. Yes!* Exhilaration overcame Simon, and he stepped closer. "Sarah, will you marry me?"

For several agonizing seconds Sarah looked right through him, made no move or gesture, stoic in the middle of the parlor, her eyes a vacant stare. The image made Simon's legs weak and her face drifted out of focus. She said something, but Simon couldn't hear it, hearing instead an odd hollow sound that seemed to come from inside his head. And then he was looking at her again, but now her brow was knitted, her arms folded across her chest, defensively.

"Sarah?" he muttered. "I have to know."

A subtle change came over her face, like her skin had just gotten colder. The private light of awareness, the one reserved just for him, dimmed slowly, and then was gone. Only Simon would have seen these changes, but to him they were as plain as a cold lamp. Simon could feel his heart hardening.

"Oh, Simon. I just don't know . . . I wish we could talk about this later."

Simon felt failure fast approaching.

"I have to know . . . now," Simon pressed, but feared her answer.

"We're not right for each other, Simon, and it would never work out. How many times have you failed to ask that question? There's a reason for that, it's just one we've never faced. We simply don't love each other enough. I'm sorry."

She said it, her voice steady and cool, as though she'd rehearsed the whole scene a hundred times. With his heart pounding against his ribs, Simon struggled to catch a breath that now came in deep gulps. She shimmered as tears blurred his vision and he realized the sweetness he needed so badly had gone sour. He turned and hurried out the door.

Sarah remained motionless, drained of emotion, and looked at where Simon had stood, knowing she had done what she had to do and she let her heart retreat into the stony shell she'd carefully built over the last few weeks.

Buell, silent, looked out at the river from where he and Simon sat in their favorite spot on the bank. Simon had just finished telling him of his encounter with David, and the visit with Sarah.

"Oh, God, Buell, what am I going to do without her? I feel like walking into the water and floating away." He paused, shaking his head back and forth and moaning. "I can't imagine what changed. Three weeks ago everything was fine. She said I should go to school and she'd wait. What did I do?" Simon leaned forward and wrapped his arms around his knees, then, putting his head down, he started to cry softly.

Buell continued to stare at the river, his jaw muscles working furiously.

Simon wept for nearly half an hour. "I thought I understood what I was going to do." Red-eyed and beaten, he looked directly at Buell. "All the things I learned from Ma and Pa. The talks we had with your father. The stuff John and Judge Kingsley told me. And Miss Everett and Nathan Greene. I watched Ma cry because we were hungry, and Pa work so hard he couldn't sleep. But they stuck with it and made it good. I learned that, and worked hard and honest for Mr. Swartz, and I'm labeled a thief. Explain that. Even my own father doubted me. So there's the pay for honesty and hard work. Gus Swartz cheats his pa and his pa gets an extra two hundred dollars for the trouble, most of it my money. And David? He's been abusing people all his life, and now he has the time and the money, somehow, to work when he feels like it. And Avery. How many people did he cheat? Yet he travels freely to Saint Louis, his uncle picking up the fare. So what did I get out of it? Huh? I'm leaving, Buell. I'm getting out of this godforsaken place. There's nothing here. You're the only one who has never doubted me or cheated me." He loosed a small sigh and his head dropped, like he was tired of talking or simply resigned to failure.

"I'm goin' with you," Buell said quietly. "When?"

"Huh?"

"Let's go. Just get some things together, saddle our horses, and leave."

"But your pa, what about Mace?"

"He'll understand. It's the same way he came to Carlisle. Where we goin'?"

Simon stared at him for a long time, trying to see past the emotionless mask set hard on Buell's face. "West? Fort Laramie or Denver City or Oregon. I don't really care. Long as it's out of here."

Simon and Buell stared at the familiar sight, the trees and the slowly moving river and sat silent for another hour. Then, on some unknown cue, they got up and went to their horses.

CHAPTER 44

Buell waited in the trees by the road to Kendrick. He'd followed David that far out of town, well out of sight. Now, the full moon cast a pale but bright light over the rough road, and the cold prairie perfumed the air with the dew-dampened leaves. He thought it must be close to two o'clock and he adjusted his seat a little, ears alert. One other rider had ridden past at about eleven. Buell had easily recognized him, a new man, but someone he'd seen around. A coyote hailed a neighbor, the long trailing cry carried clearly across the prairie, and was ignored. And then he heard the unmistakable click of horseshoe on rock. Buell touched his horse on the neck, murmured to it and waited another few seconds.

"Hello, David." Buell moved his horse from the shadow onto the road, blocking David's way.

"Sonuvabitch!" David bawled. "Scare the

shit outta me." He looked at Buell. "What the hell you want?"

"Thought we might finish our discussion from the livery."

"Get out of my way," snarled David. He attempted to turn his horse around Buell's and his face froze when he saw the Remington pistol pointed at his chest.

"Get down." Buell waved the pistol. "Now."

David got off his horse.

"Get off the road." Again the pistol moved. Buell dismounted, and looped his reins across a branch. "I'm leavin' town, and I want to get something straight with ya. I heard you threaten Pa. And I heard you're beating your ma. Either one could get you killed. Except Pa won't kill you. He's a decent man, and I think you're counting on that. Feller once told me to take care of stuff like this with a chunk a wood. And to do it private. I got this instead." He waved his pistol. "And this spot's nice and private."

"You ain't gonna use that." David tilted his head toward the pistol.

"Didn't say I was, but it'll keep your attention. I'm just telling you, Simon and I won't forget our way back. If I hear you've said one more sideways word to Pa, or your ma catches another bruise, I will come back." Buell holstered his pistol. "That's a promise."

David's eyes went to the holstered gun and Buell watched him measure the distance between them. *Go ahead and try it.* With two long strides, David covered the ground, cocking his fist as he came. Buell laid the heavy steel weapon into the side of David's head and David staggered sideways, blood gushing from a cut on his eyebrow. Blinking slowly, he shook his head a few times, then put his hand to his brow and stared at the blood. "You little bastard." He charged again, and this time Buell laid the Remington's barrel across the top of David's head. He sagged to his hands and knees and stayed there, head down like a tired animal.

Buell watched him, smiling and hoping. *Come on, David, one more time.*

"Ya better do a good job, cuz I ain't gonna stop," David muttered, still on his knees. Then he looked up, his face contorted in rage, the blood running down his neck and into his shirt black in the moonlight. "And when I'm done with you, I'll burn your pa in his bed." He struggled to his feet, swaying drunkenly. "And then I'll get Simon. And maybe get another look at that dainty little red mark on his girlfriend's ass." Head back, mouth wide open and lips stretched tight over his teeth, he laughed; a demented, soulless howl.

Buell's eyes narrowed as he heard again in his mind David's last words, *"Dainty little red mark on his girlfriend's ass,"* and his teeth ground hard together. He focused on the laughing face with its wide open mouth, and felt his entire body go slack and relaxed. He didn't hear his pistol go off, nor did he see David's head snap back in the silence.

The sound of drumming hooves reached him, and Buell realized David's horse had run off, headed for home. He looked down at David, now flat on his back in a large pool of black that spread away from his head. He stepped closer. The mouth was open in a scream, and the eyes stared at the night sky, but David was silent and saw nothing.

Buell glanced at the gun in his hand and then slowly put it away. *"That dainty little red mark . . . on his girlfriend's ass."* He looked at the dead man again, and then reached down and felt for money in David's front pants pocket. He found seven small coins, then checked the shirt pockets for paper money and found nothing. He grabbed him by his waist to roll him over and felt the belt under his shirt. Two buttons and the buckle freed it, and he stripped it from underneath the body. Buell felt the weight and unsnapped one pouch. Three fifty-dollar gold pieces dropped into his hand.

"Damn it," he muttered. He put the coins back, and then felt around for a back-pocket wallet but found nothing. He climbed into his saddle, and still holding the money belt, he headed for town, angling toward the river.

His whole day had started out wrong-footed when he'd spilled half a cup of coffee in the middle of his corn fritters and eggs, and now this. Sheriff Staker looked down at David Steele, mouth gaped open, black blood all over his face, neck and shirt. A dark patch of drying blood spread out a couple of feet from his head. He's been worked over some, with a pretty good cut over his brow and a lump on top his head that would've raised his hat. Staker felt the front pockets, and then probed under David's right buttock for a wallet. *Nothing. Not a dime. Had to have been more than one. Don't know anyone stupid enough to take on David alone, much less get the chance to hit him twice. And his horse is gone. How'd they talk him off his horse, at night?* Doc Princher approached in his wagon.

"Beat him to death, looks like," Staker

said as the doctor climbed down stiffly.

"Uh-huh." Doc Princher walked over to the body. Kneeling, he looked closely at the cut on David's head. "Huh-uh," Doc said, shaking his head. "Too much blood."

"What do you mean?" Staker peered closer.

Doc looked up at the sheriff. "You done looking at him?"

"Yeah."

"Help me turn him over, then. Easy like."

"Good Lord." Staker looked at the mess that was the back of David's head: black blood, small rocks and dirt, and pink-white bits of bone mixed in a sticky blob. "Shot 'im behind the ear, back of his head is gone. He was executed."

Doc Princher nodded, then looked at the farmer who had found the body. "Parley, help the sheriff load him up." Princher went to his wagon and removed the tailgate. Together, the farmer and the sheriff picked up the heavy body and managed to scoot it into the wagon.

Princher headed back to town, and Staker started to look around, methodically searching for whatever he might find. Trying not to hurry, he moved a quickly as possible, but dreading his visit with Ruth Steele.

■ ■ ■ ■

Mace, standing in front of the livery, saw Sheriff Staker step out of Shirley Moir's shop and head his way.

"Mace." The sheriff nodded when he got to him.

"Loren." He looked closely at the sheriff's face, trying to judge the mood.

"Nasty business."

"Yep."

"Can we go inside a minute and talk?" The sheriff headed for the livery door without waiting for an answer and Mace followed. "Shirley says you chucked David out in the street yesterday." He shook his head and puffed out his cheeks. "Again."

"Doesn't look good, but yeah, I threw him out. I'm not going to go into the details, enough to say he got my goat, again, and we had words, again. I didn't hit him, well . . . maybe once, and kicked his butt out. Same old threats about making me pay and burning the barn."

"And about his mother's accident?"

"Yeah. How'd you know about that?"

"Doc Princher. He had his doubts. No other bruises like you'd get in a fall."

"Yeah, I thought the same thing, and told

David about it. I'll admit, if I knew for sure, I just might've planted 'im. But I don't, and I didn't."

"You never have owned a pistol have you?"

"Nope. Got a shotgun. Want to see it?"

"Nope. No need. Where was Buell last night?"

"Now don't start on Buell. He's not the only man in town that has a gun and knows how to use it." Mace's voice had started to rise.

"And he's not the only one I'm going to talk to either. Was he here?"

"I don't know. You know as well as I do he comes and goes at all hours. And you know where he goes. You've checked on him. He said so." Mace smiled at the surprised look on Staker's face. "Didn't think he saw you, did you? Well, he did. So you know he sometimes just sits out there and thinks. And you know where he practices, because you been there too."

"It's my business to know, Mace, you understand that."

"Sure it is. And knowing your business, you know damn well Buell wouldn't shoot someone in the back of the head."

"How'd you know that? That's not common knowledge."

"Shit, it's all over town. Parley Profitt's

talked to everybody he's seen this morning. David was bushwhacked and robbed."

"And you're not all that upset about it, are you?"

"Matter of fact, I'm not. If it weren't for Ruth, I'd dance on his grave. Lots of folks would."

"A man's died in a way no man should, Mace. He wasn't very pleasant to be around but . . . Tell Buell I'd like to see him." He turned to go.

"Loren." Mace put out his hand. The sheriff looked at it for a moment and then stepped back and took it.

"Mace."

Buell stepped into the jailhouse. "Pa said you wanted to see me."

"Yep, thanks for stopping. Take a chair." Staker pointed at the one closest to the desk.

Buell sat.

"Is your pistol always fully loaded?"

"Of course." Buell looked a little surprised.

"Can I see it for a minute?"

Buell drew his gun and handed it butt-first to the sheriff.

Staker pulled the hammer back one click and turned the cylinder. Then he turned in his chair a little to get full light on the pistol and inspected it carefully. "Where were you last night? I mean after you left Luger's."

Buell's eyebrows went up.

"I checked. You left there about seven," Staker said. A slight smile crossed his face.

"Went down to the river and sat for a while."

"For how long?"

"Can't tell. Until eleven or so I guess."

"See anybody?"

"Nope. Wait a minute. Nobody at the river, but a fella rode in from the west just as I went into the livery. New guy, lives past Simon's place about a half mile."

"He see you?" Staker sat up straight in his chair.

"I don't think so. I was in the barn."

"Would you recognize him again?"

"Sure. He lives in that old soddy that used to belong to the Piersons."

"All right," Staker said. He handed Buell his pistol. "Thanks for stopping."

"Sure." Buell stood up and nodded. "We'll see you."

Paul felt angry and disappointed and Ana, shoulders slumped, sat silently, her hands clasped.

Simon sat with them at the kitchen table. "She simply doesn't want me. She was as

524

cold as a frog. I've lost her, that's all there is to it." Simon paused, his gaze moving from one parent to the other.

Ana's eyes told Paul there was nothing she could say, her heartache plain to see.

"I can't stay," Simon said. "Every time I walk through town I get a look or two."

"So what!" Paul replied. "You know what you are. Why would you care what they think?"

"Because they determine my reputation. They make me feel what I am in this place. And if the feeling I get makes me this miserable, I can't stay."

"But to just leave with no plans, or destination. That's crazy. Wait until we can work something out. Go to school. Anything, but don't just leave." Paul could see he was not making any difference. And he understood. He had taught his children to think for themselves, load all the weights, and go where the balance tilted. For the past hour, Simon had shown them the weights: Matt, Avery, David, Sarah and Swartz. And Paul had no trouble seeing the balance. He got up and put his arm around Ana. She burst into tears.

Mace listened and nodded. "I wanted a lot more than this, son, but I'll settle for you being satisfied. I came here just like you're leaving. And you'll know where you're going when you get there."

"It's not because I don't want to stay. I kinda do, but I want to leave more. You been good to me. And I ain't goin' forever. I expect I'll be back, and I'll keep in touch."

"Make sure you do, Buell. We'll be here, Ruth and I."

"That would be good. I like her. And Pa . . . don't be up when I leave, okay?"

"All right, son. But I'm gonna listen."

Mace stared at his son as though to imprint the image of his youthful yet somehow wise face on his mind. He stepped forward and grasped him in his arms and hugged him hard. "I love you, boy." Buell's body went tense and then suddenly relaxed.

"I love you too, Pa."

Simon rode slowly in the early morning light, past the Kingsleys' one last time. He glanced up at Sarah's window and it mocked him with its stoic stare. He urged his horse into a canter and did not see her standing in the shadows by the porch.

Buell sat waiting astride his horse and swung alongside as Simon rode by the livery. Side by side they rode, the town meeting their passage with silence as even the roosters stayed their morning call, past the last house and into the prairie, heading west.

ABOUT THE AUTHOR

Wallace J. Swenson was born and raised in rural Idaho. The fourth of eight children, he learned early about hard work and the value of things not material. After a twenty-year military career as a weatherman, he returned home to Idaho where he finished his degree in computer science and went to work for the US Department of Energy. After retiring, he wrote full-time as he and his wife of fifty-plus years tended to their grandchildren and to each other.

Wallace's first novel in the Journey to the White Cloud series, *Buell,* was published in June 2015 by Five Star Publishing. He also published short stories in *Idaho Magazine* and presented his craft on radio and TV. Past state officer in the Idaho Writer's League, Wallace felt strongly about giving back some of what he had been granted.

The employees of Thorndike Press hope you have enjoyed this Large Print book. All our Thorndike, Wheeler, and Kennebec Large Print titles are designed for easy reading, and all our books are made to last. Other Thorndike Press Large Print books are available at your library, through selected bookstores, or directly from us.

For information about titles, please call:
   (800) 223-1244

or visit our Web site at:
   http://gale.cengage.com/thorndike

To share your comments, please write:
   Publisher
   Thorndike Press
   10 Water St., Suite 310
   Waterville, ME 04901